From the Pages of
Sailing Alone Around the World

The wonderful sea charmed me from the first. (page 17)

The *Spray's* dimensions were, when finished, thirty-six feet nine inches long, over all, fourteen feet two inches wide, and four feet two inches deep in the hold. (page 22)

During these days a feeling of awe crept over me. My memory worked with startling power. The ominous, the insignificant, the great, the small, the wonderful, the commonplace—all appeared before my mental vision in magical succession. Pages of my history were recalled which had been so long forgotten that they seemed to belong to a previous existence. I heard all the voices of the past laughing, crying, telling what I had heard them tell in many corners of the earth. (page 36)

I saw clearly that if I failed now all might be lost. I sprang from the oars to my feet, and lifting the anchor above my head, threw it clear just as she was turning over. I grasped her gunwale and held on as she turned bottom up, for I suddenly remembered that I could not swim. (page 66)

"Hurrah for the *Spray!*" I shouted to seals, sea-gulls, and penguins; for there were no other living creatures about, and she had weathered all the dangers of Cape Horn. (page 113)

At last she reached port in safety, and there at 1 A. M. on June 27, 1898, cast anchor, after the cruise of more than forty-six thousand miles round the world, during an absence of three years and two months, with two days over for coming up. (pages 222–223)

The days passed happily with me wherever my ship sailed. (page 236)

The Spray

From a photograph taken in Australian waters.

SAILING ALONE AROUND THE WORLD

Captain Joshua Slocum

With an Introduction and Notes
by Dennis A. Berthold

Illustrated by Thomas Fogarty
and George Varian

George Stade
Consulting Editorial Director

JB

BARNES & NOBLE CLASSICS
NEW YORK

ℬ

Barnes & Noble Classics

New York

Published by Barnes & Noble Books
122 Fifth Avenue
New York, NY 10011

www.barnesandnoble.com/classics

Sailing Alone Around the World was first published in 1900.

Published in 2005 by Barnes & Noble Classics with new Introduction,
Notes, Biography, Chronology, Glossary, Inspired By, Comments & Questions,
and For Further Reading.

Introduction, Notes, Glossary of Nautical Terms, and For Further Reading
Copyright © 2005 by Dennis A. Berthold.

Note on Joshua Slocum, The World of Joshua Slocum and *Sailing Alone
Around the World*, Three Maps of Slocum's Voyage, Inspired by *Sailing Alone
Around the World*, Comments & Questions, and For Further Reading
Copyright © 2005 by Barnes & Noble, Inc.

Sailing Alone Around the World
ISBN-13: 978-1-59308-303-8
ISBN-10: 1-59308-303-3
LC Control Number 2005922119

Produced and published in conjunction with:
Fine Creative Media, Inc.
322 Eighth Avenue
New York, NY 10001

Michael J. Fine, President and Publisher

Printed in the United States of America

QM

16   18   20   19   17   15

Joshua Slocum

Joshua Slocum was born in Nova Scotia on February 20, 1844. As one of eleven children, he was expected to help support the family, and after they moved to Briar Island in the Bay of Fundy, ten-year-old Joshua was taken from school to work with his father, making leather boots for the local sailors and fishermen.

For young Joshua, the lure of the sea was powerful. He ran away at fourteen to work as a cook on a fishing schooner, and when his mother died two years later he left home for good, enlisting as an ordinary seaman on a British merchant ship bound for Ireland. From Britain, he shipped again, this time sailing for China, the Philippines, and Singapore. By the age of eighteen he had been awarded the certificate of second mate.

Around 1870 Slocum was given command of the bark *Washington*, a merchant ship that he sailed out of San Francisco to Japan, China, the Spice Islands, and Sydney, Australia. In Sydney, he met an American woman, Virginia Albertina Walker, whom he married in 1871. The two were well matched and well suited for life at sea. For thirteen years, Virginia would accompany her husband on his voyages, giving birth to and schooling their seven children (only four survived) while on shipboard.

For the next decade, Slocum commanded large sailing ships through many adventures and misadventures across the Pacific. A skilled shipwright, he was contracted to build the hull of an 80-ton steamship while stranded in the Philippines in 1875; although he received none of the money he had been promised, a year later he was given a schooner, the *Pato*, which he sailed homeward. With profits from the sale of the *Pato*, Slocum purchased his first ship, the *Amethyst*.

In 1886, less than two years after Virginia's death, Slocum married his cousin Henrietta "Hettie" Elliott; with a crew of ten, including two of Slocum's sons, the two newlyweds set out for South America aboard the *Aquidneck*. Slocum's considerable resourcefulness was put to the test on this voyage, during which he endured a cholera outbreak, a smallpox epidemic, and a mutinous crew before finally running aground near Paranaguá, Brazil. Stranded and without means, Slocum salvaged what he could from the wreck and built the *Liberdade*, a 35-foot-long "canoe" that he sailed the 5,500 miles home. He published an account of his adventures, *Voyage of the Liberdade*, in 1890.

Over the next several years, with steamships taking over the sailing routes, Slocum met with hard financial times. In 1892 an acquaintance offered him the rotting shell of an old oyster boat, the *Spray*. Slocum rebuilt the 37-foot sloop from the keel up, and resolved to sail it alone around the world. His journey, the world's first solo circumnavigation, lasted three years, covered 46,000 miles, and made him a celebrity. Captain Slocum chronicled his voyage in the instant seafaring classic *Sailing Alone Around the World* (1900).

The success of his book brought him moderate wealth and fame, and financed a home for Hettie. Slocum, however, grew restless for the sea, and he began making winter voyages to the West Indies. On November 14, 1909, he set out on the *Spray* in rough seas and was never seen again.

Table of Contents

The World of Joshua Slocum and
Sailing Alone Around the World
ix

Introduction by Dennis A. Berthold
xiii

SAILING ALONE AROUND THE WORLD
1

Endnotes
237

Glossary of Nautical Terms
249

Inspired by Sailing Alone Around the World
261

Comments & Questions
263

For Further Reading
267

The World of Joshua Slocum and Sailing Alone Around the World

1840   The first Cunard steamship (owned by Nova Scotian–born Sir Samuel Cunard) crosses the Atlantic Ocean in twelve days.

1844   Joshua Slocum is born the son of a farmer on February 20 in Nova Scotia, Canada.

1852   The family moves to Briar Island in the Bay of Fundy, where Joshua works with his father making leather boots for the local fishermen.

1858   Joshua runs away to work as a cook on a local fishing schooner but soon returns home. The *Great Eastern*, hailed as the world's largest steamship, is launched in England.

1860   Slocum's mother dies, and Joshua leaves home for good, shipping out on a deep-water vessel heading to Ireland. He begins working as an ordinary seaman for British merchant ships, sailing to China and Southeast Asia. Abraham Lincoln is elected president of the United States.

1862   After passing an examination, Slocum is certified as second mate. American author Henry David Thoreau, author of *Walden, or Life in the Woods*, dies.

1865   Slocum becomes an American citizen.

1869–   Assuming command of the sailing bark *Washington*, Slocum
1870   crosses the Pacific Ocean to Australia, Japan, China, and the Spice Islands. In Sydney, Australia, he meets Virginia Albertina Walker, a fellow American.

1871   While in Sydney, Joshua Slocum and Virginia Walker are married. On their return to San Francisco, the *Washington* is wrecked off the coast of Alaska. Slocum saves the cargo and crew, and his company rewards him with command of the *Constitution*. The first large luxury ocean liner is launched.

1872   On January 10 Victor Joshua Slocum is born aboard the *Constitution*, berthed in San Francisco Bay.

1873   Benjamin Aymar Slocum is born aboard Slocum's command, the *B. Aymar*, in Melbourne, Australia.

1875   Stranded in the Philippines, Slocum puts his considerable shipbuilding skills to work constructing the hull of an 80-ton steamer in Subic Bay. In lieu of payment, he is given the schooner *Pato*, which he sails home across the Pacific.

1875   A daughter, Jessie Helena, is born aboard the *B. Aymar*, in Philippine waters.

1881   A son, James Garfield (after the current president), is born aboard the *Amethyst*, an old sailing bark Slocum had purchased after selling the *Pato*. In Hong Kong, Slocum sells the *Amethyst* and buys a part interest in the *Northern Light*, an imposing three-masted ship.

1882   After leaving New York for the Orient aboard the *Northern Light*, Slocum's crew mutinies, leaving the first mate wounded. English naturalist Charles Darwin dies.

1883   On the return journey aboard the *Northern Light*, the captain overcomes another mutinous conspiracy and narrowly avoids the eruption of the volcano Krakatoa (one of the largest volcanic eruptions in modern times) in the Sunda Strait, Indonesia.

1884   Slocum sells his shares in the *Northern Light* and buys the smaller *Aquidneck*, a 326-ton sailing bark, which he sails to Buenos Aires. Virginia Slocum dies in July; not yet thirty-five years old, she is buried in Buenos Aires. Irish engineer Sir Charles Parsons invents a revolutionary steam engine, fueling the rise of efficient steamship marine travel.

1886   Slocum marries his first cousin Henrietta "Hettie" Elliott in Boston on February 2. With a crew of ten, including two of his sons, the newlyweds set out aboard the *Aquidneck* to South America.

1887   The *Aquidneck* is wrecked on a sandbar off Brazil just after Christmas.

1888   Salvaging what he can from the uninsured wreck, Slocum constructs a 35-foot-long "canoe" modeled after a Cape Ann dory. With sampan-style sails sewn by Hettie, the castaways set sail in June on the newly christened *Liberdade*, journeying 5,500 miles to Washington, D.C.

1889   After wintering in Washington, D.C., Slocum sails the *Liberdade* to Boston.

1890   Slocum writes and publishes *Voyage of the Liberdade*, an account of his honeymoon trip.

1892   Slocum is given the creaky hull of an old oyster sloop, the *Spray*. An able shipwright, he restores the sailboat to its former glory.

1893   He receives a commission to deliver the warship *Destroyer* to Brazil. Upon landing in Brazil, the ship is scuttled by the authorities.

1894   Unpaid for the job and in hopes of some remuneration, Slocum chronicles his command of the *Destroyer* in *Voyage of the Destroyer from New York to Brazil*.

1895   On April 24 Slocum sets out aboard the *Spray* on a journey alone around the world. He has almost no money and lacks critical navigational equipment. Italian physicist and inventor Guglielmo Marconi sends and receives the first radio signals.

1898   The Spanish-American War breaks out. On June 27 Slocum sails into Newport, Rhode Island, completing the world's first solo circumnavigation, a passage of 46,000 miles.

1899   He begins publishing a chronicle of his voyage in serial form.

1900   Slocum's account of his journey is published as *Sailing Alone Around the World*. Novelist Joseph Conrad publishes *Lord Jim*.

1901   The Commonwealth of Australia is created.

1902   Slocum uses the proceeds from his book to buy a house on the island of Martha's Vineyard, Massachusetts, off Cape Cod.

1905   Growing restless on land, Slocum sails the *Spray* to the Caribbean for the winter.

1906   Returning from the Caribbean, he is arrested on suspicion of raping a young girl in New Jersey; the rape charge is reduced to one of indecency, and Slocum is jailed for more than a month. That winter Slocum returns with the *Spray* to the Caribbean, on the way delivering rare Caribbean orchids to President Theodore Roosevelt.

1909   On November 14 Slocum sets out on the aging *Spray* for South America. Captain Slocum and the *Spray* are never seen again.

Introduction

I

There is nothing in sea literature like *Sailing Alone Around the World*, nor can there ever be again. Only one man was the first to sail around the world alone, and only one book recounts that astonishing voyage in his own words. This is that book.

When Joshua Slocum left Boston on April 24, 1895, to sail around the world alone in the *Spray*, a 37-foot sloop he reconstructed himself, Mabel Wagnalls wrote in his log, "The Spray will come back" (Teller, *Joshua Slocum*, p. 77; see "For Further Reading"). Those words proved prophetic in more ways than one. Of course the *Spray* did come back three years later, anchoring on June 27, 1898, in Newport, Rhode Island. No one had ever circumnavigated the globe alone until Slocum did it, and not many have done so since. The *Spray* has also returned in the hundreds of full-sized replicas Slocum fans have built over the last century, many of them amazingly precise. Two books, Kenneth Slack's *In the Wake of the Spray* (1966) and R. Bruce Roberts-Goodson's *Spray: The Ultimate Cruising Boat* (1995), have documented this phenomenon, which began in 1903 and continues to the present. Between 1969 and 1995, Roberts-Goodson sold more than 5,000 sets of plans for *Spray* replicas of various sizes, and more than 800 of these have actually been built (Roberts-Goodson, p. viii). Hundreds of additional pleasure craft have been based on the *Spray*'s general lines and rig, and there are probably several thousand more inspired, to one degree or another, by Slocum's modest sloop. Less ambitious Slocum fans can find kits in any good hobby store and build their own model at home. Right now, somewhere on the world's oceans, someone is sailing a version of the *Spray* and keeping alive the remarkable story of a little boat that sailed around the world with only one crew member, the dauntless Yankee skipper Joshua Slocum.

As important as the material reincarnations of the *Spray* are, her voyage would be far less memorable if she had not also returned as a literary artifact, the inspiration and heroine, if you will, of one of the greatest sea narratives ever written. Like the *Spray*, *Sailing Alone Around the World* is Slocum's original creation, and it has enjoyed a long life in many editions, reprintings, and retellings. It first appeared in serial form in *Century Illustrated Monthly Magazine*, a popular periodical published in New York. As soon as the magazine series ended, Slocum's tale was produced in book form, complete with the *Century* illustrations by Thomas Fogarty and George Varian. It sold 7,000 copies in its first year, and its original edition eventually sold more than 27,000 copies (Teller, pp. 179, 176). Since 1956 it has been widely available in paperback editions, including a dozen or so for young readers. Excerpts are frequently included in anthologies of nautical writing. It has been translated into Swedish, Polish, French, German, Dutch, Spanish, Czech, and in 2003 and 2004, Japanese and Chinese. There is probably no time during its history that it has been out of print, an honor it shares with such American classics as Harriet Beecher Stowe's *Uncle Tom's Cabin* (1852) and Mark Twain's *Adventures of Huckleberry Finn* (1884). Portions of the book are frequently anthologized, and its durability has kept Slocum's other extended sea narrative, *Voyage of the Liberdade* (1890), before the public as well. Slocum has his own author society, an active group of sailors, shipbuilders, and lovers of nautical literature who honor his boat, his book, and his remarkable feat with regattas, awards, a journal and newsletter, and various memorabilia, all available on the society's website (see "For Further Reading").

So for all his seeming obscurity in the world of American literature, Slocum's journey has fostered a world unto itself, a place where dedicated men and women spend years studying details of his boat; rebuilding it out of wood, fiberglass, reinforced concrete, aluminum, or steel; replicating his journey in whole or in part; and reading again and again the story of his amazing voyage.

Given such interest in the man and his boat, one would think we would know more about him today. He has been favored with a tireless biographer, Walter Magnes Teller, who assembled most of the key facts and documents in Slocum's life and interviewed Slocum's remaining family in the 1950s. Besides *Sailing Alone*, Slocum left a small published legacy of two additional accounts of voyages; a souvenir pamphlet about the *Spray*; a few unpublished letters to his editors, government officials, family, and friends; and scattered newspaper interviews with inquisitive journalists. Teller has collected and published most of this material, and after reading it our first impression is that we know this man as we would a traveling companion. Throughout *Sailing Alone* Slocum appears honest, forthright, and direct, like Henry David Thoreau in *Walden* (1854), a man who cared more for truth than money, love, or fame. Slocum is much more modest and unassuming than Thoreau, however. His writing style is straightforward and lucid, his nautical terminology is appropriate and precise, and he achieves a consistent humor by gently mocking himself as well as others. He admits his shortcomings as well as his accomplishments, as when he confesses to getting lost at Cape Horn, or feeling anxious about lecturing, or being so afraid of meeting pirates in the Mediterranean that he completely reverses his itinerary by sailing west around Cape Horn instead of going east through the Suez Canal. Thoreau described how he single-handedly built a cabin for only $28.12½; similarly, Slocum describes building the *Spray* for only $553.62. But Thoreau does not include any plans. Slocum does, along with a detailed account of how he built the boat. His diagrams of the *Spray*'s profile, deck plan, and rigging are reprinted in nearly every edition. They lend his narrative authenticity and credibility and reinforce the impression of Slocum's sincerity. He presents himself as the real thing, an honest-to-goodness Yankee ship captain with a yarn to share and the salty language for telling it.

A more reflective and contextualized reading, however, suggests that these strengths of language and nautical detail mask the inner man, and veil him from the reader rather than reveal him. Like Benjamin Franklin in his famous autobiography, the prototype for all American stories of the self-made man, Slocum seldom indulges in the introspection and personal revelation that lead to psychological understanding. Readers must pierce through the descriptions of shipboard routine and daily survival to perceive the man as well as the voyage. Appreciating the intangibles of motive, purpose, philosophy, self-image, sense of accomplishment—all those elements that comprise one's true self—are key to recognizing Slocum's literary accomplishment. Had he not achieved as much in prose as he did at sea, he would be little more than a footnote in nautical history. His deceptively simple narrative brings the man, the voyage, and the boat together as one, welded as one piece from stem to stern in a book that concludes not with a picture of the man, but a cross section of a boat. Even though *Sailing Alone* records a voyage, it also memorializes a life, and constitutes an autobiography in which both the author and his boat are constructed representations, one of words, one of wood.

Joshua Slocum has no grave, no headstone, no final resting place. On November 14, 1909, after having achieved more worldly fame and success than almost any man of his class and profession, he sailed off in the *Spray* one stormy day and never returned. He was not declared legally dead until 1924 (Teller, p. 236). Even today theories abound about his demise, some as fanciful as those surrounding Amelia Earhart, the aviator who never returned from an around-the-world flight in 1937. Was the *Spray* no longer seaworthy, and had it simply broken up in a gale? Did Slocum, who couldn't swim, fall overboard? Or did he sail down to the West Indies, as he had done for three winters between 1905 and 1908, and collide with a steamship in the night? Did he commit suicide? No one knows for sure. His most recent biographer, Ann Spencer, argues persuasively that he actually died in 1908, not 1909 (*Alone at Sea: The Adventures of Joshua Slocum*, pp. 237–249), further adding to the mystery of his death. Such questions are only the most obvious clues to a greater mystery: the voyage itself. We can read *Sailing Alone* as a great adventure story, or a detailed and factual guide to single-handed sailing, or a lesson in cross-cultural encounters, or a global geography lesson. One version of the book was actually edited for use as a geography primer in public schools. *Sailing Alone* is all these, and more. Yet by themselves these features do not explain the book's attraction for generations of readers, many of whom have never sailed or built a ship model. Slocum's story is most compelling, I think, as a personal account of one man's midlife quest for meaning and personal fulfillment in a world that no longer needed him. Joshua Slocum, setting out alone at fifty-one years of age on a voyage many deemed impossible and most thought foolish, sought a new basis for constructing a self to withstand the onslaught of a new century. By 1895 steam had replaced sail, and Slocum could no longer practice the profession he had learned at sixteen and mastered by thirty-seven. By constructing his own reality, even at the expense of friends, family, and colleagues, he might find his true self.

Like the author, readers must also search for Slocum's true self, for he does not reveal it readily. To find the inner Slocum we must read his narrative as closely as we would a novel or poem, navigating our course not only by surfaces but also by undercurrents. Slocum describes commonplace occurrences at length yet omits major events that alter the whole cruise. For example, he describes how he collects tallow (animal fat) at Cape Horn and why he trades it, yet he mentions nothing about his wife's refusal to accompany him or why he decided to round Cape Horn rather than cross the Panamanian isthmus as he originally intended (Teller, p. 98). Whether or not he gathered tallow was irrelevant to his accomplishment; but voyaging alone via Cape Horn was crucial. In autobiography, both inclusions and exclusions provide meaning and help shape our perception of the whole person. Slocum's candor is apparent, not real, and his literary judgments about what to include and what to omit, as well as the manner in which he relates them, make him an even more fascinating and intriguing author. Early newspapers disbelieved his tale, and while later students have demonstrated its veracity, few have comprehended its inner truth. Slocum, whose narrative seems straightforward and direct, is actually quite subtle. Comic, ironic, understated, metaphorical, and as calculating with words as its author was with tallow, *Sailing Alone Around the World* has literary value that must be recognized and understood if we are to grasp the full significance of Slocum's life and craft.

II

When Slocum wrote *Sailing Alone Around the World*, he already had two books to his credit, *Voyage of the Liberdade* and *Voyage of the Destroyer from New York to Brazil* (1894), the latter only thirty-seven pages long. Although Slocum attended school for only three years, he brought to his best-known sea narrative not only a wealth of nautical experience but also some basic literary experience. As the age of sail faded under the onslaught of steam, nostalgia drove a renewed interest in tales of wind-driven ships and the men who commanded them. Slocum was well placed to satisfy this demand, for he had been at sea since he was sixteen and had sailed a variety of vessels to most of the world's major ports. He started out as a deckhand on a lumber boat bound for Dublin, then signed on the *Tanjore*, a British freighter, and sailed around the Cape of Good Hope to Hong Kong and back. He returned via Batavia in the Dutch East Indies (present-day Indonesia), where he was promoted to second mate (Teller, pp. 8–9). Always the individualist, he taught himself navigation and shipbuilding, two skills essential for his famous voyage. In 1864, with two Cape Horn passages under his belt, he became a naturalized American citizen and began calling San Francisco his home port. At the fairly young age of twenty-five, he gained his first command, and in 1870 he sailed the bark *Washington* to Sydney, Australia, where he met and married Virginia Walker (Teller, pp. 10–11). Virginia, a sturdy and adventuresome American whose family had emigrated to Australia, accompanied him on every one of his voyages for the next fourteen years. She bore him seven children: three sons, Victor, Benjamin Aymar, and Garfield; one daughter, Jessie; and a set of twins and one daughter who all died in infancy. All were born on board one of the many vessels Slocum commanded between 1870 and 1884. This was truly a nautical family, voyaging together across the Pacific to catch fish and transport coal, timber, ice, and other commodities, and visiting such exotic ports as Manila, Honolulu, Shanghai, Vladivostok, and Yokohama. Of Slocum's twenty-eight years in the merchant service, seventeen of them were spent with his family aboard.

Slocum demonstrated his shipbuilding skills in 1874 when he constructed a wooden steamer for a British architect in the Philippines. As part payment he received the *Pato*, a schooner he took on an 8,000-mile cruise to the North Pacific cod banks. He sold the catch in Portland, Oregon, and then sailed on to Honolulu, where he sold the boat for a profit (Teller, pp. 15–17). Clearly enjoying the independence conferred by ownership, Slocum purchased the 350-ton ship *Amethyst* in San Francisco around 1875, and in 1881 moved up to his finest command, the 1,857-ton full-rigged ship *Northern Light* (Teller, pp. 17, 21). As a part owner, Slocum was at the peak of his career, commanding a ship he considered "the finest American sailing vessel afloat" (quoted in Teller, p. 21). He took possession in Hong Kong and sailed her to New York, making enough of a splash to earn a feature article in the *New York Tribune*. Unfortunately, his command of this notable three-master was short-lived. Only a few days out on his first voyage, a round-the-world cruise to Yokohama, Slocum had to put in for repairs, and a mutinous sailor fatally stabbed the first mate in a dispute over pay. Virginia covered the captain with a revolver while Slocum searched the crew for the weapon. On the homeward journey Slocum clapped in irons the second mate, Henry A. Slater, apparently to prevent a mutiny. On his return to New York, Slocum was convicted of false and cruel imprisonment and fined $500, and soon sold his shares in the *Northern Light* in order to return to smaller ships with smaller and hopefully more manageable crews (Teller, pp. 25–28).

Slocum's fourth ship, the *Aquidneck*, was only 326 tons, and was mostly suitable for the coasting trade between the northeastern United States and South America, one of the few remaining routes open to sailing ships. Steamers were taking over the transatlantic and transpacific routes, and the transcontinental railroad and Suez Canal had made the dangerous trips around the southern Capes uneconomical and impractical. Slocum was only one of many late-nineteenth-century sailing captains who watched steam crowd out sail and saw their personal fortunes decline as they stubbornly clung to a dying trade. Although the *Aquidneck* was a well-appointed ship with plenty of room for the family—it even had a square piano bolted to the deck in the saloon (Teller, p. 30)—it proved to be the last vessel on which the seagoing Slocums sailed together. In 1884 Virginia took ill in the anchorage off Buenos Aires and died as she had lived, at sea aboard her husband's ship. On his return to Baltimore, Joshua left his three youngest children with his sisters in Natick, Massachusetts (Teller, p. 45). Only Victor, his oldest son, remained with him. Virginia's death and the family's separation must have affected the forty-year-old Slocum deeply. He sailed for fourteen years with his wife and children, attended seven births at sea, and carefully arranged his vessels to serve the needs of both home and business. Virginia proved a supportive and dauntless wife and mother, educating their children and withstanding the rigors of commercial sailing with its harsh weather, surly crews, social isolation, and uncertain future. He would never find a companion like her again.

Slocum now began to experience the profound isolation so characteristic of command, the kind of loneliness, separation, and anxiety Joseph Conrad explores in *The Nigger of the "Narcissus"* (1897) and "The Secret Sharer" (1909), stories set during the same era as Slocum's. With Victor as mate, Slocum made several trading voyages between Baltimore and Buenos Aires on the *Aquidneck*. Early in 1886 he married Henrietta ("Hettie") Elliott, a first cousin who was, at twenty-four, eighteen years his junior (Teller, pp. 45–46). For a time, it looked as though he might reconstitute his previous family life, as Hettie, Victor, and little Garfield joined him and a crew of six men for a voyage from New York to Montevideo, Uruguay. Benjamin Aymar and Jessie stayed behind in Massachusetts, an early sign that Slocum's family life was diminishing. This would be Hettie's introduction to seafaring, and a more rigorous introduction would be hard to imagine. As Slocum lightheartedly recounts in *Voyage of the Liberdade*, within three days the *Aquidneck* encountered a hurricane with 90-mile-an-hour winds driving huge waves that destroyed the galley and almost drowned the hapless cook (Slocum, *The Voyages of Joshua Slocum*, pp. 42–43). After reaching Montevideo, Slocum plied the coastal trade between Buenos Aires and Rio de Janeiro, shipping whatever odd cargo he could find, including wine salvaged from a shipwreck. When a cholera epidemic struck late in 1886, he spent six months in quarantine trying to deliver a load of alfalfa to Rio, and went through three crews before he managed to complete the unprofitable contract (*Voyages*, pp. 48–58). On the return trip south, four men tried to take over the ship, and when two of these "pirates" attacked Slocum with knives, he shot them both, killing one of them (*Voyages*, pp. 60–64). Although he was acquitted of murder, his troubles on the *Aquidneck* were not over. The next crew he recruited turned out to be infected with smallpox, and three of the men died. Slocum spent more than a thousand dollars disinfecting the ship, but what it cost him "in health and mental anxiety," he writes, "cannot be estimated by such value" (*Voyages*, p. 71). The *Aquidneck*, the unluckiest ship Slocum ever owned, finally went aground on a sandbar in Brazil's Bay of Paranaguá, about 300 miles south of Rio de Janeiro, shortly after Christmas in 1887. After three days of buffeting by high seas, the ship's keel broke apart and left her a useless wreck. The last commercial vessel Slocum would ever own had to be sold for salvage, leaving the family homeless, destitute, in exile, and with no way to return to their native land.

At this point, lesser men might have called it quits. But Slocum's Yankee ingenuity and self-reliance prompted him to try once more to provide for his seafaring family. Hettie and Garfield had been living in Antonina, a little Brazilian town on the inland edge of Paranaguá Bay. Across the bay was the village of Guaraqueçaba (which Slocum spells phonetically as Guarakasava), a place with plenty of cheap native wood and willing labor. Slocum determined to build a boat from scratch that would take him and his family back to America, more than 5,000 miles away. The proud result was the 35-foot sailboat *Liberdade*, so named because she was launched on May 13, 1888, the day Brazil freed its slaves. After a few trial runs in the Bay of Paranaguá, the *Liberdade* set sail on June 24 with a crew of four—Victor, sixteen; Garfield, seven; and Hettie, whose first voyage was teaching her some hard lessons about the sea and sailors. She must have been getting disillusioned with sailing and perhaps her marriage as well, but she knew the *Liberdade* offered the only hope for her family to return home. Moreover, with no hired hands to bring aboard trouble or infection, she and Joshua could avoid the chief difficulties they had previously encountered. Compared to her time on the *Aquidneck*, Hettie's voyage on the *Liberdade* was peaceful indeed. A whale twice the size of the boat threatened to ram it, a gale snapped all the masts, and an onshore wind drove the boat into breaking seas that nearly swamped it; but at least there were no mutinies, homicides, or shipwrecks. Four months later the *Liberdade* anchored at Cape Roman, South Carolina, having spent fifty-five days at sea and traveled 5,510 miles, not counting what Slocum called "all the distances of the ins and outs" (*Voyages*, p. 114). The Slocums continued up the eastern seaboard to Washington, D.C., arriving there on December 27, 1888. By now word of the amazing voyage had reached the newspapers, and after spending the winter in Washington, they sailed to New York in May 1889, and were greeted by journalists eager to interview the intrepid family. One of them asked Hettie if she planned to take another voyage, and her reply spoke volumes: "Oh, I hope not. I haven't been home in over three years, and this was my wedding journey" (Teller, p. 56). True to her word, she never took a voyage with her husband again.

For Slocum, the *Liberdade* was suitably named, for this voyage liberated him from his exclusive reliance on the merchant service and led him to the vocation that would make his name a household word: writing. Despite his limited education, he had always sailed with a well-stocked library. Victor remembered that "one of the cabins of the *Northern Light* contained a library of at least five hundred volumes representing the standard works of the great writers" (Victor Slocum, *Capt. Joshua Slocum*, p. 146), including famous essayists, historians, poets, scientists, and novelists. "The cabin, with its orderly and well-fitted bookcases looked very much like the study of a literary worker or a college professor" (p. 147). The *Aquidneck* was similarly equipped, especially with three children for Virginia to educate. All sea captains wrote regularly in logs, of course, and corresponded frequently with merchants and ship owners, so Slocum was no stranger to pen and paper. After his return from South America, in fact, he pursued a six-year correspondence with the U.S. State Department in a fruitless attempt to win reparations from the Brazilian government for the loss of the *Aquidneck* (*Voyages*, pp. 125–153).

Although Slocum never learned to spell and punctuate properly, he had a keen eye for lively detail and fast-paced narrative, and omitted much tedious nautical detail in order to focus on colorful incidents and characters. He put these skills to work in *Voyage of the Liberdade*, a 175-page volume that he published at his own expense in 1890. "This literary craft of mine," he wrote self-consciously in the foreword, "in its native model and rig, goes out laden with the facts of the strange happenings on a home afloat" (*Voyages*, p. 39). Beneath its simple surface, this sentence demonstrates Slocum's instinctive literary sensibility. First, it develops an elaborate metaphor, comparing the construction of a ship to the construction of a book. Slocum knew the poetry of Henry Wadsworth Longfellow (Teller, p. 74), a writer who fully realized the metaphorical possibilities of shipbuilding in his popular poem "The Building of the Ship" (1849). Second, Slocum supports his metaphor with authentic nautical language: "craft" (a wonderful pun), "rig," "laden," "afloat," all contribute to our sense that we are entering a seafaring world. Third, he appeals to the sanctity of the "home," a cherished theme of Victorian readers. He fashions himself as at once captain, husband, and father, presenting a familiar face before he embarks on a foreign voyage. Most important, Slocum combines "facts" with "strange happenings," a blend characteristic of all great sea narratives, from Homer's *Odyssey* through Herman Melville's *Moby-Dick* (1851) right up to Sebastian Junger's *The Perfect Storm* (1997). At sea, everyday routine is spiked with unpredictable and astonishing events that keep readers on edge as they await the next abrupt change in wind and weather or in the attitudes of surly crewmen, not to mention the uncertain reactions of strangers in exotic ports.

Although *Voyage of the Liberdade* was little read, it proved to Slocum that he could write a book just as he had built a boat. His literary references show that he was familiar with a wide variety of literature. He alludes at length to classics such as Miguel de Cervantes Saavedra's *Don Quixote de la Mancha* (1605, 1615), Jonathan Swift's *Gulliver's Travels* (1726), and Samuel Taylor Coleridge's "The Rime of the Ancient Mariner" (1798). He describes scenes from numerous sea narratives, for instance Daniel Defoe's *Robinson Crusoe* (1719), Richard Henry Dana's *Two Years Before the Mast* (1840), Washington Irving's *History of the Life and Voyages of Christopher Columbus* (1828), and Owen Chase's *Narrative of the Most Extraordinary and Distressing Shipwreck of the Whale-Ship Essex* (1821), one of the books that inspired *Moby-Dick*. He also knew current literature: he mentions having read Mark Twain's *Life on the Mississippi* (1883) and quotes from popular poetry by Amelia B. Welby, Charles Kingsley, Daniel Auber, and Charles G. Leland. *Voyage of the Liberdade* made a fine trial run for *Sailing Alone Around the World*, and it merits the attention of readers who want a full picture of Slocum's literary achievement. Composing it gave him confidence in his shaky writing abilities that he would put to good use a decade later.

Still, authorship didn't pay the bills. Slocum spent the next three years wandering around shipyards looking for temporary jobs, some of them dirty and demeaning for a man who had once commanded "the finest American sailing vessel afloat." As Walter Teller puts it, "Within a span of five years Slocum had lost his wife, his home, his money and now, at age forty-five, his profession as well" (p. 56). The only good jobs were aboard steamships, but he wouldn't take one even when the White Star Line offered him a command: "I followed the sea in sailing ships since I was fourteen years old," he told his son Garfield. "If I accepted this offer, I would have to get used to steamships, and I do not like steamships" (Teller, p. 59). Slocum hoped he might win a settlement over the loss of the *Aquidneck* from the Brazilian government or find a position on a sailing vessel. He was too young and too poor to retire, yet too curious and too energetic to accept life on land. He and Hettie now lived in separate residences in East Boston, presumably by choice, he with an aunt and she with a sister and the two youngest children, Garfield and Jessie (Teller, p. 56). Benjamin Aymar was on his own, and Victor had become a sailor. At this critical time in Slocum's life, an old friend, Captain Eben Pierce, offered to give him a boat. Slocum went down to Fairhaven, Massachusetts, about 40 miles south of Boston on the Acushnet River, and there found the rotting, century-old hulk of an oyster sloop. It was the *Spray*. Pierce had played a bad joke on Slocum, but Slocum considered the boat carefully and decided to re-build her in his spare time, the one thing he had in abundance. He moved in with Pierce and spent the next thirteen months completely reframing the *Spray*, altering her lines, adding a cabin, raising her bulwarks, and strengthening her bows. By the time he was finished, he had built an entirely new craft from the remains of the old.

Cabin of the Spray, *looking for'd (left) and looking aft (right) drawn by Robbert Das. Slocum used two berths: The starboard one was used when at anchor in calm water; the port one, his sea berth, allowed him to see the wheel and mainsail. The picture on the right shows his depth sounding lead on the port side and his chart table opposite with his compass above, visible also from the cockpit. Slocum's clock/chronometer, his mug, pipe, and tobacco are on his chest. As a trained seaman he would have rigged his lee cloth with a slip knot so that he could get out in a hurry. Illustrations courtesy of Bruce Roberts Yacht Design, www.bruceroberts.com.*

Once again in command of his own vessel, albeit much reduced from the *Northern Light* and the *Aquidneck*, Slocum spent a season fishing in 1893 but decided, with characteristic self-directed humor, that he "had not the cunning properly to bait a hook." Still in need of cash, he agreed to serve as navigator aboard the *Destroyer*, an experimental American warship with a lethal undersea cannon. The new Brazilian Republic had ordered the ship to suppress a rebellion led by naval commanders. The *Destroyer*, a steamship, was towed to Brazil and delivered as promised despite a trip Slocum called "the hardest voyage that I ever made, without any exception at all" (*Voyages*, p. 186). Unfortunately, for a second time Slocum received no compensation from Brazil. Fearing the ship might fall into rebel hands or provoke a more destructive conflict, the government scuttled her and refused to pay Slocum for his work, an incident he recounts in *Sailing Alone* (pp. 62–63). In revenge he wrote *Voyage of the Destroyer from New York to Brazil*, a comic account that satirizes Brazil's incompetent navy and venal politicians as well as one of Slocum's crew, a foppish British soldier of fortune who challenged Slocum to a duel. This slender book gave Slocum a second opportunity to sharpen his literary tools and hone the wit that marks his masterpiece. Only thirty-seven pages long, it records his first lengthy voyage without his family and reveals a sardonic, even fatalistic side to his personality that his earlier book had largely masked.

In *Voyage of the Liberdade* Slocum offers a clue to his unplumbed depths when he describes his reunion with Hettie and Garfield in Antonina, after the smallpox incident: "Sorrows of the past took flight, or were locked in the closet at home, the fittest place for past misfortunes" (*Voyages*, p. 72). The sorrow locked in Slocum's heart was his grief over Virginia's death, for only a few lines before this he describes being becalmed at a little island on the return trip to his wife and son: "A spell seemed to hang over us. I recognized the place as one that I knew well; a very dear friend had stood by me on deck, looking at this island, some years before. It was the last land that my friend ever saw" (*Voyages*, p. 72). His "friend," Virginia, had given him seven children, a sailing partner, companionship, and unflinching support for fourteen years. Hettie, however much she tried, could not fill this void. By rhetorically juxtaposing the day of Virginia's death with the day of his return to Hettie, Slocum reveals his inability to construct a full relationship with his second wife and exposes an emotional isolation as profound as the physical isolation of his life aboard the *Spray*. His love for Virginia, in the words of one distant relative, had been "vital," but his feelings for Hettie were merely "kind and courtly" (quoted in Spencer, *Alone at Sea*, p. 78). The fact that Slocum and Hettie never had any children suggests a less intimate and committed relationship than he enjoyed with Virginia, and their living arrangements were more like those of a formally separated couple than a loving husband and wife. Using documents Walter Teller suppressed, Ann Spencer stresses the differences between Hettie and Virginia, and hypothesizes that, after the voyage of the *Liberdade*, Hettie may have realized "that her husband's heart was too often with his 'dear friend' Virginia" (p. 72). It was fitting that Slocum wrote *Voyage of the Destroyer* while he lived alone on the *Spray*, almost as though he was practicing for the great work of his life, an event and a book that share the same name and the same metaphorical significance in Slocum's life: *Sailing Alone Around the World*.

III

Why did Slocum undertake his perilous voyage? No one knows for sure. Certainly, he needed money, and told reporters that he hoped to make enough to buy a farm and settle down, the dream of every sailor (Teller, p. 76). In *Voyage of the Liberdade*, however, he explicitly rejected such a fate when he witnessed the poverty and resignation of a South Carolina farm family: "My own misfortunes passed into shade as the harder luck of the Andersons came before my mind, and the resolution which I had made to buy a farm was now shaken and finally dissolved into doubts of the wisdom of such a course" (*Voyages*, p. 117). He did some trading along the way and sold curios when he returned, but neither of these enterprises amounted to much financially. He made arrangements to serialize his travel adventures in several newspapers, a scheme Mark Twain used effectively when he toured Europe and the Holy Land in 1867 and compiled his letters into the wildly successful travel book *The Innocents Abroad* (1869). Within a few months of starting out, however, Slocum had written such sporadic, dull accounts that his editors quickly lost interest, and only three of the proposed installments ever appeared. For most of his three-year voyage, he ended up writing almost nothing.

Whether he knew it at the time or not, Slocum's true motives had little to do with financial gain or an alternate career. "Slocum's long journey," Ann Spencer surmises, "was as much an inner voyage through the psyche as an outward voyage over ocean waters" (p. 148). His deepest motives, I suggest, were more like those of one of his favorite literary heroes, Don Quixote, who decided in middle age to start life anew as a knight-errant. This decision isolated Quixote from his family and took him on bizarre, far-flung adventures. He appeared to many a fool, to some insane, but in his lonely idealism Quixote found the courage to confront mortality with action, however absurd it seemed to others. Victor Slocum believed that "all the people in 'Don Quixote' were to [my father] living characters" (p. 147). When Slocum decided on his solo voyage he was fifty-one, about Quixote's age. Rather than grieve over losing the *Liberdade*, the *Destroyer*, his livelihood, and the companionship of wife and family, he set a goal for himself that seemed to some people as mad as Quixote's tilting at windmills. No one had ever sailed alone around the world, let alone in a 37-foot sloop. Before sailing, he endured some of the same ostracism and skepticism society directed at the Don. He asked Hettie to accompany him, but she predictably declined, simply telling him in her Boston accent, "Joshua, I've had a v'yage" (Teller, p. 76). Shipyard friends questioned the *Spray*'s seaworthiness and Slocum's shipbuilding skills. They knew that sailing required attention twenty-four hours a day, and couldn't understand when Slocum would cook, eat, or sleep. Even after he completed his voyage, journalists questioned his veracity. Not until he produced his yacht license showing the ports he had visited did people believe that Slocum's quixotic dream had indeed come true (Teller, p. 158).

Slocum tells his own tale of his three-year voyage better than anyone, and there is no need to summarize it here. Readers must board the *Spray* and sail off on their own literary journey to savor the thrill of Slocum's accomplishment. What can be supplied is a better sense of how Slocum's narrative achieves its aim of making the impossible dream a credible reality. There is little evidence to suggest that Slocum planned to write an entire book about his journey before he started. After all, neither of his previous books had sold well. In the South Seas, however, he discovered a gift for spinning yarns about his perilous encounters with Black Pedro in the Straits of Magellan and the *Spray*'s amazing ability to steer herself. One lecture in Cape Town, South Africa, brought him enough money for his "needs in port and for the homeward voyage" (p. 200), and he still had enough South African gold in his pocket when he returned to Boston to pay his old debts (Teller, p. 161). In the Keeling, or Cocos, Islands, on August 20, 1897, he wrote a letter to Joseph B. Gilder, editor of the New York *Critic*, and asked whether he would "care for a story of the voyage around?" (Teller, p. 149), presumably a short magazine piece. When Slocum completed his voyage in Newport Harbor a year later, he received a telegram from Joseph's older brother, Richard Watson Gilder of the *Century Illustrated Monthly Magazine*, inviting Slocum to write an account for the magazine (Teller, p. 159). By this time, Slocum had decided on a book, and with R. W. Gilder's support he wrote his first draft over the winter of 1898–1899. The following summer he revised it with the help of *Century*'s editors, and it appeared serially between September 1899 and March 1900. Gilder, one of America's most powerful publishers, promoted the book with full-page advertisements in the *New York Times*, contributing mightily to the book's sales and Slocum's notoriety.

Sailing Alone Around the World is not a log or a journal or even a casual yarn, but a well-crafted narrative designed for maximum audience appeal. Central to its appeal is Slocum's persona, the image of himself that he presents to his readers. He learned on the lecture stage the value of humor, understatement, even self-deprecation, and put them to good use in constructing a colloquial voice for his narrative. Mark Twain, whose *Life on the Mississippi* had a permanent place in Slocum's shipboard library, developed such a persona into high art, a voice literary critics now call a "vernacular narrator." By employing the vernacular—the spoken language of ordinary people—writers can create a folksy narrator who sounds like he's telling a story over the backyard fence. Such deceptive simplicity encourages belief, no matter how strange the tale might be. And Slocum certainly had plenty of strange things to relate. When he was mistaken for the Antichrist at Rodriguez Island in the Indian Ocean, Slocum remarked, "It was a curious thing that at all of the islands some reality was insisted on as unreal, while improbabilities were clothed as hard facts" (p. 182). His job as a writer is to make the unreal real, to dazzle readers with the astonishing nature of his voyage while maintaining their trust. When he admits to his fears of pirates in the Mediterranean (p. 54), or confesses "a weakness" of hugging the shore too closely and beaching his boat in Uruguay (p. 65), or tells us "confidentially" that he gets seasick at Cape Horn (p. 90), he seems like one of us, an approachable and candid individual re-counting problems many mariners and ship passengers have faced. He attributes most of his success to his boat, not himself, and de-scribes at length the help he receives wherever he lands. His letter to Joseph Gilder is considerably more self-centered: He brags that he has made a voyage "such as, even the emperor of Germany could not do and first building his own ship," and adds that "the finest work I have done would be called fine even in the navy" (Teller, p. 160). In his finished book, such egotism is largely sup-pressed.

Like Twain, Slocum knew the value of humor. He considered himself "always fond of mirth" (*Voyages*, p. 120) and like Twain di-rects much of his humor at the pretentious fools he meets on his journey. The three Australian novices who refuse his help present "a case of babes in the wood or butterflies at sea," and their captain seems more distinguished by his "enormous yachtsman's cap" than his seamanship (p. 157). They are bound for New Guinea, which prompts Slocum to pun slyly on the alleged dangers of South Seas cannibalism: "Perhaps it was as well that three tenderfeet so tender as those never reached that destination" (p. 157). Always alert for funny stories and comic incidents, Slocum found "that American humor was never at a discount" in South Africa (p. 193), and some of his best jokes come at the expense of people he meets there. He mocks the famous journalist Henry M. Stanley's pretensions to nau-tical knowledge by repeating his absurd questions about the dangers posed by swordfish and rocks (p. 194). Slocum trusts his readers to understand that the first is highly unlikely, and the second so obvi-ous that it's not worth answering. He meets a clergyman who uses scripture to prove the world is flat and blandly notes that the Bible the good man carries is "not different from the one I had read" (p. 194). Slocum knows the world is round and that the Bible says nothing to contradict that, two points lost on the ignorant minister. Like any good vernacular narrator, Slocum punctures authority by appealing to common sense. Twain's vernacular hero Huckleberry Finn once decided to give up prayer after he asked for fish-hooks and didn't get any. Similarly, Slocum satirizes those who believe God answers prayers for fair winds by noting that a fair wind for one ship is necessarily foul for another (p. 215). Besides, the captain was in "one of the variables which will change when you ask it, if you ask long enough" (p. 215).

Victor Slocum found that even professional navigators missed one of Slocum's best jokes, the running gag about his tin clock. Slocum purchases the clock only because, "in our newfangled notions of navigation it is supposed that a mariner cannot find his way without one; and I had myself drifted into this way of thinking" (p. 28). Yet he knew that even the best chronometer can fail, and that real mariners can navigate in a number of ways. When the *Constitution*'s fancy chronometer failed in the Pacific, Slocum found his way home by employing lunar navigation, a lost art that allows a knowledgeable captain to determine his time anywhere in the world (Victor Slocum, p. 61). The pathetic tin clock confirms Slocum's skepticism of modern sailing methods and highlights his own navigational skills. In *Sailing Alone*, Slocum relies on lunar navigation to sail the 4,000 miles from Juan Fernández to Nuka Hiva and hits his destination within 5 miles with his "tin clock fast asleep" (p. 125), that is, not working. He even detects an error in the published tables. Slocum may have boiled his tin clock to keep it running for a short time, but only the most gullible readers will believe that he needed it to find his way. Through the tin clock, Slocum satirizes "newfangled notions of navigation" and demonstrates his self-reliance and the superiority of traditional seamanship.

Slocum also pokes fun at himself, an important technique that maintains his readers' trust. When the *Spray* strands on a beach in Uruguay, he launches his lifeboat, a homemade dory, to drop an anchor. The dory leaks badly, hardly testifying to his shipbuilding skill, and as it sinks he suddenly remembers that he cannot swim (p. 66). This time, the joke is on him. This piece of slapstick compounds his poor seamanship in getting beached in the first place with poor preparation and an absurd forgetfulness that momentarily undermine his nautical competence. He mocks his air of superiority again in Mauritius when he takes a boatload of young ladies for a sail and devilishly attempts to make them frightened and seasick. He hopes to discourage them and return to shore in time for dinner. His guests, however, "just stood up and laughed at seas tumbling aboard" (p. 188), and urged him so far out that he missed his dinner engagement. He jokes about his baldness when a Tongan princess gives him a bottle of coconut-oil for his hair (p. 134), and mocks his shark-fishing ability when he realizes he appears more heroic if he stays away from his exhibit in Tasmania (p. 149). Like Benjamin Franklin in his autobiography, Slocum makes fun of himself in order to maintain the reader's trust and avoid charges of egotism and self-promotion. (In his letter to R. W. Gilder agreeing to write for *Century* magazine, Slocum said he wanted to write "without saying Slocum Slocum all the time—that I do not care for" (quoted in Teller, p. 160).

Much of Slocum's humor comes from his ironic tone throughout, as when he refers to himself as the ship's "crew" or describes his companions: a "spider and his wife," a "cannibal" cricket (p. 209), and a goat that eats his chart of the West Indies (p. 207). He inflates his vision of the ghostly pilot from the *Pinta* into a comical musical interlude, quoting the pilot's "wild song" and his own peevish reply to the ghost to "tie a rope-yarn on the rest of the song, if there was any more of it" (p. 47). The best example of such ironic wit comes near the end, when Slocum encounters the immense United States battleship *Oregon* steaming her way around the Horn in the opening phases of the Spanish-American War, a conflict he hasn't even heard about. Using flag signals, the mighty *Oregon*, perhaps a thousand times the size of the *Spray*, asks if Slocum has seen any Spanish warships. "No," he answers, and then signals his countrymen, "Let us keep together for mutual protection" (p. 213), as if he could offer protection to a steel battleship! Such understated Yankee humor endears Slocum to his readers and makes his narrative much more than a tale of heroism and adventure.

The *Oregon's* appearance suggests another reason for Slocum's literary success, and may very well be something his editors at the *Century* encouraged. At the end of the nineteenth century, America was embarking on its imperial mission, extending its reach around the world through both trade and military might. Slocum's patriotism is a quiet undercurrent in his narrative, yet it is one that would have appealed greatly to a country that, in 1900, had just driven Spain out of the Western Hemisphere and extended its dominions across the Pacific to Hawaii and the Philippines. When Slocum takes possession of the *Spray*'s decayed hulk, she rests near the grave of John Cook, "a revered Pilgrim father. So the new *Spray* rose from hallowed ground" (p. 20). Such details, irrelevant to the voyage itself, firmly place the little sloop's voyage within the larger currents of American history. Slocum's repeated references to the "Stars and Stripes" expand this history to global proportions and remind us that the *Spray* is an American ship flying the American flag. In the Straits of Magellan he feels comforted by the presence of the *Colombia*, "a great steamship . . . with a lofty bearing" (p. 102) that he recognizes on sight. The two vessels salute each other by hoisting the American flag in nationalistic self-recognition. The harbormaster at Devonport, Tasmania, tells Slocum that "the *Spray* was the first vessel to bring the Stars and Stripes to the port" (p. 153), effectively placing the captain in the vanguard of transpacific American expansion. And at a celebration of Queen Victoria's jubilee, the local magistrate assures him that Australians "do not consider the Stars and Stripes a foreign flag" (p. 169). At this point, readers might recall Slocum's opening account of his Canadian birth and recognize his self-conscious role as a goodwill ambassador between the British Commonwealth and the newly imperialistic United States. While Slocum generally avoids politics, they are nonetheless present and were, perhaps, more noticed by readers in 1900 than today.

The same may be said for Slocum's philosophical views. His respectful attitude toward nature in an era when "the survival of the fittest" dominated social discourse must have struck early readers as unusual. Although he enjoys killing sharks (pp. 60, 127), most of the time he hesitates to kill for his food. "I seldom or never put a hook over during the whole voyage," he writes, and he refuses to shoot a large bird he sees in the Straits of Magellan: "In the loneliness of life about the dreary country I found myself in no mood to make one life less, except in self-defense" (p. 88). By the time he reaches Samoa, "a new self" rebels at the idea of carrying chickens to slaughter along the way for food, and by the end of his voyage "the mention of killing food-animals was revolting to me" (p. 208). Slocum is willing to rely on the bounty of the sea, as in the flying fish that land on his deck at night, but he is unwilling to take life himself.

Slocum never seems to have been a conventionally religious person, and Ann Spencer even speaks of his "somewhat irreligious attitude" toward missionaries and narrow-minded Christians (p. 159). She balances this view by exploring Slocum's spirituality and the numerous "moments of epiphany and awakening" that make his voyage truly "a journey of the soul" (pp. 148–149). He confirms his reckonings "by reading the clock aloft made by the Great Architect" (p. 123), and after surviving the Straits of Magellan he affirms that "the Hand that held [the waves] held also the *Spray*" (p. 89). When he enters the Pacific Ocean he adds movingly, "Then was the time to uncover my head, for I sailed alone with God" (p. 114). While Slocum certainly believed in God, his references to the deity are actually quite infrequent and often seem mere rhetorical gestures. We are always more aware that he sails "alone" than that he sails with "God." He seems to be, in fact, his own god, a self-reliant individual who discovers within himself the physical, mental, and spiritual strength to challenge the world's oceans and succeed. He refers nearly as often to "Neptune" as to "God," and his oneness with the sea echoes the nature-worship of such American transcendentalists as Ralph Waldo Emerson and Thoreau. Slocum's religion is broad, nondogmatic, humanistic, and intensely personal, not something to impose on others but rather something for all readers to discover within themselves.

It is, finally, this drive into the innermost self that marks Slocum's lasting significance. His story is at once a tale of personal triumph and a tale of personal discontent. While his book sold well, it didn't make as much money as he hoped. He was famous enough to speak at the same podium as his literary mentor, Mark Twain (*New York Times*, December 15, 1900), but had to trade on that fame by lecturing and exhibiting the *Spray* at the Pan-American Exhibition in 1901, giving tours, selling souvenirs, and marketing himself like any good American huckster (Spencer, pp. 202–203). He promoted himself aggressively, taking reporters out on the

Spray, pointing out the merits of his automatic steering apparatus, and giving lectures illustrated with 300 "lantern slides" (Spencer, p. 193). He finally made enough money to purchase his first home on the island of Martha's Vineyard, Massachusetts, in 1902 (Spencer, pp. 207–208). He and Hettie set up housekeeping, and he tried farming, but he clearly hated it. Audiences gradually lost interest in his lectures, and he soon "gained a reputation for being opinionated, acerbic, and difficult to befriend" (Spencer, pp. 212–213). By 1905 he began taking extended solo voyages to the West Indies in the winter months. His three years circumnavigating the world had confirmed the isolation all commanders feel and cemented it into his personality. Looking back at *Sailing Alone*, one notices great silences, such as the seventy-two days between Juan Fernández and Samoa, the forty-two days between Samoa and Australia, or the long reaches across the Indian Ocean. Slocum has difficulty describing his thoughts during these stretches, as though he cannot articulate his deepest feelings. Much of the narrative actually takes place on land, as when he spends an entire winter in Tasmania and Australia waiting for better weather through the Torres Strait, or when he takes a three-month trek through South Africa while the *Spray* is laid up for repairs. Even though he assures readers early on that "the acute pain of solitude experienced at first never returned" (p. 38), he mentions his "loneliness" and "solitude" again and again, particularly when the weather is fine and he has little to distract him from his isolation (pp. 36, 105). One feels Slocum is hiding something, using his humorous persona to mask feelings that surface only when he confronts the reality of an unhappy marriage and fractured family. Like his literary mentor Mark Twain, who also cloaked his despair with humor, Slocum felt increasingly isolated from the very world that had made him famous, and spent more and more time by himself. As he had advised in *Voyage of the Liberdade*, it seemed best to lock his emotions "in the closet at home" (*Voyages*, p. 72).

In 1906 Slocum was arrested in New Jersey and charged with raping a twelve-year-old girl who visited the *Spray* (Teller, p. 220). It was the lowest moment of his life. The charges were dismissed, but only after the captain had spent forty-two days in jail, apparently without any family coming to his aid. He had, biographers think, probably left his trousers unbuttoned while showing the girl around the boat, and she had overreacted (Spencer, p. 222). The event was nonetheless demeaning and embarrassing, something that Walter Teller privately considered "almost a Greek tragedy" (Spencer, p. 223). By this time, Slocum was spending most of his time on the *Spray*, either living there alone or sailing alone to the West Indies. More than Walter Teller, Ann Spencer emphasizes Slocum's loneliness and discontent in these final years. She quotes a letter from Victor Slocum that Teller left unpublished that summarizes the real cost of Slocum's voyage: "Father was a changed man when he returned from his lone voyage—he acted to me like he wanted to be alone. That voyage was a terrible strain on him. Father was so different when he returned from sailing alone, he did not talk to me much. He appeared to be deep in thought so I stayed far" (Spencer, p. 230). In the last photographs we have of Joshua Slocum, he looks drawn, tired, exhausted, unhappy, even a bit foolish and distracted, as when he shows off the *Spray* to a young admirer, Winfield Scott Clime, in 1907. Slocum wears a straw hat with its wide brim turned up to reveal a haggard, unsmiling face for the camera, and he strikes awkward poses with a hammer and axe in a vain attempt to lend authenticity to the pictures (Teller, pp. 193–194). The *Spray* appears equally disheveled and downcast, and the final descriptions we have of it suggest that Slocum had neglected his sloop as much as his family and himself (Teller, pp. 233–235). We have little writing in Slocum's own words in his final years and can only surmise what drove him to make his final voyage in such unseaworthy shape. Ann Spencer believes he ended his life "a troubled, misunderstood, and desperately insecure man" (p. 249), a view one can find beneath the surface of *Sailing Alone*. It is almost as if Slocum resisted the hard lesson of his voyage: he loved sailing and solitude more than he loved society, wealth, children, wife, or fame. It is to his lasting glory that he not only made one of the most amazing voyages in history, but also left a book to tell us about it, a book that deserves to be read closely both for what it says and what it omits, a work of literature on which Slocum lavished more care than anything in his life except the boat that carried him to his greatest fame and final doom, the 37-foot sloop *Spray*.

Dennis A. Berthold, Professor of English, has taught at Texas A&M University in College Station, Texas, since 1972. He specializes in nineteenth-century American literature and has published scholarly articles and books on Charles Brockden Brown, Ralph Waldo Emerson, Nathaniel Hawthorne, Margaret Fuller, Herman Melville, Mark Twain, Walt Whitman, and Constance Fenimore Woolson. He also writes on nautical literature, with two essays in *Literature and Lore of the Sea* (1986), a chapter on contemporary American sea fiction in *America and the Sea: A Literary History* (1995), entries in the *Encyclopedia of American Literature of the Sea and Great Lakes* (2001), and an introduction to maritime fiction in the forthcoming *Oxford Encyclopedia of Maritime History*. He has been teaching an undergraduate course in sea literature at Texas A&M since 1976.

SAILING ALONE
AROUND THE WORLD

To the one who said:
"The Spray will come back."

Contents

CHAPTER I

A blue-nose ancestry with Yankee proclivities—Youthful fondness for the sea—Master of the ship Northern Light*—Loss of the* Aquidneck*—Return home from Brazil in the canoe* Liberdade*—The gift of a "ship"—The rebuilding of the* Spray*—Conundrums in regard to finance and calking—The launching of the* Spray*   17*

CHAPTER II

Failure as a fisherman—A voyage around the world projected—From Boston to Gloucester—Fitting out for the ocean voyage—Half of a dory for a ship's boat—The run from Gloucester to Nova Scotia—A shaking up in home waters—Among old friends   25

CHAPTER III

Good-by to the American coast—Off Sable Island in a fog—In the open sea—The man in the moon takes an interest in the voyage—The first fit of loneliness—The Spray *encounters* La Vaguisa*—A bottle of wine from the Spaniard—A bout of words with the captain of the* Java*—The steamship* Olympia *spoken—Arrival at the Azores   34*

CHAPTER IV

Squally weather in the Azores—High living—Delirious from cheese and plums—The pilot of the Pinta*—At Gibraltar—Compliments exchanged with the British navy—A picnic on the Morocco shore   44*

CHAPTER V

Sailing from Gibraltar with the assistance of her Majesty's tug—The Spray's *course changed from the Suez Canal to Cape Horn—Chased by a Moorish pirate—A comparison with Columbus—The Canary Islands—The Cape Verde Islands—Sea life—Arrival at Pernambuco—A bill against the Brazilian government—Preparing for the stormy weather of the cape   54*

CHAPTER VI

Departure from Rio de Janeiro—The Spray *ashore on the sands of Uruguay—A narrow escape from shipwreck—The boy who found a sloop—The* Spray *floated but somewhat damaged—Courtesies from the British consul at Maldonado—A warm greeting at Montevideo—An excursion to Buenos Aires—Shortening the mast and bowsprit* 65

CHAPTER VII

Weighing anchor at Buenos Aires—An outburst of emotion at the mouth of the Plate—Submerged by a great wave—A stormy entrance to the strait—Captain Samblich's happy gift of a bag of carpet-tacks—Off Cape Froward—Chased by Indians from Fortescue Bay—A miss-shot for "Black Pedro"—Taking in supplies of wood and water at Three Island Cove— Animal life 75

CHAPTER VIII

From Cape Pillar into the Pacific—Driven by a tempest toward Cape Horn—Captain Slocum's greatest sea adventure—Reaching the strait again by way of Cockburn Channel—Some savages find the carpet-tacks— Danger from firebrands—A series of fierce williwaws—Again sailing westward 89

CHAPTER IX

Repairing the Spray's *sails—Savages and an obstreperous anchor—A spider-fight—An encounter with Black Pedro—A visit to the steamship* Colombia*—On the defensive against a fleet of canoes—A record of voyages through the strait—A chance cargo of tallow* 97

CHAPTER X

Running to Port Angosto in a snow-storm—A defective sheet-rope places the Spray *in peril—The* Spray *as a target for a Fuegian arrow—The island of Alan Erric—Again in the open Pacific—The run to the island of Juan Fernandez—An absentee king—At Robinson Crusoe's anchorage* 109

CHAPTER XI

The islanders of Juan Fernandez entertained with Yankee doughnuts— The beauties of Robinson Crusoe's realm—The mountain monument to Alexander Selkirk—Robinson Crusoe's cave—A stroll with the children of

*the island—Westward ho! with a friendly gale—A month's free sailing with
the Southern Cross and the sun for guides—Sighting the Marquesas—
Experience in reckoning*   118

CHAPTER XII

*Seventy-two days without a port—Whales and birds—A peep into the
Spray's galley—Flying-fish for breakfast—A welcome at Apia—A visit
from Mrs. Robert Louis Stevenson—At Vailima—Samoan hospitality—
Arrested for fast riding—An amusing merry-go-round—Teachers and
pupils of Papauta College—At the mercy of sea-nymphs*   127

CHAPTER XIII

*Samoan royalty—King Malietoa—Good-by to friends at Vailima—Leav-
ing Fiji to the south—Arrival at Newcastle, Australia—The yachts of
Sydney—A ducking on the Spray—Commodore Foy presents the sloop with
a new suit of sails—On to Melbourne—A shark that proved to be valuable—A change of course—The "Rain of Blood"—In Tasmania*   138

CHAPTER XIV

*A testimonial from a lady—Cruising round Tasmania—The skipper de-
livers his first lecture on the voyage—Abundant provisions—An inspection
of the Spray for safety at Devonport—Again at Sydney—Northward
bound for Torres Strait—An amateur shipwreck—Friends on the Australian coast—Perils of a coral sea*   152

CHAPTER XV

*Arrival at Port Denison, Queensland—A lecture—Reminiscences of Cap-
tain Cook—Lecturing for charity at Cooktown—A happy escape from a
coral reef—Home Island, Sunday Island, Bird Island—An American pearl-
fisherman—Jubilee at Thursday Island—A new ensign for the Spray—
Booby Island—Across the Indian Ocean—Christmas Island*   162

CHAPTER XVI

*A call for careful navigation—Three hours' steering in twenty-three
days—Arrival at the Keeling Cocos Islands—A curious chapter of social
history—A welcome from the children of the islands—Cleaning and
painting the Spray on the beach—A Mohammedan blessing for a pot of
jam—Keeling as a paradise—A risky adventure in a small boat—Away to*

Rodriguez—Taken for Antichrist—The governor calms the fears of the people—A lecture—A convent in the hills   173

Chapter XVII

A clean bill of health at Mauritius—Sailing the voyage over again in the opera-house—A newly discovered plant named in honor of the Spray's skipper—A party of young ladies out for a sail—A bivouac on deck—A warm reception at Durban—A friendly cross-examination by Henry M. Stanley—Three wise Boers seek proof of the flatness of the earth—Leaving South Africa   185

Chapter XVIII

Rounding the "Cape of Storms" in olden time—A rough Christmas—The Spray ties up for a three months' rest at Cape Town—A railway trip to the Transvaal—President Kruger's odd definition of the Spray's voyage—His terse sayings—Distinguished guests on the Spray—Cocoanut fiber as a padlock—Courtesies from the admiral of the Queen's navy—Off for St. Helena—Land in sight   196

Chapter XIX

In the isle of Napoleon's exile—Two lectures—A guest in the ghost-room at Plantation House—An excursion to historic Longwood—Coffee in the husk, and a goat to shell it—The Spray's ill luck with animals—A prejudice against small dogs—A rat, the Boston spider, and the cannibal cricket—Ascension Island   205

Chapter XX

In the favoring current off Cape St. Roque, Brazil—All at sea regarding the Spanish-American war—An exchange of signals with the battle-ship Oregon—Off Dreyfus's prison on Devil's Island—Reappearance to the Spray of the north star—The light on Trinidad—A charming introduction to Grenada—Talks to friendly auditors   212

Chapter XXI

Clearing for home—In the calm belt—A sea covered with sargasso—The jibstay parts in a gale—Welcomed by a tornado off Fire Island—A change of plan—Arrival at Newport—End of a cruise of over forty-six thousand miles—The Spray again at Fairhaven   219

APPENDIX

LINES AND SAIL-PLAN OF THE SPRAY

Her pedigree so far as known—The lines of the Spray—*Her self-steering qualities—Sail-plan and steering-gear—An unprecedented feat—A final word of cheer to would-be navigators* 227

List of Illustrations

The *Spray* .... *Frontispiece*
    From a photograph taken in Australian waters.
The *Northern Light,* Captain Joshua Slocum, bound
    for Liverpool, 1885 18
Cross-section of the *Spray* 21
"It'll crawl!" 23
"No dorg nor no cat" 30
The deacon's dream 31
Captain Slocum's Chronometer 33
"Good evening, sir" 36
"He also sent his card" 38
Chart of the *Spray's* course around the world—April 24,
    1895, to July 3, 1898 39
The island of Pico 41
Chart of the *Spray's* Atlantic voyages from Boston to Gibraltar,
    thence to the Strait of Magellan, in 1895, and finally
    homeward bound from the Cape of Good Hope in 1898 . . . 42
The apparition at the wheel 46
Coming to anchor at Gibraltar 50
The *Spray* at anchor off Gibraltar 51
Chased by pirates 56
"I suddenly remembered that I could not swim" 66
A double surprise 69
At the sign of the comet 73
A great wave off the Patagonian coast 76
Entrance to the Strait of Magellan 78
The course of the *Spray* through the Strait of Magellan 79
The man who wouldn't ship without another
    "mon and a doog" 80
A Fuegian girl 82
Looking west from Fortescue Bay, where the *Spray* was
    chased by Indians 83

A brush with Fuegians. 85
A bit of friendly assistance 87
Cape Pillar 90
They howled like a pack of hounds 93
A glimpse of Sandy Point (Punta Arenas) in the Strait
     of Magellan. 95
"Yammerschooner!" 100
A contrast in lighting—the electric lights of the *Colombia*
     and the canoe fires of the Fortescue Indians 104
Records of passages through the strait at the Head
     of Borgia Bay 106
Salving wreckage 108
The first shot uncovered three Fuegians. 111
The *Spray* approaching Juan Fernandez, Robinson Crusoe's
     island. 115
The house of the king 119
Robinson Crusoe's cave. 120
The man who called a cabra a goat. 122
Meeting with the whale. 128
First exchange of courtesies in Samoa 130
Vailima, the home of Robert Louis Stevenson 131
The *Spray's* course from Australia to South Africa 135
The accident at Sydney 144
Captain Slocum working the *Spray* out of the Yarrow River,
     a part of Melbourne Harbor 146
The shark on the deck of the *Spray*. 147
On board at St. Kilda. Retracing on the chart the course
     of the *Spray* from Boston 150
The *Spray* in her port duster at Devonport, Tasmania,
     February 22, 1897. 154
"Is it a-goin' to blow?". 158
The *Spray* leaving Sydney, Australia, in the new suit
     of sails given by Commodore Foy of Australia 164
The *Spray* ashore for "boot-topping" at the Keeling Islands . . . 177
Captain Slocum drifting out to sea. 180
The *Spray* at Mauritius 186
Captain Joshua Slocum. 192

Cartoon printed in the Cape Town "Owl" of March 5, 1898,
in connection with an item about Captain Slocum's trip
to Pretoria 199
Captain Slocum, Sir Alfred Milner (with the tall hat),
and Colonel Saunderson, M. P., on the bow of the *Spray* at
Cape Town 201
Reading day and night. 203
The *Spray* passed by the *Oregon* 214
The *Spray* in the storm off New York 224
Again tied to the old stake at Fairhaven 226
Plan of the after cabin of the *Spray*. 229
Deck-plan of the *Spray* 230
Sail-plan of the *Spray* 231
Steering-gear of the *Spray* 232
Body-plan of the *Spray* 233
Lines of the *Spray* 235

SAILING ALONE

AROUND THE WORLD

CHAPTER I

A blue-nose ancestry with Yankee proclivities—Youthful fondness for the sea—Master of the ship *Northern Light*—Loss of the *Aquidneck*—Return home from Brazil in the canoe *Liberdade*—The gift of a "ship"—The rebuilding of the *Spray*—Conundrums in regard to finance and calking—The launching of the *Spray*.

In the fair land of Nova Scotia, a maritime province, there is a ridge called North Mountain, overlooking the Bay of Fundy on one side and the fertile Annapolis valley on the other. On the northern slope of the range grows the hardy spruce-tree, well adapted for ship-timbers, of which many vessels of all classes have been built. The people of this coast, hardy, robust, and strong, are disposed to compete in the world's commerce, and it is nothing against the master mariner if the birthplace mentioned on his certificate be Nova Scotia. I was born in a cold spot, on coldest North Mountain, on a cold February 20, though I am a citizen of the United States—a naturalized Yankee, if it may be said that Nova Scotians are not Yankees in the truest sense of the word. On both sides my family were sailors; and if any Slocum should be found not seafaring, he will show at least an inclination to whittle models of boats and contemplate voyages. My father was the sort of man who, if wrecked on a desolate island, would find his way home, if he had a jack-knife and could find a tree. He was a good judge of a boat, but the old clay farm which some calamity made his was an anchor to him. He was not afraid of a capful of wind, and he never took a back seat at a camp-meeting or a good, old-fashioned revival.

As for myself, the wonderful sea charmed me from the first. At the age of eight I had already been afloat along with other boys on the bay, with chances greatly in favor of being drowned. When a lad I filled the important post of cook on a fishing-schooner; but I was not long in the galley, for the crew mutinied at the appearance of my first duff, and "chucked me out" before I had a chance to shine as a culinary artist. The next step toward the goal of happiness found me before the mast in a full-rigged ship bound on a foreign voyage.

Thus I came "over the bows," and not in through the cabin windows, to the command of a ship.

My best command was that of the magnificent ship *Northern Light*, of which I was part-owner. I had a right to be proud of her, for at that time—in the eighties—she was the finest American sailing-vessel afloat. Afterward I owned and sailed the *Aquidneck,* a little bark which of all man's handiwork seemed to me the nearest to perfection of beauty, and which in speed, when the wind blew, asked no favors of steamers. I had been nearly twenty years a shipmaster when I quit her deck on the coast of Brazil, where she was wrecked. My home voyage to New York with my family was made in the canoe *Liberdade,* without accident.

My voyages were all foreign. I sailed as freighter and trader principally to China, Australia, and Japan, and among the Spice Islands. Mine was not the sort of life to make one long to coil up one's ropes on land, the customs and ways of which I had finally almost forgotten. And so when times for freighters got bad, as at last they did, and I tried to quit the sea, what was there for an old sailor to do? I was born in the breezes, and I had studied the sea as

Drawn by W. Taber.
The *Northern Light,* Captain Joshua Slocum,
bound for Liverpool, 1885.

perhaps few men have studied it, neglecting all else. Next in attractiveness, after seafaring, came ship-building. I longed to be master in both professions, and in a small way, in time, I accomplished my desire. From the decks of stout ships in the worst gales I had made calculations as to the size and sort of ship safest for all weather and all seas. Thus the voyage which I am now to narrate was a natural outcome not only of my love of adventure, but of my lifelong experience.

One midwinter day of 1892, in Boston, where I had been cast up from old ocean, so to speak, a year or two before, I was cogitating whether I should apply for a command, and again eat my bread and butter on the sea, or go to work at the shipyard, when I met an old acquaintance, a whaling-captain, who said: "Come to Fairhaven and I'll give you a ship. But," he added, "she wants some repairs." The captain's terms, when fully explained, were more than satisfactory to me. They included all the assistance I would require to fit the craft for sea. I was only too glad to accept, for I had already found that I could not obtain work in the shipyard without first paying fifty dollars to a society, and as for a ship to command—there were not enough ships to go round. Nearly all our tall vessels had been cut down for coal-barges, and were being ignominiously towed by the nose from port to port, while many worthy captains addressed themselves to Sailors' Snug Harbor.[1]

The next day I landed at Fairhaven, opposite New Bedford, and found that my friend had something of a joke on me. For seven years the joke had been on him. The "ship" proved to be a very antiquated sloop called the *Spray*, which the neighbors declared had been built in the year 1. She was affectionately propped up in a field, some distance from salt water, and was covered with canvas. The people of Fairhaven, I hardly need say, are thrifty and observant. For seven years they had asked, "I wonder what Captain Eben Pierce[2] is going to do with the old *Spray*?" The day I appeared there was a buzz at the gossip exchange: at last some one had come and was actually at work on the old *Spray*. "Breaking her up, I s'pose?" "No; going to rebuild her." Great was the amazement. "Will it pay?" was the question which for a year or more I answered by declaring that I would make it pay.

My ax felled a stout oak-tree near by for a keel, and Farmer Howard, for a small sum of money, hauled in this and enough timbers for the frame of the new vessel. I rigged a steam-box and a pot for a boiler. The timbers for ribs, being straight saplings, were dressed and steamed till supple, and then bent over a log, where they were secured till set. Something tangible appeared every day to show for my labor, and the neighbors made the work sociable. It was a great day in the *Spray* shipyard when her new stem was set up and fastened to the new keel. Whaling-captains came from far to survey it. With one voice they pronounced it "A1," and in their opinion "fit to smash ice." The oldest captain shook my hand warmly when the breast-hooks were put in, declaring that he could see no reason why the *Spray* should not "cut in bow-head" yet off the coast of Greenland.[3] The much-esteemed stem-piece was from the butt of the smartest kind of a pasture oak. It afterward split a coral patch in two at the Keeling Islands, and did not receive a blemish. Better timber for a ship than pasture white oak never grew. The breast-hooks, as well as all the ribs, were of this wood, and were steamed and bent into shape as required. It was hard upon March when I began work in earnest; the weather was cold; still, there were plenty of inspectors to back me with advice. When a whaling-captain hove in sight I just rested on my adz awhile and "gammed"* with him.

New Bedford, the home of whaling-captains, is connected with Fairhaven by a bridge, and the walking is good. They never "worked along up" to the shipyard too often for me. It was the charming tales about arctic whaling that inspired me to put a double set of breast-hooks in the *Spray,* that she might shunt ice.

The seasons came quickly while I worked. Hardly were the ribs of the sloop up before apple-trees were in bloom. Then the daisies and the cherries came soon after. Close by the place where the old *Spray* had now dissolved rested the ashes of John Cook,[4] a revered Pilgrim father. So the new *Spray* rose from hallowed ground. From the deck of the new craft I could put out my hand and pick cherries that grew over the little grave. The planks for the new vessel, which I soon came to put on, were of Georgia pine an inch and a half thick. The operation of putting them on was tedious, but, when on, the calking was easy. The outward edges stood slightly open to receive the calking,

---

*Conversed; from "gam," a meeting between two whale ships.

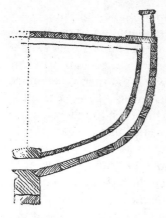

Cross-section of the *Spray.*

but the inner edges were so close that I could not see daylight between them. All the butts were fastened by through bolts, with screw-nuts tightening them to the timbers, so that there would be no complaint from them. Many bolts with screw-nuts were used in other parts of the construction, in all about a thousand. It was my purpose to make my vessel stout and strong.

Now, it is a law in Lloyd's[5] that the *Jane* repaired all out of the old until she is entirely new is still the *Jane.* The *Spray* changed her being so gradually that it was hard to say at what point the old died or the new took birth, and it was no matter. The bulwarks I built up of white-oak stanchions fourteen inches high, and covered with seven-eighth-inch white pine. These stanchions, mortised through a two-inch covering-board, I calked with thin cedar wedges. They have remained perfectly tight ever since. The deck I made of one-and-a-half-inch by three-inch white pine spiked to beams, six by six inches, of yellow or Georgia pine, placed three feet apart. The deck-inclosures were one over the aperture of the main hatch, six feet by six, for a cooking-galley, and a trunk farther aft, about ten feet by twelve, for a cabin. Both of these rose about three feet above the deck, and were sunk sufficiently into the hold to afford head-room. In the spaces along the sides of the cabin, under the deck, I arranged a berth to sleep in, and shelves for small storage, not forgetting a place for the medicine-chest. In the midship hold, that is, the space between cabin and galley, under the deck, was room for provision of water, salt beef, etc., ample for many months.

The hull of my vessel being now put together as strongly as wood and iron could make her, and the various rooms partitioned off, I set about "calking ship." Grave fears were entertained by some that at this point I should fail. I myself gave some thought to the advisability of a "professional calker." The very first blow I struck on the cotton with the calking-iron, which I thought was right, many others thought wrong. "It'll crawl!"* cried a man from Marion, passing with a basket of clams on his back. "It'll crawl!" cried another from West Island, when he saw me driving cotton into the seams. Bruno simply wagged his tail. Even Mr. Ben J———, a noted authority on whaling-ships, whose mind, however, was said to totter, asked rather confidently if I did not think "it would crawl." "How fast will it crawl?" cried my old captain friend, who had been towed by many a lively sperm-whale. "Tell us how fast," cried he, "that we may get into port in time." However, I drove a thread of oakum on top of the cotton, as from the first I had intended to do. And Bruno again wagged his tail. The cotton never "crawled." When the calking was finished, two coats of copper paint† were slapped on the bottom, two of white lead on the topsides and bulwarks. The rudder was then shipped and painted, and on the following day the *Spray* was launched. As she rode at her ancient, rust-eaten anchor, she sat on the water like a swan.

The *Spray's* dimensions were, when finished, thirty-six feet nine inches long, over all, fourteen feet two inches wide, and four feet two inches deep in the hold, her tonnage being nine tons net and twelve and seventy-one hundredths tons gross.

Then the mast, a smart New Hampshire spruce, was fitted, and likewise all the small appurtenances necessary for a short cruise. Sails were bent, and away she flew with my friend Captain Pierce and me, across Buzzard's Bay on a trial-trip—all right. The only thing that now worried my friends along the beach was, "Will she pay?" The cost of my new vessel was $553.62 for materials, and thirteen months of my own labor. I was several months more than that at Fairhaven, for I got work now and then on an occasional whale-ship fitting farther down the harbor, and that kept me the overtime.

---

*Meaning the caulk will gradually work out of the joint.
†Used to prevent the formation of organisms and wood-borers on the ship's bottom; see pp. 27 and 155.

"It'll crawl"

Thomas Fogarty.

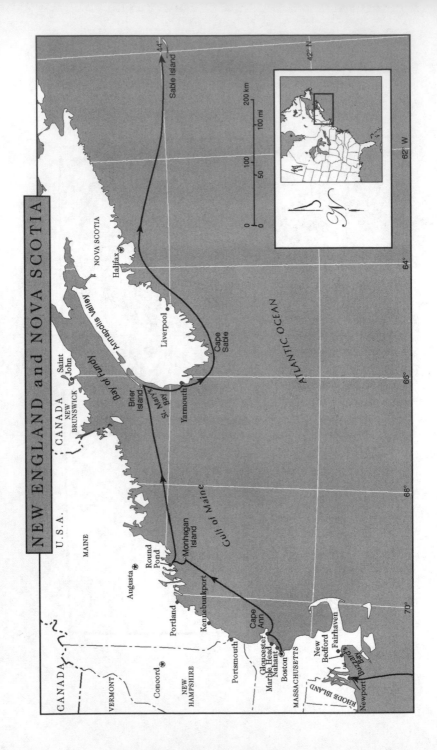

NEW ENGLAND and NOVA SCOTIA

U.S.A.

CANADA

VERMONT

NEW
HAMPSHIRE

Concord ⊛

MAINE

Augusta ⊛

Round
Pond

Portland

Kennebunkport

Portsmouth

Cape
Ann

Gloucester
Marble Head
Nahant

Boston ⊛

MASSACHUSETTS

New
Bedford

Fairhaven

Buzzard's
Bay

RHODE ISLAND

Newport

CANADA

NEW
BRUNSWICK

Saint
John

Bay of Fundy

Annapolis Valley

NOVA SCOTIA

Halifax ⊛

Liverpool

Cape
Sable

Brier
Island

St. Mary's Bay

Yarmouth

Monhegan
Island

Gulf of Maine

ATLANTIC OCEAN

Sable Island

44

42° N

62° W

64°

65°

68°

70°

200 km

100 mi

100

50

0

0

CHAPTER II

Failure as a fisherman—A voyage around the world projected—From Boston to Gloucester—Fitting out for the ocean voyage—Half of a dory for a ship's boat—The run from Gloucester to Nova Scotia—A shaking up in home waters—Among old friends.

I spent a season in my new craft fishing on the coast, only to find that I had not the cunning properly to bait a hook. But at last the time arrived to weigh anchor and get to sea in earnest. I had resolved on a voyage around the world, and as the wind on the morning of April 24, 1895, was fair, at noon I weighed anchor, set sail, and filled away from Boston, where the *Spray* had been moored snugly all winter. The twelve-o'clock whistles were blowing just as the sloop shot ahead under full sail. A short board was made up the harbor on the port tack, then coming about she stood seaward, with her boom well off to port, and swung past the ferries with lively heels. A photographer on the outer pier at East Boston got a picture of her as she swept by, her flag at the peak throwing its folds clear. A thrilling pulse beat high in me. My step was light on deck in the crisp air. I felt that there could be no turning back, and that I was engaging in an adventure the meaning of which I thoroughly understood. I had taken little advice from any one, for I had a right to my own

---

See map on opposite page: Slocum built the *Spray* in Fairhaven, Massachusetts, over a thirteen-month period from 1892–1893. He spent a season trying to make a living as a fisherman, but couldn't resist the lure of the open sea, and on April 24, 1895, he departed from Boston on his 'round-the-world voyage. He made a sentimental journey to his birthplace, Nova Scotia, and spent about six weeks among old friends. On July 2 he set sail from Yarmouth, Nova Scotia, for the long voyage across the Atlantic Ocean. This established his pattern of alternating stretches of solo sailing with lengthy stays on land, a practice that helped him ward off loneliness and maintain the *Spray*'s seaworthiness. It also provided him with numerous opportunities to describe varied cultures and locales, one of the characteristics that distinguishes his narrative from many other nautical accounts. His voyage ended three years later at Newport, Rhode Island, but he didn't consider it complete until, as he said, the *Spray* "waltzed beautifully round the coast and up the Acushnet River to Fairhaven."

opinions in matters pertaining to the sea. That the best of sailors might do worse than even I alone was borne in upon me not a league from Boston docks, where a great steamship, fully manned, officered, and piloted, lay stranded and broken. This was the *Venetian*.[1] She was broken completely in two over a ledge. So in the first hour of my lone voyage I had proof that the *Spray* could at least do better than this full-handed steamship, for I was already farther on my voyage than she. "Take warning, *Spray*, and have a care," I uttered aloud to my bark, passing fairylike silently down the bay.

The wind freshened, and the *Spray* rounded Deer Island light at the rate of seven knots.

Passing it, she squared away direct for Gloucester to procure there some fishermen's stores. Waves dancing joyously across Massachusetts Bay met her coming out of the harbor to dash them into myriads of sparkling gems that hung about her at every surge. The day was perfect, the sunlight clear and strong. Every particle of water thrown into the air became a gem, and the *Spray*, bounding ahead, snatched necklace after necklace from the sea, and as often threw them away. We have all seen miniature rainbows about a ship's prow, but the *Spray* flung out a bow of her own that day, such as I had never seen before. Her good angel had embarked on the voyage; I so read it in the sea.

Bold Nahant was soon abeam, then Marblehead was put astern. Other vessels were outward bound, but none of them passed the *Spray* flying along on her course. I heard the clanking of the dismal bell on Norman's Woe as we went by; and the reef where the schooner *Hesperus* struck[2] I passed close aboard. The "bones" of a wreck tossed up lay bleaching on the shore abreast. The wind still freshening, I settled the throat of the mainsail to ease the sloop's helm, for I could hardly hold her before it with the whole mainsail set. A schooner ahead of me lowered all sail and ran into port under bare poles, the wind being fair. As the *Spray* brushed by the stranger, I saw that some of his sails were gone, and much broken canvas hung in his rigging, from the effects of a squall.

I made for the cove, a lovely branch of Gloucester's fine harbor, again to look the *Spray* over and again to weigh the voyage, and my feelings, and all that. The bay was feather-white as my little vessel tore in, smothered in foam. It was my first experience of coming into port alone, with a craft of any size, and in among shipping. Old fishermen ran down to the wharf for which the *Spray* was heading, apparently intent upon braining herself there. I hardly know how a calamity was averted, but with my heart in my mouth, almost, I let go the wheel, stepped quickly forward, and downed the jib. The sloop naturally rounded in the wind, and just ranging ahead, laid her cheek against a mooring-pile at the windward corner of the wharf, so quietly, after all, that she would not have broken an egg. Very leisurely I passed a rope around the post, and she was moored. Then a cheer went up from the little crowd on the wharf. "You couldn't 'a' done it better," cried an old skipper, "if you weighed a ton!" Now, my weight was rather less than the fifteenth part of a ton, but I said nothing, only putting on a look of careless indifference to say for me, "Oh, that's nothing"; for some of the ablest sailors in the world were looking at me, and my wish was not to appear green, for I had a mind to stay in Gloucester several days. Had I uttered a word it surely would have betrayed me, for I was still quite nervous and short of breath.

I remained in Gloucester about two weeks, fitting out with the various articles for the voyage most readily obtained there. The owners of the wharf where I lay, and of many fishing-vessels, put on board dry cod galore, also a barrel of oil to calm the waves.* They were old skippers themselves, and took a great interest in the voyage. They also made the *Spray* a present of a "fisherman's own" lantern, which I found would throw a light a great distance round. Indeed, a ship that would run another down having such a good light aboard would be capable of running into a light-ship. A gaff, a pugh, and a dip-net, all of which an old fisherman declared I could not sail without, were also put aboard. Then, too, from across the cove came a case of copper paint, a famous antifouling article, which stood me in good stead long after. I slapped two coats of this paint on the bottom of the *Spray* while she lay a tide or so on the hard beach.

For a boat to take along, I made shift to cut a castaway dory in two athwartships, boarding up the end where it was cut. This half-dory I could hoist in and out by the nose easily enough, by hooking

---

*Oil forms a thin slick that increases the water's surface tension and suppresses the force of the waves.

the throat-halyards into a strop fitted for the purpose. A whole dory would be heavy and awkward to handle alone. Manifestly there was not room on deck for more than the half of a boat, which, after all, was better than no boat at all, and was large enough for one man. I perceived, moreover, that the newly arranged craft would answer for a washing-machine when placed athwartships, and also for a bath-tub. Indeed, for the former office my razeed dory gained such a rep-utation on the voyage that my washerwoman at Samoa would not take no for an answer. She could see with one eye that it was a new invention which beat any Yankee notion ever brought by missionar-ies to the islands, and she had to have it.

The want of a chronometer for the voyage was all that now wor-ried me. In our newfangled notions of navigation it is supposed that a mariner cannot find his way without one; and I had myself drifted into this way of thinking. My old chronometer, a good one, had been long in disuse. It would cost fifteen dollars to clean and rate it. Fif-teen dollars! For sufficient reasons I left that timepiece at home, where the Dutchman left his anchor.[3] I had the great lantern, and a lady in Boston sent me the price of a large two-burner cabin lamp, which lighted the cabin at night, and by some small contriving served for a stove through the day.

Being thus refitted I was once more ready for sea, and on May 7 again made sail. With little room in which to turn, the *Spray,* in gath-ering headway, scratched the paint off an old, fine-weather craft in the fairway, being puttied and painted for a summer voyage. "Who'll pay for that?" growled the painters. "I will," said I. "With the main-sheet," echoed the captain of the *Bluebird,* close by, which was his way of saying that I was off. There was nothing to pay for above five cents' worth of paint, maybe, but such a din was raised between the old "hooker" and the *Bluebird,* which now took up my case, that the first cause of it was forgotten altogether. Anyhow, no bill was sent after me.

The weather was mild on the day of my departure from Glouces-ter. On the point ahead, as the *Spray* stood out of the cove, was a lively picture, for the front of a tall factory was a flutter of handker-chiefs and caps. Pretty faces peered out of the windows from the top to the bottom of the building, all smiling *bon voyage.* Some hailed me to know where away and why alone. Why? When I made as if to stand in, a hundred pairs of arms reached out, and said come, but the shore was dangerous! The sloop worked out of the bay against a light southwest wind, and about noon squared away off Eastern Point, receiving at the same time a hearty salute—the last of many kindnesses to her at Gloucester. The wind freshened off the point, and skipping along smoothly, the *Spray* was soon off Thatcher's Island lights. Thence shaping her course east, by compass, to go north of Cashes Ledge and the Amen Rocks, I sat and considered the matter all over again, and asked myself once more whether it were best to sail beyond the ledge and rocks at all. I had only said that I would sail round the world in the *Spray*, "dangers of the sea excepted," but I must have said it very much in earnest. The "charter-party" with myself seemed to bind me, and so I sailed on. Toward night I hauled the sloop to the wind, and baiting a hook, sounded for bottom-fish, in thirty fathoms of water, on the edge of Cashes Ledge. With fair success I hauled till dark, landing on deck three cod and two haddocks, one hake, and, best of all, a small halibut, all plump and spry. This, I thought, would be the place to take in a good stock of provisions above what I already had; so I put out a sea-anchor that would hold her head to windward. The current being southwest, against the wind, I felt quite sure I would find the *Spray* still on the bank or near it in the morning. Then "stradding" the cable and putting my great lantern in the rigging, I lay down, for the first time at sea alone, not to sleep, but to doze and to dream.

I had read somewhere of a fishing-schooner hooking her anchor into a whale, and being towed a long way and at great speed. This was exactly what happened to the *Spray*—in my dream! I could not shake it off entirely when I awoke and found that it was the wind blowing and the heavy sea now running that had disturbed my short rest. A scud was flying across the moon. A storm was brewing; indeed, it was already stormy. I reefed the sails, then hauled in my sea-anchor, and setting what canvas the sloop could carry, headed her away for Monhegan light, which she made before daylight on the morning of the 8th. The wind being free, I ran on into Round Pond harbor, which is a little port east from Pemaquid. Here I rested a day, while the wind rattled among the pine-trees on shore. But the

"No dorg nor no cat."

following day was fine enough, and I put to sea, first writing up my
log from Cape Ann, not omitting a full account of my adventure
with the whale.

The *Spray,* heading east, stretched along the coast among many
islands and over a tranquil sea. At evening of this day, May 10, she
came up with a considerable island, which I shall always think of as
the Island of Frogs, for the *Spray* was charmed by a million voices.
From the Island of Frogs we made for the Island of Birds, called
Gannet Island, and sometimes Gannet Rock, whereon is a bright, in-
termittent light, which flashed fitfully across the *Spray's* deck as she

The deacon's dream.

coasted along under its light and shade. Thence shaping a course for Briar's Island, I came among vessels the following afternoon on the western fishing-grounds, and after speaking a fisherman at anchor, who gave me a wrong course, the *Spray* sailed directly over the southwest ledge through the worst tide-race in the Bay of Fundy, and got into Westport harbor in Nova Scotia, where I had spent eight years of my life as a lad.

The fisherman may have said "east-southeast," the course I was steering when I hailed him; but I thought he said "east-northeast," and I accordingly changed it to that. Before he made up his mind to answer me at all, he improved the occasion of his own curiosity to know where I was from, and if I was alone, and if I didn't have "no dorg nor no cat." It was the first time in all my life at sea that I had heard a hail for information answered by a question. I think the chap belonged to the Foreign Islands. There was one thing I was sure of, and that was that he did not belong to Briar's Island, because he dodged a sea that slopped over the rail, and stopping to brush the water from his face, lost a fine cod which he was about to ship. My islander would not have done that. It is known that a Briar Islander, fish or no fish on his hook, never flinches from a sea. He just tends

to his lines and hauls or "saws." Nay, have I not seen my old friend
Deacon W. D————, a good man of the island, while listening to
a sermon in the little church on the hill, reach out his hand over
the door of his pew and "jig" imaginary squid in the aisle, to the
intense delight of the young people, who did not realize that to
catch good fish one must have good bait, the thing most on the
deacon's mind.

I was delighted to reach Westport. Any port at all would have
been delightful after the terrible thrashing I got in the fierce sou'west
rip, and to find myself among old schoolmates now was charming.
It was the 13th of the month, and 13 is my lucky number—a fact
registered long before Dr. Nansen sailed in search of the north pole
with his crew of thirteen. Perhaps he had heard of my success in taking a most extraordinary ship successfully to Brazil with that number of crew.[4] The very stones on Briar's Island I was glad to see again,
and I knew them all. The little shop round the corner, which for
thirty-five years I had not seen, was the same, except that it looked
a deal smaller. It wore the same shingles—I was sure of it; for did
not I know the roof where we boys, night after night, hunted for
the skin of a black cat, to be taken on a dark night, to make a plas-
ter for a poor lame man? Lowry the tailor lived there when boys
were boys. In his day he was fond of the gun. He always carried
his powder loose in the tail pocket of his coat. He usually had in
his mouth a short dudeen;* but in an evil moment he put the
dudeen, lighted, in the pocket among the powder. Mr. Lowry was
an eccentric man.

At Briar's Island I overhauled the *Spray* once more and tried her
seams, but found that even the test of the sou'west rip had started
nothing. Bad weather and much head wind prevailing outside, I was
in no hurry to round Cape Sable. I made a short excursion with
some friends to St. Mary's Bay, an old cruising-ground, and back to
the island. Then I sailed, putting into Yarmouth the following day on
account of fog and head wind. I spent some days pleasantly enough
in Yarmouth, took in some butter for the voyage, also a barrel of potatoes, filled six barrels of water, and stowed all under deck. At

---

*Tobacco pipe.

Captain Slocum's chronometer.

Yarmouth, too, I got my famous tin clock, the only timepiece I carried on the whole voyage. The price of it was a dollar and a half, but on account of the face being smashed the merchant let me have it for a dollar.

CHAPTER III

Good-by to the American coast—Off Sable Island in a fog—In the open sea—The man in the moon takes an interest in the voyage—The first fit of loneliness—The *Spray* encounters *La Vaguisa*—A bottle of wine from the Spaniard—A bout of words with the captain of the *Java*—The steamship *Olympia* spoken—Arrival at the Azores.

I now stowed all my goods securely, for the boisterous Atlantic was before me, and I sent the topmast down, knowing that the *Spray* would be the wholesomer with it on deck. Then I gave the lanyards a pull and hitched them afresh, and saw that the gammon was secure, also that the boat was lashed, for even in summer one may meet with bad weather in the crossing.

In fact, many weeks of bad weather had prevailed. On July 1, however, after a rude gale, the wind came out nor'west and clear, propitious for a good run. On the following day, the head sea having gone down, I sailed from Yarmouth, and let go my last hold on America. The log of my first day on the Atlantic in the *Spray* reads briefly: "9:30 A. M. sailed from Yarmouth. 4:30 P. M. passed Cape Sable; distance, three cables from the land. The sloop making eight knots. Fresh breeze N. W." Before the sun went down I was taking my supper of strawberries and tea in smooth water under the lee* of the east-coast land, along which the *Spray* was now leisurely skirting.

At noon on July 3 Ironbound Island was abeam. The *Spray* was again at her best. A large schooner came out of Liverpool, Nova Scotia, this morning, steering eastward. The *Spray* put her hull down astern in five hours. At 6:45 P. M. I was in close under Chebucto Head light, near Halifax harbor. I set my flag and squared away, taking my departure from George's Island before dark to sail east of Sable Island. There are many beacon lights along the coast. Sambro, the Rock of Lamentations, carries a noble light, which, however, the liner *Atlantic,* on the night of her terrible disaster,[1] did not see. I watched light after light sink astern as I sailed into the unbounded

---

*Protected from the wind.

34

sea, till Sambro, the last of them all, was below the horizon. The
Spray was then alone, and sailing on, she held her course. July 4, at
6 A. M., I put in double reefs, and at 8:30 A. M. turned out all reefs. At
9:40 P. M. I raised the sheen* only of the light on the west end of
Sable Island, which may also be called the Island of Tragedies. The
fog, which till this moment had held off, now lowered over the sea
like a pall. I was in a world of fog, shut off from the universe. I did
not see any more of the light. By the lead, which I cast often, I
found that a little after midnight I was passing the east point of the
island, and should soon be clear of dangers of land and shoals. The
wind was holding free, though it was from the foggy point, south-
southwest. It is said that within a few years Sable Island has been reduced from forty miles in length to twenty, and that of three
lighthouses built on it since 1880, two have been washed away and
the third will soon be engulfed.

On the evening of July 5 the *Spray,* after having steered all day
over a lumpy sea, took it into her head to go without the helmsman's
aid. I had been steering southeast by south, but the wind hauling
forward a bit, she dropped into a smooth lane, heading southeast,
and making about eight knots, her very best work. I crowded on sail
to cross the track of the liners without loss of time, and to reach as
soon as possible the friendly Gulf Stream.[2] The fog lifting before
night, I was afforded a look at the sun just as it was touching the sea.
I watched it go down and out of sight. Then I turned my face eastward, and there, apparently at the very end of the bowsprit, was the
smiling full moon rising out of the sea. Neptune[†] himself coming
over the bows could not have startled me more. "Good evening, sir,"
I cried; "I'm glad to see you." Many a long talk since then I have had
with the man in the moon; he had my confidence on the voyage.

About midnight the fog shut down again denser than ever before.
One could almost "stand on it." It continued so for a number of
days, the wind increasing to a gale. The waves rose high, but I had a
good ship. Still, in the dismal fog I felt myself drifting into loneliness, an insect on a straw in the midst of the elements. I lashed the
helm, and my vessel held her course, and while she sailed I slept.

---

*Luster or glow.
†Roman god of the sea.

"Good evening, sir."

During these days a feeling of awe crept over me. My memory worked with startling power. The ominous, the insignificant, the great, the small, the wonderful, the commonplace—all appeared before my mental vision in magical succession. Pages of my history were recalled which had been so long forgotten that they seemed to belong to a previous existence. I heard all the voices of the past laughing, crying, telling what I had heard them tell in many corners of the earth.

The loneliness of my state wore off when the gale was high and I found much work to do. When fine weather returned, then came the sense of solitude, which I could not shake off. I used my voice often, at first giving some order about the affairs of a ship, for I had been told that from disuse I should lose my speech. At the meridian altitude of the sun I called aloud, "Eight bells," after the custom on a ship at sea. Again from my cabin I cried to an imaginary man at the helm, "How does she head, there?" and again, "Is she on her course?" But getting no reply, I was reminded the more palpably of my condition. My voice sounded hollow on the empty air, and I dropped the practice. However, it was not long before the thought came to me that when I was a lad I used to sing; why not try that now, where it would disturb no one? My musical talent had never bred envy in others, but out on the Atlantic, to realize what it meant, you should have heard me sing. You should have seen the porpoises leap when I pitched my voice for the waves and the sea and all that was in it. Old turtles, with large eyes, poked their heads up out of the sea as I sang "Johnny Boker," and "We'll Pay Darby Doyl for his Boots," and the like. But the porpoises were, on the whole, vastly more appreciative than the turtles; they jumped a deal higher. One day when I was humming a favorite chant, I think it was "Babylon's a-Fallin',"[3] a porpoise jumped higher than the bowsprit. Had the *Spray* been going a little faster she would have scooped him in. The sea-birds sailed around rather shy.

July 10, eight days at sea, the *Spray* was twelve hundred miles east of Cape Sable. One hundred and fifty miles a day for so small a vessel must be considered good sailing. It was the greatest run the *Spray* ever made before or since in so few days. On the evening of July 14, in better humor than ever before, all hands cried, "Sail ho!" The sail was a barkantine, three points on the weather bow, hull down. Then came the night. My ship was sailing along now without attention to the helm. The wind was south; she was heading east. Her sails were trimmed like the sails of the nautilus.[4] They drew steadily all night. I went frequently on deck, but found all well. A merry breeze kept on from the south. Early in the morning of the 15th the *Spray* was close aboard the stranger, which proved to be *La Vaguisa* of Vigo, twenty-three days from Philadelphia, bound for Vigo. A lookout from his masthead had spied the *Spray* the evening before. The captain, when I came near enough, threw a line to me and sent a bottle of wine across slung by the neck, and very good wine it was. He also sent his card, which bore the name of Juan Gantes. I think he was a good man, as Spaniards go. But when I asked him to report me "all well" (the *Spray* passing him in a lively manner), he hauled his

"He also sent his card."

shoulders much above his head; and when his mate, who knew of my expedition, told him that I was alone, he crossed himself and made for his cabin. I did not see him again. By sundown he was as far astern as he had been ahead the evening before.

There was now less and less monotony. On July 16 the wind was northwest and clear, the sea smooth, and a large bark, hull down, came in sight on the lee bow, and at 2:30 P. M. I spoke the stranger. She was the bark *Java* of Glasgow, from Peru for Queenstown for orders. Her old captain was bearish, but I met a bear once in Alaska that looked pleasanter. At least, the bear seemed pleased to meet me, but this grizzly old man! Well, I suppose my hail disturbed his siesta, and my little sloop passing his great ship had somewhat the effect on him that a red rag has upon a bull. I had the advantage over heavy ships, by long odds, in the light winds of this and the two previous days. The wind was light; his ship was heavy and foul, making poor headway, while the *Spray,* with a great mainsail bellying even to light winds, was just skipping along as nimbly as one could wish. "How long has it been calm about here?" roared the captain of the *Java,* as I came within hail of him. "Dunno, cap'n," I shouted back as loud as I could bawl. "I haven't been here long." At this the mate on the forecastle wore a broad grin. "I left Cape Sable fourteen days ago," I added. (I was now well across toward the Azores.) "Mate," he roared to his chief officer—"mate, come here and listen to the Yankee's yarn. Haul down the flag, mate, haul down the flag!" In the best of humor, after all, the *Java* surrendered to the *Spray.*

The acute pain of solitude experienced at first never returned. I had penetrated a mystery, and, by the way, I had sailed through a fog. I had met Neptune in his wrath, but he found that I had not treated him with contempt, and so he suffered me to go on and explore.

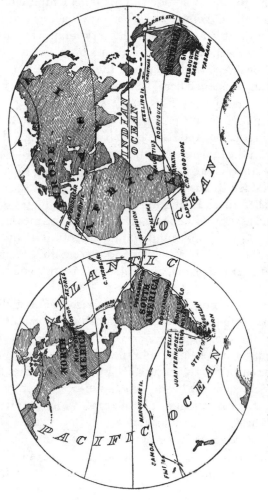

Chart of the *Spray's* course around the world—April 24, 1895, to July 3, 1898.

In the log for July 18 there is this entry: "Fine weather, wind south-southwest. Porpoises gamboling all about. The S. S. *Olympia* passed at 11:30 A. M, long. W. 34° 50'."

"It lacks now three minutes of the half-hour," shouted the captain, as he gave me the longitude and the time. I admired the businesslike air of the *Olympia;* but I have the feeling still that the captain was just a little too precise in his reckoning. That may be all well enough, however, where there is plenty of sea-room. But overconfidence, I believe, was the cause of the disaster to the liner *Atlantic,* and many more like her. The captain knew too well where he was. There were no porpoises at all skipping along with the *Olympia!* Porpoises always prefer sailing-ships. The captain was a young man, I observed, and had before him, I hope, a good record.

Land ho! On the morning of July 19 a mystic dome like a mountain of silver stood alone in the sea ahead. Although the land was completely hidden by the white, glistening haze that shone in the sun like polished silver, I felt quite sure that it was Flores Island. At half-past four P. M. it was abeam. The haze in the meantime had disappeared. Flores is one hundred and seventy-four miles from Fayal, and although it is a high island, it remained many years undiscovered after the principal group of the islands had been colonized.

Early on the morning of July 20 I saw Pico looming above the clouds on the starboard bow. Lower lands burst forth as the sun burned away the morning fog, and island after island came into view. As I approached nearer, cultivated fields appeared, "and oh, how green the corn!"[5] Only those who have seen the Azores from the deck of a vessel realize the beauty of the mid-ocean picture.

At 4:30 P. M. I cast anchor at Fayal, exactly eighteen days from Cape Sable. The American consul, in a smart boat, came alongside before the *Spray* reached the breakwater, and a young naval officer, who feared for the safety of my vessel, boarded, and offered his services as pilot. The youngster, I have no good reason to doubt, could have handled a man-of-war, but the *Spray* was too small for the amount of uniform he wore. However, after fouling all the craft in port and sinking a lighter, she was moored without much damage to herself. This wonderful pilot expected a "gratification," I understood, but whether for the reason that his government, and not I,

The island of Pico.

would have to pay the cost of raising the lighter, or because he did not sink the *Spray*, I could never make out. But I forgive him.

It was the season for fruit when I arrived at the Azores, and there was soon more of all kinds of it put on board than I knew what to do with. Islanders are always the kindest people in the world, and I met none anywhere kinder than the good hearts of this place. The people of the Azores are not a very rich community. The burden of taxes is heavy, with scant privileges in return, the air they breathe being about the only thing that is not taxed. The mother-country* does not even allow them a port of entry for a foreign mail service. A packet passing never so close with mails for Horta must deliver them first in Lisbon, ostensibly to be fumigated, but really for the tariff from the packet. My own letters posted at Horta reached the United States six days behind my letter from Gibraltar, mailed thirteen days later.

The day after my arrival at Horta was the feast of a great saint. Boats loaded with people came from other islands to celebrate at Horta, the capital, or Jerusalem, of the Azores. The deck of the *Spray* was crowded from morning till night with men, women, and children. On the day after the feast a kind-hearted native harnessed a team and drove me a day over the beautiful roads all about Fayal, "because," said he, in broken English, "when I was in America and couldn't speak a word of English, I found it hard till I met some one who seemed to have time to listen to my story, and I promised my good saint then that if ever a stranger came to my country I would try to make him happy." Unfortunately, this gentleman brought along an interpreter, that I might "learn more of the country." The

---

*Portugal.

Chart of the *Spray's* Atlantic voyages from Boston to Gibraltar, thence to the Strait of Magellan, in 1895, and finally homeward bound from the Cape of Good Hope in 1898.

fellow was nearly the death of me, talking of ships and voyages, and of the boats he had steered, the last thing in the world I wished to hear. He had sailed out of New Bedford, so he said, for "that Joe Wing they call 'John.' "[6] My friend and host found hardly a chance to edge in a word. Before we parted my host dined me with a cheer that would have gladdened the heart of a prince, but he was quite alone in his house. "My wife and children all rest there," said he, pointing to the churchyard across the way. "I moved to this house from far off," he added, "to be near the spot, where I pray every morning."

I remained four days at Fayal, and that was two days more than I had intended to stay. It was the kindness of the islanders and their touching simplicity which detained me. A damsel, as innocent as an angel, came alongside one day, and said she would embark on the *Spray* if I would land her at Lisbon. She could cook flying-fish, she thought, but her forte was dressing *bacalhao*.* Her brother Antonio, who served as interpreter, hinted that, anyhow, he would like to make the trip. Antonio's heart went out to one John Wilson, and he was ready to sail for America by way of the two capes to meet his friend. "Do you know John Wilson of Boston?" he cried. "I knew a John Wilson," I said, "but not of Boston." "He had one daughter and one son," said Antonio, by way of identifying his friend. If this reaches the right John Wilson, I am told to say that "Antonio of Pico remembers him."

---

*Or *bacalhau*; codfish (Portuguese).

CHAPTER IV

Squally weather in the Azores—High living—Delirious from cheese and plums—The pilot of the *Pinta*—At Gibraltar—Compliments exchanged with the British navy—A picnic on the Morocco shore.

I set sail from Horta early on July 24. The southwest wind at the time was light, but squalls came up with the sun, and I was glad enough to get reefs in my sails before I had gone a mile. I had hardly set the mainsail, double-reefed, when a squall of wind down the mountains struck the sloop with such violence that I thought her mast would go. However, a quick helm brought her to the wind. As it was, one of the weather lanyards was carried away and the other was stranded. My tin basin, caught up by the wind, went flying across a French school-ship to leeward. It was more or less squally all day, sailing along under high land; but rounding close under a bluff, I found an opportunity to mend the lanyards broken in the squall. No sooner had I lowered my sails when a four-oared boat shot out from some gully in the rocks, with a customs officer on board, who thought he had come upon a smuggler. I had some difficulty in making him comprehend the true case. However, one of his crew, a sailorly chap, who understood how matters were, while we palavered jumped on board and rove off the new lanyards I had already prepared, and with a friendly hand helped me "set up the rigging." This incident gave the turn in my favor. My story was then clear to all. I have found this the way of the world. Let one be without a friend, and see what will happen!

Passing the island of Pico, after the rigging was mended, the *Spray* stretched across to leeward of the island of St. Michael's, which she was up with early on the morning of July 26, the wind blowing hard. Later in the day she passed the Prince of Monaco's fine steam-yacht bound to Fayal, where, on a previous voyage, the prince had slipped his cables to "escape a reception" which the padres of the island wished to give him. Why he so dreaded the "ovation" I could not make out. At Horta they did not know. Since reaching the islands I had lived most luxuriously on fresh bread, butter, vegetables, and fruits of all kinds. Plums seemed the most plentiful on the *Spray,* and these I ate without stint. I had also a Pico white cheese that General Manning, the American consul-general, had given me, which I supposed was to be eaten, and of this I partook with the plums. Alas! by night-time I was doubled up with cramps. The wind, which was already a smart breeze, was increasing somewhat, with a heavy sky to the sou'west. Reefs had been turned out, and I must turn them in again somehow. Between cramps I got the mainsail down, hauled out the earings as best I could, and tied away point by point, in the double reef. There being sea-room, I should, in strict prudence, have made all snug and gone down at once to my cabin. I am a careful man at sea, but this night, in the coming storm, I swayed up my sails, which, reefed though they were, were still too much in such heavy weather; and I saw to it that the sheets were securely belayed. In a word, I should have laid to, but did not. I gave her the double-reefed mainsail and whole jib instead, and set her on her course. Then I went below, and threw myself upon the cabin floor in great pain. How long I lay there I could not tell, for I became delirious. When I came to, as I thought, from my swoon, I realized that the sloop was plunging into a heavy sea, and looking out of the companionway, to my amazement I saw a tall man at the helm. His rigid hand, grasping the spokes of the wheel, held them as in a vise. One may imagine my astonishment. His rig was that of a foreign sailor, and the large red cap he wore was cockbilled* over his left ear, and all was set off with shaggy black whiskers. He would have been taken for a pirate in any part of the world. While I gazed upon his threatening aspect I forgot the storm, and wondered if he had come to cut my throat. This he seemed to divine. "Señor," said he, doffing his cap, "I have come to do you no harm." And a smile, the faintest in the world, but still a smile, played on his face, which seemed not unkind when he spoke. "I have come to do you no harm. I have sailed free," he said, "but was never worse than a *contrabandista.*† I am one of Columbus's crew," he continued. "I am the pilot of the *Pinta* come

---

*Set vertically.
†Smuggler (Spanish).

The apparition at the wheel.

to aid you. Lie quiet, señor captain," he added, "and I will guide your ship to-night. You have a *calentura*,* but you will be all right to-morrow." I thought what a very devil he was to carry sail. Again, as if he read my mind, he exclaimed: "Yonder is the *Pinta* ahead; we must overtake her. Give her sail; give her sail! *Vale, vale, muy vale!*"† Biting

---

*Fever (Spanish); in English, a calenture is a fever that causes delirium and was once thought to affect sailors in the tropics.
†Properly, *vela, vela, muy vela*, Spanish for "sail, sail, more sail."

off a large quid of black twist,* he said: "You did wrong, captain, to mix cheese with plums. White cheese is never safe unless you know whence it comes. *Quien sabe,*† it may have been from *leche de Capra*‡ and becoming capricious——"

"Avast, there!" I cried. "I have no mind for moralizing."

I made shift to spread a mattress and lie on that instead of the hard floor, my eyes all the while fastened on my strange guest, who, remarking again that I would have "only pains and calentura," chuckled as he chanted a wild song:

> High are the waves, fierce, gleaming,
>   High is the tempest roar!
> High the sea-bird screaming!
>   High the Azore!

I suppose I was now on the mend, for I was peevish, and complained: "I detest your jingle. Your Azore should be at roost, and would have been were it a respectable bird!" I begged he would tie a rope-yarn on the rest of the song, if there was any more of it. I was still in agony. Great seas were boarding the *Spray*, but in my fevered brain I thought they were boats falling on deck, that careless draymen were throwing from wagons on the pier to which I imagined the *Spray* was now moored, and without fenders to breast her off. "You'll smash your boats!" I called out again and again, as the seas crashed on the cabin over my head. "You'll smash your boats, but you can't hurt the *Spray*. She is strong!" I cried.

I found, when my pains and calentura had gone, that the deck, now as white as a shark's tooth from seas washing over it, had been swept of everything movable. To my astonishment, I saw now at broad day that the *Spray* was still heading as I had left her, and was going like a race-horse. Columbus himself could not have held her more exactly on her course. The sloop had made ninety miles in the night through a rough sea. I felt grateful to the old pilot, but I marveled some that he had not taken in the jib. The gale was moderating,

---

*Big piece of chewing tobacco.
†Who knows (Spanish).
‡Properly, *leche de cabra*, Spanish for "goat's milk."

and by noon the sun was shining. A meridian altitude and the distance on the patent log, which I always kept towing, told me that she had made a true course throughout the twenty-four hours. I was getting much better now, but was very weak, and did not turn out reefs that day or the night following, although the wind fell light; but I just put my wet clothes out in the sun when it was shining, and lying down there myself, fell asleep. Then who should visit me again but my old friend of the night before, this time, of course, in a dream. "You did well last night to take my advice," said he, "and if you would, I should like to be with you often on the voyage, for the love of adventure alone." Finishing what he had to say, he again doffed his cap and disappeared as mysteriously as he came, returning, I suppose, to the phantom *Pinta*. I awoke much refreshed, and with the feeling that I had been in the presence of a friend and a seaman of vast experience. I gathered up my clothes, which by this time were dry, then, by inspiration, I threw overboard all the plums in the vessel.

July 28 was exceptionally fine. The wind from the northwest was light and the air balmy. I overhauled my wardrobe, and bent on a white shirt against nearing some coasting-packet with genteel folk on board. I also did some washing to get the salt out of my clothes. After it all I was hungry, so I made a fire and very cautiously stewed a dish of pears and set them carefully aside till I had made a pot of delicious coffee, for both of which I could afford sugar and cream. But the crowning dish of all was a fish-hash, and there was enough of it for two. I was in good health again, and my appetite was simply ravenous. While I was dining I had a large onion over the double lamp stewing for a luncheon later in the day. High living to-day!

In the afternoon the *Spray* came upon a large turtle asleep on the sea. He awoke with my harpoon through his neck, if he awoke at all. I had much difficulty in landing him on deck, which I finally accomplished by hooking the throat-halyards to one of his flippers, for he was about as heavy as my boat. I saw more turtles, and I rigged a burton ready with which to hoist them in; for I was obliged to lower the mainsail whenever the halyards were used for such purposes, and it was no small matter to hoist the large sail again. But the turtle-steak was good. I found no fault with the cook, and it was the rule of the voyage that the cook found no fault with me. There was never a ship's crew so well agreed. The bill of fare that evening was turtle-steak, tea and toast, fried potatoes, stewed onions; with dessert of stewed pears and cream.

Sometime in the afternoon I passed a barrel-buoy adrift, floating light on the water. It was painted red, and rigged with a signal-staff about six feet high. A sudden change in the weather coming on, I got no more turtle or fish of any sort before reaching port. July 31 a gale sprang up suddenly from the north, with heavy seas, and I shortened sail. The *Spray* made only fifty-one miles on her course that day. August 1 the gale continued, with heavy seas. Through the night the sloop was reaching, under close-reefed mainsail and bobbed jib. At 3 P. M. the jib was washed off the bowsprit and blown to rags and ribbons. I bent the "jumbo" on a stay at the night-heads. As for the jib, let it go; I saved pieces of it, and, after all, I was in want of pot-rags.

On August 3 the gale broke, and I saw many signs of land. Bad weather having made itself felt in the galley, I was minded to try my hand at a loaf of bread, and so rigging a pot of fire on deck by which to bake it, a loaf soon became an accomplished fact. One great feature about ship's cooking is that one's appetite on the sea is always good— a fact that I realized when I cooked for the crew of fishermen in the before-mentioned boyhood days. Dinner being over, I sat for hours reading the life of Columbus,[1] and as the day wore on I watched the birds all flying in one direction, and said, "Land lies there."

Early the next morning, August 4, I discovered Spain. I saw fires on shore, and knew that the country was inhabited. The *Spray* continued on her course till well in with the land, which was that about Trafalgar. Then keeping away a point, she passed through the Strait of Gibraltar, where she cast anchor at 3 P. M. of the same day, less than twenty-nine days from Cape Sable. At the finish of this preliminary trip I found myself in excellent health, not overworked or cramped, but as well as ever in my life, though I was as thin as a reef-point.

Two Italian barks, which had been close alongside at daylight, I saw long after I had anchored, passing up the African side of the strait. The *Spray* had sailed them both hull down before she reached Tarifa. So far as I know, the *Spray* beat everything going across the Atlantic except the steamers.

All was well, but I had forgotten to bring a bill of health from Horta, and so when the fierce old port doctor came to inspect there was a row. That, however, was the very thing needed. If you want to

Coming to anchor at Gibraltar.

get on well with a true Britisher you must first have a deuce of a row with him. I knew that well enough, and so I fired away, shot for shot, as best I could. "Well, yes," the doctor admitted at last, "your crew are healthy enough, no doubt, but who knows the diseases of your last port?"—a reasonable enough remark. "We ought to put you in the fort, sir!" he blustered; "but never mind. Free pratique,* sir! Shove off, cockswain!" And that was the last I saw of the port doctor.

But on the following morning a steam-launch, much longer than the *Spray,* came alongside,—or as much of her as could get alongside,—with compliments from the senior naval officer, Admiral Bruce, saying there was a berth for the *Spray* at the arsenal. This was around at the new mole.† I had anchored at the old mole, among the native craft, where it was rough and uncomfortable. Of course I was glad to shift, and did so as soon as possible, thinking of the great company the *Spray* would be in among battle-ships such as

---

*Certificate of health given to an incoming ship.
†Artificial breakwater of stone or masonry.

the *Collingwood, Balfleur,* and *Cormorant,* which were at that time stationed there, and on board all of which I was entertained, later, most royally.

" 'Put it thar!' as the Americans say," was the salute I got from Admiral Bruce, when I called at the admiralty to thank him for his courtesy of the berth, and for the use of the steam-launch which towed me into dock. "About the berth, it is all right if it suits, and we'll tow you out when you are ready to go. But, say, what repairs do you want? Ahoy the *Hebe,* can you spare your sailmaker? The *Spray* wants a new jib. Construction and repair, there! will you see to the *Spray?* Say, old man, you must have knocked the devil out of her coming over alone in twenty-nine days! But we'll make it smooth for you here!" Not even her Majesty's ship the *Collingwood* was better looked after than the *Spray* at Gibraltar.

Later in the day came the hail: "*Spray* ahoy! Mrs. Bruce would like to come on board and shake hands with the *Spray.* Will it be convenient to-day?" "Very!" I joyfully shouted. On the following day Sir F. Carrington, at the time governor of Gibraltar, with other

The *Spray* at anchor off Gibraltar.

high officers of the garrison, and all the commanders of the battle-ships, came on board and signed their names in the *Spray's* log-book. Again there was a hail, "*Spray* ahoy!" "Hello!" "Commander Reynolds's compliments. You are invited on board H. M. S. *Collingwood,* 'at home' at 4:30 P. M. Not later than 5:30 P. M." I had already hinted at the limited amount of my wardrobe, and that I could never succeed as a dude. "You are expected, sir, in a stovepipe hat and a claw-hammer coat!"* "Then I can't come." "Dash it! come in what you have on; that is what we mean." "Aye, aye, sir!" The *Collingwood's* cheer was good, and had I worn a silk hat as high as the moon I could not have had a better time or been made more at home. An En-glishman, even on his great battle-ship, unbends when the stranger passes his gangway, and when he says "at home" he means it.

That one should like Gibraltar would go without saying. How could one help loving so hospitable a place? Vegetables twice a week and milk every morning came from the palatial grounds of the ad-miralty. "*Spray* ahoy!" would hail the admiral. "*Spray* ahoy!" "Hello!" "To-morrow is your vegetable day, sir." "Aye, aye, sir!"

I rambled much about the old city, and a gunner piloted me through the galleries of the rock as far as a stranger is permitted to go. There is no excavation in the world, for military purposes, at all approaching these of Gibraltar in conception or execution. Viewing the stupendous works, it became hard to realize that one was within the Gibraltar of his little old Morse geography.[2]

Before sailing I was invited on a picnic with the governor, the of-ficers of the garrison, and the commanders of the war-ships at the station; and a royal affair it was. Torpedo-boat No. 91, going twenty-two knots, carried our party to the Morocco shore and back. The day was perfect—too fine, in fact, for comfort on shore, and so no one landed at Morocco. No. 91 trembled like an aspen-leaf as she raced through the sea at top speed. Sublieutenant Boucher, apparently a mere lad, was in command, and handled his ship with the skill of an older sailor. On the following day I lunched with General Carrington, the governor, at Line Wall House, which was once the Franciscan convent. In this interesting edifice are preserved relics of the fourteen

---

*Top hat and tails, formal attire.

sieges which Gibraltar has seen. On the next day I supped with the admiral at his residence, the palace, which was once the convent of the Mercenaries.* At each place, and all about, I felt the friendly grasp of a manly hand, that lent me vital strength to pass the coming long days at sea. I must confess that the perfect discipline, order, and cheerfulness at Gibraltar were only a second wonder in the great stronghold. The vast amount of business going forward caused no more excitement than the quiet sailing of a well-appointed ship in a smooth sea. No one spoke above his natural voice, save a boatswain's mate now and then. The Hon. Horatio J. Sprague, the venerable United States consul at Gibraltar, honored the *Spray* with a visit on Sunday, August 24, and was much pleased to find that our British cousins had been so kind to her.

---

*Or Mercenarians, a Spanish religious order.

CHAPTER V

Sailing from Gibraltar with the assistance of her Majesty's tug—The *Spray's* course changed from the Suez Canal to Cape Horn—Chased by a Moorish pirate—A comparison with Columbus—The Canary Islands—The Cape Verde Islands—Sea life—Arrival at Pernambuco—A bill against the Brazilian government—Preparing for the stormy weather of the cape.

Monday, August 25, the *Spray* sailed from Gibraltar, well repaid for whatever deviation she had made from a direct course to reach the place. A tug belonging to her Majesty towed the sloop into the steady breeze clear of the mount, where her sails caught a volant* wind, which carried her once more to the Atlantic, where it rose rapidly to a furious gale. My plan was, in going down this coast, to haul offshore, well clear of the land, which hereabouts is the home of pirates; but I had hardly accomplished this when I perceived a felucca† making out of the nearest port, and finally following in the wake of the *Spray*. Now, my course to Gibraltar had been taken with a view to proceed up the Mediterranean Sea, through the Suez Canal, down the Red Sea, and east about, instead of a western route, which I finally adopted. By officers of vast experience in navigating these seas, I was influenced to make the change. Longshore pirates on both coasts being numerous, I could not afford to make light of the advice. But here I was, after all, evidently in the midst of pirates and thieves! I changed my course; the felucca did the same, both vessels sailing very fast, but the distance growing less and less between us. The *Spray* was doing nobly; she was even more than at her best; but, in spite of all I could do, she would broach now and then. She was carrying too much sail for safety. I must reef or be dismasted and lose all, pirate or no pirate. I must reef, even if I had to grapple with him for my life.

I was not long in reefing the mainsail and sweating it up— probably not more than fifteen minutes; but the felucca had in the

---

*Light or sudden.
†Two-masted ship with triangular sails.

meantime so shortened the distance between us that I now saw the tuft of hair on the heads of the crew,—by which, it is said, Mohammed will pull the villains up into heaven,—and they were coming on like the wind. From what I could clearly make out now, I felt them to be the sons of generations of pirates, and I saw by their movements that they were now preparing to strike a blow. The exultation on their faces, however, was changed in an instant to a look of fear and rage. Their craft, with too much sail on, broached to on the crest of a great wave. This one great sea changed the aspect of affairs suddenly as the flash of a gun. Three minutes later the same wave overtook the *Spray* and shook her in every timber. At the same moment the sheet-strop parted, and away went the main-boom, broken short at the rigging. Impulsively I sprang to the jib-halyards and down-haul, and instantly downed the jib. The head-sail being off, and the helm put hard down, the sloop came in the wind with a bound. While shivering there, but a moment though it was, I got the mainsail down and secured inboard, broken boom and all. How I got the boom in before the sail was torn I hardly know; but not a stitch of it was broken. The mainsail being secured, I hoisted away the jib, and, without looking round, stepped quickly to the cabin and snatched down my loaded rifle and cartridges at hand; for I made mental calculations that the pirate would by this time have recovered his course and be close aboard, and that when I saw him it would be better for me to be looking at him along the barrel of a gun. The piece was at my shoulder when I peered into the mist, but there was no pirate within a mile. The wave and squall that carried away my boom dismasted the felucca outright. I perceived his thieving crew, some dozen or more of them, struggling to recover their rigging from the sea. Allah blacken their faces!

I sailed comfortably on under the jib and forestaysail, which I now set. I fished the boom and furled the sail snug for the night; then hauled the sloop's head two points offshore to allow for the set of current and heavy rollers toward the land. This gave me the wind three points on the starboard quarter and a steady pull in the headsails. By the time I had things in this order it was dark, and a flyingfish had already fallen on deck. I took him below for my supper, but found myself too tired to cook, or even to eat a thing already prepared. I do not remember to have been more tired before or since in

Chased by pirates.

all my life than I was at the finish of that day. Too fatigued to sleep, I rolled about with the motion of the vessel till near midnight, when I made shift to dress my fish and prepare a dish of tea. I fully realized now, if I had not before, that the voyage ahead would call for exertions ardent and lasting. On August 27 nothing could be seen of the Moor, or his country either, except two peaks, away in the east through the clear atmosphere of morning. Soon after the sun rose even these were obscured by haze, much to my satisfaction.

The wind, for a few days following my escape from the pirates, blew a steady but moderate gale, and the sea, though agitated into long rollers, was not uncomfortably rough or dangerous, and while sitting in my cabin I could hardly realize that any sea was running at all, so easy was the long, swinging motion of the sloop over the waves. All distracting uneasiness and excitement being now over, I was once more alone with myself in the realization that I was on the mighty sea and in the hands of the elements. But I was happy, and was becoming more and more interested in the voyage.

Columbus, in the *Santa Maria*, sailing these seas more than four hundred years before, was not so happy as I, nor so sure of success in what he had undertaken. His first troubles at sea had already begun. His crew had managed, by foul play or otherwise, to break the ship's rudder while running before probably just such a gale as the *Spray* had passed through; and there was dissension on the *Santa Maria*, something that was unknown on the *Spray*.

After three days of squalls and shifting winds I threw myself down to rest and sleep, while, with helm lashed, the sloop sailed steadily on her course.

September 1, in the early morning, land-clouds rising ahead told of the Canary Islands not far away. A change in the weather came next day: storm-clouds stretched their arms across the sky; from the east, to all appearances, might come a fierce harmattan,* or from the south might come the fierce hurricane. Every point of the compass threatened a wild storm. My attention was turned to reefing sails, and no time was to be lost over it, either, for the sea in a moment was confusion itself, and I was glad to head the sloop three points or more away from her true course that she might ride safely over the waves. I was now scudding her for the channel between Africa and the island of Fuerteventura, the easternmost of the Canary Islands, for which I was on the lookout. At 2 P. M., the weather becoming suddenly fine, the island stood in view, already abeam to starboard, and not more than seven miles off. Fuerteventura is twenty-seven hundred feet high, and in fine weather is visible many leagues away.

The wind freshened in the night, and the *Spray* had a fine run through the channel. By daylight, September 3, she was twenty-five miles clear of all the islands, when a calm ensued, which was the precursor of another gale of wind that soon came on, bringing with it dust from the African shore. It howled dismally while it lasted, and though it was not the season of the harmattan, the sea in the course of an hour was discolored with a reddish-brown dust. The air remained thick with flying dust all the afternoon, but the wind, veering northwest at night, swept it back to land, and afforded the *Spray* once more a clear sky. Her mast now bent under a strong, steady pressure, and her bellying sail swept the sea as she rolled scuppers under, courtesying to the waves. These rolling waves thrilled me as they tossed my ship, passing quickly under her keel. This was grand sailing.

---

*Dry, dust-laden wind from the North African desert.

September 4, the wind, still fresh, blew from the north-northeast, and the sea surged along with the sloop. About noon a steamship, a bullock-droger,* from the river Plate hove in sight, steering northeast, and making bad weather of it. I signaled her, but got no answer. She was plunging into the head sea and rolling in a most astonishing manner, and from the way she yawed one might have said that a wild steer was at the helm.

On the morning of September 6 I found three flying-fish on deck, and a fourth one down the fore-scuttle as close as possible to the frying-pan. It was the best haul yet, and afforded me a sumptuous breakfast and dinner.

The *Spray* had now settled down to the trade-winds and to the business of her voyage. Later in the day another droger hove in sight, rolling as badly as her predecessor. I threw out no flag to this one, but got the worst of it for passing under her lee. She was, indeed, a stale one! And the poor cattle, how they bellowed! The time was when ships passing one another at sea backed their topsails and had a "gam," and on parting fired guns; but those good old days have gone. People have hardly time nowadays to speak even on the broad ocean, where news is news, and as for a salute of guns, they cannot afford the powder. There are no poetry-enshrined freighters on the sea now; it is a prosy life when we have no time to bid one another good morning.

My ship, running now in the full swing of the trades,† left me days to myself for rest and recuperation. I employed the time in reading and writing, or in whatever I found to do about the rigging and the sails to keep them all in order. The cooking was always done quickly, and was a small matter, as the bill of fare consisted mostly of flying-fish, hot biscuits and butter, potatoes, coffee and cream—dishes readily prepared.

On September 10 the *Spray* passed the island of St. Antonio, the northwesternmost of the Cape Verdes, close aboard. The landfall was wonderfully true, considering that no observations for longitude had been made. The wind, northeast, as the sloop drew by the island,

---

*Clumsy cattle boat.
†Trade winds (see "Glossary of Nautical Terms").

was very squally, but I reefed her sails snug, and steered broad from the highland of blustering St. Antonio. Then leaving the Cape Verde Islands out of sight astern, I found myself once more sailing a lonely sea and in a solitude supreme all around. When I slept I dreamed that I was alone. This feeling never left me; but, sleeping or waking, I seemed always to know the position of the sloop, and I saw my vessel moving across the chart, which became a picture before me.

One night while I sat in the cabin under this spell, the profound stillness all about was broken by human voices alongside! I sprang instantly to the deck, startled beyond my power to tell. Passing close under lee, like an apparition, was a white bark under full sail. The sailors on board of her were hauling on ropes to brace the yards, which just cleared the sloop's mast as she swept by. No one hailed from the white-winged flier, but I heard some one on board say that he saw lights on the sloop, and that he made her out to be a fisherman. I sat long on the starlit deck that night, thinking of ships, and watching the constellations on their voyage.

On the following day, September 13, a large four-masted ship passed some distance to windward, heading north.

The sloop was now rapidly drawing toward the region of doldrums,* and the force of the trade-winds was lessening. I could see by the ripples that a counter-current had set in. This I estimated to be about sixteen miles a day. In the heart of the counter-stream the rate was more than that setting eastward.

September 14 a lofty three-masted ship, heading north, was seen from the masthead. Neither this ship nor the one seen yesterday was within signal distance, yet it was good even to see them. On the following day heavy rain-clouds rose in the south, obscuring the sun; this was ominous of doldrums. On the 16th the *Spray* entered this gloomy region, to battle with squalls and to be harassed by fitful calms; for this is the state of the elements between the northeast and the southeast trades, where each wind, struggling in turn for mastery, expends its force whirling about in all directions. Making this still more trying to one's nerve and patience, the sea was tossed into confused cross-lumps and fretted by eddying currents. As if something

---

*Area of the ocean near the equator where there is little wind.

more were needed to complete a sailor's discomfort in this state, the rain poured down in torrents day and night. The *Spray* struggled and tossed for ten days, making only three hundred miles on her course in all that time. I didn't say anything!

On September 23 the fine schooner *Nantasket* of Boston, from Bear River, for the river Plate, lumber-laden, and just through the doldrums, came up with the *Spray,* and her captain passing a few words, she sailed on. Being much fouled on the bottom by shell-fish, she drew along with her fishes which had been following the *Spray,* which was less provided with that sort of food. Fishes will always follow a foul ship. A barnacle-grown log adrift has the same attraction for deep-sea fishes. One of this little school of deserters was a dolphin that had followed the *Spray* about a thousand miles, and had been content to eat scraps of food thrown overboard from my table; for, having been wounded, it could not dart through the sea to prey on other fishes. I had become accustomed to seeing the dolphin, which I knew by its scars, and missed it whenever it took occasional excursions away from the sloop. One day, after it had been off some hours, it returned in company with three yellowtails, a sort of cousin to the dolphin. This little school kept together, except when in danger and when foraging about the sea. Their lives were often threatened by hungry sharks that came round the vessel, and more than once they had narrow escapes. Their mode of escape interested me greatly, and I passed hours watching them. They would dart away, each in a different direction, so that the wolf of the sea, the shark, pursuing one, would be led away from the others; then after a while they would all return and rendezvous under one side or the other of the sloop. Twice their pursuers were diverted by a tin pan, which I towed astern of the sloop, and which was mistaken for a bright fish; and while turning, in the peculiar way that sharks have when about to devour their prey, I shot them through the head.

Their precarious life seemed to concern the yellowtails very little, if at all. All living beings, without doubt, are afraid of death. Nevertheless, some of the species I saw huddle together as though they knew they were created for the larger fishes, and wished to give the least possible trouble to their captors. I have seen, on the other hand, whales swimming in a circle around a school of herrings, and with mighty exertion "bunching" them together in a whirlpool set in motion by their flukes, and when the small fry were all whirled nicely together, one or the other of the leviathans, lunging through the center with open jaws, take in a boat-load or so at a single mouthful. Off the Cape of Good Hope I saw schools of sardines or other small fish being treated in this way by great numbers of cavally-fish. There was not the slightest chance of escape for the sardines, while the cavally circled round and round, feeding from the edge of the mass. It was interesting to note how rapidly the small fry disappeared; and though it was repeated before my eyes over and over, I could hardly perceive the capture of a single sardine, so dexterously was it done.

Along the equatorial limit of the southeast trade-winds the air was heavily charged with electricity, and there was much thunder and lightning. It was hereabout I remembered that, a few years before, the American ship *Alert* was destroyed by lightning. Her people, by wonderful good fortune, were rescued on the same day and brought to Pernambuco, where I then met them.

On September 25, in the latitude of 5° N., longitude 26° 30' W., I spoke the ship *North Star* of London. The great ship was out forty-eight days from Norfolk, Virginia, and was bound for Rio, where we met again about two months later. The *Spray* was now thirty days from Gibraltar.

The *Spray's* next companion of the voyage was a swordfish, that swam alongside, showing its tall fin out of the water, till I made a stir for my harpoon, when it hauled its black flag down and disappeared. September 30, at half-past eleven in the morning, the *Spray* crossed the equator in longitude 29° 30' W. At noon she was two miles south of the line.* The southeast trade-winds, met, rather light, in about 4° N., gave her sails now a stiff full sending her handsomely over the sea toward the coast of Brazil, where on October 5, just north of Olinda Point, without further incident, she made the land, casting anchor in Pernambuco harbor about noon: forty days from Gibraltar, and all well on board. Did I tire of the voyage in all that time? Not a bit of it! I was never in better trim in all my life, and was eager for the more perilous experience of rounding the Horn.

---

*Equator.

It was not at all strange in a life common to sailors that, having already crossed the Atlantic twice and being now half-way from Boston to the Horn, I should find myself still among friends. My determination to sail westward from Gibraltar not only enabled me to escape the pirates of the Red Sea, but, in bringing me to Pernambuco, landed me on familiar shores. I had made many voyages to this and other ports in Brazil. In 1893 I was employed as master to take the famous Ericsson ship *Destroyer* from New York to Brazil to go against the rebel Mello[1] and his party. The *Destroyer,* by the way, carried a submarine cannon of enormous length.

In the same expedition went the *Nictheroy,* the ship purchased by the United States government during the Spanish war and renamed the *Buffalo.* The *Destroyer* was in many ways the better ship of the two, but the Brazilians in their curious war sank her themselves at Bahia. With her sank my hope of recovering wages due me; still, I could but try to recover, for to me it meant a great deal. But now within two years the whirligig of time had brought the Mello party into power, and although it was the legal government which had employed me, the so-called "rebels" felt under less obligation to me than I could have wished.

During these visits to Brazil I had made the acquaintance of Dr. Perera, owner and editor of "El Commercio Jornal," and soon after the *Spray* was safely moored in Upper Topsail Reach, the doctor, who is a very enthusiastic yachtsman, came to pay me a visit and to carry me up the waterway of the lagoon to his country residence. The approach to his mansion by the waterside was guarded by his armada, a fleet of boats including a Chinese sampan, a Norwegian pram, and a Cape Ann dory,[2] the last of which he obtained from the *Destroyer.* The doctor dined me often on good Brazilian fare, that I might, as he said, "salle gordo"* for the voyage; but he found that even on the best I fattened slowly.

Fruits and vegetables and all other provisions necessary for the voyage having been taken in, on the 23d of October I unmoored and made ready for sea. Here I encountered one of the unforgiving Mello faction in the person of the collector of customs, who charged the

---

*Leave fat (Spanish).

Spray tonnage dues when she cleared, notwithstanding that she sailed with a yacht license and should have been exempt from port charges. Our consul reminded the collector of this and of the fact— without much diplomacy, I thought—that it was I who brought the *Destroyer* to Brazil. "Oh, yes," said the bland collector; "we remember it very well," for it was now in a small way his turn.

Mr. Lungrin, a merchant, to help me out of the trifling difficulty, offered to freight the *Spray* with a cargo of gunpowder for Bahia, which would have put me in funds; and when the insurance companies refused to take the risk on cargo shipped on a vessel manned by a crew of only one, he offered to ship it without insurance, taking all the risk himself. This was perhaps paying me a greater compliment than I deserved. The reason why I did not accept the business was that in so doing I found that I should vitiate my yacht license and run into more expense for harbor dues around the world than the freight would amount to. Instead of all this, another old merchant friend came to my assistance, advancing the cash direct.

While at Pernambuco I shortened the boom, which had been broken when off the coast of Morocco, by removing the broken piece, which took about four feet off the inboard end; I also refitted the jaws. On October 24, 1895, a fine day even as days go in Brazil, the *Spray* sailed, having had abundant good cheer. Making about one hundred miles a day along the coast, I arrived at Rio de Janeiro November 5, without any event worth mentioning, and about noon cast anchor near Villaganon, to await the official port visit. On the following day I bestirred myself to meet the highest lord of the admiralty and the ministers, to inquire concerning the matter of wages due me from the beloved *Destroyer*. The high official I met said: "Captain, so far as we are concerned, you may have the ship, and if you care to accept her we will send an officer to show you where she is." I knew well enough where she was at that moment. The top of her smoke-stack being awash in Bahia, it was more than likely that she rested on the bottom there. I thanked the kind officer, but declined his offer.

The *Spray*, with a number of old shipmasters on board, sailed about the harbor of Rio the day before she put to sea. As I had decided to give the *Spray* a yawl rig for the tempestuous waters of Patagonia, I here placed on the stern a semicircular brace to support a jigger mast. These old captains inspected the *Spray's* rigging, and each one contributed something to her outfit. Captain Jones, who had acted as my interpreter at Rio, gave her an anchor, and one of the steamers gave her a cable to match it. She never dragged Jones's anchor once on the voyage, and the cable not only stood the strain on a lee shore, but when towed off Cape Horn helped break combing seas astern that threatened to board her.

CHAPTER VI

Departure from Rio de Janeiro—The *Spray* ashore on the sands of Uruguay—A narrow escape from shipwreck—The boy who found a sloop—The *Spray* floated but somewhat damaged—Courtesies from the British consul at Maldonado—A warm greeting at Montevideo—An excursion to Buenos Aires—Shortening the mast and bowsprit.

On November 28 the *Spray* sailed from Rio de Janeiro, and first of all ran into a gale of wind, which tore up things generally along the coast, doing considerable damage to shipping. It was well for her, perhaps, that she was clear of the land. Coasting along on this part of the voyage, I observed that while some of the small vessels I fell in with were able to outsail the *Spray* by day, they fell astern of her by night. To the *Spray* day and night were the same; to the others clearly there was a difference. On one of the very fine days experienced after leaving Rio, the steamship *South Wales* spoke the *Spray* and unsolicited gave the longitude by chronometer as 48° W., "as near as I can make it," the captain said. The *Spray*, with her tin clock, had exactly the same reckoning. I was feeling at ease in my primitive method of navigation, but it startled me not a little to find my position by account verified by the ship's chronometer.

On December 5 a barkantine hove in sight, and for several days the two vessels sailed along the coast together. Right here a current was experienced setting north, making it necessary to hug the shore, with which the *Spray* became rather familiar. Here I confess a weakness: I hugged the shore entirely too close. In a word, at daybreak on the morning of December 11 the *Spray* ran hard and fast on the beach. This was annoying; but I soon found that the sloop was in no great danger. The false appearance of the sand-hills under a bright moon had deceived me, and I lamented now that I had trusted to appearances at all. The sea, though moderately smooth, still carried a swell which broke with some force on the shore. I managed to launch my small dory from the deck, and ran out a kedge-anchor and warp; but it was too late to kedge the sloop off, for the tide was falling and she had already sewed a foot. Then I went about "laying out" the larger anchor, which was no easy matter, for my only lifeboat, the frail dory, when the anchor and cable were in it, was swamped at once in the surf, the load being too great for her. Then I cut the cable and made two loads of it instead of one. The anchor, with forty fathoms bent and already buoyed, I now took and succeeded in getting through the surf; but my dory was leaking fast, and by the time I had rowed far enough to drop the anchor she was full to the gunwale and sinking. There was not a moment to spare, and I saw clearly that if I failed now all might be lost. I sprang from the oars to my feet, and lifting the anchor above my head, threw it clear just as she was turning over. I grasped her gunwale and held on as she turned bottom up, for I suddenly remembered that I could not swim. Then I tried to right her, but with too much eagerness, for she rolled clean over, and left me as before, clinging to her gunwale, while my body was still in the water. Giving a moment to cool reflection, I found that although the wind was blowing moderately toward the land, the current was carrying me to sea, and that something would have to be done. Three times I had been under water, in trying to right the dory, and I was just saying, "Now I lay me," when I was seized by a determination to try yet once more, so that no one of the prophets of evil I had left behind me could say, "I told you so." Whatever the danger may have been, much or little, I can truly say that the moment was the most serene of my life.

After righting the dory for the fourth time, I finally succeeded by the utmost care in keeping her upright while I hauled myself into her and with one of the oars, which I had recovered, paddled to the shore, somewhat the worse for wear and pretty full of salt water. The position of my

"I suddenly remembered that I could not swim."

vessel, now high and dry, gave me anxiety. To get her afloat again was all I thought of or cared for. I had little difficulty in carrying the sec ond part of my cable out and securing it to the first, which I had taken the precaution to buoy before I put it into the boat. To bring the end back to the sloop was a smaller matter still, and I believe I chuckled above my sorrows when I found that in all the haphazard my judgment or my good genius had faithfully stood by me. The cable reached from the anchor in deep water to the sloop's windlass by just enough to secure a turn and no more. The anchor had been dropped at the right distance from the vessel. To heave all taut now and wait for the coming tide was all I could do.

I had already done enough work to tire a stouter man, and was only too glad to throw myself on the sand above the tide and rest; for the sun was already up, and pouring a generous warmth over the land. While my state could have been worse, I was on the wild coast of a foreign country, and not entirely secure in my property, as I soon found out. I had not been long on the shore when I heard the patter, patter of a horse's feet approaching along the hard beach, which ceased as it came abreast of the sand-ridge where I lay sheltered from the wind. Looking up cautiously, I saw mounted on a nag probably the most astonished boy on the whole coast. He had found a sloop! "It must be mine," he thought, "for am I not the first to see it on the beach?" Sure enough, there it was all high and dry and painted white. He trotted his horse around it, and finding no owner, hitched the nag to the sloop's bobstay and hauled as though he would take her home; but of course she was too heavy for one horse to move. With my skiff, however, it was different; this he hauled some distance, and concealed behind a dune in a bunch of tall grass. He had made up his mind, I dare say, to bring more horses and drag his bigger prize away, anyhow, and was starting off for the settlement a mile or so away for the reinforcement when I discovered myself to him, at which he seemed displeased and disappointed. "Buenos dias, muchacho,"* I said. He grunted a reply, and eyed me keenly from head to foot. Then bursting into a volley of questions,—more than six Yankees could ask,—he wanted to know, first, where my ship was

---

*Good morning, boy (Spanish).

from, and how many days she had been coming. Then he asked what I was doing here ashore so early in the morning. "Your questions are easily answered," I replied; "my ship is from the moon, it has taken her a month to come, and she is here for a cargo of boys." But the intimation of this enterprise, had I not been on the alert, might have cost me dearly; for while I spoke this child of the campo* coiled his lariat ready to throw, and instead of being himself carried to the moon, he was apparently thinking of towing me home by the neck, astern of his wild cayuse, over the fields of Uruguay.

The exact spot where I was stranded was at the Castillo Chicos, about seven miles south of the dividing-line of Uruguay and Brazil, and of course the natives there speak Spanish. To reconcile my early visitor, I told him that I had on my ship biscuits, and that I wished to trade them for butter and milk. On hearing this a broad grin lighted up his face, and showed that he was greatly interested, and that even in Uruguay a ship's biscuit will cheer the heart of a boy and make him your bosom friend. The lad almost flew home, and returned quickly with butter, milk, and eggs. I was, after all, in a land of plenty. With the boy came others, old and young, from neighboring ranches, among them a German settler, who was of great assistance to me in many ways.

A coast-guard from Fort Teresa, a few miles away, also came, "to protect your property from the natives of the plains," he said. I took occasion to tell him, however, that if he would look after the people of his own village, I would take care of those from the plains, pointing, as I spoke, to the nondescript "merchant" who had already stolen my revolver and several small articles from my cabin, which by a bold front I had recovered. The chap was not a native Uruguayan. Here, as in many other places that I visited, the natives themselves were not the ones discreditable to the country.

Early in the day a despatch came from the port captain of Montevideo, commanding the coast-guards to render the *Spray* every assistance. This, however, was not necessary, for a guard was already on the alert, and making all the ado that would become the wreck of a steamer with a thousand emigrants aboard. The same messenger

---

*Grassy plain in South America.

A double surprise.

brought word from the port captain that he would despatch a steam-tug to tow the *Spray* to Montevideo. The officer was as good as his word; a powerful tug arrived on the following day; but, to make a long story short, with the help of the German and one soldier and one Italian, called "Angel of Milan," I had already floated the sloop and was sailing for port with the boom off before a fair wind. The adventure cost the *Spray* no small amount of pounding on the hard sand; she lost her shoe and part of her false keel, and received other damage, which, however, was readily mended afterward in dock.

On the following day I anchored at Maldonado. The British consul, his daughter, and another young lady came on board, bringing with them a basket of fresh eggs, strawberries, bottles of milk, and a great loaf of sweet bread. This was a good landfall, and better cheer than I had found at Maldonado once upon a time when I entered the port with a stricken crew in my bark, the *Aquidneck*.[1]

In the waters of Maldonado Bay a variety of fishes abound, and fur-seals in their season haul out on the island abreast the bay to breed. Currents on this coast are greatly affected by the prevailing winds, and a tidal wave higher than that ordinarily produced by the moon is sent up the whole shore of Uruguay before a southwest gale, or lowered by a northeaster, as may happen. One of these waves having just receded before the northeast wind which brought the *Spray* in left the tide now at low ebb, with oyster-rocks laid bare for some distance along the shore. Other shellfish of good flavor were also plentiful, though small in size. I gathered a mess of oysters and mussels here, while a native with hook and line, and with mussels for bait, fished from a point of detached rocks for bream, landing several good-sized ones.

The fisherman's nephew, a lad about seven years old, deserves mention as the tallest blasphemer, for a short boy, that I met on the voyage. He called his old uncle all the vile names under the sun for not helping him across the gully. While he swore roundly in all the moods and tenses of the Spanish language, his uncle fished on, now and then congratulating his hopeful nephew on his accomplishment. At the end of his rich vocabulary the urchin sauntered off into the fields, and shortly returned with a bunch of flowers, and with all smiles handed them to me with the innocence of an angel. I remembered having seen the same flower on the banks of the river farther up, some years before. I asked the young pirate why he had brought them to me. Said he, "I don't know; I only wished to do so." Whatever the influence was that put so amiable a wish in this wild pampa boy, it must be far-reaching, thought I, and potent, seas over.

Shortly after, the *Spray* sailed for Montevideo, where she arrived on the following day and was greeted by steam-whistles till I felt embarrassed and wished that I had arrived unobserved. The voyage so far alone may have seemed to the Uruguayans a feat worthy of some recognition; but there was so much of it yet ahead, and of such an arduous nature, that any demonstration at this point seemed, somehow, like boasting prematurely.

The *Spray* had barely come to anchor at Montevideo when the agents of the Royal Mail Steamship Company, Messrs. Humphreys & Co., sent word that they would dock and repair her free of expense and give me twenty pounds sterling, which they did to the letter, and more besides. The calkers at Montevideo paid very careful attention to the work of making the sloop tight. Carpenters mended the keel and also the life-boat (the dory), painting it till I hardly knew it from a butterfly.

Christmas of 1895 found the *Spray* refitted even to a wonderful makeshift stove which was contrived from a large iron drum of some sort punched full of holes to give it a draft; the pipe reached straight up through the top of the forecastle. Now, this was not a stove by mere courtesy. It was always hungry, even for green wood; and in cold, wet days off the coast of Tierra del Fuego it stood me in good stead. Its one door swung on copper hinges, which one of the yard apprentices, with laudable pride, polished till the whole thing blushed like the brass binnacle of a P. & O. steamer.*

The *Spray* was now ready for sea. Instead of proceeding at once on her voyage, however, she made an excursion up the river, sailing December 29. An old friend of mine, Captain Howard of Cape Cod and of River Plate fame, took the trip in her to Buenos Aires, where she arrived early on the following day, with a gale of wind and a current so much in her favor that she outdid herself. I was glad to have

---

*Steamship of the Pacific and Orient Steam Navigation Company, which ran the first cruise ships.

a sailor of Howard's experience on board to witness her perfor-
mance of sailing with no living being at the helm. Howard sat near
the binnacle and watched the compass while the sloop held her
course so steadily that one would have declared that the card was
nailed fast. Not a quarter of a point did she deviate from her course.
My old friend had owned and sailed a pilot-sloop on the river for
many years, but this feat took the wind out of his sails at last, and he
cried, "I'll be stranded on Chico Bank if ever I saw the like of it!" Perhaps he had never given his sloop a chance to show what she could
do. The point I make for the *Spray* here, above all other points, is that
she sailed in shoal water and in a strong current, with other difficult
and unusual conditions. Captain Howard took all this into account.

In all the years away from his native home Howard had not forgotten the art of making fish chowders; and to prove this he brought
along some fine rockfish and prepared a mess fit for kings. When the
savory chowder was done, chocking the pot securely between two
boxes on the cabin floor, so that it could not roll over, we helped
ourselves and swapped yarns over it while the *Spray* made her own
way through the darkness on the river. Howard told me stories
about the Fuegian cannibals as she reeled along, and I told him
about the pilot of the *Pinta* steering my vessel through the storm off
the coast of the Azores, and that I looked for him at the helm in a gale
such as this. I do not charge Howard with superstition,—we are none
of us superstitious,—but when I spoke about his returning to Montevideo on the *Spray* he shook his head and took a steam-packet instead.

I had not been in Buenos Aires for a number of years. The place
where I had once landed from packets, in a cart, was now built up
with magnificent docks. Vast fortunes had been spent in remodeling
the harbor; London bankers could tell you that. The port captain,
after assigning the *Spray* a safe berth, with his compliments, sent me
word to call on him for anything I might want while in port, and I
felt quite sure that his friendship was sincere. The sloop was well
cared for at Buenos Aires; her dockage and tonnage dues were all
free, and the yachting fraternity of the city welcomed her with a
good will. In town I found things not so greatly changed as about
the docks, and I soon felt myself more at home.

From Montevideo I had forwarded a letter from Sir Edward
Hairby to the owner of the "Standard," Mr. Mulhall, and in reply to

it was assured of a warm welcome to the warmest heart, I think, outside of Ireland. Mr. Mulhall, with a prancing team, came down to the docks as soon as the *Spray* was berthed, and would have me go to his house at once, where a room was waiting. And it was New Year's day, 1896. The course of the *Spray* had been followed in the columns of the "Standard."

Mr. Mulhall kindly drove me to see many improvements about the city, and we went in search of some of the old landmarks. The man who sold "lemonade" on the plaza when first I visited this wonderful city I found selling lemonade still at two cents a glass; he had made a fortune by it. His stock in trade was a wash-tub and a neighboring hydrant, a moderate supply of brown sugar, and about six lemons that floated on the sweetened water. The water from time to time was renewed from the friendly pump, but the lemon "went on forever,"[2] and all at two cents a glass.

But we looked in vain for the man who once sold whisky and coffins in Buenos Aires; the march of civilization had crushed him—memory only clung to his name. Enterprising man that he was, I

At the sign of the comet.

fain would have looked him up. I remember the tiers of whisky-barrels, ranged on end, on one side of the store, while on the other side, and divided by a thin partition, were the coffins in the same order, of all sizes and in great numbers. The unique arrangement seemed in order, for as a cask was emptied a coffin might be filled. Besides cheap whisky and many other liquors, he sold "cider," which he manufactured from damaged Malaga raisins. Within the scope of his enterprise was also the sale of mineral waters, not entirely blameless of the germs of disease. This man surely catered to all the tastes, wants, and conditions of his customers.

Farther along in the city, however, survived the good man who wrote on the side of his store, where thoughtful men might read and learn: "This wicked world will be destroyed by a comet! The owner of this store is therefore bound to sell out at any price and avoid the catastrophe." My friend Mr. Mulhall drove me round to view the fearful comet with streaming tail pictured large on the trembling merchant's walls.

I unshipped the sloop's mast at Buenos Aires and shortened it by seven feet. I reduced the length of the bowsprit by about five feet, and even then I found it reaching far enough from home; and more than once, when on the end of it reefing the jib, I regretted that I had not shortened it another foot.

CHAPTER VII

Weighing anchor at Buenos Aires—An outburst of emotion at the mouth of the Plate—Submerged by a great wave—A stormy entrance to the strait—Captain Samblich's happy gift of a bag of carpet-tacks—Off Cape Froward—Chased by Indians from Fortescue Bay—A miss-shot for "Black Pedro"—Taking in supplies of wood and water at Three Island Cove—Animal life.

O n January 26, 1896, the *Spray*, being refitted and well provisioned in every way, sailed from Buenos Aires. There was little wind at the start; the surface of the great river was like a silver disk, and I was glad of a tow from a harbor tug to clear the port entrance. But a gale came up soon after, and caused an ugly sea, and instead of being all silver, as before, the river was now all mud. The Plate is a treacherous place for storms. One sailing there should always be on the alert for squalls. I cast anchor before dark in the best lee I could find near the land, but was tossed miserably all night, heartsore of choppy seas. On the following morning I got the sloop under way, and with reefed sails worked her down the river against a head wind. Standing in that night to the place where pilot Howard joined me for the up-river sail, I took a departure, shaping my course to clear Point Indio on the one hand, and the English Bank on the other.

I had not for many years been south of these regions. I will not say that I expected all fine sailing on the course for Cape Horn direct, but while I worked at the sails and rigging I thought only of onward and forward. It was when I anchored in the lonely places that a feeling of awe crept over me. At the last anchorage on the monotonous and muddy river, weak as it may seem, I gave way to my feelings. I resolved then that I would anchor no more north of the Strait of Magellan.

On the 28th of January the *Spray* was clear of Point Indio, English Bank, and all the other dangers of the River Plate. With a fair wind she then bore away for the Strait of Magellan, under all sail, pressing farther and farther toward the wonderland of the South, till I forgot the blessings of our milder North.

My ship passed in safety Bahia Blanca, also the Gulf of St. Matias and the mighty Gulf of St. George. Hoping that she might go clear of

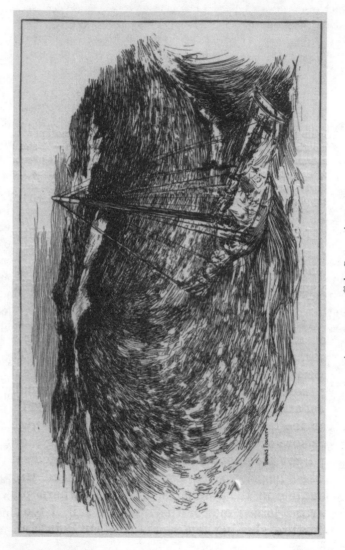

A great wave off the Patagonian coast.

the destructive tide-races, the dread of big craft or little along this coast, I gave all the capes a berth of about fifty miles, for these dangers extend many miles from the land. But where the sloop avoided one danger she encountered another. For, one day, well off the Patagonian coast, while the sloop was reaching under short sail, a tremendous wave, the culmination, it seemed, of many waves, rolled down upon her in a storm, roaring as it came. I had only a moment to get all sail down and myself up on the peak halliards, out of danger, when I saw the mighty crest towering masthead-high above me. The mountain of water submerged my vessel. She shook in every timber and reeled under the weight of the sea, but rose quickly out of it, and rode grandly over the rollers that followed. It may have been a minute that from my hold in the rigging I could see no part of the *Spray's* hull. Perhaps it was even less time than that, but it seemed a long while, for under great excitement one lives fast, and in a few seconds one may think a great deal of one's past life. Not only did the past, with electric speed, flash before me, but I had time while in my hazardous position for resolutions for the future that would take a long time to fulfil. The first one was, I remember, that if the *Spray* came through this danger I would dedicate my best energies to building a larger ship on her lines, which I hope yet to do. Other promises, less easily kept, I should have made under protest. However, the incident, which filled me with fear, was only one more test of the *Spray's* seaworthiness. It reassured me against rude Cape Horn.

From the time the great wave swept over the *Spray* until she reached Cape Virgins nothing occurred to move a pulse and set blood in motion. On the contrary, the weather became fine and the sea smooth and life tranquil. The phenomenon of mirage frequently occurred. An albatross sitting on the water one day loomed up like a large ship; two fur-seals asleep on the surface of the sea appeared like great whales, and a bank of haze I could have sworn was high land. The kaleidoscope then changed, and on the following day I sailed in a world peopled by dwarfs.

On February 11 the *Spray* rounded Cape Virgins and entered the Strait of Magellan. The scene was again real and gloomy; the wind, northeast, and blowing a gale, sent feather-white spume along the coast; such a sea ran as would swamp an ill-appointed ship. As the sloop neared the entrance to the strait I observed that two great

Entrance to the Strait of Magellan.

tide-races made ahead, one very close to the point of the land and one farther offshore. Between the two, in a sort of channel, through combers, went the *Spray* with close-reefed sails. But a rolling sea followed her a long way in, and a fierce current swept around the cape against her; but this she stemmed, and was soon chirruping under the lee of Cape Virgins and running every minute into smoother water. However, long trailing kelp from sunken rocks waved forebodingly under her keel, and the wreck of a great steamship smashed on the beach abreast gave a gloomy aspect to the scene.

I was not to be let off easy. The Virgins would collect tribute even from the *Spray* passing their promontory. Fitful rain-squalls from the northwest followed the northeast gale. I reefed the sloop's sails, and sitting in the cabin to rest my eyes, I was so strongly impressed with what in all nature I might expect that as I dozed the very air I breathed seemed to warn me of danger. My senses heard "*Spray* ahoy!" shouted in warning. I sprang to the deck, wondering who could be there that knew the *Spray* so well as to call out her name passing in the dark; for it was now the blackest of nights all around, except away in the southwest, where the old familiar white arch,* the terror of Cape Horn, rapidly pushed up by a southwest gale. I had only a moment to douse sail and lash all solid when it struck like a shot from a cannon, and for the first half-hour it was something to be remembered by way of a gale. For thirty hours it kept on blowing hard. The sloop could carry no more than a three-reefed mainsail and forestaysail; with these she held on stoutly and was not blown

---

*White squall, a sudden gale marked by whitecaps.

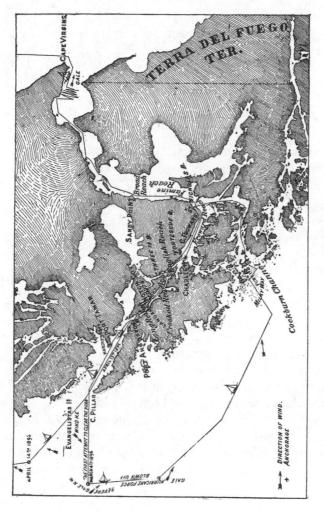

The course of the *Spray* through the Strait of Magellan.

out of the strait. In the height of the squalls in this gale she doused all sail, and this occurred often enough.

After this gale followed only a smart breeze, and the *Spray*, passing through the narrows without mishap, cast anchor at Sandy Point on February 14, 1896.

Sandy Point (Punta Arenas) is a Chilean coaling-station, and boasts about two thousand inhabitants, of mixed nationality, but mostly Chileans. What with sheep-farming, gold-mining, and hunting, the settlers in this dreary land seemed not the worst off in the world. But the natives, Patagonian and Fuegian, on the other hand, were as squalid as contact with unscrupulous traders could make them. A large percentage of the business there was traffic in "fire-water." If there was a law against selling the poisonous stuff to the natives, it was not enforced.

The man who wouldn't ship without another "mon and a doog."

Fine specimens of the Patagonian race, looking smart in the morning when they came into town, had repented before night of ever having seen a white man, so beastly drunk were they, to say nothing about the peltry of which they had been robbed.

The port at that time was free, but a customhouse was in course of construction, and when it is finished, port and tariff dues are to be collected. A soldier police guarded the place, and a sort of vigilante force besides took down its guns now and then; but as a general thing, to my mind, whenever an execution was made they killed the wrong man. Just previous to my arrival the governor, himself of a jovial turn of mind, had sent a party of young bloods to foray a Fuegian settlement and wipe out what they could of it on account of the recent massacre of a schooner's crew somewhere else. Altogether the place was quite newsy and supported two papers—dailies, I think. The port captain, a Chilean naval officer, advised me to ship hands to fight Indians in the strait farther west, and spoke of my stopping until a gunboat should be going through, which would give me a tow. After canvassing the place, however, I found only one man willing to embark, and he on condition that I should ship another "mon and a doog." But as no one else was willing to come along, and as I drew the line at dogs, I said no more about the matter, but simply loaded my guns. At this point in my dilemma Captain Pedro Samblich, a good Austrian of large experience, coming along, gave me a bag of carpet-tacks, worth more than all the fighting men and dogs of Tierra del Fuego. I protested that I had no use for carpet-tacks on board. Samblich smiled at my want of experience, and maintained stoutly that I would have use for them. "You must use them with discretion," he said; "that is to say, don't step on them yourself." With this remote hint about the use of the tacks I got on all right, and saw the way to maintain clear decks at night without the care of watching.

Samblich was greatly interested in my voyage, and after giving me the tacks he put on board bags of biscuits and a large quantity of smoked venison. He declared that my bread, which was ordinary sea-biscuits and easily broken, was not nutritious as his, which was so hard that I could break it only with a stout blow from a maul. Then he gave me, from his own sloop, a compass which was certainly better than mine, and offered to unbend her mainsail for me if I would accept it. Last of all, this large-hearted man brought out a bottle of Fuegian gold-dust from a place where it had been *cached* and begged me to help myself from it, for use farther along on the voyage. But I felt sure of success without this draft on a friend, and I was right. Samblich's tacks, as it turned out, were of more value than gold.

The port captain finding that I was resolved to go, even alone, since there was no help for it, set up no further objections, but advised me, in case the savages tried to surround me with their canoes, to shoot straight, and begin to do it in time, but to avoid killing them if possible, which I heartily agreed to do. With these simple injunctions the officer gave me my port clearance free of charge, and I sailed on the same day, February 19, 1896. It was not without thoughts of strange and stirring adventure beyond all I had yet encountered that

A Fuegian girl.

I now sailed into the country and very core of the savage Fuegians.

A fair wind from Sandy Point brought me on the first day to St. Nicholas Bay, where, so I was told, I might expect to meet savages; but seeing no signs of life, I came to anchor in eight fathoms of water, where I lay all night under a high mountain. Here I had my first experience with the terrific squalls, called williwaws, which extended from this point on through the strait to the Pacific. They were compressed gales of wind that Boreas* handed down over the hills in chunks. A full-blown williwaw will throw a ship, even without sail on, over on her beam ends; but, like other gales, they cease now and then, if only for a short time.

February 20 was my birthday, and I found myself alone, with hardly so much as a bird in sight, off Cape Froward, the southernmost point of the continent of America. By daylight in the morning I was getting my ship under way for the bout ahead.

The sloop held the wind fair while she ran thirty miles farther on her course, which brought her to Fortescue Bay, and at once among the natives' signal-fires, which blazed up now on all sides. Clouds flew over the mountain from the west all day; at night my good east wind failed, and in its stead a gale from the west soon came on. I gained anchorage at twelve o'clock that night, under the lee of a little island, and then prepared myself a cup of coffee, of which I was sorely in need; for, to tell the truth, hard beating in the heavy squalls and against the current had told on my strength. Finding that the anchor held, I drank my beverage, and named the place Coffee Island. It lies to the south of Charles Island, with only a narrow channel between.

---

*Greek god of the north wind.

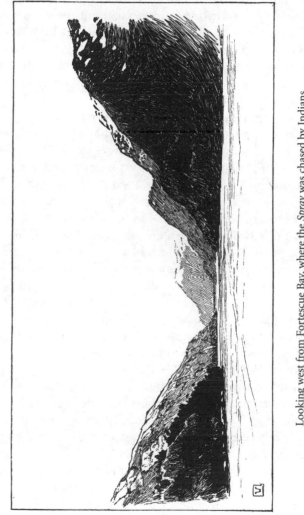

Looking west from Fortescue Bay, where the *Spray* was chased by Indians.

(From a photograph.)

By daylight the next morning the *Spray* was again under way, beating hard; but she came to in a cove in Charles Island, two and a half miles along on her course. Here she remained undisturbed two days, with both anchors down in a bed of kelp. Indeed, she might have remained undisturbed indefinitely had not the wind moderated; for during these two days it blew so hard that no boat could venture out on the strait, and the natives being away to other hunting-grounds, the island anchorage was safe. But at the end of the fierce wind-storm fair weather came; then I got my anchors, and again sailed out upon the strait.

Canoes manned by savages from Fortescue now came in pursuit. The wind falling light, they gained on me rapidly till coming within hail, when they ceased paddling, and a bow-legged savage stood up and called to me, "Yammerschooner! yammerschooner!" which is their begging term. I said, "No!" Now, I was not for letting on that I was alone, and so I stepped into the cabin, and, passing through the hold, came out at the fore-scuttle, changing my clothes as I went along. That made two men. Then the piece of bowsprit which I had sawed off at Buenos Aires, and which I had still on board, I arranged forward on the lookout, dressed as a seaman, attaching a line by which I could pull it into motion. That made three of us, and we didn't want to "yammerschooner"; but for all that the savages came on faster than before. I saw that besides four at the paddles in the canoe nearest to me, there were others in the bottom, and that they were shifting hands often. At eighty yards I fired a shot across the bows of the nearest canoe, at which they all stopped, but only for a moment. Seeing that they persisted in coming nearer, I fired the second shot so close to the chap who wanted to "yammerschooner" that he changed his mind quickly enough and bellowed with fear, "Bueno jo via Isla,"* and sitting down in his canoe, he rubbed his starboard cat-head for some time. I was thinking of the good port captain's advice when I pulled the trigger, and must have aimed pretty straight; however, a miss was as good as a mile for Mr. "Black Pedro," as he it was, and no other, a leader in several bloody massacres. He made for the island now, and the others followed him. I knew by his Spanish lingo and by his full

---

*Properly, *Bueno, yo voy a Isla*, Spanish for "Okay, I'll go to the island."

A brush with Fuegians.

beard that he was the villain I have named, a renegade mongrel, and the worst murderer in Tierra del Fuego. The authorities had been in search of him for two years. The Fuegians are not bearded.

So much for the first day among the savages. I came to anchor at midnight in Three Island Cove, about twenty miles along from Fortescue Bay. I saw on the opposite side of the strait signal-fires, and heard the barking of dogs, but where I lay it was quite deserted by natives. I have always taken it as a sign that where I found birds sitting about, or seals on the rocks, I should not find savage Indians. Seals are never plentiful in these waters, but in Three Island Cove I saw one on the rocks, and other signs of the absence of savage men.

On the next day the wind was again blowing a gale, and although she was in the lee of the land, the sloop dragged her anchors, so that I had to get her under way and beat farther into the cove, where I came to in a landlocked pool. At another time or place this would have been a rash thing to do, and it was safe now only from the fact that the gale which drove me to shelter would keep the Indians from crossing the strait. Seeing this was the case, I went ashore with gun and ax on an island, where I could not in any event be surprised, and there felled trees and split about a cord of fire-wood, which loaded my small boat several times.

While I carried the wood, though I was morally sure there were no savages near, I never once went to or from the skiff without my gun. While I had that and a clear field of over eighty yards about me I felt safe.

The trees on the island, very scattering, were a sort of beech and a stunted cedar, both of which made good fuel. Even the green limbs of the beech, which seemed to possess a resinous quality, burned readily in my great drum-stove. I have described my method of wooding up in detail, that the reader who has kindly borne with me so far may see that in this, as in all other particulars of my voyage, I took great care against all kinds of surprises, whether by animals or by the elements. In the Strait of Magellan the greatest vigilance was necessary. In this instance I reasoned that I had all about me the greatest danger of the whole voyage—the treachery of cunning savages, for which I must be particularly on the alert.

The *Spray* sailed from Three Island Cove in the morning after the gale went down, but was glad to return for shelter from another

A bit of friendly assistance.
(After a sketch by Miguel Arenas.)

sudden gale. Sailing again on the following day, she fetched Borgia Bay, a few miles on her course, where vessels had anchored from time to time and had nailed boards on the trees ashore with name and date of harboring carved or painted. Nothing else could I see to indicate that civilized man had ever been there. I had taken a survey of the gloomy place with my spy-glass, and was getting my boat out to land and take notes, when the Chilean gunboat *Huemel* came in, and officers, coming on board, advised me to leave the place at once, a thing that required little eloquence to persuade me to do. I accepted the captain's kind offer of a tow to the next anchorage, at the place called Notch Cove, eight miles farther along, where I should be clear of the worst of the Fuegians.

We made anchorage at the cove about dark that night, while the wind came down in fierce williwaws from the mountains. An instance of Magellan weather was afforded when the *Huemel,* a well-appointed gunboat of great power, after attempting on the following day to proceed on her voyage, was obliged by sheer force of the wind to return and take up anchorage again and remain till the gale abated; and lucky she was to get back!

Meeting this vessel was a little godsend. She was commanded and officered by high-class sailors and educated gentlemen. An entertainment that was gotten up on her, impromptu, at the Notch would be hard to beat anywhere. One of her midshipmen sang popular songs in French, German, and Spanish, and one (so he said) in Russian. If the audience did not know the lingo of one song from another, it was no drawback to the merriment.

I was left alone the next day, for then the *Huemel* put out on her voyage, the gale having abated. I spent a day taking in wood and water; by the end of that time the weather was fine. Then I sailed from the desolate place.

There is little more to be said concerning the *Spray's* first passage through the strait that would differ from what I have already recorded. She anchored and weighed many times, and beat many days against the current, with now and then a "slant" for a few miles, till finally she gained anchorage and shelter for the night at Port Tamar, with Cape Pillar in sight to the west. Here I felt the throb of the great ocean that lay before me. I knew now that I had put a world behind me, and that I was opening out another world ahead. I had passed the haunts of savages. Great piles of granite mountains of bleak and lifeless aspect were now astern; on some of them not even a speck of moss had ever grown. There was an unfinished newness all about the land. On the hill back of Port Tamar a small beacon had been thrown up, showing that some man had been there. But how could one tell but that he had died of loneliness and grief? In a bleak land is not the place to enjoy solitude.

Throughout the whole of the strait west of Cape Froward I saw no animals except dogs owned by savages. These I saw often enough, and heard them yelping night and day. Birds were not plentiful. The scream of a wild fowl, which I took for a loon, sometimes startled me with its piercing cry. The steamboat duck, so called because it propels itself over the sea with its wings, and resembles a miniature side-wheel steamer in its motion, was sometimes seen scurrying on out of danger. It never flies, but, hitting the water instead of the air with its wings, it moves faster than a rowboat or a canoe. The few fur-seals I saw were very shy; and of fishes I saw next to none at all. I did not catch one; indeed, I seldom or never put a hook over during the whole voyage. Here in the strait I found great abundance of mussels of an excellent quality. I fared sumptuously on them. There was a sort of swan, smaller than a Muscovy duck, which might have been brought down with the gun, but in the loneliness of life about the dreary country I found myself in no mood to make one life less, except in self-defense.

CHAPTER VIII

From Cape Pillar into the Pacific—Driven by a tempest toward Cape Horn—Captain Slocum's greatest sea adventure—Reaching the strait again by way of Cockburn Channel—Some savages find the carpet-tacks —Danger from firebrands—A series of fierce williwaws—Again sailing westward.

It was the 3d of March when the *Spray* sailed from Port Tamar direct for Cape Pillar, with the wind from the northeast, which I fervently hoped might hold till she cleared the land; but there was no such good luck in store. It soon began to rain and thicken in the northwest, boding no good. The *Spray* neared Cape Pillar rapidly, and, nothing loath, plunged into the Pacific Ocean at once, taking her first bath of it in the gathering storm. There was no turning back even had I wished to do so, for the land was now shut out by the darkness of night. The wind freshened, and I took in a third reef. The sea was confused and treacherous. In such a time as this the old fisherman prayed, "Remember, Lord, my ship is small and thy sea is so wide!"[1] I saw now only the gleaming crests of the waves. They showed white teeth while the sloop balanced over them. "Everything for an offing," I cried, and to this end I carried on all the sail she would bear. She ran all night with a free sheet, but on the morning of March 4 the wind shifted to southwest, then back suddenly to northwest, and blew with terrific force. The *Spray*, stripped of her sails, then bore off under bare poles. No ship in the world could have stood up against so violent a gale. Knowing that this storm might continue for many days, and that it would be impossible to work back to the westward along the coast outside of Tierra del Fuego, there seemed nothing to do but to keep on and go east about, after all. Anyhow, for my present safety the only course lay in keeping her before the wind. And so she drove southeast, as though about to round the Horn, while the waves rose and fell and bellowed their never-ending story of the sea; but the Hand that held these held also the *Spray*. She was running now with a reefed forestaysail, the sheets flat amidship. I paid out two long ropes to steady her course and to

Cape Pillar.

break combing seas astern, and I lashed the helm amidship. In this trim she ran before it, shipping never a sea. Even while the storm raged at its worst, my ship was wholesome and noble. My mind as to her seaworthiness was put at ease for aye.

When all had been done that I could do for the safety of the vessel, I got to the fore-scuttle, between seas, and prepared a pot of coffee over a wood fire, and made a good Irish stew. Then, as before and afterward on the *Spray,* I insisted on warm meals. In the tide-race off Cape Pillar, however, where the sea was marvelously high, uneven, and crooked, my appetite was slim, and for a time I postponed cooking. (Confidentially, I was seasick!)

The first day of the storm gave the *Spray* her actual test in the worst sea that Cape Horn or its wild regions could afford, and in no part of the world could a rougher sea be found than at this particular point, namely, off Cape Pillar, the grim sentinel of the Horn.

Farther offshore, while the sea was majestic, there was less apprehension of danger. There the *Spray* rode, now like a bird on the crest of a wave, and now like a waif deep down in the hollow between seas; and so she drove on. Whole days passed, counted as other days, but with always a thrill—yes, of delight.

On the fourth day of the gale, rapidly nearing the pitch of Cape Horn, I inspected my chart and pricked off the course and distance to Port Stanley, in the Falkland Islands, where I might find my way and refit, when I saw through a rift in the clouds a high mountain, about seven leagues away on the port beam. The fierce edge of the gale by this time had blown off, and I had already bent a squarcsail on the boom in place of the mainsail, which was torn to rags. I hauled in the trailing ropes, hoisted this awkward sail reefed, the forestaysail being already set, and under this sail brought her at once on the wind heading for the land, which appeared as an island in the sea. So it turned out to be, though not the one I had supposed.

I was exultant over the prospect of once more entering the Strait of Magellan and beating through again into the Pacific, for it was more than rough on the outside coast of Tierra del Fuego. It was indeed a mountainous sea. When the sloop was in the fiercest squalls, with only the reefed forestaysail set, even that small sail shook her from keelson to truck when it shivered by the leech. Had I harbored the shadow of a doubt for her safety, it would have been that she might spring a leak in the garboard at the heel of the mast; but she never called me once to the pump. Under pressure of the smallest sail I could set she made for the land like a race-horse, and steering her over the crests of the waves so that she might not trip was nice work. I stood at the helm now and made the most of it.

Night closed in before the sloop reached the land, leaving her feeling the way in pitchy darkness. I saw breakers ahead before long. At this I wore ship and stood offshore, but was immediately startled by the tremendous roaring of breakers again ahead and on the lee bow. This puzzled me, for there should have been no broken water where I supposed myself to be. I kept off a good bit, then wore round, but finding broken water also there, threw her head again offshore. In this way, among dangers, I spent the rest of the night. Hail and sleet in the fierce squalls cut my flesh till the blood trickled over my face; but what of that? It was daylight, and the sloop was in the midst of the Milky Way of the sea, which is northwest of Cape Horn, and it was the white breakers of a huge sea over sunken rocks which had threatened to engulf her through the night. It was Fury Island I had sighted and steered for, and what a panorama was before me now and all around! It was not the time to complain of a broken skin. What could I do but fill away among the breakers and find a channel between them, now that it was day? Since she had escaped the rocks through the night, surely she would find her way by daylight. This was the greatest sea adventure of my life. God knows how my vessel escaped.

The sloop at last reached inside of small islands that sheltered her in smooth water. Then I climbed the mast to survey the wild scene astern. The great naturalist Darwin looked over this seascape from the deck of the *Beagle,* and wrote in his journal, "Any landsman seeing the Milky Way would have nightmare for a week."[2] He might have added, "or seaman" as well.

The *Spray's* good luck followed fast. I discovered, as she sailed along through a labyrinth of islands, that she was in the Cockburn Channel, which leads into the Strait of Magellan at a point opposite Cape Froward, and that she was already passing Thieves' Bay, suggestively named. And at night, March 8, behold, she was at anchor in a snug cove at the Turn! Every heart-beat on the *Spray* now counted thanks.

Here I pondered on the events of the last few days, and, strangely enough, instead of feeling rested from sitting or lying down, I now began to feel jaded and worn; but a hot meal of venison stew soon put me right, so that I could sleep. As drowsiness came on I sprinkled the deck with tacks, and then I turned in, bearing in mind the advice of my old friend Samblich that I was not to step on them myself. I saw to it that not a few of them stood "business end" up; for when the *Spray* passed Thieves' Bay two canoes had put out and followed in her wake, and there was no disguising the fact any longer that I was alone.

Now, it is well known that one cannot step on a tack without saying something about it. A pretty good Christian will whistle when he steps on the "commercial end" of a carpet-tack; a savage will howl and claw the air, and that was just what happened that night about twelve o'clock, while I was asleep in the cabin, where the savages thought they "had me," sloop and all, but changed their minds when they stepped on deck, for then they thought that I or somebody else had them. I had no need of a dog; they howled like a pack of hounds. I had hardly use for a gun. They jumped pell-mell, some into their canoes and some into the sea, to cool off, I suppose, and there was a deal of free language over it as they went. I fired several guns when I came on deck, to let the rascals know that I was home, and then I turned in again, feeling sure I should not be disturbed any more by people who left in so great a hurry.

The Fuegians, being cruel, are naturally cowards; they regard a rifle with superstitious fear. The only real danger one could see that might come from their quarter would be from allowing them to surround one within bow-shot, or to anchor within range where they might lie in ambush. As for their coming on deck at night, even had I not put tacks about, I could have cleared them off by shots from the cabin and hold. I always kept a quantity of ammunition within reach in the hold and in the cabin and in the forepeak, so that retreating to any of these places I could "hold the fort" simply by shooting up through the deck.

Perhaps the greatest danger to be apprehended was from the use of fire. Every canoe carries fire; nothing is thought of that, for it is their custom to communicate by smoke-signals. The harmless brand that lies smoldering in the bottom of one of their canoes might be ablaze in one's cabin if he were not on the alert. The port captain of

"They howled like a pack of hounds."

Sandy Point warned me particularly of this danger. Only a short time before they had fired a Chilean gunboat by throwing brands in through the stern windows of the cabin. The *Spray* had no openings in the cabin or deck, except two scuttles, and these were guarded by fastenings which could not be undone without waking me if I were asleep.

On the morning of the 9th, after a refreshing rest and a warm breakfast, and after I had swept the deck of tacks, I got out what spare canvas there was on board, and began to sew the pieces together in the shape of a peak for my square-mainsail, the tarpaulin. The day to all appearances promised fine weather and light winds, but appearances in Tierra del Fuego do not always count. While I was wondering why no trees grew on the slope abreast of the anchorage, half minded to lay by the sail-making and land with my gun for some game and to inspect a white boulder on the beach, near the brook, a williwaw came down with such terrific force as to carry the *Spray,* with two anchors down, like a feather out of the cove and away into deep water. No wonder trees did not grow on the side of that hill! Great Boreas! a tree would need to be all roots to hold on against such a furious wind.

From the cove to the nearest land to leeward was a long drift, however, and I had ample time to weigh both anchors before the sloop came near any danger, and so no harm came of it. I saw no more savages that day or the next; they probably had some sign by which they knew of the coming williwaws; at least, they were wise in not being afloat even on the second day, for I had no sooner gotten to work at sail-making again, after the anchor was down, than the wind, as on the day before, picked the sloop up and flung her seaward with a vengeance, anchor and all, as before. This fierce wind, usual to the Magellan country, continued on through the day, and swept the sloop by several miles of steep bluffs and precipices overhanging a bold shore of wild and uninviting appearance. I was not sorry to get away from it, though in doing so it was no Elysian shore[3] to which I shaped my course. I kept on sailing in hope, since I had no choice but to go on, heading across for St. Nicholas Bay, where I had cast anchor February 19. It was now the 10th of March! Upon reaching the bay the second time I had circumnavigated the wildest part of desolate Tierra del Fuego. But the *Spray* had not yet arrived at St. Nicholas, and by the merest accident her bones were saved from resting there when she did arrive. The parting of a staysail-sheet in a williwaw, when the sea was turbulent and she was plunging into the storm, brought me forward to see instantly a dark cliff ahead and breakers so close under the bows that I felt surely lost, and in my thoughts cried, "Is the hand of fate against me, after all, leading me in the end to this dark spot?" I sprang aft again, unheeding the flapping sail, and threw the wheel over, expecting, as the sloop came down into the hollow of a wave, to feel her timbers smash under me on the rocks. But at the touch of her helm she swung clear of the danger, and in the next moment she was in the lee of the land.

It was the small island in the middle of the bay for which the sloop had been steering, and which she made with such unerring aim as nearly to run it down. Farther along in the bay was the anchorage, which I managed to reach, but before I could get the anchor down another squall caught the sloop and whirled her round like a top and carried her away, altogether to leeward of the bay. Still farther to leeward was a great headland, and I bore off for that. This was

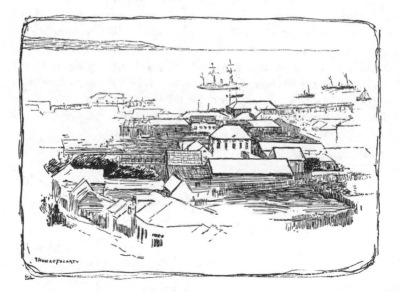

A glimpse of Sandy Point (Punta Arenas) in the Strait of Magellan.

retracing my course toward Sandy Point, for the gale was from the southwest.

I had the sloop soon under good control, however, and in a short time rounded to under the lee of a mountain, where the sea was as smooth as a mill-pond, and the sails flapped and hung limp while she carried her way close in. Here I thought I would anchor and rest till morning, the depth being eight fathoms very close to the shore. But it was interesting to see, as I let go the anchor, that it did not reach the bottom before another williwaw struck down from this mountain and carried the sloop off faster than I could pay out cable. Therefore, instead of resting, I had to "man the windlass" and heave up the anchor with fifty fathoms of cable hanging up and down in deep water. This was in that part of the strait called Famine Reach. Dismal Famine Reach! On the sloop's crab-windlass I worked the rest of the night, thinking how much easier it was for me when I could say, "Do that thing or the other," than now doing all myself. But I hove away and sang the old chants[4] that I sang when I was a sailor. Within the last few days I had passed through much and was now thankful that my state was no worse.

It was daybreak when the anchor was at the hawse. By this time the wind had gone down, and cat's-paws took the place of williwaws, while the sloop drifted slowly toward Sandy Point. She came within sight of ships at anchor in the roads, and I was more than half minded to put in for new sails, but the wind coming out from the northeast, which was fair for the other direction, I turned the prow of the *Spray* westward once more for the Pacific, to traverse a second time the second half of my first course through the strait.

CHAPTER IX

Repairing the *Spray's* sails—Savages and an obstreperous anchor—A spider-fight—An encounter with Black Pedro—A visit to the steamship *Colombia*—On the defensive against a fleet of canoes—A record of voyages through the strait—A chance cargo of tallow.

I was determined to rely on my own small resources to repair the damages of the great gale which drove me southward toward the Horn, after I had passed from the Strait of Magellan out into the Pacific. So when I had got back into the strait, by way of Cockburn Channel, I did not proceed eastward for help at the Sandy Point settlement, but turning again into the northwestward reach of the strait, set to work with my palm and needle at every opportunity, when at anchor and when sailing. It was slow work; but little by little the squaresail on the boom expanded to the dimensions of a serviceable mainsail with a peak to it and a leech besides. If it was not the best-setting sail afloat, it was at least very strongly made and would stand a hard blow. A ship, meeting the *Spray* long afterward, reported her as wearing a mainsail of some improved design and patent reefer, but that was not the case.

The *Spray* for a few days after the storm enjoyed fine weather, and made fair time through the strait for the distance of twenty miles, which, in these days of many adversities, I called a long run. The weather, I say, was fine for a few days; but it brought little rest. Care for the safety of my vessel, and even for my own life, was in no wise lessened by the absence of heavy weather. Indeed, the peril was even greater, inasmuch as the savages on comparatively fine days ventured forth on their marauding excursions, and in boisterous weather disappeared from sight, their wretched canoes being frail and undeserving the name of craft at all. This being so, I now enjoyed gales of wind as never before, and the *Spray* was never long without them during her struggles about Cape Horn. I became in a measure inured to the life, and began to think that one more trip through the strait, if perchance the sloop should be blown off again, would make me the aggressor, and put the Fuegians entirely on the defensive. This feeling was forcibly borne in on me at Snug Bay, where I anchored at gray morning after passing Cape Froward, to find, when broad day appeared, that two canoes which I had eluded by sailing all night were now entering the same bay stealthily under the shadow of the high headland. They were well manned, and the savages were well armed with spears and bows. At a shot from my rifle across the bows, both turned aside into a small creek out of range. In danger now of being flanked by the savages in the bush close aboard, I was obliged to hoist the sails, which I had barely lowered, and make across to the opposite side of the strait, a distance of six miles. But now I was put to my wit's end as to how I should weigh anchor, for through an accident to the windlass right here I could not budge it. However, I set all sail and filled away, first hauling short by hand. The sloop carried her anchor away, as though it was meant to be always towed in this way underfoot, and with it she towed a ton or more of kelp from a reef in the bay, the wind blowing a wholesale breeze.

Meanwhile I worked till blood started from my fingers, and with one eye over my shoulder for savages, I watched at the same time, and sent a bullet whistling whenever I saw a limb or a twig move; for I kept a gun always at hand, and an Indian appearing then within range would have been taken as a declaration of war. As it was, however, my own blood was all that was spilt—and from the trifling accident of sometimes breaking the flesh against a cleat or a pin which came in the way when I was in haste. Sea-cuts in my hands from pulling on hard, wet ropes were sometimes painful and often bled freely; but these healed when I finally got away from the strait into fine weather.

After clearing Snug Bay I hauled the sloop to the wind, repaired the windlass, and hove the anchor to the hawse, catted it, and then stretched across to a port of refuge under a high mountain about six miles away, and came to in nine fathoms close under the face of a perpendicular cliff. Here my own voice answered back, and I named the place "Echo Mountain." Seeing dead trees farther along where the shore was broken, I made a landing for fuel, taking, besides my ax, a rifle, which on these days I never left far from hand; but I saw no living thing here, except a small spider, which had nested in a dry log that I boated to the sloop. The conduct of this insect interested me now more than anything else around the wild place. In my cabin it met, oddly enough, a spider of its own size and species that had come all the way from Boston—a very civil little chap, too, but mighty spry. Well, the Fuegian threw up its antennæ for a fight; but my little Bostonian downed it at once, then broke its legs, and pulled them off, one by one, so dexterously that in less than three minutes from the time the battle began the Fuegian spider didn't know itself from a fly.

I made haste the following morning to be under way after a night of wakefulness on the weird shore. Before weighing anchor, however, I prepared a cup of warm coffee over a smart wood fire in my great Montevideo stove. In the same fire was cremated the Fuegian spider, slain the day before by the little warrior from Boston, which a Scots lady at Cape Town long after named "Bruce"[1] upon hearing of its prowess at Echo Mountain. The *Spray* now reached away for Coffee Island, which I sighted on my birthday, February 20, 1896.

There she encountered another gale, that brought her in the lee of great Charles Island for shelter. On a bluff point on Charles were signal-fires, and a tribe of savages, mustered here since my first trip through the strait, manned their canoes to put off for the sloop. It was not prudent to come to, the anchorage being within bow-shot of the shore, which was thickly wooded; but I made signs that one canoe might come alongside, while the sloop ranged about under sail in the lee of the land. The others I motioned to keep off, and incidentally laid a smart Martini-Henry rifle[2] in sight, close at hand, on the top of the cabin. In the canoe that came alongside, crying their never-ending begging word "yammerschooner," were two squaws and one Indian, the hardest specimens of humanity I had ever seen in any of my travels. "Yammerschooner" was their plaint when they pushed off from the shore, and "yammerschooner" it was when they got alongside. The squaws beckoned for food, while the Indian, a black-visaged savage, stood sulkily as if he took no interest at all in the matter, but on my turning my back for some biscuits and jerked beef for the squaws, the "buck" sprang on deck and confronted me, saying in Spanish jargon that we had met before. I thought I recognized the tone of his "yammerschooner," and his full beard identified him as the Black Pedro whom, it was true, I had met before. "Where are the rest of the crew?" he asked, as he looked uneasily around, expecting hands, maybe, to come out of the forescuttle and deal him his just deserts for many murders. "About three

"Yammerschooner!"

weeks ago," said he, "when you passed up here, I saw three men on board. Where are the other two?" I answered him briefly that the same crew was still on board. "But," said he, "I see you are doing all the work," and with a leer he added, as he glanced at the mainsail, "hombre valiente."* I explained that I did all the work in the day, while the rest of the crew slept, so that they would be fresh to watch for Indians at night. I was interested in the subtle cunning of this savage, knowing him, as I did, better perhaps than he was aware. Even had I not been advised before I sailed from Sandy Point, I should have measured him for an arch-villain now. Moreover, one of the squaws, with that spark of kindliness which is somehow found in the breast of even the lowest savage, warned me by a sign to be on my guard, or Black Pedro would do me harm. There was no need of the warning, however, for I was on my guard from the first, and at that moment held a smart revolver in my hand ready for instant service.

"When you sailed through here before," he said, "you fired a shot at me," adding with some warmth that it was "muy malo."† I affected not to understand, and said, "You have lived at Sandy Point, have you not?" He answered frankly, "Yes," and appeared delighted to meet one who had come from the dear old place. "At the mission?" I queried. "Why, yes," he replied, stepping forward as if to embrace an old friend. I motioned him back, for I did not share his flattering humor. "And you know Captain Pedro Samblich?" continued I. "Yes," said the villain, who had killed a kinsman of Samblich—"yes, indeed; he is a great friend of mine." "I know it," said I. Samblich had told me to shoot him on sight. Pointing to my rifle on the cabin, he wanted to know how many times it fired. "Cuantos?"‡ said he. When I explained to him that that gun kept right on shooting, his jaw fell, and he spoke of getting away. I did not hinder him from going. I gave the squaws biscuits and beef, and one of them gave me several lumps of tallow§ in exchange, and I think it worth mentioning that she did not offer me the smallest pieces, but with some extra trouble handed

---

*Brave man (Spanish).
†Very bad (Spanish).
‡How many? (Spanish).
§Animal fat used in soaps, candles, and lubricants.

me the largest of all the pieces in the canoe. No Christian could have done more. Before pushing off from the sloop the cunning savage asked for matches, and made as if to reach with the end of his spear the box I was about to give him; but I held it toward him on the muzzle of my rifle, the one that "kept on shooting." The chap picked the box off the gun gingerly enough, to be sure, but he jumped when I said, "Quedao [Look out]," at which the squaws laughed and seemed not at all displeased. Perhaps the wretch had clubbed them that morning for not gathering mussels enough for his breakfast. There was a good understanding among us all.

From Charles Island the *Spray* crossed over to Fortescue Bay, where she anchored and spent a comfortable night under the lee of high land, while the wind howled outside. The bay was deserted now. They were Fortescue Indians whom I had seen at the island, and I felt quite sure they could not follow the *Spray* in the present hard blow. Not to neglect a precaution, however, I sprinkled tacks on deck before I turned in.

On the following day the loneliness of the place was broken by the appearance of a great steamship, making for the anchorage with a lofty bearing. She was no Diego* craft. I knew the sheer, the model, and the poise. I threw out my flag, and directly saw the Stars and Stripes flung to the breeze from the great ship.

The wind had then abated, and toward night the savages made their appearance from the island, going direct to the steamer to "yammer-schooner." Then they came to the *Spray* to beg more, or to steal all, declaring that they got nothing from the steamer. Black Pedro here came alongside again. My own brother could not have been more delighted to see me, and he begged me to lend him my rifle to shoot a guanaco† for me in the morning. I assured the fellow that if I remained there another day I would lend him the gun, but I had no mind to remain. I gave him a cooper's draw-knife‡ and some other small implements which would be of service in canoe-making, and bade him be off.

Under the cover of darkness that night I went to the steamer, which I found to be the *Colombia*, Captain Henderson, from New York, bound for San Francisco. I carried all my guns along with me,

---

*Slang for "Spanish."
†South American mammal similar to a llama.
‡Blade with a handle on either end used by barrel-makers.

in case it should be necessary to fight my way back. In the chief mate of the *Colombia*, Mr. Hannibal, I found an old friend, and he referred affectionately to days in Manila when we were there together, he in the *Southern Cross* and I in the *Northern Light*, both ships as beautiful as their names.

The *Colombia* had an abundance of fresh stores on board. The captain gave his steward some order, and I remember that the guileless young man asked me if I could manage, besides other things, a few cans of milk and a cheese. When I offered my Montevideo gold for the supplies, the captain roared like a lion and told me to put my money up. It was a glorious outfit of provisions of all kinds that I got.

Returning to the *Spray*, where I found all secure, I prepared for an early start in the morning. It was agreed that the steamer should blow her whistle for me if first on the move. I watched the steamer, off and on, through the night for the pleasure alone of seeing her electric lights, a pleasing sight in contrast to the ordinary Fuegian canoe with a brand of fire in it. The sloop was the first under way, but the *Colombia*, soon following, passed, and saluted as she went by. Had the captain given me his steamer, his company would have been no worse off than they were two or three months later. I read afterward, in a late California paper, "The *Colombia* will be a total loss." On her second trip to Panama she was wrecked on the rocks of the California coast.[3]

The *Spray* was then beating against wind and current, as usual in the strait. At this point the tides from the Atlantic and the Pacific meet, and in the strait, as on the outside coast, their meeting makes a commotion of whirlpools and combers that in a gale of wind is dangerous to canoes and other frail craft.

A few miles farther along was a large steamer ashore, bottom up. Passing this place, the sloop ran into a streak of light wind, and then—a most remarkable condition for strait weather—it fell entirely calm. Signal-fires sprang up at once on all sides, and then more than twenty canoes hove in sight, all heading for the *Spray*. As they came within hail, their savage crews cried, "Amigo yammerschooner," "Anclas aqui," "Bueno puerto aqui,"* and like scraps of Spanish

---

Amigo: friend; *anclas aqui*: anchor here; *bueno puerto aqui*: good harbor here (Spanish).

A contrast in lighting—the electric lights of the *Colombia* and the canoe fires of the Fortescue Indians.

mixed with their own jargon. I had no thought of anchoring in their "good port." I hoisted the sloop's flag and fired a gun, all of which they might construe as a friendly salute or an invitation to come on. They drew up in a semicircle, but kept outside of eighty yards, which in self-defense would have been the death-line.

In their mosquito fleet was a ship's boat stolen probably from a murdered crew. Six savages paddled this rather awkwardly with the blades of oars which had been broken off. Two of the savages standing erect wore sea-boots, and this sustained the suspicion that they had fallen upon some luckless ship's crew, and also added a hint that they had already visited the *Spray's* deck, and would now, if they could, try her again. Their sea-boots, I have no doubt, would have protected their feet and rendered carpet-tacks harmless. Paddling clumsily, they passed down the strait at a distance of a hundred yards from the sloop, in an offhand manner and as if bound to Fortescue Bay. This I judged to be a piece of strategy, and so kept a sharp lookout over a small island which soon came in range between them and the sloop, completely hiding them from view, and toward which the *Spray* was now drifting helplessly with the tide, and with every prospect of going on the rocks, for there was no anchorage, at least, none that my cables would reach. And, sure enough, I soon saw a movement in the grass just on top of the island, which is called Bonet Island and is one hundred and thirty-six feet high. I fired several shots over the place, but saw no other sign of the savages. It was they that had moved the grass, for as the sloop swept past the island, the rebound of the tide carrying her clear, there on the other side was the boat, surely enough exposing their cunning and treachery. A stiff breeze, coming up suddenly, now scattered the canoes while it extricated the sloop from a dangerous position, albeit the wind, though friendly, was still ahead.

The *Spray*, flogging against current and wind, made Borgia Bay on the following afternoon, and cast anchor there for the second time. I would now, if I could, describe the moonlit scene on the strait at midnight after I had cleared the savages and Bonet Island. A heavy cloud-bank that had swept across the sky then cleared away, and the night became suddenly as light as day, or nearly so. A high mountain was mirrored in the channel ahead, and the *Spray* sailing along with her shadow was as two sloops on the sea.

The sloop being moored, I threw out my skiff, and with ax and gun landed at the head of the cove, and filled a barrel of water from a stream. Then, as before, there was no sign of Indians at the place. Finding it quite deserted, I rambled about near the beach for an hour or more. The fine weather seemed, somehow, to add loneliness to the place, and when I came upon a spot where a grave was marked I went no farther. Returning to the head of the cove, I came to a sort of Calvary, it appeared to me, where navigators, carrying their cross, had each set one up as a beacon to others coming after. They had anchored here and gone on, all except the one under the little mound. One of the simple marks, curiously enough, had been left there by the steamship *Colimbia*, sister ship to the *Colombia*, my neighbor of that morning.

I read the names of many other vessels; some of them I copied in my journal, others were illegible. Many of the crosses had decayed and fallen, and many a hand that put them there I had known, many a hand now still. The air of depression was about the place, and I hurried back to the sloop to forget myself again in the voyage.

Early the next morning I stood out from Borgia Bay, and off Cape Quod, where the wind fell light, I moored the sloop by kelp in twenty fathoms of water, and held her there a few hours against a three-knot current. That night I anchored in Langara Cove, a few miles farther along, where on the following day I discovered wreckage and goods washed up from the sea. I worked all day now, salving and boating off a cargo to the sloop. The bulk of the goods was tallow in casks and in lumps from which the casks had broken away; and embedded in the seaweed was a barrel of wine, which I also towed alongside. I hoisted them all in with the throat-halyards, which I took to the windlass. The weight of some of the casks was a little over eight hundred pounds.

There were no Indians about Langara; evidently there had not been any since the great gale which had washed the wreckage on shore. Probably it was the same gale that drove the *Spray* off Cape Horn, from March 3 to 8. Hundreds of tons of kelp had been torn from beds in deep water and rolled up into ridges on the beach. A specimen stalk which I found entire, roots, leaves, and all, measured one hundred and thirty-one feet in length. At this place I filled a barrel of water at night, and on the following day sailed with a fair wind at last.

I had not sailed far, however, when I came abreast of more tallow in a small cove, where I anchored, and boated

Records of passages through the Strait at the head of Borgia Bay.
NOTE: On a small bush nearer the water there was a board bearing several other inscriptions, to which were added the words "Sloop *Spray*, March, 1896."

off as before. It rained and snowed hard all that day, and it was no light work carrying tallow in my arms over the boulders on the beach. But I worked on till the *Spray* was loaded with a full cargo. I was happy then in the prospect of doing a good business farther along on the voyage, for the habits of an old trader would come to the surface. I sailed from the cove about noon, greased from top to toe, while my vessel was tallowed from keelson to truck. My cabin, as well as the hold and deck, was stowed full of tallow, and all were thoroughly smeared.

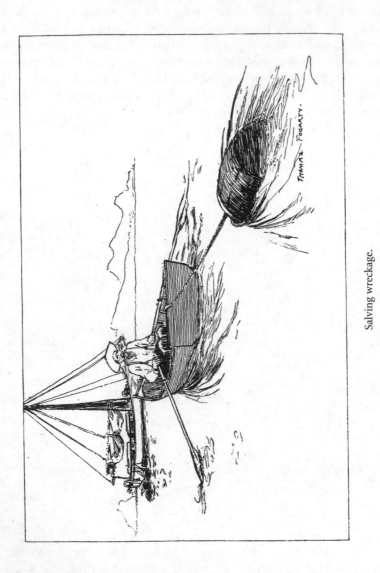

Salving wreckage.

CHAPTER X

Running to Port Angosto in a snow-storm—A defective sheet-rope places the *Spray* in peril—The *Spray* as a target for a Fuegian arrow—The island of Alan Erric—Again in the open Pacific—The run to the island of Juan Fernandez—An absentee king—At Robinson Crusoe's anchorage.

Another gale had then sprung up, but the wind was still fair, and I had only twenty-six miles to run for Port Angosto, a dreary enough place, where, however, I would find a safe harbor in which to refit and stow cargo. I carried on sail to make the harbor before dark, and she fairly flew along, all covered with snow, which fell thick and fast, till she looked like a white winter bird. Between the storm-bursts I saw the headland of my port, and was steering for it when a flaw of wind caught the mainsail by the lee, jibed it over, and dear! dear! how nearly was this the cause of disaster; for the sheet parted and the boom unshipped, and it was then close upon night. I worked till the perspiration poured from my body to get things adjusted and in working order before dark, and, above all, to get it done before the sloop drove to leeward of the port of refuge. Even then I did not get the boom shipped in its saddle. I was at the entrance of the harbor before I could get this done, and it was time to haul her to or lose the port; but in that condition, like a bird with a broken wing, she made the haven. The accident which so jeopardized my vessel and cargo came of a defective sheet-rope, one made from sisal, a treacherous fiber which has caused a deal of strong language among sailors.

I did not run the *Spray* into the inner harbor of Port Angosto, but came to inside a bed of kelp under a steep bluff on the port hand going in. It was an exceedingly snug nook, and to make doubly sure of holding on here against all williwaws I moored her with two anchors and secured her, besides, by cables to trees. However, no wind ever reached there except back flaws from the mountains on the opposite side of the harbor. There, as elsewhere in that region, the country was made up of mountains. This was the place where I was to refit and whence I was to sail direct, once more, for Cape Pillar and the Pacific.

I remained at Port Angosto some days, busily employed about the sloop. I stowed the tallow from the deck to the hold, arranged my cabin in better order, and took in a good supply of wood and water. I also mended the sloop's sails and rigging, and fitted a jigger, which changed the rig to a yawl, though I called the boat a sloop just the same, the jigger being merely a temporary affair.

I never forgot, even at the busiest time of my work there, to have my rifle by me ready for instant use; for I was of necessity within range of savages, and I had seen Fuegian canoes at this place when I anchored in the port, farther down the reach, on the first trip through the strait. I think it was on the second day, while I was busily employed about decks, that I heard the swish of something through the air close by my ear, and heard a "zip"-like sound in the water, but saw nothing. Presently, however, I suspected that it was an arrow of some sort, for just then one passing not far from me struck the mainmast, where it stuck fast, vibrating from the shock—a Fuegian autograph. A savage was somewhere near, there could be no doubt about that. I did not know but he might be shooting at me, with a view to getting my sloop and her cargo; and so I threw up my old Martini-Henry, the rifle that kept on shooting, and the first shot uncovered three Fuegians, who scampered from a clump of bushes where they had been concealed, and made over the hills. I fired away a good many cartridges, aiming under their feet to encourage their climbing. My dear old gun woke up the hills, and at every report all three of the savages jumped as if shot; but they kept on, and put Fuego real estate between themselves and the *Spray* as fast as their legs could carry them. I took care then, more than ever before, that all my firearms should be in order and that a supply of ammunition should always be ready at hand. But the savages did not return, and although I put tacks on deck every night, I never discovered that any more visitors came, and I had only to sweep the deck of tacks carefully every morning after.

As the days went by, the season became more favorable for a chance to clear the strait with a fair wind, and so I made up my mind after six attempts, being driven back each time, to be in no further haste to sail. The bad weather on my last return to Port

"The first shot uncovered three Fuegians."

Angosto for shelter brought the Chilean gunboat *Condor* and the
Argentine cruiser *Azopardo* into port. As soon as the latter came to
anchor, Captain Mascarella, the commander, sent a boat to the
Spray with the message that he would take me in tow for Sandy
Point if I would give up the voyage and return—the thing farthest
from my mind. The officers of the *Azopardo* told me that, coming

up the strait after the *Spray* on her first passage through, they saw Black Pedro and learned that he had visited me. The *Azopardo,* being a foreign man-of-war, had no right to arrest the Fuegian outlaw, but her captain blamed me for not shooting the rascal when he came to my sloop.

I procured some cordage and other small supplies from these vessels, and the officers of each of them mustered a supply of warm flannels, of which I was most in need. With these additions to my outfit, and with the vessel in good trim, though somewhat deeply laden, I was well prepared for another bout with the Southern, misnamed Pacific, Ocean.

In the first week in April southeast winds, such as appear about Cape Horn in the fall and winter seasons, bringing better weather than that experienced in the summer, began to disturb the upper clouds; a little more patience, and the time would come for sailing with a fair wind.

At Port Angosto I met Professor Dusen[1] of the Swedish scientific expedition to South America and the Pacific Islands. The professor was camped by the side of a brook at the head of the harbor, where there were many varieties of moss, in which he was interested, and where the water was, as his Argentine cook said, "muy rico."* The professor had three well-armed Argentines along in his camp to fight savages. They seemed disgusted when I filled water at a small stream near the vessel, slighting their advice to go farther up to the greater brook, where it was "muy rico." But they were all fine fellows, though it was a wonder that they did not all die of rheumatic pains from living on wet ground.

Of all the little haps and mishaps to the *Spray* at Port Angosto, of the many attempts to put to sea, and of each return for shelter, it is not my purpose to speak. Of hindrances there were many to keep her back, but on the thirteenth day of April, and for the seventh and last time, she weighed anchor from that port. Difficulties, however, multiplied all about in so strange a manner that had I been given to superstitious fears I should not have persisted in sailing on a thirteenth day, notwithstanding that a fair wind blew in the offing.

---

*Literally, "very rich" (Spanish), here meaning "very delicious."

Many of the incidents were ludicrous. When I found myself, for instance, disentangling the sloop's mast from the branches of a tree after she had drifted three times around a small island, against my will, it seemed more than one's nerves could bear, and I had to speak about it, so I thought, or die of lockjaw, and I apostrophized the *Spray* as an impatient farmer might his horse or his ox. "Didn't you know," cried I—"didn't you know that you couldn't climb a tree?" But the poor old *Spray* had essayed, and successfully too, nearly everything else in the Strait of Magellan, and my heart softened toward her when I thought of what she had gone through. Moreover, she had discovered an island. On the charts this one that she had sailed around was traced as a point of land. I named it Alan Erric Island, after a worthy literary friend whom I had met in strange byplaces, and I put up a sign, "Keep off the grass," which, as discoverer, was within my rights.

Now at last the *Spray* carried me free of Tierra del Fuego. If by a close shave only, still she carried me clear, though her boom actually hit the beacon rocks to leeward as she lugged on sail to clear the point. The thing was done on the 13th of April, 1896. But a close shave and a narrow escape were nothing new to the *Spray*.

The waves doffed their white caps beautifully to her in the strait that day before the southeast wind, the first true winter breeze of the season from that quarter, and here she was out on the first of it, with every prospect of clearing Cape Pillar before it should shift. So it turned out; the wind blew hard, as it always blows about Cape Horn, but she had cleared the great tide-race off Cape Pillar and the Evangelistas, the outermost rocks of all, before the change came. I remained at the helm, humoring my vessel in the cross seas, for it was rough, and I did not dare to let her take a straight course. It was necessary to change her course in the combing seas, to meet them with what skill I could when they rolled up ahead, and to keep off when they came up abeam.

On the following morning, April 14, only the tops of the highest mountains were in sight, and the *Spray*, making good headway on a northwest course, soon sank these out of sight. "Hurrah for the *Spray!*" I shouted to seals, sea-gulls, and penguins; for there were no other living creatures about, and she had weathered all the dangers of Cape Horn. Moreover, she had on her voyage round the Horn salved a cargo of which she had not jettisoned a pound. And why should not one rejoice also in the main chance* coming so of itself?

I shook out a reef, and set the whole jib, for, having sea-room, I could square away two points. This brought the sea more on her quarter, and she was the wholesomer under a press of sail. Occasionally an old southwest sea, rolling up, combed athwart her, but did no harm. The wind freshened as the sun rose half-mast or more, and the air, a bit chilly in the morning, softened later in the day; but I gave little thought to such things as these.

One wave, in the evening, larger than others that had threatened all day,—one such as sailors call "fine-weather seas,"—broke over the sloop fore and aft. It washed over me at the helm, the last that swept over the *Spray* off Cape Horn. It seemed to wash away old regrets. All my troubles were now astern; summer was ahead; all the world was again before me. The wind was even literally fair. My "trick" at the wheel was now up, and it was 5 P. M. I had stood at the helm since eleven o'clock the morning before, or thirty hours.

Then was the time to uncover my head, for I sailed alone with God. The vast ocean was again around me, and the horizon was unbroken by land. A few days later the *Spray* was under full sail, and I saw her for the first time with a jigger spread. This was indeed a small incident, but it was the incident following a triumph. The wind was still southwest, but it had moderated, and roaring seas had turned to gossiping waves that rippled and pattered against her sides as she rolled among them, delighted with their story. Rapid changes went on, those days, in things all about while she headed for the tropics. New species of birds came around; albatrosses fell back and became scarcer and scarcer; lighter gulls came in their stead, and pecked for crumbs in the sloop's wake.

On the tenth day from Cape Pillar a shark came along, the first of its kind on this part of the voyage to get into trouble. I harpooned him and took out his ugly jaws. I had not till then felt inclined to take the life of any animal, but when John Shark hove in sight my sympathy flew to the winds. It is a fact that in Magellan I let pass many ducks that would have made a good stew, for I had no mind in the lonesome strait to take the life of any living thing.

---

*Good opportunity.

From Cape Pillar I steered for Juan Fernandez, and on the 26th of April, fifteen days out, made that historic island right ahead.

The blue hills of Juan Fernandez, high among the clouds, could be seen about thirty miles off. A thousand emotions thrilled me when I

The *Spray* approaching Juan Fernandez, Robinson Crusoe's Island.

saw the island, and I bowed my head to the deck. We may mock the Oriental salaam, but for my part I could find no other way of expressing myself.

The wind being light through the day, the *Spray* did not reach the island till night. With what wind there was to fill her sails she stood close in to shore on the northeast side, where it fell calm and remained so all night. I saw the twinkling of a small light farther along in a cove, and fired a gun, but got no answer, and soon the light disappeared altogether. I heard the sea booming against the cliffs all night, and realized that the ocean swell was still great, although from the deck of my little ship it was apparently small. From the cry of animals in the hills, which sounded fainter and fainter through the night, I judged that a light current was drifting the sloop from the land, though she seemed all night dangerously near the shore, for, the land being very high, appearances were deceptive.

Soon after daylight I saw a boat putting out toward me. As it pulled near, it so happened that I picked up my gun, which was on the deck, meaning only to put it below; but the people in the boat, seeing the piece in my hands, quickly turned and pulled back for shore, which was about four miles distant. There were six rowers in her, and I observed that they pulled with oars in oar-locks, after the manner of trained seamen, and so I knew they belonged to a civilized race; but their opinion of me must have been anything but flattering when they mistook my purpose with the gun and pulled away with all their might. I made them understand by signs, but not without difficulty, that I did not intend to shoot, that I was simply putting the piece in the cabin, and that I wished them to return. When they understood my meaning they came back and were soon on board.

One of the party, whom the rest called "king," spoke English; the others spoke Spanish. They had all heard of the voyage of the *Spray* through the papers of Valparaiso, and were hungry for news concerning it. They told me of a war between Chile and the Argentine, which I had not heard of when I was there. I had just visited both countries, and I told them that according to the latest reports, while I was in Chile, their own island was sunk. (This same report that Juan Fernandez had sunk was current in Australia when I arrived there three months later.)

I had already prepared a pot of coffee and a plate of doughnuts, which, after some words of civility, the islanders stood up to and discussed with a will, after which they took the *Spray* in tow of their boat and made toward the island with her at the rate of a good three knots. The man they called king took the helm, and with whirling it up and down he so rattled the *Spray* that I thought she would never carry herself straight again. The others pulled away lustily with their oars. The king, I soon learned, was king only by courtesy. Having lived longer on the island than any other man in the world,—thirty years,—he was so dubbed. Juan Fernandez was then under the administration of a governor of Swedish nobility, so I was told. I was also told that his daughter could ride the wildest goat on the island. The governor, at the time of my visit, was away at Valparaiso with his family, to place his children at school. The king had been away once for a year or two, and in Rio de Janeiro had married a Brazilian woman who followed his fortunes to the far-off island. He was himself a Portuguese and a native of the Azores. He had sailed in New Bedford whale-ships and had steered a boat. All this I learned, and more too, before we reached the anchorage. The sea-breeze, coming in before long, filled the *Spray's* sails, and the experienced Portuguese mariner piloted her to a safe berth in the bay, where she was moored to a buoy abreast the settlement.

CHAPTER XI

The islanders at Juan Fernandez entertained with Yankee doughnuts—
The beauties of Robinson Crusoe's realm—The mountain monument to
Alexander Selkirk—Robinson Crusoe's cave—A stroll with the
children of the island—Westward ho! with a friendly gale—A month's
free sailing with the Southern Cross and the sun for guides—Sighting
the Marquesas—Experience in reckoning.

The *Spray* being secured, the islanders returned to the coffee
and doughnuts, and I was more than flattered when they did
not slight my buns, as the professor had done in the Strait of
Magellan. Between buns and doughnuts there was little difference
except in name. Both had been fried in tallow, which was the strong
point in both, for there was nothing on the island fatter than a goat,
and a goat is but a lean beast, to make the best of it. So with a view
to business I hooked my steelyards to the boom at once, ready to
weigh out tallow, there being no customs officer to say, "Why do you
do so?" and before the sun went down the islanders had learned the
art of making buns and doughnuts. I did not charge a high price for
what I sold, but the ancient and curious coins I got in payment,
some of them from the wreck of a galleon sunk in the bay no one
knows when, I sold afterward to antiquarians for more than face-
value. In this way I made a reasonable profit. I brought away money
of all denominations from the island, and nearly all there was, so far
as I could find out.

Juan Fernandez, as a place of call, is a lovely spot. The hills are
well wooded, the valleys fertile, and pouring down through many
ravines are streams of pure water. There are no serpents on the island, and no wild beasts other than pigs and goats, of which I saw a
number, with possibly a dog or two. The people lived without the
use of rum or beer of any sort. There was not a police officer or a
lawyer among them. The domestic economy of the island was simplicity itself. The fashions of Paris did not affect the inhabitants;
each dressed according to his own taste. Although there was no doctor, the people were all healthy, and the children were all beautiful.
There were about forty-five souls on the island all told. The adults

The house of the king.

were mostly from the mainland of South America. One lady there, from Chile, who made a flying-jib for the *Spray*, taking her pay in tallow, would be called a belle at Newport. Blessed island of Juan Fernandez! Why Alexander Selkirk ever left you was more than I could make out.

A large ship which had arrived some time before, on fire, had been stranded at the head of the bay, and as the sea smashed her to pieces on the rocks, after the fire was drowned, the islanders picked up the timbers and utilized them in the construction of houses, which naturally presented a ship-like appearance. The house of the king of Juan Fernandez, Manuel Carroza by name, besides resembling the ark, wore a polished brass knocker on its only door, which was painted green. In front of this gorgeous entrance was a flag-mast all ataunto, and near it a smart whale-boat painted red and blue, the delight of the king's old age.

I of course made a pilgrimage to the old lookout place at the top of the mountain, where Selkirk spent many days peering into the distance for the ship which came at last. From a tablet fixed into the face of the rock I copied these words, inscribed in Arabic capitals:

Robinson Crusoe's cave.

IN MEMORY

OF

ALEXANDER SELKIRK,

MARINER,

A native of Largo, in the county of Fife, Scotland, who lived on this island in complete solitude for four years and four months. He was landed from the *Cinque Ports* galley, 96 tons, 18 guns, A. D. 1704, and was taken off in the *Duke,* privateer, 12th February, 1709. He died Lieutenant of H. M. S. *Weymouth,* A. D. 1723,* aged 47. This tablet is

---

*Mr. J. Cuthbert Hadden, in the "Century Magazine" for July 1899, shows that the tablet is in error as to the year of Selkirk's death. It should be 1721 [author's note].

erected near Selkirk's lookout, by Commodore Powell and the officers of H. M. S. *Topaze,* A. D. 1868.

The cave in which Selkirk dwelt while on the island is at the head of the bay now called Robinson Crusoe Bay.[1] It is around a bold headland west of the present anchorage and landing. Ships have anchored there, but it affords a very indifferent berth. Both of these anchorages are exposed to north winds, which, however, do not reach home with much violence. The holding-ground being good in the first-named bay to the eastward, the anchorage there may be considered safe, although the undertow at times makes it wild riding.

I visited Robinson Crusoe Bay in a boat, and with some difficulty landed through the surf near the cave, which I entered. I found it dry and inhabitable. It is located in a beautiful nook sheltered by high mountains from all the severe storms that sweep over the island, which are not many; for it lies near the limits of the trade-wind regions, being in latitude 35½° S. The island is about fourteen miles in length, east and west, and eight miles in width; its height is over three thousand feet. Its distance from Chile, to which country it belongs, is about three hundred and forty miles.

Juan Fernandez was once a convict station. A number of caves in which the prisoners were kept, damp, unwholesome dens, are no longer in use, and no more prisoners are sent to the island.

The pleasantest day I spent on the island, if not the pleasantest on my whole voyage, was my last day on shore,—but by no means because it was the last,—when the children of the little community, one and all, went out with me to gather wild fruits for the voyage. We found quinces, peaches, and figs, and the children gathered a basket of each. It takes very little to please children, and these little ones, never hearing a word in their lives except Spanish, made the hills ring with mirth at the sound of words in English. They asked me the names of all manner of things on the island. We came to a wild fig-tree loaded with fruit, of which I gave them the English name. "Figgies, figgies!" they cried, while they picked till their baskets were full. But when I told them that the *cabra* they pointed out was only a goat, they screamed with laughter, and rolled on the grass in wild delight to think that a man had come to their island who would call a cabra a goat.

The first child born on Juan Fernandez, I was told, had become a

The man who called a cabra a goat.

beautiful woman and was now a mother. Manuel Carroza and the good soul who followed him here from Brazil had laid away their only child, a girl, at the age of seven, in the little churchyard on the point. In the same half-acre were other mounds among the rough lava rocks, some marking the burial-place of native-born children, some the resting-places of seamen from passing ships, landed here to end days of sickness and get into a sailors' heaven.

The greatest drawback I saw in the island was the want of a school. A class there would necessarily be small, but to some kind soul who loved teaching and quietude life on Juan Fernandez would, for a limited time, be one of delight.

On the morning of May 5, 1896, I sailed from Juan Fernandez, having feasted on many things, but on nothing sweeter than the adventure itself of a visit to the home and to the very cave of Robinson Crusoe. From the island the *Spray* bore away to the north, passing the island of St. Felix before she gained the trade-winds, which seemed slow in reaching their limits.

If the trades were tardy, however, when they did come they came with a bang, and made up for lost time; and the *Spray*, under reefs, sometimes one, sometimes two, flew before a gale for a great many days, with a bone in her mouth, toward the Marquesas, in the west, which she made on the forty-third day out, and still kept on sailing. My time was all taken up those days—not by standing at the helm; no man, I think, could stand or sit and steer a vessel round the world: I did better than that; for I sat and read my books, mended my clothes, or cooked my meals and ate them in peace. I had already found that it was not good to be alone, and so I made companionship with what there was around me, sometimes with the universe and sometimes with my own insignificant self; but my books were always my friends, let fail all else. Nothing could be easier or more restful than my voyage in the trade-winds.

I sailed with a free wind day after day, marking the position of my ship on the chart with considerable precision; but this was done by intuition, I think, more than by slavish calculations. For one whole month my vessel held her course true; I had not, the while, so much as a light in the binnacle. The Southern Cross I saw every night abeam. The sun every morning came up astern; every evening it went down ahead. I wished for no other compass to guide me, for these were true. If I doubted my reckoning after a long time at sea I verified it by reading the clock aloft made by the Great Architect, and it was right.

There was no denying that the comical side of the strange life appeared. I awoke, sometimes, to find the sun already shining into my cabin. I heard water rushing by, with only a thin plank between me and the depths, and I said, "How is this?" But it was all right; it was my ship on her course, sailing as no other ship had ever sailed before in the world. The rushing water along her side told me that she was sailing at full speed. I knew that no human hand was at the helm; I knew that all was well with "the hands" forward, and that there was no mutiny on board.

The phenomena of ocean meteorology were interesting studies even here in the trade-winds. I observed that about every seven days the wind freshened and drew several points farther than usual from the direction of the pole; that is, it went round from east-southeast to south-southeast, while at the same time a heavy swell rolled up from the southwest. All this indicated that gales were going on in the anti-trades. The wind then hauled day after day as it moderated, till it stood again at the normal point, east-southeast. This is more or less the constant state of the winter trades in latitude 12° S., where I "ran down the longitude"* for weeks. The sun, we all know, is the creator of the trade-winds and of the wind system over all the earth. But ocean meteorology is, I think, the most fascinating of all. From Juan Fernandez to the Marquesas I experienced six changes of these great palpitations of sea-winds and of the sea itself, the effect of far-off gales. To know the laws that govern the winds, and to know that you know them, will give you an easy mind on your voyage round the world; otherwise you may tremble at the appearance of every cloud. What is true of this in the trade-winds is much more so in the variables, where changes run more to extremes.

To cross the Pacific Ocean, even under the most favorable circumstances, brings you for many days close to nature, and you realize the vastness of the sea. Slowly but surely the mark of my little ship's course on the track-chart reached out on the ocean and across it, while at her utmost speed she marked with her keel still slowly the sea that carried her. On the forty-third day from land,—a long time to be at sea alone,—the sky being beautifully clear and the moon being "in distance" with the sun, I threw up my sextant for sights.[2] I found from the result of three observations, after long wrestling with lunar tables, that her longitude by observation agreed within five miles of that by dead-reckoning.

This was wonderful; both, however, might be in error, but somehow I felt confident that both were nearly true, and that in a few hours more I should see land; and so it happened, for then I made the island of Nukahiva, the southernmost of the Marquesas group, clear-cut and lofty. The verified longitude when abreast was

---

*Sailed due west until reaching the desired longitude.

somewhere between the two reckonings; this was extraordinary. All navigators will tell you that from one day to another a ship may lose or gain more than five miles in her sailing-account, and again, in the matter of lunars, even expert lunarians are considered as doing clever work when they average within eight miles of the truth.

I hope I am making it clear that I do not lay claim to cleverness or to slavish calculations in my reckonings. I think I have already stated that I kept my longitude, at least, mostly by intuition. A rotator log always towed astern, but so much has to be allowed for currents and for drift, which the log never shows, that it is only an approximation, after all, to be corrected by one's own judgment from data of a thousand voyages; and even then the master of the ship, if he be wise, cries out for the lead and the lookout.

Unique was my experience in nautical astronomy from the deck of the *Spray*—so much so that I feel justified in briefly telling it here. The first set of sights, just spoken of, put her many hundred miles west of my reckoning by account. I knew that this could not be correct. In about an hour's time I took another set of observations with the utmost care; the mean result of these was about the same as that of the first set. I asked myself why, with my boasted self-dependence, I had not done at least better than this. Then I went in search of a discrepancy in the tables, and I found it. In the tables I found that the column of figures from which I had got an important logarithm was in error. It was a matter I could prove beyond a doubt, and it made the difference as already stated. The tables being corrected, I sailed on with self-reliance unshaken, and with my tin clock fast asleep. The result of these observations naturally tickled my vanity, for I knew that it was something to stand on a great ship's deck and with two assistants take lunar observations approximately near the truth. As one of the poorest of American sailors, I was proud of the little achievement alone on the sloop, even by chance though it may have been.

I was *en rapport** now with my surroundings, and was carried on a vast stream where I felt the buoyancy of His hand who made all the worlds. I realized the mathematical truth of their motions, so well

---

*In harmony (French).

known that astronomers compile tables of their positions through the years and the days, and the minutes of a day, with such precision that one coming along over the sea even five years later may, by their aid, find the standard time of any given meridian on the earth.

To find local time is a simpler matter. The difference between local and standard time is longitude expressed in time—four minutes, we all know, representing one degree. This, briefly, is the principle on which longitude is found independent of chronometers. The work of the lunarian, though seldom practised in these days of chronometers, is beautifully edifying, and there is nothing in the realm of navigation that lifts one's heart up more in adoration.

CHAPTER XII

Seventy-two days without a port—Whales and birds—A peep into the *Spray's* galley—Flying-fish for breakfast—A welcome at Apia—A visit from Mrs. Robert Louis Stevenson—At Vailima—Samoan hospitality—Arrested for fast riding—An amusing merry-go-round—Teachers and pupils of Papauta College—At the mercy of sea-nymphs.

To be alone forty-three days would seem a long time, but in reality, even here, winged moments flew lightly by, and instead of my hauling in for Nukahiva, which I could have made as well as not, I kept on for Samoa, where I wished to make my next landing. This occupied twenty-nine days more, making seventy-two days in all. I was not distressed in any way during that time. There was no end of companionship; the very coral reefs kept me company, or gave me no time to feel lonely, which is the same thing, and there were many of them now in my course to Samoa.

First among the incidents of the voyage from Juan Fernandez to Samoa (which were not many) was a narrow escape from collision with a great whale that was absent-mindedly plowing the ocean at night while I was below. The noise from his startled snort and the commotion he made in the sea, as he turned to clear my vessel, brought me on deck in time to catch a wetting from the water he threw up with his flukes. The monster was apparently frightened. He headed quickly for the east; I kept on going west. Soon another whale passed, evidently a companion, following in its wake. I saw no more on this part of the voyage, nor did I wish to.

Hungry sharks came about the vessel often when she neared islands or coral reefs. I own to a satisfaction in shooting them as one would a tiger. Sharks, after all, are the tigers of the sea. Nothing is more dreadful to the mind of a sailor, I think, than a possible encounter with a hungry shark.

A number of birds were always about; occasionally one poised on the mast to look the *Spray* over, wondering, perhaps, at her odd wings, for she now wore her Fuego mainsail, which, like Joseph's coat, was made of many pieces.[1] Ships are less common on the

Meeting with the whale.

Southern seas than formerly. I saw not one in the many days crossing the Pacific.

My diet on these long passages usually consisted of potatoes and salt cod and biscuits, which I made two or three times a week. I had always plenty of coffee, tea, sugar, and flour. I carried usually a good supply of potatoes, but before reaching Samoa I had a mishap which left me destitute of this highly prized sailors' luxury. Through meeting at Juan Fernandez the Yankee Portuguese named Manuel Carroza, who nearly traded me out of my boots, I ran out of potatoes in mid-ocean, and was wretched thereafter. I prided myself on being something of a trader; but this Portuguese from the Azores by way of New Bedford, who gave me new potatoes for the older ones I had got from the *Colombia,* a bushel or more of the best, left me no ground for boasting. He wanted mine, he said, "for changee the seed." When I got to sea I found that his tubers were rank and unedible, and full of fine yellow streaks of repulsive appearance. I tied the sack up and returned to the few left of my old stock, thinking that maybe when I got right hungry the island potatoes would improve in flavor. Three weeks later I opened the bag again, and out flew millions of winged insects! Manuel's potatoes had all turned to moths. I tied them up quickly and threw all into the sea.

Manuel had a large crop of potatoes on hand, and as a hint to whalemen, who are always eager to buy vegetables, he wished me to report whales off the island of Juan Fernandez, which I have already done, and big ones at that, but they were a long way off.

Taking things by and large, as sailors say, I got on fairly well in the matter of provisions even on the long voyage across the Pacific. I found always some small stores to help the fare of luxuries; what I lacked of fresh meat was made up in fresh fish, at least while in the trade-winds, where flying-fish crossing on the wing at night would hit the sails and fall on deck, sometimes two or three of them, sometimes a dozen. Every morning except when the moon was large I got a bountiful supply by merely picking them up from the lee scuppers. All tinned meats went begging.

On the 16th of July, after considerable care and some skill and hard work, the *Spray* cast anchor at Apia, in the kingdom of Samoa, about noon. My vessel being moored, I spread an awning, and instead of going at once on shore I sat under it till late in the evening, listening with delight to the musical voices of the Samoan men and women.

A canoe coming down the harbor, with three young women in it, rested her paddles abreast the sloop. One of the fair crew, hailing with the naïve salutation, "Talofa lee" ("Love to you, chief"), asked:

"Schoon come Melike?"

"Love to you," I answered, and said, "Yes."

"You man come 'lone?"

Again I answered, "Yes."

"I don't believe that. You had other mans, and you eat 'em."

At this sally the others laughed. "What for you come long way?" they asked.

"To hear you ladies sing," I replied.

"Oh, talofa lee!" they all cried, and sang on. Their voices filled the air with music that rolled across to the grove of tall palms on the other side of the harbor and back. Soon after this six young men came down in the United States consul-general's boat, singing in parts and beating time with their oars. In my interview with them I came off better than with the damsels in the canoe. They bore an invitation from General Churchill[2] for me to come and dine at the

First exchange of courtesies in Samoa.

consulate. There was a lady's hand in things about the consulate at Samoa. Mrs. Churchill picked the crew for the general's boat, and saw to it that they wore a smart uniform and that they could sing the Samoan boatsong, which in the first week Mrs. Churchill herself could sing like a native girl.

Next morning bright and early Mrs. Robert Louis Stevenson came to the *Spray* and invited me to Vailima[3] the following day. I was of course thrilled when I found myself, after so many days of adventure, face to face with this bright woman, so lately the companion of the author who had delighted me on the voyage. The kindly eyes, that looked me through and through, sparkled when we compared notes of adventure. I marveled at some of her experiences and escapes. She told me that, along with her husband, she had voyaged in all manner of rickety craft among the islands of the Pacific, reflectively adding, "Our tastes were similar."

Following the subject of voyages, she gave me the four beautiful

Vailima, the home of Robert Louis Stevenson.

volumes of sailing directories for the Mediterranean, writing on the fly-leaf of the first:

To Captain Slocum.

These volumes have been read and re-read many times by my husband, and I am very sure that he would be pleased that they should be passed on to the sort of seafaring man that he liked above all others.

Fanny V. de G. Stevenson.

Mrs. Stevenson also gave me a great directory of the Indian Ocean. It was not without a feeling of reverential awe that I received the books so nearly direct from the hand of Tusitala,* "who sleeps in the forest." Aolele,† the *Spray* will cherish your gift.

The novelist's stepson, Mr. Lloyd Osbourne, walked through the Vailima mansion with me and bade me write my letters at the old desk. I thought it would be presumptuous to do that; it was sufficient for me to enter the hall on the floor of which the "Writer of Tales," according to the Samoan custom, was wont to sit.

Coming through the main street of Apia one day, with my hosts,

---

*Teller of Tales (Samoan), the natives' nickname for Robert Louis Stevenson.
†Flying Cloud (Samoan), the natives' nickname for Frances Stevenson.

all bound for the *Spray*, Mrs. Stevenson on horseback, I walking by her side, and Mr. and Mrs. Osbourne close in our wake on bicycles, at a sudden turn in the road we found ourselves mixed with a remarkable native procession, with a somewhat primitive band of music, in front of us, while behind was a festival or a funeral, we could not tell which. Several of the stoutest men carried bales and bundles on poles. Some were evidently bales of tapa-cloth.* The burden of one set of poles, heavier than the rest, however, was not so easily made out. My curiosity was whetted to know whether it was a roast pig or something of a gruesome nature, and I inquired about it. "I don't know," said Mrs. Stevenson, "whether this is a wedding or a funeral. Whatever it is, though, captain, our place seems to be at the head of it."

The *Spray* being in the stream,† we boarded her from the beach abreast, in the little razeed Gloucester dory, which had been painted a smart green. Our combined weight loaded it gunwale to the water, and I was obliged to steer with great care to avoid swamping. The adventure pleased Mrs. Stevenson greatly, and as we paddled along she sang, "They went to sea in a pea-green boat."‡ I could understand her saying of her husband and herself, "Our tastes were similar."

As I sailed farther from the center of civilization I heard less and less of what would and what would not pay. Mrs. Stevenson, in speaking of my voyage, did not once ask me what I would make out of it. When I came to a Samoan village, the chief did not ask the price of gin, or say, "How much will you pay for roast pig?" but, "Dollar, dollar," said he; "white man know only dollar."

"Never mind dollar. The *tapo* has prepared ava;§ let us drink and rejoice." The tapo is the virgin hostess of the village; in this instance it was Taloa, daughter of the chief. "Our taro# is good; let us eat. On the tree there is fruit. Let the day go by; why should we mourn over

---

*Polynesian fabric made from tree bark.
†Anchored offshore.
‡Paraphrase of English poet Edward Lear's poem "The Owl and the Pussycat" (1871).
§A strong native liquor.
#Starchy root used in pastes, puddings, and other dishes.

that? There are millions of days coming. The breadfruit* is yellow in the sun, and from the cloth-tree is Taloa's gown. Our house, which is good, cost but the labor of building it, and there is no lock on the door."

While the days go thus in these Southern islands we at the North are struggling for the bare necessities of life.

For food the islanders have only to put out their hand and take what nature has provided for them; if they plant a banana-tree, their only care afterward is to see that too many trees do not grow. They have great reason to love their country and to fear the white man's yoke, for once harnessed to the plow, their life would no longer be a poem.

The chief of the village of Caini, who was a tall and dignified Tonga man, could be approached only through an interpreter and talking man. It was perfectly natural for him to inquire the object of my visit, and I was sincere when I told him that my reason for casting anchor in Samoa was to see their fine men, and fine women, too. After a considerable pause the chief said: "The captain has come a long way to see so little; but," he added, "the tapo must sit nearer the captain." "Yack," said Taloa, who had so nearly learned to say yes in English, and suiting the action to the word, she hitched a peg nearer, all hands sitting in a circle upon mats. I was no less taken with the chief's eloquence than delighted with the simplicity of all he said. About him there was nothing pompous; he might have been taken for a great scholar or statesman, the least assuming of the men I met on the voyage. As for Taloa, a sort of Queen of the May, and the other tapo girls, well, it is wise to learn as soon as possible the manners and customs of these hospitable people, and meanwhile not to mistake for over-familiarity that which is intended as honor to a guest. I was fortunate in my travels in the islands, and saw nothing to shake one's faith in native virtue.

To the unconventional mind the punctilious etiquette of Samoa is perhaps a little painful. For instance, I found that in partaking of ava, the social bowl, I was supposed to toss a little of the beverage over my shoulder, or pretend to do so, and say, "Let the gods drink,"

*Large, starchy fruit basic to the Polynesian diet.

and then drink it all myself; and the dish, invariably a cocoanut-shell, being empty, I might not pass it politely as we would do, but politely throw it twirling across the mats at the tapo.

My most grievous mistake while at the islands was made on a nag, which, inspired by a bit of good road, must needs break into a smart trot through a village. I was instantly hailed by the chief's deputy, who in an angry voice brought me to a halt. Perceiving that I was in trouble, I made signs for pardon, the safest thing to do, though I did not know what offense I had committed. My interpreter coming up, however, put me right, but not until a long palaver had ensued. The deputy's hail, liberally translated, was: "Ahoy, there, on the frantic steed! Know you not that it is against the law to ride thus through the village of our fathers?" I made what apologies I could, and offered to dismount and, like my servant, lead my nag by the bridle. This, the interpreter told me, would also be a grievous wrong, and so I again begged for pardon. I was summoned to appear before a chief; but my interpreter, being a wit as well as a bit of a rogue, explained that I was myself something of a chief, and should not be detained, being on a most important mission. In my own behalf I could only say that I was a stranger, but, pleading all this, I knew I still deserved to be roasted, at which the chief showed a fine row of teeth and seemed pleased, but allowed me to pass on.

The chief of the Tongas and his family at Caini, returning my visit, brought presents of tapa-cloth and fruits. Taloa, the princess, brought a bottle of cocoanut-oil for my hair, which another man might have regarded as coming late.

It was impossible to entertain on the *Spray* after the royal manner in which I had been received by the chief. His fare had included all that the land could afford, fruits, fowl, fishes, and flesh, a hog having been roasted whole. I set before them boiled salt pork and salt beef, with which I was well supplied, and in the evening took them all to a new amusement in the town, a rocking-horse merry-go-round, which they called a "kee-kee," meaning theater; and in a spirit of justice they pulled off the horses' tails, for the proprietors of the show, two hard-fisted countrymen of mine, I grieve to say, unceremoniously hustled them off for a new set, almost at the first spin. I was not a little proud of my Tonga friends; the chief, finest of them all, carried a portentous club. As for the theater, through the

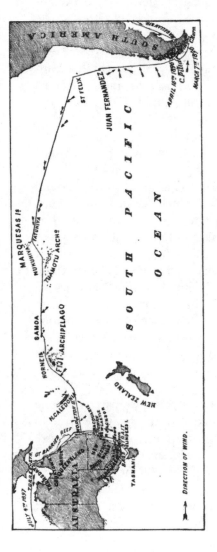

The *Spray*'s course from the Strait of Magellan to Torres Strait.

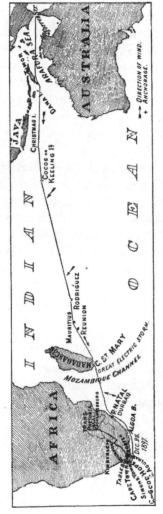

The *Spray*'s course from Australia to South Africa.

greed of the proprietors it was becoming unpopular, and the representatives of the three great powers, in want of laws which they could enforce, adopted a vigorous foreign policy, taxing it twenty-five per cent. on the gate-money. This was considered a great stroke of legislative reform!

It was the fashion of the native visitors to the *Spray* to come over the bows, where they could reach the head-gear and climb aboard with ease, and on going ashore to jump off the stern and swim away; nothing could have been more delightfully simple. The modest natives wore *lava-lava** bathing-dresses, a native cloth from the bark of the mulberry-tree, and they did no harm to the *Spray*. In summerland Samoa their coming and going was only a merry every-day scene.

One day the head teachers of Papauta College, Miss Schultze and Miss Moore, came on board with their ninety-seven young women students. They were all dressed in white, and each wore a red rose, and of course came in boats or canoes in the cold-climate style. A merrier bevy of girls it would be difficult to find. As soon as they got on deck, by request of one of the teachers, they sang "The Watch on the Rhine,"[4] which I had never heard before. "And now," said they all, "let's up anchor and away." But I had no inclination to sail from Samoa so soon. On leaving the *Spray* these accomplished young women each seized a palm-branch or paddle, or whatever else would serve the purpose, and literally paddled her own canoe. Each could have swum as readily, and would have done so, I dare say, had it not been for the holiday muslin.

It was not uncommon at Apia to see a young woman swimming alongside a small canoe with a passenger for the *Spray*. Mr. Trood,[†] an old Eton boy, came in this manner to see me, and he exclaimed, "Was ever king ferried in such state?" Then, suiting his action to the sentiment, he gave the damsel pieces of silver till the natives watching on shore yelled with envy. My own canoe, a small dugout, one day when it had rolled over with me, was seized by a party of fair bathers, and before I could get my breath, almost, was towed around

---

*Strictly, not the cloth but the style: a wraparound dress or sarong.
†Thomas Trood, British vice-consul to Samoa and author of *Island Reminiscences* (1912).

and around the *Spray*, while I sat in the bottom of it, wondering what they would do next. But in this case there were six of them, three on a side, and I could not help myself. One of the sprites, I remember, was a young English lady, who made more sport of it than any of the others.

CHAPTER XIII

Samoan royalty—King Malietoa—Good-by to friends at Vailima—
Leaving Fiji to the south—Arrival at Newcastle, Australia—The yachts
of Sydney—A ducking on the *Spray*—Commodore Foy presents the
sloop with a new suit of sails—On to Melbourne—A shark that
proved to be valuable—A change of course—The "Rain of Blood"—
In Tasmania.

A t Apia I had the pleasure of meeting Mr. A. Young, the father of the late Queen Margaret, who was Queen of Manua
from 1891 to 1895. Her grandfather was an English sailor
who married a princess. Mr. Young is now the only survivor of the
family, two of his children, the last of them all, having been lost in
an island trader which a few months before had sailed, never to return. Mr. Young was a Christian gentleman, and his daughter Margaret was accomplished in graces that would become any lady. It was
with pain that I saw in the newspapers a sensational account of her
life and death, taken evidently from a paper in the supposed interest
of a benevolent society, but without foundation in fact. And the startling head-lines saying, "Queen Margaret of Manua is dead," could
hardly be called news in 1898, the queen having then been dead
three years.

While hobnobbing, as it were, with royalty, I called on the king
himself, the late Malietoa.[1] King Malietoa was a great ruler; he never
got less than forty-five dollars a month for the job, as he told me
himself, and this amount had lately been raised, so that he could live
on the fat of the land and not any longer be called "Tin-of-salmon
Malietoa" by graceless beach-combers.

As my interpreter and I entered the front door of the palace, the
king's brother, who was viceroy, sneaked in through a taro-patch by
the back way, and sat cowering by the door while I told my story to
the king. Mr. W——— of New York,[2] a gentleman interested in
missionary work, had charged me, when I sailed, to give his re-
membrance to the king of the Cannibal Islands, other islands of
course being meant; but the good King Malietoa, notwithstanding
that his people have not eaten a missionary in a hundred years,

received the message himself, and seemed greatly pleased to hear so directly from the publishers of the "Missionary Review,"* and wished me to make his compliments in return. His Majesty then excused himself, while I talked with his daughter, the beautiful Faamu-Sami (a name signifying "To make the sea burn"), and soon reappeared in the full-dress uniform of the German commander-in-chief, Emperor William† himself; for, stupidly enough, I had not sent my credentials ahead that the king might be in full regalia to receive me. Calling a few days later to say good-by to Faamu-Sami, I saw King Malietoa for the last time.

Of the landmarks in the pleasant town of Apia, my memory rests first on the little school just back of the London Missionary Society coffee-house and reading-rooms, where Mrs. Bell taught English to about a hundred native children, boys and girls. Brighter children you will not find anywhere.

"Now, children," said Mrs. Bell, when I called one day, "let us show the captain that we know something about the Cape Horn he passed in the *Spray*," at which a lad of nine or ten years stepped nimbly forward and read Basil Hall's fine description of the great cape,³ and read it well. He afterward copied the essay for me in a clear hand.

Calling to say good-by to my friends at Vailima, I met Mrs. Stevenson in her Panama hat, and went over the estate with her. Men were at work clearing the land, and to one of them she gave an order to cut a couple of bamboo-trees for the *Spray* from a clump she had planted four years before, and which had grown to the height of sixty feet. I used them for spare spars, and the butt of one made a serviceable jib-boom on the homeward voyage. I had then only to take ava with the family and be ready for sea. This ceremony, important among Samoans, was conducted after the native fashion. A Triton horn was sounded to let us know when the beverage was ready, and in response we all clapped hands. The bout being in honor of the *Spray,* it was my turn first, after the custom of the country, to spill a little over my shoulder; but having

---

*Interdenominational journal published by Funk and Wagnalls from 1888 to 1939.
†Kaiser Wilhelm II (1859–1941; ruled 1888–1918), emperor of Germany and king of Prussia.

forgotten the Samoan for "Let the gods drink," I repeated the equivalent in Russian and Chinook, as I remembered a word in each, whereupon Mr. Osbourne pronounced me a confirmed Samoan. Then I said "Tofah!"* to my good friends of Samoa, and all wishing the *Spray bon voyage,*† she stood out of the harbor August 20, 1896, and continued on her course. A sense of loneliness seized upon me as the islands faded astern, and as a remedy for it I crowded on sail for lovely Australia, which was not a strange land to me; but for long days in my dreams Vailima stood before the prow.

The *Spray* had barely cleared the islands when a sudden burst of the trades brought her down to close reefs, and she reeled off one hundred and eighty-four miles the first day, of which I counted forty miles of current in her favor. Finding a rough sea, I swung her off free and sailed north of the Horn Islands, also north of Fiji instead of south, as I had intended, and coasted down the west side of the archipelago. Thence I sailed direct for New South Wales, passing south of New Caledonia, and arrived at Newcastle after a passage of forty-two days, mostly of storms and gales.

One particularly severe gale encountered near New Caledonia foundered the American clipper-ship *Patrician* farther south. Again, nearer the coast of Australia, when, however, I was not aware that the gale was extraordinary, a French mailsteamer from New Caledonia for Sydney, blown considerably out of her course, on her arrival reported it an awful storm, and to inquiring friends said: "Oh, my! we don't know what has become of the little sloop *Spray*. We saw her in the thick of the storm." The *Spray* was all right, lying to like a duck. She was under a goose's wing mainsail, and had had a dry deck while the passengers on the steamer, I heard later, were up to their knees in water in the saloon. When their ship arrived at Sydney they gave the captain a purse of gold for his skill and seamanship in bringing them safe into port. The captain of the *Spray* got nothing of this sort. In this gale I made the land about Seal Rocks, where the steamship *Catherton,*‡ with many lives, was lost a short time before.

---

*Properly, *tofa*, Samoan for "good-bye."
† "Good-bye" (French); literally, "good trip."
‡The Australian vessel *Catterthun* sank on August 7, 1896, with fifty-five lives lost.

I was many hours off the rocks, beating back and forth, but weathered them at last.

I arrived at Newcastle in the teeth of a gale of wind. It was a stormy season. The government pilot, Captain Cumming, met me at the harbor bar, and with the assistance of a steamer carried my vessel to a safe berth. Many visitors came on board, the first being the United States consul, Mr. Brown. Nothing was too good for the *Spray* here. All government dues were remitted, and after I had rested a few days a port pilot with a tug carried her to sea again, and she made along the coast toward the harbor of Sydney, where she arrived on the following day, October 10, 1896.

I came to in a snug cove near Manly for the night, the Sydney harbor police-boat giving me a pluck into anchorage while they gathered data from an old scrap-book of mine, which seemed to interest them.[4] Nothing escapes the vigilance of the New South Wales police; their reputation is known the world over. They made a shrewd guess that I could give them some useful information, and they were the first to meet me. Some one said they came to arrest me, and—well, let it go at that.

Summer was approaching, and the harbor of Sydney was blooming with yachts. Some of them came down to the weather-beaten *Spray* and sailed round her at Shelcote, where she took a berth for a few days. At Sydney I was at once among friends. The *Spray* remained at the various watering-places in the great port for several weeks, and was visited by many agreeable people, frequently by officers of H. M. S. *Orlando* and their friends. Captain Fisher, the commander, with a party of young ladies from the city and gentlemen belonging to his ship, came one day to pay me a visit in the midst of a deluge of rain. I never saw it rain harder even in Australia. But they were out for fun, and rain could not dampen their feelings, however hard it poured. But, as ill luck would have it, a young gentleman of another party on board, in the full uniform of a very great yacht club, with brass buttons enough to sink him, stepping quickly to get out of the wet, tumbled holus-bolus,* head and heels, into a barrel of water I had been coopering, and being a short man, was soon out

---

*All at once.

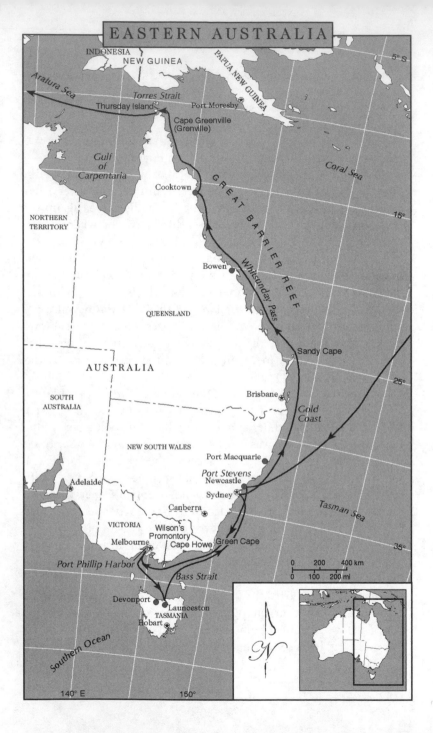

EASTERN AUSTRALIA

of sight, and nearly drowned before he was rescued. It was the nearest to a casualty on the *Spray* in her whole course, so far as I know. The young man having come on board with compliments made the mishap most embarrassing. It had been decided by his club that the *Spray* could not be officially recognized, for the reason that she brought no letters from yacht-clubs in America, and so I say it seemed all the more embarrassing and strange that I should have caught at least one of the members, in a barrel, and, too, when I was not fishing for yachtsmen.

The typical Sydney boat is a handy sloop of great beam and enormous sail-carrying power; but a capsize is not uncommon, for they carry sail like vikings. In Sydney I saw all manner of craft, from the smart steam-launch and sailing-cutter to the smaller sloop and canoe pleasuring on the bay. Everybody owned a boat. If a boy in Australia has not the means to buy him a boat he builds one, and it is usually one not to be ashamed of. The *Spray* shed her Joseph's coat, the Fuego mainsail, in Sydney, and wearing a new suit, the handsome present of Commodore Foy, she was flagship of the Johnstone's Bay Flying Squadron when the circumnavigators of Sydney harbor sailed in their annual regatta. They "recognized" the *Spray* as belonging to "a club of her own," and with more Australian sentiment than fastidiousness gave her credit for her record.

See map on opposite page: Slocum spent over eight months in Australia, more time than in any other country. Perhaps because of his birth in Nova Scotia, he felt a kinship with another member of the British Commonwealth, a feeling that was warmly reciprocated. He arrived in Newcastle in early October, 1896, and departed from Thursday Island in the Torres Strait on June 24, 1897. He originally intended to sail west around the continent's lonely southern coast, but unseasonably bad weather and adverse winds convinced him to alter his course and sail up the eastern coast and through the Torres Strait, which is filled with dangerous reefs and shallows. While he waited for better weather, he visited Melbourne, Sydney, and the exotic island of Tasmania, where he gave his first lecture to an admiring audience. He found Tasmania so appealing that, he wrote, "If there was a moment in my voyage when I could have given it up, it was there and then."

The accident at Sydney.

Time flew fast those days in Australia, and it was December 6, 1896, when the *Spray* sailed from Sydney. My intention was now to sail around Cape Leeuwin direct for Mauritius on my way home, and so I coasted along toward Bass Strait in that direction.

There was little to report on this part of the voyage, except changeable winds, "busters,"* and rough seas. The 12th of December, however, was an exceptional day, with a fine coast wind, northeast. The *Spray* early in the morning passed Twofold Bay and later Cape Bundooro† in a smooth sea with land close aboard. The lighthouse on the cape dipped a flag to the *Spray's* flag, and children on the balconies of a cottage near the shore waved handkerchiefs as she passed by. There were only a few people all told on the shore, but the scene was a happy one. I saw festoons of evergreen in token of Christmas, near at hand. I saluted the merrymakers, wishing them a "Merry Christmas," and could hear them say, "I wish you the same."

From Cape Bundooro I passed by Cliff Island in Bass Strait, and exchanged signals with the light-keepers while the *Spray* worked up under the island. The wind howled that day while the sea broke over their rocky home.

A few days later, December 17, the *Spray* came in close under Wilson's Promontory, again seeking shelter. The keeper of the light at that station, Mr. J. Clark, came on board and gave me directions for Waterloo Bay, about three miles to leeward, for which I bore up at once, finding good anchorage there in a sandy cove protected from all westerly and northerly winds.

Anchored here was the ketch *Secret*, a fisherman, and the *Mary* of Sydney, a steam ferry-boat fitted for whaling. The captain of the *Mary* was a genius, and an Australian genius at that, and smart. His crew, from a sawmill up the coast, had not one of them seen a live whale when they shipped; but they were boatmen after an Australian's own heart, and the captain had told them that to kill a whale was no more than to kill a rabbit. They believed him, and that settled it. As luck would have it, the very first one they saw on their cruise, although an ugly humpback, was a dead whale in no time, Captain Young, the master of the *Mary*, killing the monster at a single thrust of a harpoon. It was taken in tow for Sydney, where they put it on exhibition. Nothing but whales interested the crew of the gallant *Mary*, and they spent most of their time here gathering fuel along shore for a cruise on the grounds off Tasmania. Whenever the

---

*Australian slang for fierce, cold winds from the south.
†Aboriginal name for Green Cape, on Australia's southeastern coast.

Captain Slocum working the *Spray* out of the Yarrow River, a part of Melbourne harbor.

word "whale" was mentioned in the hearing of these men their eyes glistened with excitement.

We spent three days in the quiet cove, listening to the wind outside. Meanwhile Captain Young and I explored the shores, visited abandoned miners' pits, and prospected for gold ourselves.

Our vessels, parting company the morning they sailed, stood away like sea-birds each on its own course. The wind for a few days was moderate, and, with unusual luck of fine weather, the *Spray* made Melbourne Heads on the 22d of December, and, taken in tow by the steam-tug *Racer*, was brought into port.

Christmas day was spent at a berth in the river Yarrow, but I lost little time in shifting to St. Kilda, where I spent nearly a month.

The *Spray* paid no port charges in Australia or anywhere else on

The shark on the deck of the *Spray*.

the voyage, except at Pernambuco, till she poked her nose into the custom-house at Melbourne, where she was charged tonnage dues; in this instance, sixpence a ton on the gross. The collector exacted six shillings and sixpence, taking off nothing for the fraction under thirteen tons, her exact gross being 12.70 tons. I squared the matter by charging people sixpence each for coming on board, and when this business got dull I caught a shark and charged them sixpence each to look at that. The shark was twelve feet six inches in length, and carried a progeny of twenty-six, not one of them less than two feet in length. A slit of a knife let them out in a canoe full of water, which, changed constantly, kept them alive one whole day. In less than an hour from the time I heard of the ugly brute it was on deck and on exhibition, with rather more than the amount of the *Spray's* tonnage dues already collected. Then I hired a good Irishman, Tom Howard by name,—who knew all about sharks, both on the land and in the sea, and could talk about them,—to answer questions and lecture. When I found that I could not keep abreast of the questions I turned the responsibility over to him.

Returning from the bank, where I had been to deposit money early in the day, I found Howard in the midst of a very excited crowd, telling imaginary habits of the fish. It was a good show; the people wished to see it, and it was my wish that they should; but owing to his over-stimulated enthusiasm, I was obliged to let Howard resign. The income from the show and the proceeds of the tallow I had gathered in the Strait of Magellan, the last of which I had disposed of to a German soap-boiler at Samoa, put me in ample funds.

January 24, 1897, found the *Spray* again in tow of the tug *Racer*, leaving Hobson's Bay after a pleasant time in Melbourne and St. Kilda, which had been protracted by a succession of southwest winds that seemed never-ending.

In the summer months, that is, December, January, February, and sometimes March, east winds are prevalent through Bass Strait and round Cape Leeuwin; but owing to a vast amount of ice drifting up from the Antarctic, this was all changed now and emphasized with much bad weather, so much so that I considered it impracticable to pursue the course farther. Therefore, instead of thrashing round cold and stormy Cape Leeuwin, I decided to spend a pleasanter and more profitable time in Tasmania, waiting for the season for favorable winds through Torres Strait, by way of the Great Barrier Reef, the route I finally decided on. To sail this course would be taking advantage of anticyclones,* which never fail, and besides it would give me the chance to put foot on the shores of Tasmania, round which I had sailed years before.

I should mention that while I was at Melbourne there occurred one of those extraordinary storms sometimes called "rain of blood," the first of the kind in many years about Australia. The "blood" came from a fine brick-dust matter afloat in the air from the deserts. A rain-storm setting in brought down this dust simply as mud; it fell in such quantities that a bucketful was collected from the sloop's awnings, which were spread at the time. When the wind blew hard and I was obliged to furl awnings, her sails, unprotected on the booms, got mud-stained from clue to earing.

The phenomena of dust-storms, well understood by scientists, are not uncommon on the coast of Africa. Reaching some distance out over the sea, they frequently cover the track of ships, as in the case of the one through which the *Spray* passed in the earlier part of her voyage. Sailors no longer regard them with superstitious fear, but our credulous brothers on the land cry out "Rain of blood!" at the first splash of the awful mud.

The rip off Port Phillip Heads, a wild place, was rough when the *Spray* entered Hobson's Bay from the sea, and was rougher when she stood out. But, with sea-room and under sail, she made good weather immediately after passing it. It was only a few hours' sail to Tasmania across the strait, the wind being fair and blowing hard. I carried the St. Kilda shark along, stuffed with hay, and disposed of it to Professor Porter, the curator of the Victoria Museum of Launceston, which is at the head of the Tamar. For many a long day to come may be seen there the shark of St. Kilda. Alas! the good but mistaken people of St. Kilda, when the illustrated journals with pictures of my shark reached their news-stands, flew into a passion, and swept all papers containing mention of fish into the fire; for St. Kilda was a watering-place—and the idea of a shark *there!* But my show went on.

---

*Moderate winds favorable for sailing that circulate around areas of high pressure.

On board at St. Kilda. Retracing on the chart the course of the *Spray* from Boston.

The *Spray* was berthed on the beach at a small jetty at Launceston while the tide driven in by the gale that brought her up the river was unusually high; and she lay there hard and fast, with not enough water around her at any time after to wet one's feet till she was ready to sail; then, to float her, the ground was dug from under her keel.

In this snug place I left her in charge of three children, while I made journeys among the hills and rested my bones, for the coming voyage, on the moss-covered rocks at the gorge hard by, and among the ferns I found wherever I went. My vessel was well taken care of. I never returned without finding that the decks had been washed and that one of the children, my nearest neighbor's little girl from across the road, was at the gangway attending to visitors, while the others, a brother and sister, sold marine curios such as were in the cargo, on "ship's account." They were a bright, cheerful crew, and people came a long way to hear them tell the story of the voyage, and of the monsters of the deep "the captain had slain." I had only to keep myself away to be a hero of the first water; and it suited me very well to do so and to rusticate in the forests and among the streams.

CHAPTER XIV

A testimonial from a lady—Cruising round Tasmania—The skipper delivers his first lecture on the voyage—Abundant provisions—An inspection of the *Spray* for safety at Devonport—Again at Sydney—Northward bound for Torres Strait—An amateur shipwreck—Friends on the Australian coast—Perils of a coral sea.

February 1, 1897, on returning to my vessel I found waiting for me the letter of sympathy which I subjoin:

A lady sends Mr. Slocum the inclosed five-pound note as a token of her appreciation of his bravery in crossing the wide seas on so small a boat, and all alone, without human sympathy to help when danger threatened. All success to you.

To this day I do not know who wrote it or to whom I am indebted for the generous gift it contained. I could not refuse a thing so kindly meant, but promised myself to pass it on with interest at the first opportunity, and this I did before leaving Australia.

The season of fair weather around the north of Australia being yet a long way off, I sailed to other ports in Tasmania, where it is fine the year round, the first of these being Beauty Point, near which are Beaconsfield and the great Tasmania gold-mine,[1] which I visited in turn. I saw much gray, uninteresting rock being hoisted out of the mine there, and hundreds of stamps crushing it into powder. People told me there was gold in it, and I believed what they said.

I remember Beauty Point for its shady forest and for the road among the tall gum-trees. While there the governor of New South Wales, Lord Hampden, and his family came in on a steam-yacht, sight-seeing. The *Spray*, anchored near the landing-pier, threw her bunting out, of course, and probably a more insignificant craft bearing the Stars and Stripes was never seen in those waters. However, the governor's party seemed to know why it floated there, and all about the *Spray*, and when I heard his Excellency say, "Introduce me to the captain," or "Introduce the captain to me," whichever it was, I found myself at once in the presence of a gentleman and a friend, and one greatly interested in my voyage. If any one of the party was more interested than the governor himself, it was the Honorable Margaret, his daughter. On leaving, Lord and Lady Hampden promised to rendezvous with me on board the *Spray* at the Paris Exposition in 1900. "If we live," they said, and I added, for my part, "Dangers of the seas excepted."

From Beauty Point the *Spray* visited Georgetown, near the mouth of the river Tamar. This little settlement, I believe, marks the place where the first footprints were made by whites in Tasmania, though it never grew to be more than a hamlet.

Considering that I had seen something of the world, and finding people here interested in adventure, I talked the matter over before my first audience in a little hall by the country road. A piano having been brought in from a neighbor's, I was helped out by the severe thumping it got, and by a "Tommy Atkins" song[2] from a strolling comedian. People came from a great distance, and the attendance all told netted the house about three pounds sterling. The owner of the hall, a kind lady from Scotland, would take no rent, and so my lecture from the start was a success.

From this snug little place I made sail for Devonport, a thriving place on the river Mersey, a few hours' sail westward along the coast, and fast becoming the most important port in Tasmania. Large steamers enter there now and carry away great cargoes of farm produce, but the *Spray* was the first vessel to bring the Stars and Stripes to the port, the harbor-master, Captain Murray, told me, and so it is written in the port records. For the great distinction the *Spray* enjoyed many civilities while she rode comfortably at anchor in her port-duster awning that covered her from stem to stern.

From the magistrate's house, "Malunnah," on the point, she was saluted by the Jack both on coming in and on going out, and dear Mrs. Aikenhead, the mistress of Malunnah, supplied the *Spray* with jams and jellies of all sorts, by the case, prepared from the fruits of her own rich garden—enough to last all the way home and to spare. Mrs. Wood, farther up the harbor, put up bottles of raspberry wine for me. At this point, more than ever before, I was in the land of good cheer. Mrs. Powell sent on board chutney prepared "as we prepare it in India." Fish and game were plentiful here, and the voice of the gobbler was heard, and from Pardo, farther up the country, came an enormous cheese; and yet people inquire: "What did you live on? What did you eat?"

I was haunted by the beauty of the landscape all about, of the natural ferneries then disappearing, and of the domed forest-trees on the slopes, and was fortunate in meeting a gentleman intent on preserving in art the beauties of his country. He presented me with many reproductions from his collection of pictures, also many originals, to show to my friends.

By another gentleman I was charged to tell the glories of Tasmania in every land and on every occasion. This was Dr. McCall, M. L. C. The doctor gave me useful hints on lecturing. It was not without misgivings, however, that I filled away on this new course, and I am free to say that it is only by the kindness of sympathetic audiences that my oratorical bark was held on even keel. Soon after my first

The *Spray* in her port duster at Devonport, Tasmania, February 22, 1897.

talk the kind doctor came to me with words of approval. As in many other of my enterprises, I had gone about it at once and without second thought. "Man, man," said he, "great nervousness is only a sign of brain, and the more brain a man has the longer it takes him to get over the affliction; but," he added reflectively, "you will get over it." However, in my own behalf I think it only fair to say that I am not yet entirely cured.

The *Spray* was hauled out on the marine railway at Devonport and examined carefully top and bottom, but was found absolutely free from the destructive teredo,* and sound in all respects. To protect her further against the ravage of these insects the bottom was coated once more with copper paint, for she would have to sail through the Coral and Arafura seas before refitting again. Everything was done to fit her for all the known dangers. But it was not without regret that I looked forward to the day of sailing from a country of so many pleasant associations. If there was a moment in my voyage when I could have given it up, it was there and then; but no vacancies for a better post being open, I weighed anchor April 16, 1897, and again put to sea.

The season of summer was then over; winter was rolling up from the south, with fair winds for the north. A foretaste of winter wind sent the *Spray* flying round Cape Howe and as far as Cape Bundooro farther along, which she passed on the following day, retracing her course northward. This was a fine run, and boded good for the long voyage home from the antipodes. My old Christmas friends on Bundooro seemed to be up and moving when I came the second time by their cape, and we exchanged signals again, while the sloop sailed along as before in a smooth sea and close to the shore.

The weather was fine, with clear sky the rest of the passage to Port Jackson (Sydney), where the *Spray* arrived April 22, 1897, and anchored in Watson's Bay, near the heads, in eight fathoms of water. The harbor from the heads to Parramatta, up the river, was more than ever alive with boats and yachts of every class. It was, indeed, a scene of animation, hardly equaled in any other part of the world.

---

*Shipworm, a wood-borer common in tropical waters; see footnote on p. 22.

A few days later the bay was flecked with tempestuous waves, and none but stout ships carried sail. I was in a neighboring hotel then, nursing a neuralgia which I had picked up alongshore, and had only that moment got a glance of just the stern of a large, unmanageable steamship passing the range of my window as she forged in by the point, when the bell-boy burst into my room shouting that the *Spray* had "gone bung." I tumbled out quickly, to learn that "bung" meant that a large steamship had run into her, and that it was the one of which I saw the stern, the other end of her having hit the *Spray*. It turned out, however, that no damage was done beyond the loss of an anchor and chain, which from the shock of the collision had parted at the hawse. I had nothing at all to complain of, though, in the end, for the captain, after he clubbed his ship, took the *Spray* in tow up the harbor, clear of all dangers, and sent her back again, in charge of an officer and three men, to her anchorage in the bay, with a polite note saying he would repair any damages done. But what yawing about she made of it when she came with a stranger at the helm! Her old friend the pilot of the *Pinta* would not have been guilty of such lubberly work. But to my great delight they got her into a berth, and the neuralgia left me then, or was forgotten. The captain of the steamer, like a true seaman, kept his word, and his agent, Mr. Collishaw handed me on the very next day the price of the lost anchor and chain, with something over for anxiety of mind. I remember that he offered me twelve pounds at once; but my lucky number being thirteen, we made the amount thirteen pounds, which squared all accounts.

I sailed again, May 9, before a strong southwest wind, which sent the *Spray* gallantly on as far as Port Stevens, where it fell calm and then came up ahead; but the weather was fine, and so remained for many days, which was a great change from the state of the weather experienced here some months before.

Having a full set of admiralty sheet-charts of the coast and Barrier Reef, I felt easy in mind. Captain Fisher, R. N., who had steamed through the Barrier passages in H. M. S. *Orlando,* advised me from the first to take this route, and I did not regret coming back to it now.

The wind, for a few days after passing Port Stevens, Seal Rocks, and Cape Hawk, was light and dead ahead; but these points are photographed on my memory from the trial of beating round them some months before when bound the other way. But now, with a good stock of books on board, I fell to reading day and night, leaving this pleasant occupation merely to trim sails or tack, or to lie down and rest, while the *Spray* nibbled at the miles. I tried to compare my state with that of old circumnavigators, who sailed exactly over the route which I took from Cape Verde Islands or farther back to this point and beyond, but there was no comparison so far as I had got. Their hardships and romantic escapes—those of them who escaped death and worse sufferings—did not enter into my experience, sailing all alone around the world. For me is left to tell only of pleasant experiences, till finally my adventures are prosy and tame.

I had just finished reading some of the most interesting of the old voyages in woe-begone ships, and was already near Port Macquarie, on my own cruise, when I made out, May 13, a modern dandy craft in distress, anchored on the coast. Standing in for her, I found that she was the cutter-yacht *Akbar*,* which had sailed from Watson's Bay about three days ahead of the *Spray*, and that she had run at once into trouble. No wonder she did so. It was a case of babes in the wood or butterflies at sea. Her owner, on his maiden voyage, was all duck trousers; the captain, distinguished for the enormous yachtsman's cap he wore, was a Murrumbidgee† whaler before he took command of the *Akbar;* and the navigating officer, poor fellow, was almost as deaf as a post, and nearly as stiff and immovable as a post in the ground. These three jolly tars comprised the crew. None of them knew more about the sea or about a vessel than a newly born babe knows about another world. They were bound for New Guinea, so they said; perhaps it was as well that three tenderfeet so tender as those never reached that destination.

The owner, whom I had met before he sailed, wanted to race the poor old *Spray* to Thursday Island en route. I declined the challenge, naturally, on the ground of the unfairness of three young yachtsmen in a clipper against an old sailor all alone in a craft of coarse build; besides that, I would not on any account race in the Coral Sea.

---

*Akbar was not her registered name, which need not be told [author's note].[3]
†The Murrumbidgee is a small river winding among the mountains of Australia, and would be the last place in which to look for a whale [author's note].

"Is it a-goin' to blow?"

"*Spray* ahoy!" they all hailed now. "What's the weather goin' t' be? Is it a-goin' to blow? And don't you think we'd better go back t' r-r-refit?"

I thought, "If ever you get back, don't refit," but I said: "Give me the end of a rope, and I'll tow you into yon port farther along; and on your lives," I urged, "do not go back round Cape Hawk, for it's winter to the south of it."

They purposed making for Newcastle under jury-sails; for their mainsail had been blown to ribbons, even the jigger had been blown away, and her rigging flew at loose ends. The *Akbar,* in a word, was a wreck.

"Up anchor," I shouted, "up anchor, and let me tow you into Port Macquarie, twelve miles north of this."

"No," cried the owner; "we'll go back to Newcastle. We missed Newcastle on the way coming; we didn't see the light, and it was not thick, either." This he shouted very loud, ostensibly for my hearing, but closer even than necessary, I thought, to the ear of the navigating officer. Again I tried to persuade them to be towed into the port of refuge so near at hand. It would have cost them only the trouble of weighing their anchor and passing me a rope; of this I assured them, but they declined even this, in sheer ignorance of a rational course.

"What is your depth of water?" I asked.

"Don't know; we lost our lead. All the chain is out. We sounded with the anchor."

"Send your dinghy over, and I'll give you a lead."

"We've lost our dinghy, too," they cried.

"God is good, else you would have lost yourselves," and "Farewell" was all I could say.

The trifling service proffered by the *Spray* would have saved their vessel.

"Report us," they cried, as I stood on—"report us with sails blown away, and that we don't care a dash and are not afraid."

"Then there is no hope for you," and again "Farewell."

I promised I would report them, and did so at the first opportunity, and out of humane reasons I do so again. On the following day I spoke the steamship *Sherman,* bound down the coast, and reported the yacht in distress and that it would be an act of humanity to tow her somewhere away from her exposed position on an open coast. That she did not get a tow from the steamer was from no lack of funds to pay the bill; for the owner, lately heir to a few hundred pounds, had the money with him. The proposed voyage to New Guinea was to look that island over with a view to its purchase. It was about eighteen days before I heard of the *Akbar* again, which was on the 31st of May, when I reached Cooktown, on the Endeavor River, where I found this news:

May 31, the yacht *Akbar*, from Sydney for New Guinea, three hands on board, lost at Crescent Head; the crew saved.

So it took them several days to lose the yacht, after all.

After speaking the distressed *Akbar* and the *Sherman*, the voyage for many days was uneventful save in the pleasant incident on May 16 of a chat by signal with the people on South Solitary Island, a dreary stone heap in the ocean just off the coast of New South Wales, in latitude 30° 12′ south.

"What vessel is that?" they asked, as the sloop came abreast of their island. For answer I tried them with the Stars and Stripes at the peak. Down came their signals at once, and up went the British ensign instead, which they dipped heartily. I understood from this that they made out my vessel and knew all about her, for they asked no more questions. They didn't even ask if the "voyage would pay," but they threw out this friendly message, "Wishing you a pleasant voyage," which at that very moment I was having.

May 19 the *Spray*, passing the Tweed River, was signaled from Danger Point, where those on shore seemed most anxious about the state of my health, for they asked if "all hands" were well, to which I could say, "Yes."

On the following day the *Spray* rounded Great Sandy Cape, and, what is a notable event in every voyage, picked up the trade-winds, and these winds followed her now for many thousands of miles, never ceasing to blow from a moderate gale to a mild summer breeze, except at rare intervals.

From the pitch of the cape was a noble light seen twenty-seven miles; passing from this to Lady Elliott Light, which stands on an island as a sentinel at the gateway of the Barrier Reef, the *Spray* was at once in the fairway leading north. Poets have sung of beacon-light and of pharos,* but did ever poet behold a great light flash up before his path on a dark night in the midst of a coral sea? If so, he knew the meaning of his song.

The *Spray* had sailed for hours in suspense, evidently stemming a current. Almost mad with doubt, I grasped the helm to throw her

---

*Generic term for "lighthouse," derived from the ancient lighthouse at Pharos, Egypt.

head off shore, when blazing out of the sea was the light ahead. "Excalibur!"* cried "all hands," and rejoiced, and sailed on. The *Spray* was now in a protected sea and smooth water, the first she had dipped her keel into since leaving Gibraltar, and a change it was from the heaving of the misnamed "Pacific" Ocean.

The Pacific is perhaps, upon the whole, no more boisterous than other oceans, though I feel quite safe in saying that it is not more pacific except in name. It is often wild enough in one part or another. I once knew a writer who, after saying beautiful things about the sea, passed through a Pacific hurricane, and he became a changed man. But where, after all, would be the poetry of the sea were there no wild waves? At last here was the *Spray* in the midst of a sea of coral. The sea itself might be called smooth indeed, but coral rocks are always rough, sharp, and dangerous. I trusted now to the mercies of the Maker of all reefs, keeping a good lookout at the same time for perils on every hand.

Lo! the Barrier Reef and the waters of many colors studded all about with enchanted islands! I behold among them after all many safe harbors, else my vision is astray. On the 24th of May, the sloop, having made one hundred and ten miles a day from Danger Point, now entered Whitsunday Pass, and that night sailed through among the islands. When the sun rose next morning I looked back and regretted having gone by while it was dark, for the scenery far astern was varied and charming.

---

*Exclamation of delight, derived from the name of King Arthur's legendary sword.

CHAPTER XV

Arrival at Port Denison, Queensland—A lecture—Reminiscences of Captain Cook—Lecturing for charity at Cooktown—A happy escape from a coral reef—Home Island, Sunday Island, Bird Island—An American pearl-fisherman—Jubilee at Thursday Island—A new ensign for the *Spray*—Booby Island—Across the Indian Ocean—Christmas Island.

On the morning of the 26th Gloucester Island was close aboard, and the *Spray* anchored in the evening at Port Denison, where rests, on a hill, the sweet little town of Bowen, the future watering place and health-resort of Queensland. The country all about here had a healthful appearance.

The harbor was easy of approach, spacious and safe, and afforded excellent holding-ground. It was quiet in Bowen when the *Spray* arrived, and the good people with an hour to throw away on the second evening of her arrival came down to the School of Arts to talk about the voyage, it being the latest event. It was duly advertised in the two little papers, "Boomerang" and "Nully Nully," in the one the day before the affair came off, and in the other the day after, which was all the same to the editor, and, for that matter, it was the same to me.

Besides this, circulars were distributed with a flourish, and the "best bellman" in Australia was employed. But I could have keel-hauled the wretch, bell and all, when he came to the door of the little hotel where my prospective audience and I were dining, and with his clattering bell and fiendish yell made noises that would awake the dead, all over the voyage of the *Spray* from "Boston to Bowen, the two Hubs in the cart-wheels of creation," as the "Boomerang" afterward said.

Mr. Myles, magistrate, harbor-master, land commissioner, gold warden, etc., was chairman, and introduced me, for what reason I never knew, except to embarrass me with a sense of vain ostentation and embitter my life, for Heaven knows I had met every person in town the first hour ashore. I knew them all by name now, and they all knew me. However, Mr. Myles was a good talker. Indeed, I tried to induce him to go on and tell the story while I showed the pictures, but this he refused to do. I may explain that it was a talk illustrated by stereopticon.* The views were good, but the lantern, a thirty-shilling affair, was wretched, and had only an oil-lamp in it.

I sailed early the next morning before the papers came out, thinking it best to do so. They each appeared with a favorable column, however, of what they called a lecture, so I learned afterward, and they had a kind word for the bellman besides.

From Port Denison the sloop ran before the constant trade-wind, and made no stop at all, night or day, till she reached Cooktown, on the Endeavor River, where she arrived Monday, May 31, 1897, before a furious blast of wind encountered that day fifty miles down the coast. On this parallel of latitude is the high ridge and backbone of the trade-winds, which about Cooktown amount often to a hard gale.

I had been charged to navigate the route with extra care, and to feel my way over the ground. The skilled officer of the Royal Navy who advised me to take the Barrier Reef passage wrote me that H. M. S. *Orlando* steamed nights as well as days through it, but that I, under sail, would jeopardize my vessel on coral reefs if I undertook to do so.

Confidentially, it would have been no easy matter finding anchorage every night. The hard work, too, of getting the sloop under way every morning was finished, I had hoped, when she cleared the Strait of Magellan. Besides that, the best of admiralty charts made it possible to keep on sailing night and day. Indeed, with a fair wind, and in the clear weather of that season, the way through the Barrier Reef Channel, in all sincerity, was clearer than a highway in a busy city, and by all odds less dangerous. But to any one contemplating the voyage I would say, beware of reefs day or night, or, remaining on the land, be wary still.

"The *Spray* came flying into port like a bird," said the longshore daily papers of Cooktown the morning after she arrived; "and it seemed strange," they added, "that only one man could be seen on board working the craft." The *Spray* was doing her best, to be sure, for it was near night, and she was in haste to find a perch before dark.

---

*Early device for projecting photographs.

Tacking inside of all the craft in port, I moored her at sunset nearly abreast the Captain Cook[1] monument, and next morning went ashore to feast my eyes on the very stones the great navigator had seen, for I was now on a seaman's consecrated ground. But there seemed a question in Cooktown's mind as to the exact spot where his ship, the *Endeavor*, hove down for repairs on her memorable voyage around the world. Some said it was not at all at the place where the monument now stood. A discussion of the subject was going on one morning where I happened to be, and a young lady present, turning to me as one of some authority in nautical matters, very flatteringly asked my opinion. Well, I could see no

The *Spray* leaving Sydney, Australia, in the new suit of sails given by Commodore Foy of Australia.
(From a photograph.)

reason why Captain Cook, if he made up his mind to repair his ship inland, couldn't have dredged out a channel to the place where the monument now stood, if he had a dredging-machine with him, and afterward fill it up again; for Captain Cook could do 'most anything, and nobody ever said that he hadn't a dredger along. The young lady seemed to lean to my way of thinking, and following up the story of the historical voyage, asked if I had visited the point farther down the harbor where the great circumnavigator was murdered. This took my breath, but a bright school-boy coming along relieved my embarrassment, for, like all boys, seeing that information was wanted, he volunteered to supply it. Said he: "Captain Cook wasn't murdered 'ere at all, ma'am; 'e was killed in Hafrica: a lion et 'im."

Here I was reminded of distressful days gone by. I think it was in 1866[2] that the old steamship *Soushay,* from Batavia for Sydney, put in at Cooktown for scurvy-grass,* as I always thought, and "incidentally" to land mails. On her sick-list was my fevered self; and so I didn't see the place till I came back on the *Spray* thirty-one years later. And now I saw coming into port the physical wrecks of miners from New Guinea, destitute and dying. Many had died on the way and had been buried at sea. He would have been a hardened wretch who could look on and not try to do something for them.

The sympathy of all went out to these sufferers, but the little town was already straitened from a long run on its benevolence. I thought of the matter, of the lady's gift to me at Tasmania, which I had promised myself I would keep only as a loan, but found now, to my embarrassment, that I had invested the money. However, the good Cooktown people wished to hear a story of the sea, and how the crew of the *Spray* fared when illness got aboard of her. Accordingly the little Presbyterian church on the hill was opened for a conversation; everybody talked, and they made a roaring success of it. Judge Chester, the magistrate, was at the head of the gam, and so it was bound to succeed. He it was who annexed the island of New Guinea to Great Britain.[3] "While I was about it," said he, "I annexed the blooming lot of it." There was a ring in the statement pleasant to the

---

*Any one of a number of plants mariners gathered and ate to prevent scurvy, a disease caused by vitamin C deficiency.

ear of an old voyager. However, the Germans made such a row over the judge's mainsail haul that they got a share in the venture.

Well, I was now indebted to the miners of Cooktown for the great privilege of adding a mite to a worthy cause, and to Judge Chester all the town was indebted for a general good time. The matter standing so, I sailed on June 6, 1897, heading away for the north as before.

Arrived at a very inviting anchorage about sundown, the 7th, I came to, for the night, abreast the Claremont light-ship. This was the only time throughout the passage of the Barrier Reef Channel that the *Spray* anchored, except at Port Denison and at Endeavor River. On the very night following this, however (the 8th), I regretted keenly, for an instant, that I had not anchored before dark, as I might have done easily under the lee of a coral reef. It happened in this way. The *Spray* had just passed M Reef light-ship, and left the light dipping astern, when, going at full speed, with sheets off, she hit the M Reef itself on the north end, where I expected to see a beacon.

She swung off quickly on her heel, however, and with one more bound on a swell cut across the shoal point so quickly that I hardly knew how it was done. The beacon wasn't there; at least, I didn't see it. I hadn't time to look for it after she struck, and certainly it didn't much matter then whether I saw it or not.

But this gave her a fine departure for Cape Greenville,* the next point ahead. I saw the ugly boulders under the sloop's keel as she flashed over them, and I made a mental note of it that the letter M, for which the reef was named, was the thirteenth one in our alphabet, and that thirteen, as noted years before, was still my lucky number. The natives of Cape Greenville are notoriously bad, and I was advised to give them the go-by. Accordingly, from M Reef I steered outside of the adjacent islands, to be on the safe side. Skipping along now, the *Spray* passed Home Island, off the pitch of the cape, soon after midnight, and squared away on a westerly course. A short time later she fell in with a steamer bound south, groping her way in the dark and making the night dismal with her own black smoke.

From Home Island I made for Sunday Island, and bringing that abeam, shortened sail, not wishing to make Bird Island, farther

---

*Properly, Cape Grenville, on Australia's northeastern coast.

along, before daylight, the wind being still fresh and the islands being low, with dangers about them. Wednesday, June 9, 1897, at daylight, Bird Island was dead ahead, distant two and a half miles, which I considered near enough. A strong current was pressing the sloop forward. I did not shorten sail too soon in the night! The first and only Australian canoe seen on the voyage was encountered here standing from the mainland, with a rag of sail set, bound for this island.

A long, slim fish that leaped on board in the night was found on deck this morning. I had it for breakfast. The spry chap was no larger around than a herring, which it resembled in every respect, except that it was three times as long; but that was so much the better, for I am rather fond of fresh herring, anyway. A great number of fisher-birds were about this day, which was one of the pleasantest on God's earth. The *Spray*, dancing over the waves, entered Albany Pass as the sun drew low in the west over the hills of Australia.

At 7:30 P. M. the *Spray*, now through the pass, came to anchor in a cove in the mainland, near a pearl-fisherman, called the *Tarawa*, which was at anchor, her captain from the deck of his vessel directing me to a berth. This done, he at once came on board to clasp hands. The *Tarawa* was a Californian, and Captain Jones, her master, was an American.

On the following morning Captain Jones brought on board two pairs of exquisite pearl shells, the most perfect ones I ever saw. They were probably the best he had, for Jones was the heart-yarn of a sailor. He assured me that if I would remain a few hours longer some friends from Somerset, near by, would pay us all a visit, and one of the crew, sorting shells on deck, "guessed" they would. The mate "guessed" so, too. The friends came, as even the second mate and cook had "guessed" they would. They were Mr. Jardine, stockman, famous throughout the land, and his family. Mrs. Jardine was the niece of King Malietoa, and cousin to the beautiful Faamu-Sami ("To make the sea burn"), who visited the *Spray* at Apia. Mr. Jardine was himself a fine specimen of a Scotsman. With his little family about him, he was content to live in this remote place, accumulating the comforts of life.

The fact of the *Tarawa* having been built in America accounted for the crew, boy Jim and all, being such good guessers. Strangely enough, though, Captain Jones himself, the only American aboard, was never heard to guess at all.

After a pleasant chat and good-by to the people of the *Tarawa*, and to Mr. and Mrs. Jardine, I again weighed anchor and stood across for Thursday Island, now in plain view, mid-channel in Torres Strait, where I arrived shortly after noon. Here the *Spray* remained over until June 24. Being the only American representative in port, this tarry was imperative, for on the 22d was the Queen's diamond jubilee.[4] The two days over were, as sailors say, for "coming up."*

Meanwhile I spent pleasant days about the island. Mr. Douglas, resident magistrate, invited me on a cruise in his steamer one day among the islands in Torres Strait. This being a scientific expedition in charge of Professor Mason Bailey,[5] botanist, we rambled over Friday and Saturday islands, where I got a glimpse of botany. Miss Bailey, the professor's daughter, accompanied the expedition, and told me of many indigenous plants with long names.

The 22d was the great day on Thursday Island, for then we had not only the jubilee, but a jubilee with a grand corroboree in it, Mr. Douglas having brought some four hundred native warriors and their wives and children across from the mainland to give the celebration the true native touch, for when they do a thing on Thursday Island they do it with a roar. The corroboree was, at any rate, a howling success. It took place at night, and the performers, painted in fantastic colors, danced or leaped about before a blazing fire. Some were rigged and painted like birds and beasts, in which the emu and kangaroo were well represented. One fellow leaped like a frog. Some had the human skeleton painted on their bodies, while they jumped about threateningly, spear in hand, ready to strike down some imaginary enemy. The kangaroo hopped and danced with natural ease and grace, making a fine figure. All kept time to music, vocal and instrumental, the instruments (save the mark!)[†] being bits of wood, which they beat one against the other, and saucer-like bones, held in the palm of the hands, which they knocked together, making a dull sound. It was a show at once amusing, spectacular, and hideous.

---

*Getting back in shape.

†Derogatory phrase implying that the natives' instruments hardly deserved the name.

The warrior aborigines that I saw in Queensland were for the most part lithe and fairly well built, but they were stamped always with repulsive features, and their women were, if possible, still more ill favored.

I observed that on the day of the jubilee no foreign flag was waving in the public grounds except the Stars and Stripes, which along with the Union Jack guarded the gateway, and floated in many places, from the tiniest to the standard size. Speaking to Mr. Douglas, I ventured a remark on this compliment to my country. "Oh," said he, "this is a family affair, and we do not consider the Stars and Stripes a foreign flag." The *Spray* of course flew her best bunting, and hoisted the Jack as well as her own noble flag as high as she could.

On June 24 the *Spray*, well fitted in every way, sailed for the long voyage ahead, down the Indian Ocean. Mr. Douglas gave her a flag as she was leaving his island. The *Spray* had now passed nearly all the dangers of the Coral Sea and Torres Strait, which, indeed, were not a few; and all ahead from this point was plain sailing and a straight course. The trade-wind was still blowing fresh, and could be safely counted on now down to the coast of Madagascar, if not beyond that, for it was still early in the season.

I had no wish to arrive off the Cape of Good Hope before midsummer, and it was now early winter. I had been off that cape once[6] in July, which was, of course, midwinter there. The stout ship I then commanded encountered only fierce hurricanes, and she bore them ill. I wished for no winter gales now. It was not that I feared them more, being in the *Spray* instead of a large ship, but that I preferred fine weather in any case. It is true that one may encounter heavy gales off the Cape of Good Hope at any season of the year, but in the summer they are less frequent and do not continue so long. And so with time enough before me to admit of a run ashore on the islands en route, I shaped the course now for Keeling Cocos, atoll islands, distant twenty-seven hundred miles. Taking a departure from Booby Island, which the sloop passed early in the day, I decided to sight Timor on the way, an island of high mountains.

Booby Island I had seen before, but only once, however, and that was when in the steamship *Soushay*, on which I was "hove-down" in a fever. When she steamed along this way I was well enough to crawl on deck to look at Booby Island. Had I died for it, I would have seen that island. In those days passing ships landed stores in a cave on the island for shipwrecked and distressed wayfarers. Captain Airy of the *Soushay*, a good man, sent a boat to the cave with his contribution to the general store. The stores were landed in safety, and the boat, returning, brought back from the improvised post-office there a dozen or more letters, most of them left by whalemen, with the request that the first homeward-bound ship would carry them along and see to their mailing, which had been the custom of this strange postal service for many years. Some of the letters brought back by our boat were directed to New Bedford, and some to Fairhaven, Massachusetts.

There is a light to-day on Booby Island, and regular packet communication with the rest of the world, and the beautiful uncertainty of the fate of letters left there is a thing of the past. I made no call at the little island, but standing close in, exchanged signals with the keeper of the light. Sailing on, the sloop was at once in the Arafura Sea, where for days she sailed in water milky white and green and purple. It was my good fortune to enter the sea on the last quarter of the moon, the advantage being that in the dark nights I witnessed the phosphorescent light effect at night in its greatest splendor. The sea, where the sloop disturbed it, seemed all ablaze, so that by its light I could see the smallest articles on deck, and her wake was a path of fire.

On the 25th of June the sloop was already clear of all the shoals and dangers, and was sailing on a smooth sea as steadily as before, but with speed somewhat slackened. I got out the flying-jib made at Juan Fernandez, and set it as a spinnaker from the stoutest bamboo that Mrs. Stevenson had given me at Samoa. The spinnaker pulled like a sodger,* and the bamboo holding its own, the *Spray* mended her pace.

Several pigeons flying across to-day from Australia toward the islands bent their course over the *Spray*. Smaller birds were seen flying in the opposite direction. In the part of the Arafura that I came to first, where it was shallow, sea-snakes writhed about on the surface and tumbled over and over in the waves. As the sloop sailed farther on, where the sea became deep, they disappeared. In the ocean, where the water is blue, not one was ever seen.

---

*Soldier; Slocum borrows this idiomatic spelling from Scottish poet Robert Burns (1759–1796), one of his favorite poets.

In the days of serene weather there was not much to do but to read and take rest on the *Spray*, to make up as much as possible for the rough time off Cape Horn, which was not yet forgotten, and to forestall the Cape of Good Hope by a store of ease. My sea journal was now much the same from day to day—something like this of June 26 and 27, for example:

June 26, in the morning, it is a bit squally; later in the day blowing a steady breeze.

On the log at noon is	.	.	.	.	.	.	.	130 miles
Subtract correction for slip	.	.	.	.	.	.	10 "
							120 "
Add for current	.	.	.	.	.	.	.	10 "
							130 "

Latitude by observation at noon, 10° 23′ S.
Longitude as per mark on the chart.

There wasn't much brain-work in that log, I'm sure. June 27 makes a better showing, when all is told:

First of all, to-day, was a flying-fish on deck; fried it in butter.
133 miles on the log.
For slip, off, and for current, on, as per guess, about equal—let it go at that.
Latitude by observation at noon, 10° 25′ S.

For several days now the *Spray* sailed west on the parallel of 10° 25′ S., as true as a hair. If she deviated at all from that, through the day or night,—and this may have happened,—she was back, strangely enough, at noon, at the same latitude. But the greatest science was in reckoning the longitude. My tin clock and only time-piece had by this time lost its minute-hand, but after I boiled her she told the hours, and that was near enough on a long stretch.

On the 2d of July the great island of Timor was in view away to the nor'ard. On the following day I saw Dana Island, not far off, and a breeze came up from the land at night, fragrant of the spices or what not of the coast.

On the 11th, with all sail set and with the spinnaker still abroad,

Christmas Island, about noon, came into view one point on the starboard bow. Before night it was abeam and distant two and a half miles. The surface of the island appeared evenly rounded from the sea to a considerable height in the center. In outline it was as smooth as a fish, and a long ocean swell, rolling up, broke against the sides, where it lay like a monster asleep, motionless on the sea. It seemed to have the proportions of a whale, and as the sloop sailed along its side to the part where the head would be, there was a nostril, even, which was a blow-hole through a ledge of rock where every wave that dashed threw up a shaft of water, lifelike and real.

It had been a long time since I last saw this island; but I remember my temporary admiration for the captain of the ship I was then in, the *Tanjore*, when he sang out one morning from the quarterdeck, well aft, "Go aloft there, one of ye, with a pair of eyes, and see Christmas Island." Sure enough, there the island was in sight from the royal-yard. Captain M———* had thus made a great hit, and he never got over it. The chief mate, terror of us ordinaries in the ship, walking never to windward of the captain, now took himself very humbly to leeward altogether. When we arrived at Hong-Kong there was a letter in the ship's mail for me. I was in the boat with the captain some hours while he had it. But do you suppose he could hand a letter to a seaman? No, indeed; not even to an ordinary seaman. When we got to the ship he gave it to the first mate; the first mate gave it to the second mate, and he laid it, michingly,† on the capstan-head, where I could get it!

---

*John P. Martin, captain of the *Tanjore* (see chapter XV, note 2).
†In a sneaky or skulking manner.

CHAPTER XVI

A call for careful navigation—Three hours' steering in twenty-three days—Arrival at the Keeling Cocos Islands—A curious chapter of social history—A welcome from the children of the islands—Cleaning and painting the *Spray* on the beach—A Mohammedan blessing for a pot of jam—Keeling as a paradise—A risky adventure in a small boat—Away to Rodriguez—Taken for Antichrist—The governor calms the fears of the people—A lecture—A convent in the hills.

To the Keeling Cocos Islands was now only five hundred and fifty miles; but even in this short run it was necessary to be extremely careful in keeping a true course else I would miss the atoll.

On the 12th, some hundred miles southwest of Christmas Island, I saw anti-trade clouds flying up from the southwest very high over the regular winds, which weakened now for a few days, while a swell heavier than usual set in also from the southwest. A winter gale was going on in the direction of the Cape of Good Hope. Accordingly, I steered higher to windward, allowing twenty miles a day while this went on, for change of current; and it was not too much, for on that course I made the Keeling Islands right ahead. The first unmistakable sign of the land was a visit one morning from a white tern that fluttered very knowingly about the vessel, and then took itself off westward with a businesslike air in its wing. The tern is called by the islanders the "pilot of Keeling Cocos." Farther on I came among a great number of birds fishing, and fighting over whatever they caught. My reckoning was up, and springing aloft, I saw from halfway up the mast cocoanut-trees standing out of the water ahead. I expected to see this; still, it thrilled me as an electric shock might have done. I slid down the mast, trembling under the strangest sensations; and not able to resist the impulse, I sat on deck and gave way to my emotions. To folks in a parlor on shore this may seem weak indeed, but I am telling the story of a voyage alone.

I didn't touch the helm, for with the current and heave of the sea the sloop found herself at the end of the run absolutely in the fairway of the channel. You couldn't have beaten it in the navy! Then

I trimmed her sails by the wind, took the helm, and flogged her up the couple of miles or so abreast the harbor landing, where I cast anchor at 3:30 P.M., July 17, 1897, twenty-three days from Thursday Island. The distance run was twenty-seven hundred miles as the crow flies. This would have been a fair Atlantic voyage. It was a delightful sail! During those twenty-three days I had not spent altogether more than three hours at the helm, including the time occupied in beating into Keeling harbor. I just lashed the helm and let her go; whether the wind was abeam or dead aft, it was all the same: she always sailed on her course. No part of the voyage up to this point, taking it by and large, had been so finished as this.*

The Keeling Cocos Islands, according to Admiral Fitzroy, R. N.,† lie between the latitudes of 11° 50′ and 12° 12′ S., and the longitudes of 96° 51′ and 96° 58′ E. They were discovered in 1608–9 by Captain William Keeling, then in the service of the East India Company. The southern group consists of seven or eight islands and islets on the atoll, which is the skeleton of what some day, according to the history of coral reefs, will be a continuous island. North Keeling has no harbor, is seldom visited, and is of no importance. The South Keelings are a strange little world, with a romantic history all their own. They

---

*Mr. Andrew J. Leach, reporting, July 21, 1897, through Governor Kynnersley of Singapore, to Joseph Chamberlain, Colonial Secretary, said concerning the *Iphegenia's* visit to the atoll: "As we left the ocean depths of deepest blue and entered the coral circle, the contrast was most remarkable. The brilliant colors of the waters, transparent to a depth of over thirty feet, now purple, now of the bluest sky-blue, and now green, with the white crests of the waves flashing under a brilliant sun, the encircling . . . palm-clad islands, the gaps between which were to the south undiscernible, the white sand shores and the whiter gaps where breakers appeared, and, lastly, the lagoon itself, seven or eight miles across from north to south, and five to six miles from east to west, presented a sight never to be forgotten. After some little delay, Mr. Sidney Ross, the eldest son of Mr. George Ross, came off to meet us, and soon after, accompanied by the doctor and another officer, we went ashore.

"On reaching the landing-stage, we found, hauled up for cleaning, etc., the *Spray* of Boston, a yawl of 12.70 tons gross, the property of Captain Joshua Slocum. He arrived at the island on the 17th of July, twenty-three days out from Thursday Island. This extraordinary solitary traveler left Boston some two years ago single-handed, crossed to Gibraltar, sailed down to Cape Horn, passed through the Strait of Magellan to the Society Islands, thence to Australia, and through the Torres Strait to Thursday Island" [author's note].

†Robert Fitzroy (1805–1865) commanded the *Beagle* during English naturalist Charles Darwin's explorations (see chapter VIII, note 2).

have been visited occasionally by the floating spar of some hurricane-swept ship, or by a tree that has drifted all the way from Australia, or by an ill-starred ship cast away, and finally by man. Even a rock once drifted to Keeling, held fast among the roots of a tree.

After the discovery of the islands by Captain Keeling, their first notable visitor was Captain John Clunis-Ross, who in 1814 touched in the ship *Borneo* on a voyage to India. Captain Ross returned two years later with his wife and family and his mother-in-law, Mrs. Dymoke, and eight sailor-artisans, to take possession of the islands, but found there already one Alexander Hare, who meanwhile had marked the little atoll as a sort of Eden for a seraglio of Malay women which he moved over from the coast of Africa. It was Ross's own brother, oddly enough, who freighted Hare and his crowd of women to the islands, not knowing of Captain John's plans to occupy the little world. And so Hare was there with his outfit, as if he had come to stay.

On his previous visit, however, Ross had nailed the English Jack to a mast on Horsburg Island, one of the group. After two years shreds of it still fluttered in the wind, and his sailors, nothing loath, began at once the invasion of the new kingdom to take possession of it, women and all. The force of forty women, with only one man to command them, was not equal to driving eight sturdy sailors back into the sea.*

From this time on Hare had a hard time of it. He and Ross did not get on well as neighbors. The islands were too small and too near for characters so widely different. Hare had "oceans of money," and might have lived well in London; but he had been governor of a wild colony in Borneo, and could not confine himself to the tame life that prosy civilization affords. And so he hung on to the atoll with his forty women, retreating little by little before Ross and his sturdy crew, till at last he found himself and his harem on the little island known to this day as Prison Island, where, like Bluebeard, he confined his wives in a castle. The channel between the islands was narrow, the water was not deep, and the eight Scotch sailors wore long

---

*In the accounts given in Findlay's "Sailing Directory"[1] of some of the events there is a chronological discrepancy.[2] I follow the accounts gathered from the old captain's grandsons and from records on the spot [author's note].

boots. Hare was now dismayed. He tried to compromise with rum and other luxuries, but these things only made matters worse. On the day following the first St. Andrew's celebration* on the island, Hare, consumed with rage, and no longer on speaking terms with the captain, dashed off a note to him, saying: "DEAR ROSS: I thought when I sent rum and roast pig to your sailors that they would stay away from my flower-garden." In reply to which the captain, burning with indignation, shouted from the center of the island, where he stood, "Ahoy, there, on Prison Island! You Hare, don't you know that rum and roast pig are not a sailor's heaven?" Hare said afterward that one might have heard the captain's roar across to Java.

The lawless establishment was soon broken up by the women deserting Prison Island and putting themselves under Ross's protection. Hare then went to Batavia, where he met his death.

My first impression upon landing was that the crime of infanticide had not reached the islands of Keeling Cocos. "The children have all come to welcome you," explained Mr. Ross, as they mustered at the jetty by hundreds, of all ages and sizes. The people of this country were all rather shy, but, young or old, they never passed one or saw one passing their door without a salutation. In their musical voices they would say, "Are you walking?" ("Jalan, jalan?")† "Will you come along?" one would answer.

For a long time after I arrived the children regarded the "one-man ship" with suspicion and fear. A native man had been blown away to sea many years before, and they hinted to one another that he might have been changed from black to white, and returned in the sloop. For some time every movement I made was closely watched. They were particularly interested in what I ate. One day, after I had been "boot-topping" the sloop with a composition of coal-tar‡ and other stuff, and while I was taking my dinner, with the luxury of blackberry jam, I heard a commotion, and then a yell and a stampede, as the children ran away yelling: "The captain is eating coal-tar! The captain is eating coal-tar!" But they soon found out that this same "coal-tar" was very good to eat, and that I had brought a quantity of

*November 30, the feast day of Andrew, the patron saint of Scotland.
†The natives of these islands speak Malay.
‡Creosote, a wood preservative distilled from coal.

The *Spray* ashore for "boot-topping" at the Keeling Islands.
(From a photograph.)

it. One day when I was spreading a sea-biscuit thick with it for a wide-awake youngster, I heard them whisper, "Chut-chut!" meaning that a shark had bitten my hand, which they observed was lame. Thenceforth they regarded me as a hero, and I had not fingers enough for the little bright-eyed tots that wanted to cling to them and follow me about. Before this, when I held out my hand and said, "Come!" they would shy off for the nearest house, and say, "Dingin" ("It's cold"), or "Ujan" ("It's going to rain"). But it was now accepted that I was not the returned spirit of the lost black, and I had plenty of friends about the island, rain or shine.

One day after this, when I tried to haul the sloop and found her

fast in the sand, the children all clapped their hands and cried that a
kpeting (crab) was holding her by the keel; and little Ophelia, ten or
twelve years of age, wrote in the *Spray's* log-book:

> A hundred men with might and main
> On the windlass hove, yeo ho!
> The cable only came in twain;
> The ship she would not go;
> For, child, to tell the strangest thing,
> The keel was held by a great kpeting.

This being so or not, it was decided that the Mohammedan priest,
Sama the Emim, for a pot of jam, should ask Mohammed to bless
the voyage and make the crab let go the sloop's keel, which it did, if
it had hold, and she floated on the very next tide.

On the 22d of July arrived H. M. S. *Iphegenia,* with Mr. Justice
Andrew J. Leech and court officers on board, on a circuit of inspection among the Straits Settlements, of which Keeling Cocos was a
dependency, to hear complaints and try cases by law, if any there
were to try. They found the *Spray* hauled ashore and tied to a
cocoanut-tree. But at the Keeling Islands there had not been a griev-
ance to complain of since the day that Hare migrated, for the Rosses
have always treated the islanders as their own family.

If there is a paradise on this earth it is Keeling. There was not a
case for a lawyer, but something had to be done, for here were two
ships in port, a great man-of-war and the *Spray.* Instead of a lawsuit
a dance was got up, and all the officers who could leave their ship
came ashore. Everybody on the island came, old and young, and the
governor's great hall was filled with people. All that could get on
their feet danced, while the babies lay in heaps in the corners of the
room, content to look on. My little friend Ophelia danced with the
judge. For music two fiddles screeched over and over again the good
old tune, "We won't go home till morning."* And we did not.

The women at the Keelings do not do all the drudgery, as in many
places visited on the voyage. It would cheer the heart of a Fuegian

---

*Folk song using the same melody as "For He's a Jolly Good Fellow."

woman to see the Keeling lord of creation up a cocoanut-tree. Besides cleverly climbing the trees, the men of Keeling build exquisitely modeled canoes. By far the best workmanship in boat-building I saw on the voyage was here. Many finished mechanics dwelt under the palms at Keeling, and the hum of the band-saw and the ring of the anvil were heard from morning till night. The first Scotch settlers left there the strength of Northern blood and the inheritance of steady habits. No benevolent society has ever done so much for any islanders as the noble Captain Ross, and his sons, who have followed his example of industry and thrift.

Admiral Fitzroy of the *Beagle*, who visited here, where many things are reversed, spoke of "these singular though small islands, where crabs eat cocoanuts, fish eat coral, dogs catch fish, men ride on turtles, and shells are dangerous man-traps,"* adding that the greater part of the sea-fowl roost on branches, and many rats make their nests in the tops of palm-trees.

My vessel being refitted, I decided to load her with the famous mammoth tridacna† shell of Keeling, found in the bayou near by. And right here, within sight of the village, I came near losing "the crew of the *Spray*"—not from putting my foot in a man-trap shell, however, but from carelessly neglecting to look after the details of a trip across the harbor in a boat. I had sailed over oceans; I have since completed a course over them all, and sailed round the whole world without so nearly meeting a fatality as on that trip across a lagoon, where I trusted all to some one else, and he, weak mortal that he was, perhaps trusted all to me. However that may be, I found myself with a thoughtless African negro in a rickety bateau that was fitted with a rotten sail, and this blew away in mid-channel in a squall, that sent us drifting helplessly to sea, where we should have been incontinently lost. With the whole ocean before us to leeward, I was dismayed to see, while we drifted, that there was not a paddle or an oar in the boat! There was an anchor, to be sure, but not enough rope to tie a cat, and we were already in deep water. By great good fortune, however, there was a pole. Plying this as a

---

*Quotation from Fitzroy's *Narrative of the Surveying Voyages of His Majesty's Ships Adventure and Beagle* (London: Henry Colburn, 1839), vol. 3, p. 635.
†Giant clam.

Captain Slocum drifting out to sea.

paddle with the utmost energy, and by the merest accidental flaw in the wind to favor us, the trap of a boat was worked into shoal water, where we could touch bottom and push her ashore. With Africa, the nearest coast to leeward, three thousand miles away, with not so much as a drop of water in the boat, and a lean and hungry negro— well, cast the lot as one might, the crew of the *Spray* in a little while would have been hard to find. It is needless to say that I took no more such chances. The tridacna were afterward procured in a safe boat, thirty of them taking the place of three tons of cement ballast, which I threw overboard to make room and give buoyancy.

On August 22, the kpeting, or whatever else it was that held the sloop in the islands, let go its hold, and she swung out to sea under all sail, heading again for home. Mounting one or two heavy rollers on the fringe of the atoll, she cleared the flashing reefs. Long before dark Keeling Cocos, with its thousand souls, as sinless in their lives as perhaps it is possible for frail mortals to be, was left out of sight, astern. Out of sight, I say, except in my strongest affection.

The sea was rugged, and the *Spray* washed heavily when hauled on the wind, which course I took for the island of Rodriguez, and which brought the sea abeam. The true course for the island was west by south, one quarter south, and the distance was nineteen hundred miles; but I steered considerably to the windward of that to allow for the heave of the sea and other leeward effects. My sloop on this course ran under reefed sails for days together. I naturally tired of the never-ending motion of the sea, and, above all, of the wetting I got whenever I showed myself on deck. Under these heavy weather conditions the *Spray* seemed to lag behind on her course; at least, I attributed to these conditions a discrepancy in the log, which by the fifteenth day out from Keeling amounted to one hundred and fifty miles between the rotator and the mental calculations I had kept of what she should have gone, and so I kept an eye lifting for land. I could see about sundown this day a bunch of clouds that stood in one spot, right ahead, while the other clouds floated on; this was a sign of something. By midnight, as the sloop sailed on, a black object appeared where I had seen the resting clouds. It was still a long way off, but there could be no mistaking this: it was the high island of Rodriguez. I hauled in the patent log, which I was now towing more from habit than from necessity, for I had learned the *Spray* and her ways long before this. If one thing was clearer than another in her voyage, it was that she could be trusted to come out right and in safety, though at the same time I always stood ready to give her the benefit of even the least doubt. The officers who are over-sure, and "know it all like a book," are the ones, I have observed, who wreck the most ships and lose the most lives. The cause of the discrepancy in the log was one often met with, namely, coming in contact with some large fish; two out of the four blades of the rotator were crushed or bent, the work probably of a shark. Being sure of the sloop's position, I lay down to rest and to think, and I felt better for it. By daylight the island was abeam, about three miles away. It wore a hard, weather-beaten appearance there, all alone, far out in the Indian Ocean, like land adrift. The windward side was uninviting, but there was a good port to lee-ward, and I hauled in now close on the wind for that. A pilot came out to take me into the inner harbor, which was reached through a narrow channel among coral reefs.

It was a curious thing that at all of the islands some reality was in-sisted on as unreal, while improbabilities were clothed as hard facts; and so it happened here that the good abbé, a few days before, had been telling his people about the coming of Antichrist, and when they saw the *Spray* sail into the harbor, all feather-white before a gale of wind, and run all standing upon the beach, and with only one man aboard, they cried, "May the Lord help us, it is he, and he has come in a boat!" which I say would have been the most improbable way of his coming. Nevertheless, the news went flying through the place. The governor of the island, Mr. Roberts, came down immedi-ately to see what it was all about, for the little town was in a great commotion. One elderly woman, when she heard of my advent, made for her house and locked herself in. When she heard that I was actually coming up the street she barricaded her doors, and did not come out while I was on the island, a period of eight days. Governor Roberts and his family did not share the fears of their people, but came on board at the jetty, where the sloop was berthed, and their example induced others to come also. The governor's young boys took charge of the *Spray's* dinghy at once, and my visit cost his Ex-cellency, besides great hospitality to me, the building of a boat for them like the one belonging to the *Spray*.

My first day at this Land of Promise* was to me like a fairy-tale. For many days I had studied the charts and counted the time of my arrival at this spot, as one might his entrance to the Islands of the Blessed,[3] looking upon it as the terminus of the last long run, made irksome by the want of many things with which, from this time on, I could keep well supplied. And behold, here was the sloop, arrived, and made securely fast to a pier in Rodriguez. On the first evening

---

*Allusion to the Bible, Hebrews 11:9 (King James Version); the "land of promise" is Canaan, now part of Palestine.

ashore, in the land of napkins and cut glass, I saw before me still the ghosts of hempen towels and of mugs with handles knocked off. Instead of tossing on the sea, however, as I might have been, here was I in a bright hall, surrounded by sparkling wit, and dining with the governor of the island! "Aladdin," I cried, "where is your lamp? My fisherman's lantern, which I got at Gloucester, has shown me better things than your smoky old burner ever revealed."

The second day in port was spent in receiving visitors. Mrs. Roberts and her children came first to "shake hands," they said, "with the *Spray*." No one was now afraid to come on board except the poor old woman, who still maintained that the *Spray* had Antichrist in the hold, if, indeed, he had not already gone ashore. The governor entertained that evening, and kindly invited the "destroyer of the world" to speak for himself. This he did, elaborating most effusively on the dangers of the sea (which, after the manner of many of our frailest mortals, he would have had smooth had he made it); also by contrivances of light and darkness he exhibited on the wall pictures of the places and countries visited on the voyage (nothing like the countries, however, that he would have made), and of the people seen, savage and other, frequently groaning, "Wicked world! Wicked world!" When this was finished his Excellency the governor, speaking words of thankfulness, distributed pieces of gold.

On the following day I accompanied his Excellency and family on a visit to San Gabriel, which was up the country among the hills. The good abbé of San Gabriel entertained us all royally at the convent, and we remained his guests until the following day. As I was leaving his place, the abbé said, "Captain, I embrace you, and of whatever religion you may be, my wish is that you succeed in making your voyage, and that our Saviour the Christ be always with you!" To this good man's words I could only say, "My dear abbé, had all religionists been so liberal there would have been less bloodshed in the world."

At Rodriguez one may now find every convenience for filling pure and wholesome water in any quantity, Governor Roberts having built a reservoir in the hills, above the village, and laid pipes to the jetty, where, at the time of my visit, there were five and a half feet at high tide. In former years well-water was used, and more or less sickness occurred from it. Beef may be had in any quantity on the island, and at a moderate price. Sweet potatoes were plentiful and cheap; the large sack of them that I bought there for about four shillings kept unusually well. I simply stored them in the sloop's dry hold. Of fruits, pomegranates were most plentiful; for two shillings I obtained a large sack of them, as many as a donkey could pack from the orchard, which, by the way, was planted by nature herself.

CHAPTER XVII

A clean bill of health at Mauritius—Sailing the voyage over again in the opera-house—A newly discovered plant named in honor of the *Spray's* skipper—A party of young ladies out for a sail—A bivouac on deck—A warm reception at Durban—A friendly cross-examination by Henry M. Stanley—Three wise Boers seek proof of the flatness of the earth—Leaving South Africa.

O n the 16th of September, after eight restful days at Rodriguez, the mid-ocean land of plenty, I set sail, and on the 19th arrived at Mauritius, anchoring at quarantine about noon. The sloop was towed in later on the same day by the doctor's launch, after he was satisfied that I had mustered all the crew for inspection. Of this he seemed in doubt until he examined the papers, which called for a crew of one all told from port to port, throughout the voyage. Then finding that I had been well enough to come thus far alone, he gave me pratique without further ado. There was still another official visit for the *Spray* to pass farther in the harbor. The governor of Rodriguez, who had most kindly given me, besides a regular mail, private letters of introduction to friends, told me I should meet, first of all, Mr. Jenkins of the postal service, a good man. "How do you do, Mr. Jenkins?" cried I, as his boat swung alongside. "You don't know me," he said. "Why not?" I replied. "From where is the sloop?" "From around the world," I again replied, very solemnly. "And alone?" "Yes; why not?" "And you know me?" "Three thousand years ago," cried I, "when you and I had a warmer job than we have now" (even this was hot). "You were then Jenkinson, but if you have changed your name I don't blame you for that." Mr. Jenkins, forbearing soul, entered into the spirit of the jest, which served the *Spray* a good turn, for on the strength of this tale it got out that if any one should go on board after dark the devil would get him at once. And so I could leave the *Spray* without the fear of her being robbed at night. The cabin, to be sure, was broken into, but it was done in daylight, and the thieves got no more than a box of smoked herrings before "Tom" Ledson, one of the port officials, caught them red-handed, as it were, and sent them to jail. This

The *Spray* at Mauritius.

was discouraging to pilferers, for they feared Ledson more than they feared Satan himself. Even Mamode Hajee Ayoob, who was the day-watchman on board,—till an empty box fell over in the cabin and frightened him out of his wits,—could not be hired to watch nights, or even till the sun went down. "Sahib,"* he cried, "there is no need of it," and what he said was perfectly true.

At Mauritius, where I drew a long breath, the *Spray* rested her wings, it being the season of fine weather. The hardships of the

---

*Hindu word used especially as a term of general respect for European men.

voyage, if there had been any, were now computed by officers of experience as nine tenths finished, and yet somehow I could not forget that the United States was still a long way off.

The kind people of Mauritius, to make me richer and happier, rigged up the opera-house, which they had named the "Ship *Pantai.*"* All decks and no bottom was this ship, but she was as stiff as a church. They gave me free use of it while I talked over the *Spray's* adventures. His Honor the mayor introduced me to his Excellency the governor from the poop-deck of the *Pantai.* In this way I was also introduced again to our good consul, General John P. Campbell, who had already introduced me to his Excellency. I was becoming well acquainted, and was in for it now to sail the voyage over again. How I got through the story I hardly know. It was a hot night, and I could have choked the tailor who made the coat I wore for this occasion. The kind governor saw that I had done my part trying to rig like a man ashore, and he invited me to Government House at Reduit, where I found myself among friends.

It was winter still off stormy Cape of Good Hope, but the storms might whistle there. I determined to see it out in milder Mauritius, visiting Rose Hill, Curipepe, and other places on the island. I spent a day with the elder Mr. Roberts, father of Governor Roberts of Rodriguez, and with his friends the Very Reverend Fathers O'Loughlin and McCarthy. Returning to the *Spray* by way of the great flower conservatory near Moka, the proprietor, having only that morning discovered a new and hardy plant, to my great honor named it "Slocum,"[1] which he said Latinized it at once, saving him some trouble on the twist of a word; and the good botanist seemed pleased that I had come. How different things are in different countries! In Boston, Massachusetts, at that time, a gentleman, so I was told, paid thirty thousand dollars to have a flower named after his wife, and it was not a big flower either, while "Slocum," which came without the asking, was bigger than a mangel-wurzel![†]

I was royally entertained at Moka, as well as at Reduit and other places—once by seven young ladies, to whom I spoke of my inability

---

*Guinea-hen [author's note].
†Large, coarse beet used to feed cattle.

to return their hospitality except in my own poor way of taking them on a sail in the sloop. "The very thing! The very thing!" they all cried. "Then please name the time," I said, as meek as Moses. "To-morrow!" they all cried. "And, aunty, we may go, mayn't we, and we'll be real good for a whole week afterward, aunty! Say yes, aunty dear!" All this after saying "To-morrow"; for girls in Mauritius are, after all, the same as our girls in America; and their dear aunt said "Me, too" about the same as any really good aunt might say in my own country.

I was then in a quandary, it having recurred to me that on the very "to-morrow" I was to dine with the harbor-master, Captain Wilson. However, I said to myself, "The *Spray* will run out quickly into rough seas; these young ladies will have *mal de mer** and a good time, and I'll get in early enough to be at the dinner, after all." But not a bit of it. We sailed almost out of sight of Mauritius, and they just stood up and laughed at seas tumbling aboard, while I was at the helm making the worst weather of it I could, and spinning yarns to the aunt about sea-serpents and whales. But she, dear lady, when I had finished with stories of monsters, only hinted at a basket of provisions they had brought along, enough to last a week, for I had told them about my wretched steward.

The more the *Spray* tried to make these young ladies seasick, the more they all clapped their hands and said, "How lovely it is!" and "How beautifully she skims over the sea!" and "How beautiful our island appears from the distance!" and they still cried, "Go on!" We were fifteen miles or more at sea before they ceased the eager cry, "Go on!" Then the sloop swung round, I still hoping to be back to Port Louis in time to keep my appointment. The *Spray* reached the island quickly, and flew along the coast fast enough; but I made a mistake in steering along the coast on the way home, for as we came abreast of Tombo Bay it enchanted my crew. "Oh, let's anchor here!" they cried. To this no sailor in the world would have said nay. The sloop came to anchor, ten minutes later, as they wished, and a young man on the cliff abreast, waving his hat, cried, *"Vive la Spray!"* My passengers said, "Aunty, mayn't we have a swim in the surf along the

---

*Seasickness (French).

shore?" Just then the harbor-master's launch hove in sight, coming out to meet us; but it was too late to get the sloop into Port Louis that night. The launch was in time, however, to land my fair crew for a swim; but they were determined not to desert the ship. Meanwhile I prepared a roof for the night on deck with the sails, and a Bengali man-servant arranged the evening meal. That night the *Spray* rode in Tombo Bay with her precious freight. Next morning bright and early, even before the stars were gone, I awoke to hear praying on deck.

The port officers' launch reappeared later in the morning, this time with Captain Wilson himself on board, to try his luck in getting the *Spray* into port, for he had heard of our predicament. It was worth something to hear a friend tell afterward how earnestly the good harbor-master of Mauritius said, "I'll find the *Spray* and I'll get her into port." A merry crew he discovered on her. They could hoist sails like old tars, and could trim them, too. They could tell all about the ship's "hoods," and one should have seen them clap a bonnet on the jib. Like the deepest of deep-water sailors, they could heave the lead, and—as I hope to see Mauritius again!—any of them could have put the sloop in stays. No ship ever had a fairer crew.

The voyage was the event of Port Louis; such a thing as young ladies sailing about the harbor, even, was almost unheard of before.

While at Mauritius the *Spray* was tendered the use of the military dock free of charge, and was thoroughly refitted by the port authorities. My sincere gratitude is also due other friends for many things needful for the voyage put on board, including bags of sugar from some of the famous old plantations.

The favorable season now set in, and thus well equipped, on the 26th of October, the *Spray* put to sea. As I sailed before a light wind the island receded slowly, and on the following day I could still see the Puce Mountain near Moka. The *Spray* arrived next day off Galets, Réunion, and a pilot came out and spoke her. I handed him a Mauritius paper and continued on my voyage; for rollers were running heavily at the time, and it was not practicable to make a landing. From Réunion I shaped a course direct for Cape St. Mary, Madagascar.

The sloop was now drawing near the limits of the trade-wind, and the strong breeze that had carried her with free sheets the many

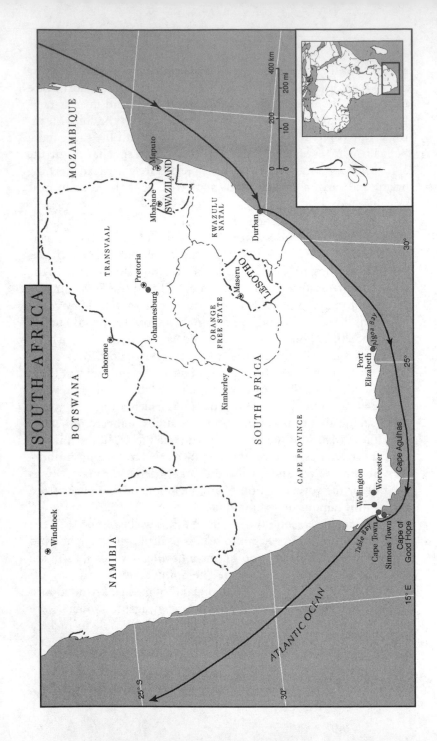

thousands of miles from Sandy Cape, Australia, fell lighter each day until October 30, when it was altogether calm, and a motionless sea held her in a hushed world. I furled the sails at evening, sat down on deck, and enjoyed the vast stillness of the night.

October 31 a light east-northeast breeze sprang up, and the sloop passed Cape St. Mary about noon. On the 6th, 7th, 8th, and 9th of November, in the Mozambique Channel, she experienced a hard gale of wind from the southwest. Here the *Spray* suffered as much as she did anywhere, except off Cape Horn. The thunder and lightning preceding this gale were very heavy. From this point until the sloop arrived off the coast of Africa, she encountered a succession of gales of wind, which drove her about in many directions, but on the 17th of November she arrived at Port Natal.*

This delightful place is the commercial center of the "Garden Colony," Durban itself, the city, being the continuation of a garden. The signalman from the bluff station reported the *Spray* fifteen miles off. The wind was freshening, and when she was within eight miles he said: "The *Spray* is shortening sail; the mainsail was reefed and set in ten minutes. One man is doing all the work."

This item of news was printed three minutes later in a Durban morning journal, which was handed to me when I arrived in port. I

See map on opposite page: Slocum spent four months visiting South Africa. He arrived in Durban on November 17, 1897, and left Cape Town on March 26, 1898. While the *Spray* underwent repairs in dry dock, Slocum traveled around the country on a free government railroad pass and visited Kimberley, Johannesburg, and Pretoria, the capital. At the time of Slocum's visit, South Africa was divided into separate countries: the British Cape Colony and the two independent republics of Transvaal and the Orange Free State, which were populated by Boers, or Afrikaners of Dutch descent. These two republics had recently formed an alliance opposing federation with the British, a conflict that was only resolved when the British won the South African War of 1899–1902. In testimony to Slocum's increasing fame, he met Paul Krüger, the president of Transvaal and the region's most determined opponent of British domination. Some of Slocum's best humor comes at the expense of the nationalistic conservative "Oom Paul," who truly did believe that the world was flat.

*Now Durban, a seaport of South Africa.

could not verify the time it had taken to reef the sail, for, as I have already said, the minute-hand of my timepiece was gone. I only knew that I reefed as quickly as I could.

The same paper, commenting on the voyage, said: "Judging from the stormy weather which has prevailed off this coast during the past few weeks, the *Spray* must have had a very stormy voyage from Mauritius to Natal." Doubtless the weather would have been called stormy by sailors in any ship, but it caused the *Spray* no more inconvenience than the delay natural to head winds generally.

The question of how I sailed the sloop alone, often asked, is best answered, perhaps, by a Durban newspaper. I would shrink from repeating the editor's words but for the reason that undue estimates have been made of the amount of skill and energy required to sail a sloop of even the *Spray's* small tonnage. I heard a man who called himself a sailor say that "it would require three men to do what it was claimed" that I did alone, and what I found perfectly easy to do over and over again; and I have heard that others made similar nonsensical remarks, adding that I would work myself to death. But here is what the Durban paper said:

As briefly noted yesterday, the *Spray,* with a crew of one man, arrived at this port yesterday afternoon on her cruise round the world. The

Captain Joshua Slocum.

Spray made quite an auspicious entrance to Natal. Her commander sailed his craft right up the channel past the main wharf, and dropped his anchor near the old *Forerunner* in the creek, before any one had a chance to get on board. The *Spray* was naturally an object of great curiosity to the Point people, and her arrival was witnessed by a large crowd. The skilful manner in which Captain Slocum steered his craft about the vessels which were occupying the waterway was a treat to witness.

The *Spray* was not sailing in among greenhorns when she came to Natal. When she arrived off the port the pilot-ship, a fine, able steam-tug, came out to meet her, and led the way in across the bar, for it was blowing a smart gale and was too rough for the sloop to be towed with safety. The trick of going in I learned by watching the steamer; it was simply to keep on the windward side of the channel and take the combers end on.

I found that Durban supported two yacht-clubs, both of them full of enterprise. I met all the members of both clubs, and sailed in the crack yacht *Florence* of the Royal Natal, with Captain Spradbrow and the Right Honorable Harry Escombe, premier of the colony. The yacht's center-board plowed furrows through the mud-banks, which, according to Mr. Escombe, Spradbrow afterward planted with potatoes. The *Florence*, however, won races while she tilled the skipper's land. After our sail on the *Florence* Mr. Escombe offered to sail the *Spray* round the Cape of Good Hope for me, and hinted at his famous cribbage-board to while away the hours. Spradbrow, in retort, warned me of it. Said he, "You would be played out of the sloop before you could round the cape." By others it was not thought probable that the premier of Natal would play cribbage off the Cape of Good Hope to win even the *Spray*.

It was a matter of no small pride to me in South Africa to find that American humor was never at a discount, and one of the best American stories I ever heard was told by the premier. At Hotel Royal one day, dining with Colonel Saunderson, M. P.,* his son, and Lieutenant Tipping, I met Mr. Stanley.[2] The great explorer was just

---

*Member of Parliament.

from Pretoria, and had already as good as flayed President Krüger[3] with his trenchant pen. But that did not signify, for everybody has a whack at Oom Paul, and no one in the world seems to stand the joke better than he, not even the Sultan of Turkey himself. The colonel introduced me to the explorer, and I hauled close to the wind, to go slow, for Mr. Stanley was a nautical man once himself,—on the *Nyanza*, I think,—and of course my desire was to appear in the best light before a man of his experience. He looked me over carefully, and said, "What an example of patience!" "Patience is all that is required," I ventured to reply. He then asked if my vessel had water-tight compartments. I explained that she was all water-tight and all compartment. "What if she should strike a rock?" he asked. "Compartments would not save her if she should hit the rocks lying along her course," said I; adding, "she must be kept away from the rocks." After a considerable pause Mr. Stanley asked, "What if a swordfish should pierce her hull with its sword?" Of course I had thought of that as one of the dangers of the sea, and also of the chance of being struck by lightning. In the case of the swordfish, I ventured to say that "the first thing would be to secure the sword." The colonel invited me to dine with the party on the following day, that we might go further into this matter, and so I had the pleasure of meeting Mr. Stanley a second time, but got no more hints in navigation from the famous explorer.

It sounds odd to hear scholars and statesmen say the world is flat; but it is a fact that three Boers favored by the opinion of President Krüger prepared a work to support that contention. While I was at Durban they came from Pretoria to obtain data from me, and they seemed annoyed when I told them that they could not prove it by my experience. With the advice to call up some ghost of the dark ages for research, I went ashore, and left these three wise men poring over the *Spray's* track on a chart of the world, which, however, proved nothing to them, for it was on Mercator's projection, and behold, it was "flat." The next morning I met one of the party in a clergyman's garb, carrying a large Bible, not different from the one I had read. He tackled me, saying, "If you respect the Word of God, you must admit that the world is flat." "If the Word of God stands on a flat world—" I began. "What!" cried he, losing himself in a passion,

and making as if he would run me through with an assagai.*
"What!" he shouted in astonishment and rage, while I jumped aside
to dodge the imaginary weapon. Had this good but misguided fa-
natic been armed with a real weapon, the crew of the *Spray* would
have died a martyr there and then. The next day, seeing him across
the street, I bowed and made curves with my hands. He responded
with a level, swimming movement of his hands, meaning "the world
is flat." A pamphlet by these Transvaal geographers, made up of ar-
guments from sources high and low to prove their theory, was
mailed to me before I sailed from Africa on my last stretch around
the globe.

While I feebly portray the ignorance of these learned men, I have
great admiration for their physical manhood. Much that I saw first
and last of the Transvaal and the Boers was admirable. It is well
known that they are the hardest of fighters, and as generous to the
fallen as they are brave before the foe. Real stubborn bigotry with
them is only found among old fogies, and will die a natural death,
and that, too, perhaps long before we ourselves are entirely free from
bigotry. Education in the Transvaal is by no means neglected, English as well as Dutch being taught to all that can afford both; but
the tariff duty on English school-books is heavy, and from necessity
the poorer people stick to the Transvaal Dutch and their flat world,
just as in Samoa and other islands a mistaken policy has kept the natives down to Kanaka.†

I visited many public schools at Durban, and had the pleasure of
meeting many bright children.

But all fine things must end, and December 14, 1897, the "crew"
of the *Spray*, after having a fine time in Natal, swung the sloop's
dinghy in on deck, and sailed with a morning land-wind, which carried her clear of the bar, and again she was "off on her alone," as they
say in Australia.

---

*South African spear.
†Properly, the Hawaiian language, but here used to mean any native Polynesian
tongue.

CHAPTER XVIII

Rounding the "Cape of Storms" in olden time—A rough Christmas—
The *Spray* ties up for a three months' rest at Cape Town—A railway
trip to the Transvaal—President Krüger's odd definition of the *Spray's*
voyage—His terse sayings—Distinguished guests on the *Spray*—
Cocoanut fiber as a padlock—Courtesies from the admiral of the
Queen's navy—Off for St. Helena—Land in sight.

The Cape of Good Hope was now the most prominent point
to pass. From Table Bay I could count on the aid of brisk
trades, and then the *Spray* would soon be at home. On the
first day out from Durban it fell calm, and I sat thinking about
these things and the end of the voyage. The distance to Table Bay,
where I intended to call, was about eight hundred miles over what
might prove a rough sea. The early Portuguese navigators, endowed with patience, were more than sixty-nine years struggling
to round this cape before they got as far as Algoa Bay, and there the
crew mutinied. They landed on a small island, now called Santa
Cruz, where they devoutly set up the cross, and swore they would
cut the captain's throat if he attempted to sail farther. Beyond this
they thought was the edge of the world, which they too believed
was flat; and fearing that their ship would sail over the brink of it,
they compelled Captain Diaz,[1] their commander, to retrace his
course, all being only too glad to get home. A year later, we are
told, Vasco da Gama sailed successfully round the "Cape of
Storms," as the Cape of Good Hope was then called, and discovered Natal on Christmas or Natal day; hence the name. From this
point the way to India was easy.[2]

Gales of wind sweeping round the cape even now were frequent
enough, one occurring, on an average, every thirty-six hours; but one
gale was much the same as another, with no more serious result than
to blow the *Spray* along on her course when it was fair, or to blow
her back somewhat when it was ahead. On Christmas, 1897, I came
to the pitch of the cape. On this day the *Spray* was trying to stand on
her head, and she gave me every reason to believe that she would ac-
complish the feat before night. She began very early in the morning

to pitch and toss about in a most unusual manner, and I have to record that, while I was at the end of the bowsprit reefing the jib, she ducked me under water three times for a Christmas box.* I got wet and did not like it a bit: never in any other sea was I put under more than once in the same short space of time, say three minutes. A large English steamer passing ran up the signal, "Wishing you a Merry Christmas." I think the captain was a humorist; his own ship was throwing her propeller out of water.

Two days later, the *Spray,* having recovered the distance lost in the gale, passed Cape Agulhas in company with the steamship *Scotsman,* now with a fair wind. The keeper of the light on Agulhas exchanged signals with the *Spray* as she passed, and afterward wrote me at New York congratulations on the completion of the voyage. He seemed to think the incident of two ships of so widely different types passing his cape together worthy of a place on canvas, and he went about having the picture made. So I gathered from his letter. At lonely stations like this hearts grow responsive and sympathetic, and even poetic. This feeling was shown toward the *Spray* along many a rugged coast, and reading many a kind signal thrown out to her gave one a grateful feeling for all the world.

One more gale of wind came down upon the *Spray* from the west after she passed Cape Agulhas, but that one she dodged by getting into Simons Bay. When it moderated she beat around the Cape of Good Hope, where they say the *Flying Dutchman*† is still sailing. The voyage then seemed as good as finished; from this time on I knew that all, or nearly all, would be plain sailing.

Here I crossed the dividing-line of weather. To the north it was clear and settled, while south it was humid and squally, with, often enough, as I have said, a treacherous gale. From the recent hard weather the *Spray* ran into a calm under Table Mountain, where she lay quietly till the generous sun rose over the land and drew a breeze in from the sea.

The steam-tug *Alert,* then out looking for ships, came to the *Spray* off the Lion's Rump,‡ and in lieu of a larger ship towed her into port.

---

*That is, a Christmas present.
†Legendary ghost ship doomed to sail stormy seas forever.
‡Promontory (now called Signal Hill) at the entrance to Table Bay, Cape Town.

The sea being smooth, she came to anchor in the bay off the city of Cape Town, where she remained a day, simply to rest clear of the bustle of commerce. The good harbor-master sent his steam-launch to bring the sloop to a berth in dock at once, but I preferred to remain for one day alone, in the quiet of a smooth sea, enjoying the retrospect of the passage of the two great capes. On the following morning the *Spray* sailed into the Alfred Dry-docks, where she remained for about three months in the care of the port authorities, while I traveled the country over from Simons Town to Pretoria, being accorded by the colonial government a free railroad pass over all the land.

The trip to Kimberley, Johannesburg, and Pretoria was a pleasant one. At the last-named place I met Mr. Krüger, the Transvaal president. His Excellency received me cordially enough; but my friend Judge Beyers, the gentleman who presented me, by mentioning that I was on a voyage around the world, unwittingly gave great offense to the venerable statesman, which we both regretted deeply. Mr. Krüger corrected the judge rather sharply, reminding him that the world is flat. "You don't mean *round* the world," said the president; "it is impossible! You mean *in* the world. Impossible!" he said, "impossible!" and not another word did he utter either to the judge or to me. The judge looked at me and I looked at the judge, who should have known his ground, so to speak, and Mr. Krüger glowered at us both. My friend the judge seemed embarrassed, but I was delighted; the incident pleased me more than anything else that could have happened. It was a nugget of information quarried out of Oom Paul, some of whose sayings are famous. Of the English he said, "They took first my coat and then my trousers." He also said, "Dynamite is the corner-stone of the South African Republic." Only unthinking people call President Krüger dull.

Soon after my arrival at the cape, Mr. Krüger's friend Colonel Saunderson,* who had arrived from Durban some time before, invited me to Newlands Vineyard, where I met many agreeable people. His Excellency Sir Alfred Milner, the governor, found time to come

---

*Colonel Saunderson was Mr. Krüger's very best friend, inasmuch as he advised the president to avast mounting guns [author's note].

Cartoon printed in the Cape Town "Owl" of March 5, 1898, in connection with an item about Captain Slocum's trip to Pretoria.

aboard with a party. The governor, after making a survey of the deck, found a seat on a box in my cabin; Lady Muriel sat on a keg, and Lady Saunderson sat by the skipper at the wheel, while the colonel, with his kodak, away in the dinghy, took snap shots of the sloop and her distinguished visitors. Dr. David Gill, astronomer royal, who was of the party, invited me the next day to the famous Cape Observatory. An hour with Dr. Gill was an hour among the stars. His discoveries in stellar photography are well known. He showed me the great astronomical clock of the observatory, and I showed him the tin clock on the *Spray,* and we went over the subject of standard time at sea, and how it was found from the deck of the little sloop without the aid of a clock of any kind. Later it was advertised that Dr. Gill would preside at a talk about the voyage of the *Spray:* that alone secured for me a full house. The hall was packed, and many were not able to get in. This success brought me sufficient money for all my needs in port and for the homeward voyage.

After visiting Kimberley and Pretoria, and finding the *Spray* all right in the docks, I returned to Worcester and Wellington, towns famous for colleges and seminaries, passed coming in, still traveling as the guest of the colony. The ladies of all these institutions of learning wished to know how one might sail round the world alone, which I thought augured of sailing-mistresses in the future instead of sailing-masters. It will come to that yet if we men-folk keep on saying we "can't."

On the plains of Africa I passed through hundreds of miles of rich but still barren land, save for scrub-bushes, on which herds of sheep were browsing. The bushes grew about the length of a sheep apart, and they, I thought, were rather long of body; but there was still room for all. My longing for a foothold on land seized upon me here, where so much of it lay waste; but instead of remaining to plant forests and reclaim vegetation, I returned again to the *Spray* at the Alfred Docks, where I found her waiting for me, with everything in order, exactly as I had left her.

I have often been asked how it was that my vessel and all appurtenances were not stolen in the various ports where I left her for days together without a watchman in charge. This is just how it was: The *Spray* seldom fell among thieves. At the Keeling Islands, at Rodriguez, and at many such places, a wisp of cocoanut fiber in the

Captain Slocum, Sir Alfred Milner (with the tall hat), and Colonel Saunderson, M. P., on the bow of the *Spray* at Cape Town.

door-latch, to indicate that the owner was away, secured the goods against even a longing glance. But when I came to a great island nearer home, stout locks were needed; the first night in port things which I had always left uncovered disappeared, as if the deck on which they were stowed had been swept by a sea.

A pleasant visit from Admiral Sir Harry Rawson of the Royal Navy and his family brought to an end the *Spray's* social relations with the Cape of Good Hope. The admiral, then commanding the South African Squadron, and now in command of the great Channel fleet, evinced the greatest interest in the diminutive *Spray* and her behavior off Cape Horn, where he was not an entire stranger. I have to admit that I was delighted with the trend of Admiral Rawson's

questions, and that I profited by some of his suggestions, notwithstanding the wide difference in our respective commands.

On March 26, 1898, the *Spray* sailed from South Africa, the land
of distances and pure air, where she had spent a pleasant and profitable time. The steam-tug *Tigre* towed her to sea from her wonted
berth at the Alfred Docks, giving her a good offing. The light morning breeze, which scantily filled her sails when the tug let go the tow-
line, soon died away altogether, and left her riding over a heavy
swell, in full view of Table Mountain and the high peaks of the Cape
of Good Hope. For a while the grand scenery served to relieve the
monotony. One of the old circumnavigators (Sir Francis Drake, I
think), when he first saw this magnificent pile, sang, " 'Tis the
fairest thing and the grandest cape I've seen in the whole circum-
ference of the earth."³

The view was certainly fine, but one has no wish to linger long to
look in a calm at anything, and I was glad to note, finally, the short
heaving sea, precursor of the wind which followed on the second
day. Seals playing about the *Spray* all day, before the breeze came,
looked with large eyes when, at evening, she sat no longer like a
lazy bird with folded wings. They parted company now, and the
Spray soon sailed the highest peaks of the mountains out of sight,
and the world changed from a mere panoramic view to the light of
a homeward-bound voyage. Porpoises and dolphins, and such other
fishes as did not mind making a hundred and fifty miles a day, were
her companions now for several days. The wind was from the southeast; this suited the *Spray* well, and she ran along steadily at her best
speed, while I dipped into the new books given me at the cape, reading day and night. March 30 was for me a fast-day in honor of them.
I read on, oblivious of hunger or wind or sea, thinking that all was
going well, when suddenly a comber rolled over the stern and
slopped saucily into the cabin, wetting the very book I was reading.
Evidently it was time to put in a reef, that she might not wallow on
her course.

March 31 the fresh southeast wind had come to stay. The *Spray*
was running under a single-reefed mainsail, a whole jib, and a
flying-jib besides, set on the Vailima bamboo, while I was reading Stevenson's delightful "Inland Voyage."⁴ The sloop was again
doing her work smoothly, hardly rolling at all, but just leaping

"Reading day and night."

along among the white horses,* a thousand gamboling porpoises keeping her company on all sides. She was again among her old friends the flying-fish, interesting denizens of the sea. Shooting out of the waves like arrows, and with outstretched wings, they sailed on the wind in graceful curves; then falling till again they touched the crest of the waves to wet their delicate wings and renew the flight. They made merry the livelong day. One of the joyful sights on the ocean of a bright day is the continual flight of these interesting fish.

---

*Cresting waves.

One could not be lonely in a sea like this. Moreover, the reading of delightful adventures enhanced the scene. I was now in the *Spray* and on the Oise in the *Arethusa* at one and the same time. And so the *Spray* reeled off the miles, showing a good run every day till April 11, which came almost before I knew it. Very early that morning I was awakened by that rare bird, the booby, with its harsh quack, which I recognized at once as a call to go on deck; it was as much as to say, "Skipper, there's land in sight." I tumbled out quickly, and sure enough, away ahead in the dim twilight, about twenty miles off, was St. Helena.

My first impulse was to call out, "Oh, what a speck in the sea!" It is in reality nine miles in length and two thousand eight hundred and twenty-three feet in height. I reached for a bottle of port-wine out of the locker, and took a long pull from it to the health of my invisible helmsman—the pilot of the *Pinta*.

CHAPTER XIX

In the isle of Napoleon's exile—Two lectures—A guest in the ghost-room at Plantation House—An excursion to historic Longwood—Coffee in the husk, and a goat to shell it—The *Spray's* ill luck with animals—A prejudice against small dogs—A rat, the Boston spider, and the cannibal cricket—Ascension Island.

I t was about noon when the *Spray* came to anchor off Jamestown, and "all hands" at once went ashore to pay respects to his Excellency the governor of the island, Sir R. A. Sterndale. His Excellency, when I landed, remarked that it was not often, nowadays, that a circumnavigator came his way, and he cordially welcomed me, and arranged that I should tell about the voyage, first at Garden Hall to the people of Jamestown, and then at Plantation House—the governor's residence, which is in the hills a mile or two back—to his Excellency and the officers of the garrison and their friends. Mr. Poole, our worthy consul, introduced me at the castle, and in the course of his remarks asserted that the sea-serpent was a Yankee.

Most royally was the crew of the *Spray* entertained by the governor. I remained at Plantation House a couple of days, and one of the rooms in the mansion, called the "west room," being haunted, the butler, by command of his Excellency, put me up in that—like a prince. Indeed, to make sure that no mistake had been made, his Excellency came later to see that I was in the right room, and to tell me all about the ghosts he had seen or heard of. He had discovered all but one, and wishing me pleasant dreams, he hoped I might have the honor of a visit from the unknown one of the west room. For the rest of the chilly night I kept the candle burning, and often looked from under the blankets, thinking that maybe I should meet the great Napoleon face to face; but I saw only furniture, and the horse-shoe that was nailed over the door opposite my bed.

St. Helena has been an island of tragedies—tragedies that have been lost sight of in wailing over the Corsican.[1] On the second day of my visit the governor took me by carriage-road through the turns over the island. At one point of our journey the road, in winding around spurs and ravines, formed a perfect W within the distance of a few rods. The roads, though tortuous and steep, were fairly good, and I was struck with the amount of labor it must have cost to build them. The air on the heights was cool and bracing. It is said that, since hanging for trivial offenses went out of fashion, no one has died there, except from falling over the cliffs in old age, or from being crushed by stones rolling on them from the steep mountains! Witches at one time were persistent at St. Helena, as with us in America in the days of Cotton Mather.[2] At the present day crime is rare in the island. While I was there, Governor Sterndale, in token of the fact that not one criminal case had come to court within the year, was presented with a pair of white gloves by the officers of justice.

Returning from the governor's house to Jamestown, I drove with Mr. Clark, a countryman of mine, to "Longwood," the home of Napoleon. M. Morilleau, French consular agent in charge, keeps the place respectable and the buildings in good repair. His family at Longwood, consisting of wife and grown daughters, are natives of courtly and refined manners, and spend here days, months, and years of contentment, though they have never seen the world beyond the horizon of St. Helena.

On the 20th of April the *Spray* was again ready for sea. Before going on board I took luncheon with the governor and his family at the castle. Lady Sterndale had sent a large fruit-cake, early in the morning, from Plantation House, to be taken along on the voyage. It was a great high-decker, and I ate sparingly of it, as I thought, but it did not keep as I had hoped it would. I ate the last of it along with my first cup of coffee at Antigua, West Indies, which, after all, was quite a record. The one my own sister made me at the little island in the Bay of Fundy, at the first of the voyage, kept about the same length of time, namely, forty-two days.

After luncheon a royal mail was made up for Ascension, the island next on my way. Then Mr. Poole and his daughter paid the *Spray* a farewell visit, bringing me a basket of fruit. It was late in the evening before the anchor was up, and I bore off for the west, loath to leave my new friends. But fresh winds filled the sloop's sails once more, and I watched the beacon-light at Plantation House, the governor's parting signal for the *Spray,* till the island faded in the darkness astern and became one with the night, and by midnight the light itself had disappeared below the horizon.

When morning came there was no land in sight, but the day went on the same as days before, save for one small incident. Governor Sterndale had given me a bag of coffee in the husk, and Clark, the American, in an evil moment, had put a goat on board, "to butt the sack and hustle the coffee-beans out of the pods." He urged that the animal, besides being useful, would be as companionable as a dog. I soon found that my sailing-companion, this sort of dog with horns, had to be tied up entirely. The mistake I made was that I did not chain him to the mast instead of tying him with grass ropes less securely, and this I learned to my cost. Except for the first day, before the beast got his sea-legs on, I had no peace of mind. After that, actuated by a spirit born, maybe, of his pasturage, this incarnation of evil threatened to devour everything from flying-jib to stern-davits. He was the worst pirate I met on the whole voyage. He began depredations by eating my chart of the West Indies, in the cabin, one day, while I was about my work for'ard, thinking that the critter was securely tied on deck by the pumps. Alas! there was not a rope in the sloop proof against that goat's awful teeth!

It was clear from the very first that I was having no luck with animals on board. There was the tree-crab from the Keeling Islands. No sooner had it got a claw through its prison-box than my sea-jacket, hanging within reach, was torn to ribbons. Encouraged by this success, it smashed the box open and escaped into my cabin, tearing up things generally, and finally threatening my life in the dark. I had hoped to bring the creature home alive, but this did not prove feasible. Next the goat devoured my straw hat, and so when I arrived in port I had nothing to wear ashore on my head. This last unkind stroke decided his fate. On the 27th of April the *Spray* arrived at Ascension, which is garrisoned by a man-of-war crew, and the boatswain of the island came on board. As he stepped out of his boat the mutinous goat climbed into it, and defied boatswain and crew. I hired them to land the wretch at once, which they were only too willing to do, and there he fell into the hands of a most excellent Scotchman, with the chances that he would never get away. I was destined to sail once more into the depths of solitude, but these experiences had no bad effect upon me; on the contrary, a spirit of charity and even benevolence grew stronger in my nature through the meditations of these supreme hours on the sea.

In the loneliness of the dreary country about Cape Horn I found myself in no mood to make one life less in the world, except in self-defense, and as I sailed this trait of the hermit character grew till the mention of killing food-animals was revolting to me. However well I may have enjoyed a chicken stew afterward at Samoa, a new self rebelled at the thought suggested there of carrying chickens to be slain for my table on the voyage, and Mrs. Stevenson, hearing my protest, agreed with me that to kill the companions of my voyage and eat them would be indeed next to murder and cannibalism.

As to pet animals, there was no room for a noble large dog on the *Spray* on so long a voyage, and a small cur was for many years associated in my mind with hydrophobia. I witnessed once the death of a sterling young German from that dreadful disease, and about the same time heard of the death, also by hydrophobia, of the young gentleman who had just written a line of insurance in his company's books for me. I have seen the whole crew of a ship scamper up the rigging to avoid a dog racing about the decks in a fit. It would never do, I thought, for the crew of the *Spray* to take a canine risk, and with these just prejudices indelibly stamped on my mind, I have, I am afraid, answered impatiently too often the query, "Didn't you have a dog?" with, "I and the dog wouldn't have been very long in the same boat, in any sense." A cat would have been a harmless animal, I dare say, but there was nothing for puss to do on board, and she is an unsociable animal at best. True, a rat got into my vessel at the Keeling Cocos Islands, and another at Rodriguez, along with a centiped stowed away in the hold; but one of them I drove out of the ship, and the other I caught. This is how it was: for the first one with infinite pains I made a trap, looking to its capture and destruction; but the wily rodent, not to be deluded, took the hint and got ashore the day the thing was completed.

It is, according to tradition, a most reassuring sign to find rats coming to a ship, and I had a mind to abide the knowing one of Rodriguez; but a breach of discipline decided the matter against him. While I slept one night, my ship sailing on, he undertook to walk over me, beginning at the crown of my head, concerning which I am always sensitive. I sleep lightly. Before his impertinence had got him even to my nose I cried "Rat!" had him by the tail, and threw him out of the companionway into the sea.

As for the centiped, I was not aware of its presence till the wretched insect, all feet and venom, beginning, like the rat, at my head, wakened me by a sharp bite on the scalp. This also was more than I could tolerate. After a few applications of kerosene the poisonous bite, painful at first, gave me no further inconvenience.

From this on for a time no living thing disturbed my solitude; no insect even was present in my vessel, except the spider and his wife, from Boston, now with a family of young spiders. Nothing, I say, till sailing down the last stretch of the Indian Ocean, where mosquitos came by hundreds from rain-water poured out of the heavens. Simply a barrel of rain-water stood on deck five days, I think, in the sun, then music began. I knew the sound at once; it was the same as heard from Alaska to New Orleans.

Again at Cape Town, while dining out one day, I was taken with the song of a cricket, and Mr. Branscombe, my host, volunteered to capture a pair of them for me. They were sent on board next day in a box labeled, "Pluto and Scamp." Stowing them away in the binnacle in their own snug box, I left them there without food till I got to sea—a few days. I had never heard of a cricket eating anything. It seems that Pluto was a cannibal, for only the wings of poor Scamp were visible when I opened the lid, and they lay broken on the floor of the prison-box. Even with Pluto it had gone hard, for he lay on his back stark and stiff, never to chirrup again.

Ascension Island, where the goat was marooned, is called the Stone Frigate, R. N., and is rated "tender"* to the South African Squadron. It lies in 7° 55′ south latitude and 14° 25′ west longitude, being in the very heart of the southeast trade-winds and about eight hundred and forty miles from the coast of Liberia. It is a mass of volcanic matter, thrown up from the bed of the ocean to the height of two thousand eight hundred and eighteen feet at the highest point above sea-level. It is a strategic point, and belonged to Great Britain before it got cold.[3] In the limited but rich soil at the top of the island, among the clouds, vegetation has taken root, and a little scientific farming is carried on under the supervision of a gentleman from Canada. Also a few cattle and sheep are pastured there for the garrison

---

*Port for supplies or repair.

mess. Water storage is made on a large scale. In a word, this heap of cinders and lava rock is stored and fortified, and would stand a siege.

Very soon after the *Spray* arrived I received a note from Captain Blaxland, the commander of the island, conveying his thanks for the royal mail brought from St. Helena, and inviting me to luncheon with him and his wife and sister at headquarters, not far away. It is hardly necessary to say that I availed myself of the captain's hospitality at once. A carriage was waiting at the jetty when I landed, and a sailor, with a broad grin, led the horse carefully up the hill to the captain's house, as if I were a lord of the admiralty, and a governor besides; and he led it as carefully down again when I returned. On the following day I visited the summit among the clouds, the same team being provided, and the same old sailor leading the horse. There was probably not a man on the island at that moment better able to walk than I. The sailor knew that. I finally suggested that we change places. "Let me take the bridle," I said, "and keep the horse from bolting." "Great Stone Frigate!" he exclaimed, as he burst into a laugh, "this 'ere 'oss wouldn't bolt no faster nor a turtle. If I didn't tow 'im 'ard we'd never get into port." I walked most of the way over the steep grades, whereupon my guide, every inch a sailor, became my friend. Arriving at the summit of the island, I met Mr. Schank, the farmer from Canada, and his sister, living very cozily in a house among the rocks, as snug as conies,* and as safe. He showed me over the farm, taking me through a tunnel which led from one field to the other, divided by an inaccessible spur of mountain. Mr. Schank said that he had lost many cows and bullocks, as well as sheep, from breakneck over the steep cliffs and precipices. One cow, he said, would sometimes hook another right over a precipice to destruction, and go on feeding unconcernedly. It seemed that the animals on the island farm, like mankind in the wide world, found it all too small.

On the 26th of April, while I was ashore, rollers came in which rendered launching a boat impossible. However, the sloop being securely moored to a buoy in deep water outside of all breakers, she was safe, while I, in the best of quarters, listened to well-told stories

---

*Rabbits.

among the officers of the Stone Frigate. On the evening of the 29th, the sea having gone down, I went on board and made preparations to start again on my voyage early next day, the boatswain of the island and his crew giving me a hearty handshake as I embarked at the jetty.

For reasons of scientific interest, I invited in mid-ocean the most thorough investigation concerning the crew-list of the *Spray*. Very few had challenged it, and perhaps few ever will do so henceforth; but for the benefit of the few that may, I wished to clench beyond doubt the fact that it was not at all necessary in the expedition of a sloop around the world to have more than one man for the crew, all told, and that the *Spray* sailed with only one person on board. And so, by appointment, Lieutenant Eagles, the executive officer, in the morning, just as I was ready to sail, fumigated the sloop, rendering it impossible for a person to live concealed below, and proving that only one person was on board when she arrived. A certificate to this effect, besides the official documents from the many consulates, health offices, and custom-houses, will seem to many superfluous; but this story of the voyage may find its way into hands unfamiliar with the business of these offices and of their ways of seeing that a vessel's papers, and, above all, her bills of health, are in order.

The lieutenant's certificate being made out, the *Spray*, nothing loath, now filled away clear of the sea-beaten rocks, and the trade-winds, comfortably cool and bracing, sent her flying along on her course. On May 8, 1898, she crossed the track, homeward bound, that she had made October 2, 1895, on the voyage out. She passed Fernando de Noronha at night, going some miles south of it, and so I did not see the island. I felt a contentment in knowing that the *Spray* had encircled the globe, and even as an adventure alone I was in no way discouraged as to its utility, and said to myself, "Let what will happen, the voyage is now on record." A period was made.

CHAPTER XX

In the favoring current off Cape St. Roque, Brazil—All at sea regarding the Spanish-American war—An exchange of signals with the battleship *Oregon*—Off Dreyfus's prison on Devil's Island—Reappearance to the *Spray* of the north star—The light on Trinidad—A charming introduction to Grenada—Talks to friendly auditors.

On May 10 there was a great change in the condition of the sea; there could be no doubt of my longitude now, if any had before existed in my mind. Strange and long-forgotten current ripples pattered against the sloop's sides in grateful music; the tune arrested the ear, and I sat quietly listening to it while the *Spray* kept on her course. By these current ripples I was assured that she was now off St. Roque and had struck the current which sweeps around that cape. The trade-winds, we old sailors say, produce this current, which, in its course from this point forward, is governed by the coastline of Brazil, Guiana, Venezuela, and, as some would say, by the Monroe Doctrine.[1]

The trades had been blowing fresh for some time, and the current, now at its height, amounted to forty miles a day. This, added to the sloop's run by the log, made the handsome day's work of one hundred and eighty miles on several consecutive days. I saw nothing of the coast of Brazil, though I was not many leagues off and was always in the Brazil current.

I did not know that war with Spain had been declared,[2] and that I might be liable, right there, to meet the enemy and be captured. Many had told me at Cape Town that, in their opinion, war was inevitable, and they said: "The Spaniard will get you! The Spaniard will get you!" To all this I could only say that, even so, he would not get much. Even in the fever-heat over the disaster to the *Maine* I did not think there would be war; but I am no politician. Indeed, I had hardly given the matter a serious thought when, on the 14th of May, just north of the equator, and near the longitude of the river Amazon, I saw first a mast, with the Stars and Stripes floating from it, rising astern as if poked up out of the sea, and then rapidly appearing on the horizon, like a citadel, the *Oregon!*[3] As she came near I saw that the great ship was flying the signals "C B T," which read, "Are there any men-of-war about?" Right under these flags, and larger than the *Spray's* mainsail, so it appeared, was the yellowest Spanish flag[4] I ever saw. It gave me nightmare some time after when I reflected on it in my dreams.

I did not make out the *Oregon's* signals till she passed ahead, where I could read them better, for she was two miles away, and I had no binoculars. When I had read her flags I hoisted the signal "No," for I had not seen any Spanish men-of-war; I had not been looking for any. My final signal, "Let us keep together for mutual protection," Captain Clark did not seem to regard as necessary. Perhaps my small flags were not made out; anyhow, the *Oregon* steamed on with a rush, looking for Spanish men-of-war, as I learned afterward. The *Oregon's* great flag was dipped beautifully three times to the *Spray's* lowered flag as she passed on. Both had crossed the line only a few hours before. I pondered long that night over the probability of a war risk now coming upon the *Spray* after she had cleared all, or nearly all, the dangers of the sea, but finally a strong hope mastered my fears.

On the 17th of May, the *Spray,* coming out of a storm at daylight, made Devil's Island,* two points on the lee bow, not far off. The wind was still blowing a stiff breeze on shore. I could clearly see the dark-gray buildings on the island as the sloop brought it abeam. No flag or sign of life was seen on the dreary place.

Later in the day a French bark on the port tack, making for Cayenne, hove in sight, close-hauled on the wind. She was falling to leeward fast. The *Spray* was also closed-hauled, and was lugging on sail to secure an offing on the starboard tack, a heavy swell in the night having thrown her too near the shore, and now I considered the matter of supplicating a change of wind. I had already enjoyed my share of favoring breezes over the great oceans, and I asked myself if it would be right to have the wind turned now all into my sails while the Frenchman was bound the other way. A head current, which he stemmed, together with a scant wind, was bad enough for him. And so I could only say, in my heart, "Lord, let matters stand as

---

*French penal colony.

THOMAS FOGARTY.

The *Spray* passed by the *Oregon*.

they are, but do not help the Frenchman any more just now, for what would suit him well would ruin me!"

I remembered that when a lad I heard a captain often say in meeting that in answer to a prayer of his own the wind changed from southeast to northwest, entirely to his satisfaction. He was a good man, but did this glorify the Architect—the Ruler of the winds and the waves? Moreover, it was not a trade-wind, as I remember it, that changed for him, but one of the variables which will change when you ask it, if you ask long enough. Again, this man's brother maybe was not bound the opposite way, well content with a fair wind himself, which made all the difference in the world.*

On May 18, 1898, is written large in the *Spray's* log-book: "To-night, in latitude 7° 13′ N., for the first time in nearly three years I see the north star." The *Spray* on the day following logged one hundred and forty-seven miles. To this I add thirty-five miles for current sweeping her onward. On the 20th of May, about sunset, the island of Tobago, off the Orinoco, came into view, bearing west by north, distant twenty-two miles. The *Spray* was drawing rapidly toward her home destination. Later at night, while running free along the coast of Tobago, the wind still blowing fresh, I was startled by the sudden flash of breakers on the port bow and not far off. I luffed instantly offshore, and then tacked, heading in for the island. Finding myself, shortly after, close in with the land, I tacked again offshore, but without much altering the bearings of the danger. Sail whichever way I would, it seemed clear that if the sloop weathered the rocks at all it would be a close shave, and I watched with anxiety, while beating against the current, always losing ground. So the matter stood hour after hour, while I watched the flashes of light thrown up as regularly as the beats of the long ocean swells, and always they seemed just a little nearer. It was evidently a coral reef,—of this I had not the slightest doubt,—and a bad reef at that. Worse still, there might be other reefs ahead forming a bight into which the current would sweep me, and where I should be hemmed in and finally wrecked.

---

*The Bishop of Melbourne (commend me to his teachings) refused to set aside a day of prayer for rain, recommending his people to husband water when the rainy season was on. In like manner, a navigator husbands the wind, keeping a weather-gage where practicable [author's note].

I had not sailed these waters since a lad, and lamented the day I had allowed on board the goat that ate my chart. I taxed my memory of sea lore, of wrecks on sunken reefs, and of pirates harbored among coral reefs where other ships might not come, but nothing that I could think of applied to the island of Tobago, save the one wreck of Robinson Crusoe's ship in the fiction, and that gave me little information about reefs. I remembered only that in Crusoe's case he kept his powder dry. "But there she booms again," I cried, "and how close the flash is now! Almost aboard was that last breaker! But you'll go by, *Spray,* old girl! 'Tis abeam now! One surge more! and oh, one more like that will clear your ribs and keel!" And I slapped her on the transom, proud of her last noble effort to leap clear of the danger, when a wave greater than the rest threw her higher than before, and, behold, from the crest of it was revealed at once all there was of the reef. I fell back in a coil of rope, speechless and amazed, not distressed, but rejoiced. Aladdin's lamp! My fisherman's own lantern! It was the great revolving light on the island of Trinidad, thirty miles away, throwing flashes over the waves, which had deceived me! The orb of the light was now dipping on the horizon, and how glorious was the sight of it! But, dear Father Neptune, as I live, after a long life at sea, and much among corals, I would have made a solemn declaration to that reef! Through all the rest of the night I saw imaginary reefs, and not knowing what moment the sloop might fetch up on a real one, I tacked off and on till daylight, as nearly as possible in the same track, all for the want of a chart. I could have nailed the St. Helena goat's pelt to the deck.

My course was now for Grenada, to which I carried letters from Mauritius. About midnight of the 22d of May I arrived at the island, and cast anchor in the roads off the town of St. George, entering the inner harbor at daylight on the morning of the 23d, which made forty-two days' sailing from the Cape of Good Hope. It was a good run, and I doffed my cap again to the pilot of the *Pinta.*

Lady Bruce, in a note to the *Spray* at Port Louis, said Grenada was a lovely island, and she wished the sloop might call there on the voyage home. When the *Spray* arrived, I found that she had been fully expected. "How so?" I asked. "Oh, we heard that you were at Mauritius," they said, "and from Mauritius, after meeting Sir Charles Bruce, our old governor, we knew you would come to Grenada."

This was a charming introduction, and it brought me in contact with people worth knowing.

The *Spray* sailed from Grenada on the 28th of May, and coasted along under the lee of the Antilles, arriving at the island of Dominica on the 30th, where, for the want of knowing better, I cast anchor at the quarantine ground; for I was still without a chart of the islands, not having been able to get one even at Grenada. Here I not only met with further disappointment in the matter, but was threatened with a fine for the mistake I made in the anchorage. There were no ships either at the quarantine or at the commercial roads, and I could not see that it made much difference where I anchored. But a negro chap, a sort of deputy harbor-master, coming along, thought it did, and he ordered me to shift to the other anchorage, which, in truth, I had already investigated and did not like, because of the heavier roll there from the sea. And so instead of springing to the sails at once to shift, I said I would leave outright as soon as I could procure a chart, which I begged he would send and get for me. "But I say you mus' move befo' you gets anyt'ing 't all," he insisted, and raising his voice so that all the people alongshore could hear him, he added, "An' jes now!" Then he flew into a towering passion when they on shore snickered to see the crew of the *Spray* sitting calmly by the bulwark instead of hoisting sail. "I tell you dis am quarantine," he shouted, very much louder than before. "That's all right, general," I replied; "I want to be quarantined anyhow." "That's right, boss," some one on the beach cried, "that's right; you get quarantined," while others shouted to the deputy to "make de white trash move 'long out o' dat." They were about equally divided on the island for and against me. The man who had made so much fuss over the matter gave it up when he found that I wished to be quarantined, and sent for an all-important half-white, who soon came alongside, starched from clue to earing. He stood in the boat as straight up and down as a fathom of pump-water—a marvel of importance. "Charts!" cried I, as soon as his shirt-collar appeared over the sloop's rail; "have you any charts?" "No, sah," he replied with much-stiffened dignity; "no, sah; cha'ts do'sn't grow on dis island." Not doubting the information, I tripped anchor immediately, as I had intended to do from the first, and made all sail for St. John, Antigua, where I arrived on the 1st of June, having sailed with great caution in midchannel all the way.

The *Spray,* always in good company, now fell in with the port officers' steam-launch at the harbor entrance, having on board Sir Francis Fleming, governor of the Leeward Islands, who, to the delight of "all hands," gave the officer in charge instructions to tow my ship into port. On the following day his Excellency and Lady Fleming, along with Captain Burr, R. N., paid me a visit. The court-house was tendered free to me at Antigua, as was done also at Grenada, and at each place a highly intelligent audience filled the hall to listen to a talk about the seas the *Spray* had crossed, and the countries she had visited.

CHAPTER XXI

Clearing for home—In the calm belt—A sea covered with sargasso—
The jibstay parts in a gale—Welcomed by a tornado off Fire Island—A
change of plan—Arrival at Newport—End of a cruise of over forty-six
thousand miles—The *Spray* again at Fairhaven.

O n the 4th of June, 1898, the *Spray* cleared from the United
States consulate, and her license to sail single-handed, even
round the world, was returned to her for the last time. The
United States consul, Mr. Hunt, before handing the paper to me,
wrote on it, as General Roberts had done at Cape Town, a short
commentary on the voyage. The document, by regular course, is
now lodged in the Treasury Department at Washington, D. C.

On June 5, 1898, the *Spray* sailed for a home port, heading first
direct for Cape Hatteras. On the 8th of June she passed under the
sun from south to north; the sun's declination on that day was
22° 54′, and the latitude of the *Spray* was the same just before noon.
Many think it is excessively hot right under the sun. It is not necessarily so. As a matter of fact the thermometer stands at a bearable
point whenever there is a breeze and a ripple on the sea, even exactly
under the sun. It is often hotter in cities and on sandy shores in
higher latitudes.

The *Spray* was booming joyously along for home now, making
her usual good time, when of a sudden she struck the horse latitudes, and her sail flapped limp in a calm.[1] I had almost forgotten
this calm belt, or had come to regard it as a myth. I now found it
real, however, and difficult to cross. This was as it should have been,
for, after all of the dangers of the sea, the dust-storm on the coast of
Africa, the "rain of blood" in Australia, and the war risk when nearing home, a natural experience would have been missing had the
calm of the horse latitudes been left out. Anyhow, a philosophical
turn of thought now was not amiss, else one's patience would have
given out almost at the harbor entrance. The term of her probation
was eight days. Evening after evening during this time I read by the
light of a candle on deck. There was no wind at all, and the sea became

smooth and monotonous. For three days I saw a full-rigged ship on the horizon, also becalmed.

Sargasso,* scattered over the sea in bunches, or trailed curiously along down the wind in narrow lanes, now gathered together in great fields, strange sea-animals, little and big, swimming in and out, the most curious among them being a tiny sea-horse which I captured and brought home preserved in a bottle. But on the 18th of June a gale began to blow from the southwest, and the sargasso was dispersed again in windrows and lanes.

On this day there was soon wind enough and to spare. The same might have been said of the sea The *Spray* was in the midst of the turbulent Gulf Stream itself. She was jumping like a porpoise over the uneasy waves. As if to make up for lost time, she seemed to touch only the high places. Under a sudden shock and strain her rigging began to give out. First the main-sheet strap was carried away, and then the peak halyard-block broke from the gaff. It was time to reef and refit, and so when "all hands" came on deck I went about doing that.

The 19th of June was fine, but on the morning of the 20th another gale was blowing, accompanied by cross-seas that tumbled about and shook things up with great confusion. Just as I was thinking about taking in sail the jibstay broke at the masthead, and fell, jib and all, into the sea. It gave me the strangest sensation to see the bellying sail fall, and where it had been suddenly to see only space. However, I was at the bows, with presence of mind to gather it in on the first wave that rolled up, before it was torn or trailed under the sloop's bottom. I found by the amount of work done in three minutes' or less time that I had by no means grown stiff-jointed on the voyage; anyhow, scurvy had not set in, and being now within a few degrees of home, I might complete the voyage, I thought, without the aid of a doctor. Yes, my health was still good, and I could skip about the decks in a lively manner, but could I climb? The great King Neptune tested me severely at this time, for the stay being gone, the mast itself switched about like a reed, and was not easy to climb; but a gun-tackle purchase was got up, and the stay set taut from the

---

*Floating masses of seaweed, common in warm gulf waters.

masthead, for I had spare blocks and rope on board with which to rig it, and the jib, with a reef in it, was soon pulling again like a "sodger" for home. Had the *Spray's* mast not been well stepped, however, it would have been "John Walker" when the stay broke. Good work in the building of my vessel stood me always in good stead.

On the 23d of June I was at last tired, tired, tired of baffling squalls and fretful cobble-seas. I had not seen a vessel for days and days, where I had expected the company of at least a schooner now and then. As to the whistling of the wind through the rigging, and the slopping of the sea against the sloop's sides, that was well enough in its way, and we could not have got on without it, the *Spray* and I; but there was so much of it now, and it lasted so long! At noon of that day a winterish storm was upon us from the nor'west. In the Gulf Stream, thus late in June, hailstones were pelting the *Spray,* and lightning was pouring down from the clouds, not in flashes alone, but in almost continuous streams. By slants, however, day and night I worked the sloop in toward the coast, where, on the 25th of June, off Fire Island, she fell into the tornado which, an hour earlier, had swept over New York city with lightning that wrecked buildings and sent trees flying about in splinters; even ships at docks had parted their moorings and smashed into other ships, doing great damage. It was the climax storm of the voyage, but I saw the unmistakable character of it in time to have all snug aboard and receive it under bare poles. Even so, the sloop shivered when it struck her, and she heeled over unwillingly on her beam ends; but rounding to, with a sea-anchor ahead, she righted and faced out the storm. In the midst of the gale I could do no more than look on, for what is a man in a storm like this? I had seen one electric storm on the voyage, off the coast of Madagascar, but it was unlike this one. Here the lightning kept on longer, and thunderbolts fell in the sea all about. Up to this time I was bound for New York; but when all was over I rose, made sail, and hove the sloop round from starboard to port tack, to make for a quiet harbor to think the matter over; and so, under short sail, she reached in for the coast of Long Island, while I sat thinking and watching the lights of coasting-vessels which now began to appear in sight. Reflections of the voyage so nearly finished stole in upon me now; many tunes I had hummed again and again came back once more. I found myself repeating fragments of a hymn often sung by a dear Christian woman of Fairhaven when I was rebuilding the *Spray*. I was to hear once more and only once, in profound solemnity, the metaphorical hymn:

> By waves and wind I'm tossed and driven.

And again:

> But still my little ship outbraves
> The blust'ring winds and stormy waves.[2]

After this storm I saw the pilot of the *Pinta* no more.

The experiences of the voyage of the *Spray*, reaching over three years, had been to me like reading a book, and one that was more and more interesting as I turned the pages, till I had come now to the last page of all, and the one more interesting than any of the rest.

When daylight came I saw that the sea had changed color from dark green to light. I threw the lead and got soundings in thirteen fathoms. I made the land soon after, some miles east of Fire Island, and sailing thence before a pleasant breeze along the coast, made for Newport. The weather after the furious gale was remarkably fine. The *Spray* rounded Montauk Point early in the afternoon; Point Judith was abeam at dark; she fetched in at Beavertail next. Sailing on, she had one more danger to pass—Newport harbor was mined.* The *Spray* hugged the rocks along where neither friend nor foe could come if drawing much water, and where she would not disturb the guard-ship in the channel. It was close work, but it was safe enough so long as she hugged the rocks close, and not the mines. Flitting by a low point abreast of the guard-ship, the dear old *Dexter*,† which I knew well, some one on board of her sang out, "There goes a craft!" I threw up a light at once and heard the hail, "*Spray*, ahoy!" It was the voice of a friend, and I knew that a friend would not fire on the *Spray*. I eased off the main-sheet now, and the *Spray* swung off for the beacon-lights of the inner harbor. At last she reached port in

---

*Because of the Spanish-American War (see chapter XX, note 2).
†The *Samuel Dexter*, built in 1874, was patrolling the minefields.

safety, and there at 1 A. M. on June 27, 1898, cast anchor, after the cruise of more than forty-six thousand miles round the world, during an absence of three years and two months, with two days over for coming up.

Was the crew well? Was I not? I had profited in many ways by the voyage. I had even gained flesh, and actually weighed a pound more than when I sailed from Boston. As for aging, why, the dial of my life was turned back till my friends all said, "Slocum is young again." And so I was, at least ten years younger than the day I felled the first tree for the construction of the *Spray*.

My ship was also in better condition than when she sailed from Boston on her long voyage. She was still as sound as a nut, and as tight as the best ship afloat. She did not leak a drop—not one drop! The pump, which had been little used before reaching Australia, had not been rigged since that at all.

The first name on the *Spray's* visitors' book in the home port was written by the one who always said, "The *Spray* will come back."[3] The *Spray* was not quite satisfied till I sailed her around to her birthplace, Fairhaven, Massachusetts, farther along. I had myself a desire to return to the place of the very beginning whence I had, as I have said, renewed my age. So on July 3, with a fair wind, she waltzed beautifully round the coast and up the Acushnet River to Fairhaven, where I secured her to the cedar spile driven in the bank to hold her when she was launched. I could bring her no nearer home.

If the *Spray* discovered no continents on her voyage, it may be that there were no more continents to be discovered; she did not seek new worlds, or sail to powwow about the dangers of the seas. The sea has been much maligned. To find one's way to lands already discovered is a good thing, and the *Spray* made the discovery that even the worst sea is not so terrible to a well-appointed ship. No king, no country, no treasury at all, was taxed for the voyage of the *Spray*, and she accomplished all that she undertook to do.

To succeed, however, in anything at all, one should go understandingly about his work and be prepared for every emergency. I see, as I look back over my own small achievement, a kit of not too elaborate carpenters' tools, a tin clock, and some carpet-tacks, not a great many, to facilitate the enterprise as already mentioned in the story. But above all to be taken into account were some years of

The *Spray* in the storm off New York.

schooling, where I studied with diligence Neptune's laws, and these laws I tried to obey when I sailed overseas; it was worth the while.

And now, without having wearied my friends, I hope, with detailed scientific accounts, theories, or deductions, I will only say that I have endeavored to tell just the story of the adventure itself. This, in my own poor way, having been done, I now moor ship, weather-bitt cables, and leave the sloop *Spray*, for the present, safe in port.

Again tied to the old stake at Fairhaven.

APPENDIX

Lines and Sail-Plan of the *Spray*

Her pedigree so far as known—The Lines of the *Spray*—Her self-steering qualities—Sail-plan and steering-gear—An unprecedented feat—A final word of cheer to would-be navigators.

From a feeling of diffidence toward sailors of great experience, I refrained, in the preceding chapters as prepared for serial publication in the "Century Magazine," from entering fully into the details of the *Spray's* build, and of the primitive methods employed to sail her. Having had no yachting experience at all, I had no means of knowing that the trim vessels seen in our harbors and near the land could not all do as much, or even more, than the *Spray,* sailing, for example, on a course with the helm lashed.

I was aware that no other vessel had sailed in this manner around the globe, but would have been loath to say that another could not do it, or that many men had not sailed vessels of a certain rig in that manner as far as they wished to go. I was greatly amused, therefore, by the flat assertions of an expert that it could not be done.[1]

The *Spray,* as I sailed her, was entirely a new boat, built over from a sloop which bore the same name, and which, tradition said, had first served as an oysterman, about a hundred years ago, on the coast of Delaware. There was no record in the custom-house of where she was built. She was once owned at Noank, Connecticut, afterward in New Bedford and when Captain Eben Pierce presented her to me, at the end of her natural life, she stood, as I have already described, propped up in a field at Fairhaven. Her lines were supposed to be those of a North Sea fisherman. In rebuilding timber by timber and plank by plank, I added to her freeboard twelve inches amidships, eighteen inches forward, and fourteen inches aft, thereby increasing her sheer, and making her, as I thought, a better deep-water ship. I will not repeat the history of the rebuilding of the *Spray,* which

I have detailed in my first chapter, except to say that, when finished, her dimensions were thirty-six feet nine inches over all, fourteen feet two inches wide, and four feet two inches deep in the hold, her tonnage being nine tons net, and twelve and seventy one-hundredths tons gross.

I gladly produce the lines of the *Spray*, with such hints as my really limited fore-and-aft sailing will allow, my seafaring life having been spent mostly in barks and ships. No pains have been spared to give them accurately. The *Spray* was taken from New York to Bridgeport, Connecticut, and, under the supervision of the Park City Yacht Club, was hauled out of water and very carefully measured in every way to secure a satisfactory result. Captain Robins produced the model. Our young yachtsmen, pleasuring in the "lilies of the sea,"* very naturally will not think favorably of my craft. They have a right to their opinion, while I stick to mine. They will take exceptions to her short ends, the advantage of these being most apparent in a heavy sea.

Some things about the *Spray's* deck might be fashioned differently without materially affecting the vessel. I know of no good reason why for a party-boat a cabin trunk might not be built amidships instead of far aft, like the one on her, which leaves a very narrow space between the wheel and the line of the companionway. Some even say that I might have improved the shape of her stern. I do not know about that. The water leaves her run sharp after bearing her to the last inch, and no suction is formed by undue cutaway.

Smooth-water sailors say, "Where is her overhang?" They never crossed the Gulf Stream in a nor'easter, and they do not know what is best in all weathers. For your life, build no fantail overhang on a craft going offshore. As a sailor judges his prospective ship by a "blow of the eye" when he takes interest enough to look her over at all, so I judged the *Spray*, and I was not deceived.

In a sloop-rig the *Spray* made that part of her voyage reaching from Boston through the Strait of Magellan, during which she experienced the greatest variety of weather conditions. The yawl-rig then adopted was an improvement only in that it reduced the size of a rather heavy mainsail and slightly improved her steering qualities

---

*Common phrase that Slocum applies to fancy and pretentious yachts.

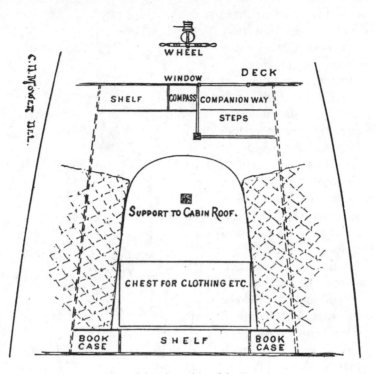

Plan of the after cabin of the *Spray*.

on the wind. When the wind was aft the jigger was not in use; invariably it was then furled. With her boom broad off and with the wind two points on the quarter the *Spray* sailed her truest course. It never took long to find the amount of helm, or angle of rudder, required to hold her on her course, and when that was found I lashed the wheel with it at that angle. The mainsail then drove her, and the main-jib, with its sheet boused flat amidships or a little to one side or the other, added greatly to the steadying power. Then if the wind was even strong or squally I would sometimes set a flying-jib also, on a pole rigged out on the bowsprit, with the sheets hauled flat amidships, which was a safe thing to do, even in a gale of wind. A stout downhaul on the gaff was a necessity, because without it the mainsail might not have come down when I wished to lower it in a breeze. The amount of helm required varied according to the amount of wind and its direction. These points are quickly gathered from practice.

Briefly I have to say that when close-hauled in a light wind under all sail she required little or no weather helm. As the wind increased I would go on deck, if below, and turn the wheel up a spoke more or less, relash it, or, as sailors say, put it in a becket, and then leave it as before.

To answer the questions that might be asked to meet every contingency would be a pleasure, but it would overburden my book. I can only say here that much comes to one in practice, and that, with such as love sailing, mother-wit is the best teacher, after experience. Labor-saving appliances? There were none. The sails were hoisted by hand; the halyards were rove through ordinary ships' blocks with common patent rollers. Of course the sheets were all belayed aft.

The windlass used was in the shape of a winch, or crab, I think it is called. I had three anchors, weighing forty pounds, one

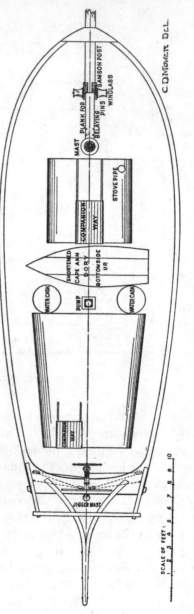

Deck-plan of the *Spray*.

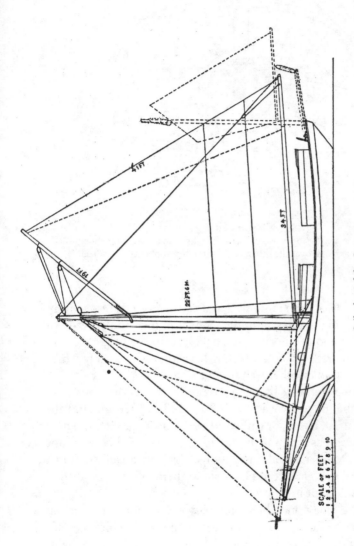

Sail-plan of the *Spray*.

The solid lines represent the sail-plan of the *Spray* on starting for the long voyage. With it she crossed the Atlantic to Gibraltar, and then crossed again southwest to Brazil. In South American waters the bowsprit and boom were shortened and the jigger-sail added to form the yawl-rig with which the rest of the trip was made, the sail-plan of which is indicated by the dotted lines. The extreme sail forward is a flying jib occasionally used, set to a bamboo stick fastened to the bowsprit. The manner of setting and bracing the jigger-mast is not indicated in this drawing, but may be partly observed in the plans on pages 230 and 232.

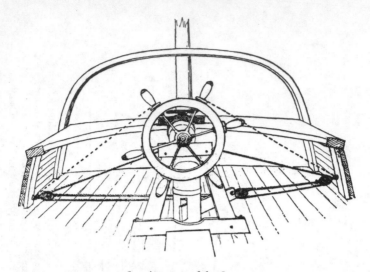

Steering-gear of the *Spray*.
The dotted lines are the ropes used to lash the wheel. In practice the loose ends
were belayed, one over the other, around the top spokes of the wheel.

hundred pounds, and one hundred and eighty pounds respectively. The windlass and the forty-pound anchor, and the "fiddle-head," or carving, on the end of the cutwater, belonged to the original *Spray*. The ballast, concrete cement, was stanchioned down securely. There was no iron or lead or other weight on the keel.

If I took measurements by rule I did not set them down, and after sailing even the longest voyage in her I could not tell offhand the length of her mast, boom, or gaff. I did not know the center of effort in her sails, except as it hit me in practice at sea, nor did I care a rope yarn about it. Mathematical calculations, however, are all right in a good boat, and the *Spray* could have stood them. She was easily balanced and easily kept in trim.

Some of the oldest and ablest shipmasters have asked how it was possible for her to hold a true course before the wind, which was just what the *Spray* did for weeks together. One of these gentlemen, a highly esteemed shipmaster and friend, testified as government expert in a famous murder trial in Boston, not long since, that a ship would not hold her course long enough for the steersman to leave the helm to cut the captain's throat.[2] Ordinarily it would be so. One might say that with a square-rigged ship it would always be so. But the *Spray*, at the moment of the tragedy in question, was sailing around the globe with no one at the helm, except at intervals more or less rare. However, I may say here that this would have had no bearing on the murder case in Boston. In all probability Justice laid her hand on the true rogue. In other words, in the case of a model and rig similar to that of the tragedy ship, I should myself testify as did the nautical experts at the trial.

But see the run the *Spray* made from Thursday Island to the Keeling Cocos Islands, twenty-seven hundred miles distant, in twenty-three days, with no one at the helm in that time, save for about one hour, from land to land. No other ship in the history of the world ever performed, under similar circumstances, the feat on so long and continuous a voyage. It was, however, a delightful midsummer sail. No one can know the pleasure of sailing free over the great oceans save those who have had the experience. It is not necessary, in order to realize the utmost enjoyment of going around the globe, to sail alone, yet for once and the first time there was a great deal of fun in it. My friend the government expert, and saltest of salt sea-captains, standing only yesterday on the deck of the *Spray*, was convinced of her famous qualities, and he spoke enthusiastically of selling his farm on Cape Cod and putting to sea again.

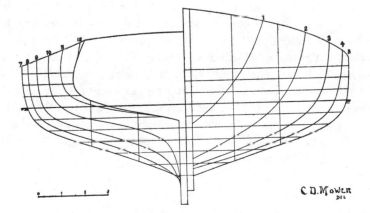

Body-plan of the *Spray*.

To young men contemplating a voyage I would say go. The tales of rough usage are for the most part exaggerations, as also are the stories of sea danger. I had a fair schooling in the so-called "hard ships" on the hard Western Ocean* and in the years there I do not remember having once been "called out of my name."† Such recollections have endeared the sea to me. I owe it further to the officers of all the ships I ever sailed in as boy and man to say that not one ever lifted so much as a finger to me. I did not live among angels, but among men who could be roused. My wish was, though, to please the officers of my ship wherever I was, and so I got on. Dangers there are, to be sure, on the sea as well as on the land, but the intelligence and skill God gives to man reduce these to a minimum. And here comes in again the skilfully modeled ship worthy to sail the seas.

To face the elements is, to be sure, no light matter when the sea is in its grandest mood. You must then know the sea, and know that you know it, and not forget that it was made to be sailed over.

I have given in the plans of the *Spray* the dimensions of such a ship as I should call seaworthy in all conditions of weather and on all seas. It is only right to say, though, that to insure a reasonable measure of success, experience should sail with the ship. But in order to be a successful navigator or sailor it is not necessary to hang a tar-bucket about one's neck. On the other hand, much thought concerning the brass buttons one should wear[3] adds nothing to the safety of the ship.

I may some day see reason to modify the model of the dear old *Spray,* but out of my limited experience I strongly recommend her wholesome lines over those of pleasure-fliers for safety. Practice in a craft such as the *Spray* will teach young sailors and fit them for the more important vessels. I myself learned more seamanship, I think, on the *Spray* than on any other ship I ever sailed, and as for patience, the greatest of all the virtues, even while sailing through the reaches of the Strait of Magellan, between the bluff mainland and dismal Fuego, where through intricate sailing I was obliged to steer, I learned to sit by the wheel, content to make ten miles a day beating

---

*The Pacific Ocean, notorious for long and difficult voyages.
†Reprimanded.

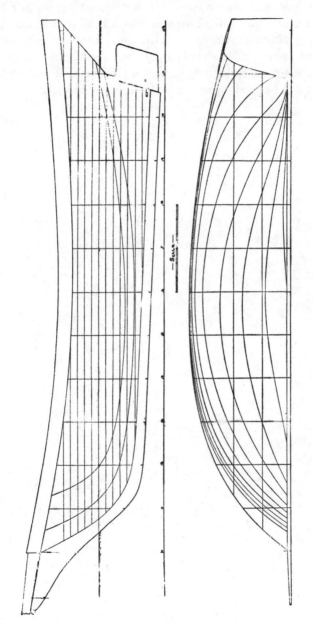

-Scale-

Lines of the *Spray.*

against the tide, and when a month at that was all lost, I could find some old tune to hum while I worked the route all over again, beating as before. Nor did thirty hours at the wheel, in storm, overtax my human endurance, and to clap a hand to an oar and pull into or out of port in a calm was no strange experience for the crew of the *Spray.* The days passed happily with me wherever my ship sailed.

Endnotes

Chapter I

1. (p. 19) *Sailors' Snug Harbor:* Founded in 1833 on Staten Island, New York, this was a privately endowed retirement home for sailors. At its peak in 1900, it had 1,000 men in residence. The institution remained active until 1976, when it was moved to North Carolina, and the original site became a National Historic Landmark and cultural center. A second retirement home with the same name was founded in Boston in 1852 and is now a private foundation. By Slocum's time, the term had become synonymous with retirement from seafaring and didn't necessarily refer to any one place.

2. (p. 19) *Captain Eben Pierce:* A former whaling captain, Pierce (c.1822–1902) had known Slocum since 1889. In 1865 Pierce invented the "darting gun," one of the first explosive devices attached to a harpoon, a device that made him wealthy.

3. (p. 20) *declaring that he could see no reason why the* Spray *should not "cut in bow-head" yet off the coast of Greenland:* The bowhead whale, also known as the Greenland right whale, inhabits Arctic and subarctic waters of the Northern Hemisphere. The captain's remark is intended to praise the *Spray*'s sturdy construction, which made it strong enough to keep a whale alongside while "cutting in" (stripping blubber from the carcass).

4. (p. 20) *John Cook:* John Cooke (c.1608–1695) was the first white inhabitant of Fairhaven, Massachusetts, and the last surviving male passenger of the *Mayflower*, which carried the Pilgrims from England to Massachusetts. The exact location of Cooke's grave is uncertain.

5. (p. 21) *Lloyd's:* Slocum does not refer to the famous English insurance company of this name, but to *Lloyd's Register of Shipping*, established in 1760. This annual register records all the ships built in a given year and certifies their dimensions, condition, quality, and so forth.

Chapter II

1. (p. 26) Venetian: This 423-foot British steamship struck submerged rocks in thick fog and snow on March 2, 1895, and broke in half two days later. No one was killed, but the ship was a total loss.

2. (p. 26) *I heard the clanking of the dismal bell on Norman's Woe as we went*

by; and the reef where the schooner Hesperus *struck:* Numerous ships were wrecked in the harbor of Gloucester, Massachusetts, in a huge blizzard on December 17, 1839. One of American poet Henry Wadsworth Longfellow's most famous ballads, "The Wreck of the Hesperus" (1842), is a fictional version of the event. Slocum, an admirer of Longfellow's poetry, probably knew the final lines by heart: "Such was the wreck of the Hesperus, / In the midnight and the snow! / Christ save us all from a death like this, / On the reef of Norman's Woe!"

3. (p. 28) *where the Dutchman left his anchor:* This is a slang naval saying for anything that has been left behind. It comes from the legend of a Dutch captain who explained that he wrecked his ship because he had an excellent anchor but had left it at home during that voyage.

4. (p. 32) *Dr. Nansen sailed in search of the north pole with his crew of thirteen. Perhaps he had heard of my success in taking a most extraordinary ship successfully to Brazil with that number of crew:* The Norwegian Arctic explorer Fridtjof Nansen (1861–1930) attempted unsuccessfully to reach the North Pole during the years 1893–1896. Slocum's "extraordinary ship" was the *Destroyer,* a warship he was commissioned to deliver to Brazil in 1893 (see "Introduction," p. xxv).

Chapter III

1. (p. 34) *the liner* Atlantic, *on the night of her terrible disaster:* On April 1, 1873, this White Star steamship collided with submerged rocks in a heavy gale off Mars Head, Nova Scotia, 22 miles west of Halifax; of its 945 passengers and crew, 562 perished, including all women and children except for one young boy. At the time, it was the worst North Atlantic shipwreck since 1707, when the British navy sank two French ships in Martinique Bay, Newfoundland.

2. (p. 35) *the friendly Gulf Stream:* This warm ocean current originates in the western Atlantic and then flows northward along the coast of South America, through the Gulf of Mexico, and up the eastern coast of the United States and Canada. Some of the densest fogs in the world form where the Gulf Stream meets the cold waters of the Labrador Current, off the Grand Banks of Newfoundland.

3. (p. 37) *I sang "Johnny Boker," and "We'll Pay Darby Doyl for his Boots,"* . . . *"Babylon's a-Fallin' ":* The first two are sea chanteys, songs sailors sing while they haul on the ropes or manage the sails. The third, "Babylon Is Fallen" (1863), was a popular song by American songwriter Henry Clay

Work that was inspired by the recruitment of slaves into the Union Army during the American Civil War.

4. (p. 37) *Her sails were trimmed like the sails of the nautilus:* The paper nautilus, or argonaut, is an octopus-like cephalopod. The female paper nautilus builds a thin shell for laying eggs and guards the eggs with sail-like flaps attached to its tentacles, which it spreads over the shell opening. Many sailors falsely believed the animal used these flaps as sails for locomotion.

5. (p. 40) *"and oh, how green the corn!":* Slocum slightly misquotes a line from Scottish author Robert Louis Stevenson's poem "The Country of the Camisards" (1879): "And O, how deep the corn."

6. (p. 42) *He had sailed out of New Bedford, so he said, for "that Joe Wing they call 'John' ":* Joseph and John Wing were members of a prominent New Bedford family that controlled the largest fleet of American whale ships by 1870.

Chapter IV

1. (p. 49) *I sat for hours reading the life of Columbus:* Slocum carried with him American author Washington Irving's popular biography *A History of the Life and Voyages of Christopher Columbus* (1828), for years considered a standard work (see "Introduction," p. xxiii).

2. (p. 52) *Morse geography:* Slocum refers to the geography textbooks of American clergyman Jedidiah Morse (1761–1826), known as "the father of American geography"; these books (the first was issued in 1784) became widely used in American schoolrooms during the nineteenth century.

Chapter V

1. (p. 62) *the rebel Mello:* Admiral Custodio de Mello (1845?–1902) led an unsuccessful rebellion against the republic of Brazil in 1893–1894. He commanded the gunboat that turned Slocum away from Rio de Janeiro in January 1887, the first of many setbacks that led to the loss of the *Aquidneck* later that year (see "Introduction," p. xx).

2. (p. 62) *his armada, a fleet of boats including a Chinese sampan, a Norwegian pram, and a Cape Ann dory:* Slocum is having some fun at the doctor's expense. These are all small, lightweight boats that are often poorly constructed and unseaworthy.

Chapter VI

1. (p. 70) *better cheer than I had found at Maldonado once upon a time when I entered the port with a stricken crew in my bark, the* Aquidneck: As he describes in *Voyage of the Liberdade* (1890), when Slocum discovered his crew was infected with smallpox, he tried to put in at Maldonado but was turned away. He had to make sail into a hurricane with a sick crew, during what he called "the most dismal of all my nights at sea" (Slocum, *The Voyages of Joshua Slocum*, p. 68; see "For Further Reading").

2. (p. 73) *the lemon "went on forever":* This is a possible allusion to "The Brook: An Idyl," by English poet Alfred, Lord Tennyson (1809–1892): "For men may come and men may go, / But I go on forever."

Chapter VIII

1. (p. 89) *the old fisherman prayed, "Remember, Lord, my ship is small and thy sea is so wide!":* Sometimes called the "Breton Fisherman's Prayer," this is a folk saying popular among sailors.

2. (p. 92) *The great naturalist Darwin . . . wrote in his journal, "Any landsman seeing the Milky Way would have nightmare for a week":* Charles Darwin (1809–1882) was the official naturalist aboard the *Beagle*, an English ship that sailed around the world from 1831 to 1836 on a famous voyage of exploration and discovery. Slocum carried Darwin's account of this expedition on the *Spray* and here paraphrases the following passage from chapter 11: "We passed out between the East and West Furies; and a little farther northward there are so many breakers that the sea is called the Milky Way. One sight of such a coast is enough to make a landsman dream for a week about shipwrecks, peril, and death" (*Narrative of the Surveying Voyages of His Majesty's Ships Adventure and Beagle*, London: Henry Colburn, 1839, vol. 3, p. 307). Darwin's account is popularly known as *Voyage of the Beagle*.

3. (p. 94) *it was no Elysian shore:* In Greek mythology, Elysium is the happy place where the souls of the good and heroic abide after death. It is sometimes portrayed as an island.

4. (p. 96) *old chants:* In the first edition of *Sailing Alone Around the World* (1900), Slocum identifies these as "Blow, Boys, Blow for Californy, O" and "The Sweet By and By." By combining a sea chantey about going to the California gold fields with a Protestant hymn about going to heaven, Slocum intermixes the secular and the sacred, as he does with his previous references to Neptune and God. The last five sentences of this paragraph are

one of the few passages in the 1901 text that revise the first edition and may reveal the hand of squeamish *Century* editors who feared offending their religious readers. A few lines before, someone substituted the sentence "Dismal Famine Reach!" for Slocum's mildly blasphemous sentence "I could have wished it Jericho!"—meaning he would have preferred to be anywhere else.

Chapter IX

1. (p. 99) *spider, slain the day before . . . "Bruce"*: The allusion is to Scottish patriot and king Robert the Bruce (1274–1329), who was supposedly so inspired by the perseverance of a spider he observed while he was in exile that he returned to Scotland and succeeded in driving out the English invaders.
2. (p. 99) *a smart Martini-Henry rifle*: This was the standard British army rifle from 1871 to 1904. It was a single-shot weapon, which means that later in the narrative (see p. 101) Slocum is lying about the rifle's capabilities.
3. (p. 103) Colombia . . . *wrecked on the rocks of the California coast*: The *Colombia* went aground between San Francisco and Santa Cruz, California, on July 14, 1896.

Chapter X

1. (p. 112) *Professor Dusen*: Botanist Per Carl Hjalmar Dusén (1855–1926) specialized in studying peat moss in Patagonia and Brazil.

Chapter XI

1. (p. 121) *The cave in which Selkirk dwelt . . . Robinson Crusoe Bay*: English novelist Daniel Defoe based his novel *The Life and Strange Surprizing Adventures of Robinson Crusoe* (1719) on Scottish sailor Alexander Selkirk's lonely sojourn on one of the Juan Fernández islands.
2. (p. 124) *the moon being "in distance" with the sun, I threw up my sextant for sights*: Both the sun and moon are clearly visible, which allows Slocum to measure the moon's distance from the sun to determine his longitude. This is a good example of lunar navigation.

Chapter XII

1. (p. 127) *which, like Joseph's coat, was made of many pieces*: The Bible, Genesis 37:3, refers to Joseph's "coat of many colours" (King James version). It may or may not have been made of "many pieces," like Slocum's patchwork mainsail.

2. (p. 129) *General Churchill:* William Churchill (1859–1920), author of three books on Polynesian migration, language, and culture, was United States consul-general to Samoa (1896–1899).

3. (p. 130) *Mrs. Robert Louis Stevenson . . . invited me to Vailima:* Frances Osbourne née Van de Grift (1840–1914), an American, divorced her husband and married Scottish author Robert Louis Stevenson in 1880. Stevenson was eleven years younger than his wife and suffered from tuberculosis. In 1889 the couple moved to Samoa for Stevenson's health. They purchased 314 acres on the slopes of Mount Vaea and built Vailima (Samoan for "Five Waters"), a spacious, modern mansion that became famous throughout the South Pacific for its hospitality and lavish lifestyle. The Samoans deeply appreciated the Stevensons, and when Robert died in 1894 he was buried atop Mount Vaea. Vailima and his grave became a shrine for literary pilgrims, of which Slocum, a great admirer of Stevenson's writing, may be counted among the first.

4. (p. 136) *"The Watch on the Rhine":* This patriotic German poem was composed in 1840 by Max Schneckenburger and set to music in 1854 by Karl Wilhelm. It became the anthem for the Prussian army in the Franco-Prussian War of 1870–1871 and was strongly associated with German nationalism and militarism. Of the three Western powers vying for control of Samoa—Germany, Britain, and the United States—Germany was the least favored by native Samoans. One reason for Robert Louis Stevenson's popularity in Samoa was his opposition to German rule. Slocum seems unaware of this irony.

Chapter XIII

1. (p. 138) *the king himself, the late Malietoa:* Malietoa Laupepa (1841–1898) was in his fourth and last term as king of Samoa, having ruled for eighteen of the last twenty-four years. Malietoa is a title, not a name.

2. (p. 138) *Mr. W——— of New York:* Adam Willis Wagnalls (1843–1924), a cofounder of the Funk and Wagnalls publishing company, was an ordained Lutheran minister before he began his business career in 1877. His daughter, Mabel, was one of Slocum's most enthusiastic supporters (see chapter XXI, note 3).

3. (p. 139) *Basil Hall's fine description of the great cape:* Basil Hall (1788–1844) was a British naval officer, explorer, and travel writer who rounded Cape Horn in 1820. His memorable description of the cape in *Extracts from a*

Journal, Written on the Coasts of Chile, Peru, and Mexico (2 volumes, 1824) was reprinted frequently throughout the nineteenth century.

4. (p. 141) *the Sydney harbor police-boat . . . gathered data from an old scrap-book of mine, which seemed to interest them:* This is a good example of Slocum's deliberate omission of uncomfortable incidents. Henry A. Slater, the mate whom Slocum had imprisoned on the *Northern Light* in 1883 (see "Introduction," p. xix), was now living in Sydney. He began attacking Slocum in public even before the *Spray* arrived, and on the eve of Slocum's arrival the *Sydney Daily Telegraph* published Slater's scurrilous accusations at length. Slocum defended himself by sharing with reporters and police a number of clippings from American newspapers that gave his side of the matter. He then confronted Slater in Water Police Court, where the judge ordered Slater to post bond and remain silent for six months. Many locals took Slater's side, but the controversy soon diminished, and Slocum enjoyed a two-month stay at Sydney.

Chapter XIV

1. (p. 152) *Beaconsfield and the great Tasmania gold-mine:* Between 1877 and 1914, the Tasmania Gold Mine produced $450 million worth of gold and made Beaconsfield one of Tasmania's most prosperous and famous towns.

2. (p. 153) *a "Tommy Atkins" song:* "Tommy Atkins" was a generic term for the typical British soldier that originated in the eighteenth century. The popular music-hall song "Private Tommy Atkins" was published in 1893, with lyrics by Henry Hamilton and music by S. Potter. It praises the "Tommy's" courage and sense of duty in carrying out England's imperial mission. Slocum may be referring to this particular song or one similar to it.

3. (p. 157) *Akbar was not her registered name, which need not be told [author's note]:* Again, Slocum avoids stating controversial facts. When he related the story to his son Victor, he maintained that the pleasure craft's real name was *Guinevere* and was owned by Mr. Moncton and crewed by his friends Burton and Cox. "They were," adds Victor, "a spectacle of both contempt and pity, the very kind that brings amateur seamanship into disrepute" (Victor Slocum, *Capt. Joshua Slocum,* p. 346).

Chapter XV

1. (p. 164) *Captain Cook:* James Cook (1728–1779), English navigator and explorer, made the first accurate maps of eastern Australia on his voyage

around the world in the *Endeavour* (1768–1771). On a later voyage, Cook was killed by natives on the island of Hawaii.

2. (p. 165) *I was reminded of distressful days gone by. I think it was in 1866:* Slocum means 1861, when he took his first voyage to the Far East on the *Tanjore* and was left ill with fever in hospital in Batavia (present-day Jakarta, Indonesia). Captain Airy of the *Soushay* rescued him and restored him to health.

3. (p. 165) *Judge Chester, . . . who annexed the island of New Guinea to Great Britain:* In another example of Western imperialism in the South Seas, Henry N. Chester, police magistrate of Thursday Island, Queensland, Australia, peremptorily claimed New Guinea for the British crown in 1883. The British government refused to accept the new territory, but changed its mind the following year and in 1885 divided the island with Germany.

4. (p. 168) *Queen's diamond jubilee:* June 22, 1897, was the sixtieth anniversary of the reign of Queen Victoria (1819–1901), the longest-reigning monarch in British history.

5. (p. 168) *a scientific expedition in charge of Professor Mason Bailey:* Frederick Manson Bailey (1827–1915) was an Australian botanist who wrote numerous books and reports on the plant life of Queensland.

6. (p. 169) *I had been off that cape once:* In 1883 Slocum was homeward bound around the Cape of Good Hope in the *Northern Light* and nearly lost her in high winds and heavy seas. The ship lost its rudder head, sprang a leak, and had to jettison much of its cargo to remain stable. It required two months in a South African port to repair the damage.

Chapter XVI

1. (p. 175) *Findlay's "Sailing Directory":* Slocum is referring to Alexander George Findlay's *A Directory for the Navigation of the Indian Ocean* (London: R. H. Laurie, 1876). This is very likely one of the volumes Slocum received from Fanny Stevenson (see pp. 130–131).

2. (p. 175) *there is a chronological discrepancy:* Slocum's note about "a chronological discrepancy" is correct. John Clunies-Ross (1786–1854), a Scottish adventurer, first touched at the Keeling, or Cocos, Islands in 1825, not 1814. He returned in 1827 with his family and established extensive coconut plantations. Ross's employer, Alexander Hare, had already settled on the islands in 1826, and both men claimed the territory for themselves. The islands have only 5.6 square miles of land area, and relations between the two claimants were poor. Hare left in 1831, and the islands were de-

clared a British possession in 1857. In 1886 they were attached to Britain's Straits Settlements (a collective name for former British colonies in Southeast Asia) and granted to the Ross family in perpetuity. This led to the popular but false idea that the family had established a monarchy. In 1978 the Ross family sold the islands to Australia.

3. (p. 182) *Islands of the Blessed:* In Greek and Roman mythology, these were imaginary islands in the far west where the favorites of the gods live after their death in eternal joy.

Chapter XVII

1. (p. 187) *having . . . discovered a new and hardy plant, to my great honor named it "Slocum":* The tropical hibiscus "Slocum" is listed among the thousands of varieties of *Hibiscus rosa-sinensis*, a widespread and popular species of plants with large, colorful, showy flowers.

2. (p. 193) *Mr. Stanley:* Henry Morton Stanley (1841–1904) was an Anglo-American journalist who became famous when he went to Africa and located the Scottish missionary David Livingstone in 1871. He navigated the Congo River from its source to the sea, circumnavigated the Victoria Nyanza (Lake Victoria), and helped the Belgians organize the Congo Free State. At the time of Slocum's visit, he had become a British subject and was a member of the British Parliament.

3. (p. 194) *President Krüger:* Paul Kruger (1825–1904), nicknamed "Oom Paul" by his countrymen, was a pioneer South African soldier and politician. As a Boer, one of the Dutch settlers of South Africa, he resisted British domination and helped achieve the independence of the Dutch-speaking Republic of Transvaal in 1881. He served as its president from 1883 to 1903. Political tensions between Britain and the Transvaal ran high in the late 1890s and erupted in the South African War of 1899–1902.

Chapter XVIII

1. (p. 196) *Captain Diaz:* Bartolomeu Dias (died 1500) was a Portuguese navigator who in 1488 was the first European to round the Cape of Good Hope.

2. (p. 196) *Vasco da Gama sailed successfully round the . . . Cape of Good Hope. . . . From this point the way to India was easy:* Portuguese navigator Vasco da Gama (c.1469–1524) sailed around the Cape of Good Hope on his voyage to India (1497–1499). He was the first European to sail to India.

3. (p. 202) *Sir Francis Drake . . . sang "'Tis the fairest thing . . . of the earth":* Drake (1540?–1596) was the first Englishman to sail around the world

(1577–1580). The quotation is not from Drake but is a rough paraphrase from Richard Hakluyt, *The Principall Navigations, Voiages, and Discoveries of the English Nation* (London, 1589), a frequently reprinted collection of narratives much read by sailors.

4. (p. 202) *Stevenson's delightful "Inland Voyage":* An *Inland Voyage* (1878) was Robert Louis Stevenson's first published book. It describes his youthful journey on the Oise and other rivers in Belgium and France in the canoe *Arethusa*.

Chapter XIX

1. (p. 205) *the great Napoleon . . . St. Helena . . . Corsican:* Napoléon Bonaparte (1769–1821) was a brilliant French general who declared himself emperor of the French in 1804. He was born in Corsica, an island in the Mediterranean, and after his defeat at Waterloo in 1815 the Allies exiled him to St. Helena, a British possession.

2. (p. 206) *Witches at one time were persistent at St. Helena, as with us in America in the days of Cotton Mather:* Mather (1663–1728) was a Puritan minister and historian in early Massachusetts who ardently believed in witchcraft. His writings helped provoke the Salem witchcraft trials (1692) and defended the execution of witches.

3. (p. 209) *Ascension Island . . . a mass of volcanic matter . . . belonged to Great Britain before it got cold:* This is a good example of Slocum's wry commentary on history and politics. He humorously implies that Britain, in its unceasing quest for imperial dominion, had claimed Ascension Island before the lava that formed it had a chance to cool.

Chapter XX

1. (p. 212) *Monroe Doctrine:* This is another joking political reference with overtones of imperialism. In his address to Congress in 1823, President James Monroe called for an end to European intervention in the Western Hemisphere. By Slocum's time, this policy was being used to justify the United States conquests in Latin America and the Pacific.

2. (p. 212) *I did not know that war with Spain had been declared:* Slocum is referring to the brief Spanish-American War of 1898, fought over Spanish policies in Cuba and U.S. expansionist policies. War fever broke out in the United States when the U.S. battleship *Maine* exploded and sank in Havana harbor on February 15, 1898, killing 260 men. Spain declared war on the United States on April 24, and Congress responded in kind the next

day. Given the fact that the Spanish fleet gathered in Havana harbor on May 19 and was blockaded there on May 28, it's unlikely Slocum was ever in any danger.

3. (p. 212) Oregon: Commissioned in 1896, the *Oregon* represented America's bid to become a great naval power. She was specifically designed for long-range cruising, and at 348 feet in length and 11,688 tons she was among the largest and swiftest ships in the fleet. When Slocum hailed her she was on her way from the Pacific Ocean to bolster the Navy in Cuba. She steamed 14,700 miles in sixty-seven days, an amazingly fast voyage that caught the imagination of the American public and made the ship a symbol of American naval power.

4. (p. 213) *yellowest Spanish flag:* The Spanish flag of 1898 had three bright-yellow horizontal stripes and two red horizontal stripes. The *Oregon* is indicating that it specifically seeks Spanish "men-o'-war" (battleships).

Chapter XXI

1. (p. 219) *she struck the horse latitudes, and her sail flapped limp in a calm:* The horse latitudes are two zones of high atmospheric pressure and light winds located approximately at latitudes 30 degrees north and south.

2. (p. 222) *the metaphorical hymn: By waves and wind . . . / . . . and stormy waves:* This hymn appears anonymously in Rice Haggard's *A Selection of Christian Hymns* (Lexington, KY: John Norvell, Printer, 1818, pp. 348–351), where it is called the "Sailor's Song" and sung to the tune "Lenox." Through thirteen stanzas the hymn develops an elaborate comparison between sailing and Christian faith. It uses such metaphors as "my anchor, hope," "a heavenly breeze," "my quadrant, faith," "my Bible is my chart," and "pilot angels." Slocum remembers almost verbatim three lines from the first two stanzas.

3. (p. 223) *The first name . . . was written by the one who always said, "The Spray will come back":* Mabel Wagnalls (1871–1946), the only daughter of Adam Willis Wagnalls (see chapter XIII, note 2), visited the *Spray* just before Slocum embarked on his voyage in 1895. When he returned she encouraged him to write up his experiences, and he gratefully dedicated *Sailing Alone* to her. See "Introduction," p. xiii.

Appendix

1. (p. 227) *the flat assertions of an expert that it could not be done:* While Slocum's narrative was appearing in the *Century*, an anonymous *New York*

Times columnist began questioning whether the *Spray* could really steer herself. Slocum defended his sloop in a letter to the *Times*, but the columnist remained unconvinced and wrote two more articles raising the same issue. The Appendix is partly intended to answer such criticisms.

2. (p. 233) *testified . . . in a famous murder trial in Boston . . . that a ship would not hold her course long enough for the steersman to leave the helm to cut the captain's throat:* In the spring of 1898, Thomas M. Bram was tried for the ax murder of his captain, the captain's wife, and the second mate while at sea on the *Herbert Fuller*. The defense claimed that the helmsman, not Bram, left his post to commit the murders, but thirty-nine shipmasters testified that no one could leave the helm long enough to kill three people without taking the ship off course. Bram was convicted and sentenced to life in prison; he was pardoned in 1919 by President Woodrow Wilson.

3. (p. 234) *to hang a tar-bucket . . . brass buttons one should wear:* Slocum contrasts the ordinary sailor who spends his days spreading pine tar on ropes with the officers who wear coats with fancy buttons. Either extreme can be a pose, and neither is required for good seamanship.

Glossary of Nautical Terms

This is a comprehensive list of all the nautical terms Slocum uses. Many terms have additional meanings, and many can be used as both nouns and verbs. The definitions below give the minimum information necessary so that general readers will understand the basic meaning of each term in the context of Slocum's narrative. These meanings may not apply in other contexts. For simplicity's sake, usually only the relevant definition is provided.

Slocum often uses obsolete or antiquated terms that might not appear in other nautical glossaries. These are not specifically noted, but sometimes more modern synonyms are given. He also uses various spellings, and variants are given only when his practice might be confusing.

Just as with modern automobiles or computers, every part of a ship has its own name. Ropes are named for their function (whether they are used for hauling or for support, for instance), and masts and sails are named for their position. Because Slocum was a shipbuilder as well as a sailor, he uses many technical terms for a ship's structure. These can be quite specific, and readers who wish to know more should consult a reference work on wooden ships that includes diagrams, plans, and cross-sections.

abeam   90 degrees off a ship's bow, or front.

aft   At or toward a ship's stern, or rear.

amidships   At a ship's midsection.

anti-trade winds (anti-trade clouds)   Wind currents above 6,000 feet found in the trade wind regions that flow from the equator toward either pole.

astern   Toward a ship's stern, or rear; used generally in place of "behind."

athwartships   At right angles to the ship.

avast   The order to stop a current activity.

bark   Three-masted vessel with square sails on the first two masts (foremast and mainmast) and fore-and-aft sails on the third mast (mizzenmast).

barkantine   Three-masted vessel with square sails on the first mast (foremast) and fore-and-aft sails on the second and third masts (mainmast and mizzenmast).

barrel-buoy   Floating barrel anchored to the bottom and used as a marker at sea.

beacon rocks   Landmarks used for guidance.

beam   A ship's greatest width.

beam ends   Ends of a ship's crossbeams; a ship that is listing so far over on its side that its beam (width) is almost vertical with the water is said to be "on her beam ends."

beating   Sailing into the wind on a zigzag course. See *tack*.

becket   Short rope used to secure the wheel, another rope, or any similar object.

before the wind   Sailing with the wind astern, or behind.

belay   (1) To wrap a rope around a cleat or belaying pin. (2) To cancel an order.

bells   Ship's days are divided into six four-hour increments, or watches; during each watch, a bell is struck every half hour, with the number of strikes increasing from one to eight times, after which a new watch begins.

bend   (1) To tie or knot ropes. (2) To fasten a sail to its yard or boom.

bight   Slight recess or shallow bay in a shoreline or line of reefs.

binnacle   Covered stand, sometimes lighted, that protects the compass.

board   Leg on a tack or zigzag course when a ship sails as directly into the wind as it can.

bobbed   Shortened or reduced.

bobstay   Rope or chain running from under the bow to the end of the bowsprit; this counteracts the pull of the forestay, the rope running from the bowsprit to the foremast.

bonnet   Additional piece of sail added to the bottom of a jib (a triangular sail on the bow).

boom   Spar that secures the bottom of a fore-and-aft sail and extends in one direction from a mast.

boot-topping   Applying a protective coating to the hull to prevent the growth of marine organisms.

bouse   Usually "bowse"; to haul a rope or tackle downward.

bow   Forepart of a ship, particularly the tapering prow or front.

bowsprit   Spar extending from a ship's bow forward and over the water.

brace   To turn the yards, or horizontal spars that secure the top and bottom of squaresails; also, the ropes used for this maneuver.

breast-hook   Wood or iron plate used to reinforce a ship's frame at the bow.

broach   When a vessel under sail with the wind astern accidentally turns so that the wind blows against its side, a maneuver that could dismast or capsize a small vessel.

bulwark(s)   Low wooden wall around the upper deck.

burton   Small tackle, or combination of ropes and pulleys used for hoisting.

butts   Two planks that meet endwise.

by and large   Sailing close to the wind but not too close; adopted more widely to mean "on the whole" or "generally."

cabin trunk   Also *cabin top*; a raised ceiling built above decks that allows more headroom below decks.

cable   Measure of distance that varies according to country; in the U.S. Navy, a cable is 120 fathoms or 720 feet.

capstan-head   Top of a winch mounted on deck and used for heavy lifting.

card   Circular card of a magnetic compass that attaches to the needles and rotates with them to indicate direction.

cat   To attach the anchor to the cat-head.

cat-head   Wooden beam on a ship's bow to which the anchor is attached; named for the cat's head carved on the end of early beams.

cat's-paw   Ripple on a calm sea caused by a light, distant breeze.

center of effort   Point on a sail through which the sum of the wind's driving forces appear to act; knowing the center of effort allows sailors to fine-tune the opposing forces of wind and wave for maximum speed.

charter-party   Contract between a ship owner and a merchant to transport goods to a particular place for a fixed sum of money.

chronometer   Very accurate clock set to Greenwich mean time and used for navigation.

cleat   Piece of wood or metal used to secure ropes.

close aboard   Nearby.

close-reefed sails   Sails with all sections, or reefs, folded, but not actually furled, so as to reduce the area.

clue   Usually "clew"; lower corner of a sail.

coasting-packet   Strictly, a mail boat sailing between coastal ports; Slocum seems to use the term more generally.

cobble-seas   Rough seas with small waves in contrary directions.

cockswain   Usually "coxswain"; person who steers a small boat.

combing seas   Rough, white-water seas with large, breaking waves.

companionway   Stairs leading from the deck into a cabin below.

crab-windlass   Small manual winch for taking in cables.

cutaway   Angle at which a ship's prow meets the water; Slocum uses the term to refer to the stern.

cutwater   Structural timber in the prow.

dead-reckoning   Estimating a ship's position from its speed and direction from the last clearly determined position.

dinghy   Small rowboat.

dip-net   Small net for scooping fish out of the water.

dory   Small, flat-bottomed rowboat.

down-haul   Rope used to pull down small sails that may not fall from their own weight, such as a jib.

duff   Simple pudding of flour, water, and various fruits or flavorings.

earing   Short piece of rope used to tie a sail to its appropriate yard or boom.

false keel   Length of wood or other cushioning material that runs outside along the centerline of a ship's bottom to protect the actual keel.

fantail overhang   Elliptical section of deck that extends over the water from a ship's stern.

fathom   Unit of measurement equal to 6 feet.

fender   Protective cushion or bumper on a ship's hull.

fiddle-head   Piece of wood carved like a scroll and used in place of a figure-head.

fill away   To manage the sails so that they catch the full force of the wind.

fish   To repair or strengthen a spar by binding additional pieces of wood to it.

flaw   Sudden burst of wind.

flying-jib   Foremost sail on a ship; a triangular sail running from the foremast to the outermost part of the bowsprit.

fore-and-aft   Sails rigged lengthwise from front to rear, as opposed to square-sails, which are rigged crosswise; may be triangular like a jib or quadrilateral like Slocum's mainsail.

forecastle   Compartment in a ship's front, or bow; usually the crew's living quarters.

forepeak   Space that is farthest forward in a ship's front, or bow.

fore-scuttle   Covered opening in the front part of the deck.

forestaysail   Triangular sail rigged along an immovable rope or stay running from the foremast to the bowsprit.

freeboard   Distance between the waterline and the upper deck.

free sheet   Mainsail with the rope tied off and unattended; possible only in steady winds and currents.

furl   To roll up a sail and secure it to its yard or boom.

gaff   (1) Hook for spearing fish and bringing them aboard. (2) Spar extending in one direction off a mast and used to hold the upper edge of a quadrilateral fore-and-aft sail.

galley   A ship's kitchen.

gammon   Rope securing the bowsprit to stout timbers in a ship's prow.

garboard   Planks of the hull that fit into the keel, the frame's central longitudinal timber.

goose's wing mainsail   Configuration that reduces sail area by pulling up the lower inside corner of the mainsail.

gun-tackle purchase   Contrivance consisting of two pulleys and one rope.

gunwale   Raised upper edge around a vessel's perimeter.

halyard   Rope used for hoisting or lowering sails or yards; also spelled "halliard."

hard down   To the full extent, usually said when putting the helm completely in one direction.

haul   Change in the direction of the wind over the bows.

hawse   Space in a ship's bow near the hawseholes, holes through which the anchor cables run.

head   Generally, the upper or front part of anything; for example, a ship's forward area.

head-gear   Any of the ropes or netting in the bow.

head-sail   General term for any of the triangular sails mounted forward and attached at one end to the bowsprit.

heart-yarn   Inner strand in a rope.

heel   As a noun, the lower part of the stern where the keel meets the rudder; as a verb, to lean to one side; in reference to masts, the base of the mast that joins the keel.

helm   Steering apparatus.

holding-ground   Place to set anchor.

hood   (1) Covering over a hatch. (2) Either end of the hull's planking (afterhood and forehood).

hooker   Contemptuous term for an antiquated or clumsy ship.

hove down   Beached and turned on its side for repair.

hull down   When a ship at sea is so distant that its hull cannot be seen but its masts are visible.

jaws   Mechanism that secures a gaff to a mast.

jib   Triangular sail extending from the foremast to the bowsprit or jib boom (spar extending forward from the bowsprit).

jibe   Sudden shift from one side to the other.

jib-halyard   Rope used to hoist the jib.

jibstay   Fixed rope from which the jib extends.

jigger mast   Mast rigged astern to set a small extra sail.

jigger spread   Sail plan that includes a jigger mast and sail.

jumbo   Largest and inmost triangular sail, set on a fixed rope or stay between the foremast and bowsprit.

jury-sail   Temporary or makeshift sail.

kedge-anchor   Light anchor that can be carried a distance from the ship and dropped; the ship may then be winched up to it.

keel   Sturdy beam that runs along the lower centerline of the frame from front to back like a backbone.

keelhauling   Punishment in which a person is bound and dragged underneath a ship from one side to the other.

keelson   Plank or beam mounted internally above the keel and floor-timbers for extra strength.

knot   When referring to speed, a knot is a nautical mile, or 6,080 feet, per hour.

lanyard   Short length of rope securing a longer rope, such as a stay.

lay to   To remain stationary.

lead   Cylindrical piece of lead tied to a rope and cast overboard to determine the water's depth; it usually has wax on one end to pick up sand or mud from the sea floor for inspection.

league   Measure of distance, used here to indicate about 3½ miles (measurement varies according to country).

lee, leeward   Direction the wind blows toward; when you face leeward, the wind is at your back.

leech   Back edge of a fore-and-aft sail (the edge farthest from the mast), or either side of a squaresail.

lighter   Boat used to transport cargo between a ship and shore.

light-ship   Permanently anchored vessel supplied with a powerful beacon to warn ships of nautical dangers; used in place of a lighthouse.

lubberly   Clumsy, unskilled in seamanship.

luff   To sail more directly into the wind.

mainsail   Largest sail, here a quadrilateral sail on the mainmast.

main-sheet   Rope attached to a lower corner of the mainsail and used to adjust it.

main-sheet strap   Rope around a pulley attached to the main-sheet.

mast   Slender vertical timber set in a ship's keel and rising above the deck to support a sail and necessary spar such as a yard or boom. Additional support comes from ropes tied to the sides, back, and front of the ship. Most masts consist of more than one section—for example, a lower mast and a topmast. Ships are identified by the number of masts they carry as well as the type and configuration of their sails.

masthead   Topmost portion of a mast.

meridian altitude   Angle or height of a celestial body, measured by an arc extending from the horizon along the observer's line of longitude.

night-heads Properly "knightheads," the timbers that hold the base of the bowsprit.

oakum Caulking made by impregnating the fibers of old hempen ropes with pine tar, or resin.

offing A position in sight of the shore while being safely away from it.

on the wind Sailing at an angle into the wind.

patent log Manufactured device towed from the stern to measure distance.

patent reefer Thick, short cloth coat, or pea jacket.

patent roller Manufactured part of a block that allows ropes to move through it smoothly.

peak halliards Usually "peak halyards," ropes used for lowering a gaff from its outer end.

peak halyard-block Pulley attached to the ropes on the outer end of a gaff.

pilot Qualified local person who knows the particular characteristics of a harbor or channel and is taken aboard as a temporary navigator.

pin Specifically, a metal axle on which blocks or pulleys revolve; Slocum may mean any sharp projection likely to cut flesh.

point Properly "reef-point"; light rope attached to a sail and used to tie up a section to reduce the overall sail area.

points The thirty-two divisions on the compass card; one point is 11 degrees and 15 minutes.

poise The way a ship holds herself in the water.

poop-deck Raised deck at the stern, sometimes doubling as the roof of a cabin.

port The left side, or in a leftward direction; the older term was "larboard."

position by account Estimated location, determined by speed and direction; similar to dead-reckoning, except the latter may include the current and other factors.

pugh Long-handled hooked prong for snaring fish; also "pew."

quarter Curved rear side of a vessel.

razeed To have the upper deck cut away; therefore, anything with a part removed to reduce its size.

reach Straight course through a bend in a channel.

reaching   Sailing any course except one with the wind behind.

reef   As a noun, the horizontal section of sail that may be folded and secured to reduce its area; as a verb, to reduce sail area by folding and securing a portion of the sail.

reeve   To pass a rope through a hole in a block, ringbolt, or other fixture.

ribs   Curving vertical frames of a ship's hull.

rope-yarn   Hemp threads twisted together to make up larger strands.

rotator   Part of the patent log that revolves and indicates distance traveled.

rove   Past tense of reeve.

rudder   Hinged device at the stern that extends into the water and controls a vessel's direction.

saddle   Block of wood fixed to a spar and forming a base for another spar.

schooner   Vessel with anywhere from two to six masts and carrying fore-and-aft sails.

scudding   Sailing with the wind behind the vessel and with sufficient speed to keep waves from breaking over the stern.

scupper   Side gutter that drains water off the deck.

sea-anchor   Any floating device, such as a canvas bag or a crossed pair of oars, that can be thrown overboard to create a drag and keep a vessel to the wind.

settle   To ease slightly or slacken.

sewed   Said of a ship that has run aground; the amount she has sewed is given as the difference between the actual water level and her floating line.

sextant   Device for measuring the height and angles of heavenly bodies, thus allowing mariners to determine their position at sea.

sheer   Sidelong curve of a ship's deck from front to back.

sheet   Rope fastened to the lower corner of a sail for adjusting it.

sheet-strop   Section of rope around a block.

ship   (1) To place in its proper position. (2) To bring onto the ship.

shoe   Plank attached underneath the false keel for additional protection.

shorten sail   To reduce the area of sail.

skiff   Any small, flat-bottomed boat with a sharp prow and square stern.

slant   Wind of short duration.

slip   As a noun, Slocum seems to use this as slang for leeway, the difference between a vessel's forward and lateral movement; as a verb, to detach an anchor's cables for a speedy departure (as opposed to hoisting the anchor aboard).

sloop   One-masted vessel with fore-and-aft sails and a headsail; this is the *Spray*'s original rig.

spinnaker   Large, baggy triangular sail set opposite to the mainsail on its own boom and used when sailing before the wind.

squall   Sudden, brief storm with heavy rain and strong winds.

squaresail   Rectangular sail that hangs from spars (yards) set perpendicularly to masts; Slocum uses one without yards in an emergency.

stanchion   To secure a load between decks by propping a timber between it and the ceiling.

starboard quarter   Right-hand rear curved section of a vessel.

stay   Any fixed rope used to support various masts, spars, and sails.

stays   To put a ship in stays is to change its direction.

stay-sail-sheet   Immovable rope on which a small triangular sail is hoisted.

steelyard   Balance scale with a counterweight at one end.

stem   As a noun, the upright beam of a vessel's bow; as a verb, to make headway against an opposing current or wind.

stem-piece   Lower beam of the stem that connects it to the keel.

stern   Rear of a vessel.

stern-davits   Projections from the stern used to raise and lower a small boat. Slocum uses the phrase figuratively, since the *Spray* carries its spare boat on deck and has no davits.

stand offshore   To hold a course away from shore.

stradding   Wrapping a portion of a cable in leather to protect it from rubbing against a hard surface.

stranded   Said of a rope that breaks from chafing or strain.

tack   Sail with the wind blowing across the front or bow of the ship.

tar-bucket   Receptacle that holds the pine sap used to waterproof ropes and other cordage.

throat-halyard   Rope used for hoisting and lowering a gaff from the inboard end.

throat (of a mainsail)   Upper forward corner of a large quadrilateral sail.

tide-race   Strong current caused by tides striking a promontory and sweeping around it at increased speed.

tonnage   Amount of weight a merchant vessel can carry as cargo; also "tons."

tonnage dues   Fees charged by port officials and assessed according to cargo capacity.

topmast   Vertical timber set above the lower mast; see *mast*.

trade winds   Winds on either side of the equator that blow consistently in predictable directions; *trade* here means "track," not "commerce."

transom   Planking across the upper part of a vessel's rear, or stern.

trim   As a noun, the horizontal angle of a ship relative to the water—a ship in ideal trim sits parallel to the water; as a verb, to adjust the sails for the desired angle to the wind.

trip   To bury a vessel's bow in an oncoming wave.

truck   Piece of wood at the top of a mast; the highest point on a ship.

warp   Cable used to winch a ship up to an anchor, dock, or other fixed point; as a verb, the act of doing so.

weather-bitt   To take an extra turn of the mooring cables around the anchor or windlass.

weather bow   Side of a ship's front facing into the wind.

weather-gage   Having the wind advantage over another vessel or a hazardous object, such as rocks. Such a ship would be windward of the other vessel or hazard.

weather helm   Degree to which the helm must be kept to windward to maintain a steady course.

wheel   Wheel attached to the rudder by ropes and used to steer the ship; part of the helm.

windlass   Winch on which the anchor cable is wound.

windward   Direction the wind blows from; when you face windward, the wind is blowing in your face.

wear ship (wore ship)   To change direction so that the wind is coming over the rear or stern; the modern term for this is "jibe."

yard   Spar mounted across a mast to carry a sail, typically used on square-rigged ships.

yaw   To steer wildly and off course.

yawl   Vessel with two masts, a large mainmast and a much smaller "jigger" mast near the rear, or stern. By adding a jigger mast, Slocum changes the *Spray* from a sloop to a yawl.

Inspired by
Sailing Alone Around the World

The amazing adventure detailed by Joshua Slocum in *Sailing Alone Around the World* inspired legions of imitators. One of the first was American author Jack London, best known for the classics *The Call of the Wild* (1903) and *White Fang* (1906). After reading Slocum's book, London resolved to learn navigation and sail across the Pacific. His entertaining account, *The Cruise of the Snark* (1911), details his island-hopping adventures across the South Seas. The narrative describes headhunters on the Solomon Islands, the seasickness of London's crew, and the disappointment the writer experienced at not seeing the flying fish Slocum had described.

In 1901, just a year after the publication of *Sailing Alone Around the World*, Canadian journalist Norman Luxton challenged sailor John Voss to circumnavigate the globe in a vessel even smaller than Slocum's *Spray*. Later that same year, Luxton and Voss set sail together aboard the 32-foot *Tilikum*—a modified 100-year-old dugout canoe 5 feet shorter than Slocum's vessel. Luxton abandoned ship in Australia, presumably fed up with Voss's heavy womanizing while docked and drinking rages while afloat. Voss continued on and eventually completed his journey around Africa to London, although his replacement crew died mysteriously. Voss's highly literate *The Venturesome Voyages of Captain Voss* (1913) is sometimes published today under the title *40,000 Miles in a Canoe*.

The Joshua Slocum Society International created the Slocum Award to recognize "the most notable single-handed passage made during the past year." The first award, given in 1956, went to Argentincan sailor Vito Dumas, who made a solo voyage around the world in 1942, setting off from Buenos Aires and traveling eastward through the notorious latitudes known as the "Roaring Forties," a route across the storm-tossed seas below South America, Africa, and Australia. He carried a minimum of provisions, sailing even without a radio, since carrying one during World War II might have branded him a spy. Dumas later recounted his journey in *Alone Through the Roaring Forties: The Voyage of Lehg II Round the World* (1960).

Many other narratives in the tradition of Slocum deserve recognition. At sixty-four years old, Francis Chichester became the first man to circumnavigate the globe with only a single stop. He recounted his journey in the classic *Gipsy Moth Circles the World* (1967). Chichester's immense fame, which began while he was still at sea, inspired the *London Times* to sponsor the Golden Globe, the first solo boat race around the world. Robin Knox-Johnston won the competition and simultaneously became the first man to sail alone around the world without a single stop, recording his adventures in *A World of My Own* (1969). Knox-Johnston won, however, only because the eccentric mastermind Bernard Moitessier, victory in hand but disgusted with the commercial nature of the contest, decided to reverse course and sail around the world again rather than stop and claim his prize (see Moitessier's book *The Long Way*, published in 1971). *A Voyage for Madmen*, the 2001 best-seller by Peter Nichols, recounts this first Golden Globe competition and the gripping stories of each of its nine participants.

Other narratives worth investigating include *The Saga of Cimba* (1939), by Richard Maury; *Once Is Enough* (1959), by Miles Smeeton; *The Strange Last Voyage of Donald Crowhurst* (1970), by Nicholas Tomalin and Ron Hall; *Godforsaken Sea: The True Story of a Race Through the World's Most Dangerous Waters* (2000), by Derek Lundy; and *Sailing Around the World: A Family Retraces Joshua Slocum's Voyage* (2002), by Guy Bernardin. Each of these unique stories describes in a different way the excitement and danger of traveling the high seas.

Comments & Questions

In this section, we aim to provide the reader with an array of perspectives on the text, as well as questions that challenge those perspectives. The commentary has been culled from sources as diverse as reviews contemporaneous with the work, letters written by the author, literary criticism of later generations, and appreciations written throughout the work's history. Following the commentary, a series of questions seeks to filter Joshua Slocum's Sailing Alone Around the World *through a variety of points of view and bring about a richer understanding of this enduring work.*

Comments

THE CRITIC

"Sailing Alone Around the World" will never win a prize for terse and trenchant titles; yet it is hard to see how it could be briefer and still adequate. As for the story itself, which appeared in book form toward the end of March, the Evening Post summarizes it in saying that, to match it, one must go back to Marryat [English naval commander and novelist Frederick Marryat, 1792–1848], and remember that the gallant English captain dealt in fiction, while the American, Captain Slocum, sticks to fact. The skipper of the *Spray* not only officered his little sloop, but manned it—not only manned it, but built it. Never were the words of the "Bab Ballad" so applicable as in this case:—

> "For I am the cook, and the captain bold,
>   And the mate of the *Nancy* brig,
>   And the bosun tight, and midshipmite,
>   And the crew of the captain's gig."

The shipbuilders have put a million years between the fleets of Columbus and Magellan and the ocean greyhounds of the year 1900; but Captain Slocum is inspired by the spirit of those early ages, and shows himself a close kinsman of the dauntless navigator who discovered America, and of him who made a yet more marvellous voyage which led to the discovery of the Philippines. All his experiences were not so terrifying and disheartening as his two cruises through Magellan Strait, nor yet so idyllic as the run from Africa to the Keeling or Cocos Islands, when for three weeks not more than sixty minutes were spent in steering. A friend of the Captain's, connected with the Century Co., who had kept track of the *Spray* on its 46,000-mile adventure, received in November, 1897, a long letter dated, "The *Spray*, tied to a tree at Keeling-Cocos Islands, August 20th, 1897." "Do you think," asked the modest skipper, "our people will care for a story of the voyage around?" The answer to this question is the reception the "story" has had as it appeared in the *Century*, where it was planned to run for three months, the period being extended first to four, then to five, and again to six months— with a supplementary paper in the seventh number describing the structure and rig of the gallant little ship. There is an abundance of salt in this "personal narrative," and not all of it is the salt of the sea. Much of it is Attic. The Captain is a stylist as well as a wit.

—April 1900

CHICAGO DAILY TRIBUNE

Captain Slocum's simple and delightful narrative of his voyage around the world alone in the little sloop Spray combines the adventurous charm of "Robinson Crusoe" with the life and humor of Marryat. It is a rare good book for lovers of sea travels and adventure. The Captain is a literary artist as well as a daring and skillful sailor, and he tells his experiences with a delightful combination of modesty and delicate humor. Best of all, his story is true, and as remarkable for what it tells as for the way he tells it.

A Nova Scotian by birth and a naturalized Yankee by nationality, Captain Slocum is a retired shipmaster. He built the Spray with his own hands at New Bedford and started on his unprecedented single-handed voyage in the summer of 1895. The Spray is less than thirty-seven feet long and fourteen feet wide, sloop rigged; in this little vessel Captain Slocum circumnavigated the globe in three years with no other crew than himself alone. He traveled 46,000 miles and came back to Boston weighing more than when he left, and without a drop of water in the snug hold of the Spray. . . . The whole book is one to delight the heart of all who know anything of the charm and mystery of the sea.

—April 7, 1900

LIVING AGE

When a sea-captain who can both build his own boat and take it alone from one end of the world to the other has also the ability to write a breezy account of his adventures on the voyage, a good book naturally results. Captain Joshua Slocum's "Sailing Alone Around the World" is of this class. The skipper of the Spray saw Stevenson's island, saluted the Oregon on her famous trip, got impressions of St. Helena, and had an interview with President Krüger, among a hundred other interesting experiences. A good-humored sense of the ridiculous adds much to the entertaining quality of the book, and the illustrations enable one to picture the sloop at many points of interest.

—May 5, 1900

Questions

1. Can we at this distance reconstruct Joshua Slocum's character? What kind of man would not just enjoy the fantasy of sailing alone around the world, but actually do it? There's his courage and skill, of course, but what else?

2. Is there anything about Slocum's voyage you would like to know that he doesn't tell us? If so, what?

3. How is it different psychologically to sail the seas alone and, say, walk alone through the uninhabited heights of the Rocky Mountains or rocket alone to the moon?

4. Although he was born in Nova Scotia, Slocum has been described as a quintessential American. Does he seem that way to you?

For Further Reading

Biographies and Primary Materials

Joshua Slocum Society International. *http://www.joshuaslocum societyintl.org/*. A well-maintained website with links to much additional Slocum material, especially regarding the *Spray*.

Joyce, Jessie Slocum. *Joshua Slocum, Sailor: A Biography Written by Beth Day, from the Story told by His Daughter Jessie Slocum Joyce*. Boston, MA: Houghton Mifflin, 1953.

Slack, Kenneth. *In the Wake of the Spray*. New Brunswick, NJ: Rutgers University Press, 1966. Analyzes the design of the *Spray* and describes various replicas.

Historical and Geographical Context

Bernardin, Guy. *Sailing Around the World: A Family Retraces Joshua Slocum's Voyage*. Dobbs Ferry, NY: Sheridan House, 2002.

Great Voyages in Small Boats: Solo Circumnavigations. Clinton Corners, NY: J. de Graff, 1976.

Riesenberg, Felix. *Cape Horn*. New York: Dodd, Mead, 1939. A history of the region and its explorers.

Slocum, Joshua. *Around the World in the Sloop Spray: A Geographical Reader Describing Captain Slocum's Voyage Alone Around the World*. New York: C. Scribner's Sons, 1903. Abridged and annotated by Edward R. Shaw for schoolroom use, with a preface by Joshua Slocum.

Smeeton, Miles. *Because the Horn Is There*. London: Nautical Publishing Company, 1970. A history of voyages around Cape Horn.

Teller, Walter Magnes. *Five Sea Captains: Amasa Delano, Edmund Fanning, Richard Cleveland, George Coggeshall, Joshua Slocum: Their Own Accounts of Voyages Under Sail*. New York: Atheneum, 1960. Reprints Slocum's narrative along with four others to place Slocum in the genre of New England seafaring narratives.

Works Cited in the Introduction

Roberts-Goodson, R. Bruce. *Spray: The Ultimate Cruising Boat.* Dobbs Ferry, NY: Sheridan House, 1995. A technical account of the *Spray*'s design and construction along with detailed descriptions and photographs of later boats based on her lines.

Slocum, Joshua. *The Voyages of Joshua Slocum.* Collected and introduced by Walter Magnes Teller. New Brunswick, NJ: Rutgers University Press, 1958. Contains virtually everything Slocum wrote, including many letters.

Slocum, Victor. *Capt. Joshua Slocum: The Life and Voyages of America's Best Known Sailor.* New York: Sheridan House, 1950. A personal account by Captain Slocum's oldest son, told from a valuable nautical perspective but not always reliable in its historical facts.

Spencer, Ann. *Alone at Sea: The Adventures of Joshua Slocum.* Buffalo, NY: Firefly Books, 1999. A readable and sensitive biography that corrects some of Teller's omissions and appends four unpublished letters, one by Joshua and three by Hettie.

Teller, Walter Magnes. *Joshua Slocum.* New Brunswick, NJ: Rutgers University Press, 1971. A revised version of Teller's *The Search for Captain Slocum: A Biography*, New York: Charles Scribner's Sons, 1956. The most authoritative biography, but unfortunately does not include references, for which one must consult the earlier volume.